THE HIDDEN CHILD

ALSO BY CAMILLA LÄCKBERG

The Ice Princess

The Preacher

The Stonecutter

The Stranger

THE
HIDDEN CHILD

CAMILLA LÄCKBERG

Translated by Marlaine Delargy

PEGASUS CRIME

NEW YORK LONDON

This novel is entirely a work of fiction. The names, characters, and incidents portrayed in it are the work of the author's imagination. Any resemblance to actual persons, living or dead, or events is entirely coincidental.

THE HIDDEN CHILD

Pegasus Books LLC
80 Broad Street, 5th Floor
New York, NY 10004

Copyright © 2007 Camilla Läckberg

English translation © 2014 by Marlaine Delargy

First Pegasus Books edition 2014

First published in Swedish as *Tyskungen* in 2007

Published by agreement with Bengt Nordin Agency, Sweden

Interior design by Maria Fernandez

Camilla Läckberg asserts the moral right to be identified as the author of this work.

Library of Congress Cataloging-in-Publication Data is available.

ISBN: 978-1-60598-553-4

10 9 8 7 6 5 4 3 2 1

Printed in the United States of America
Distributed by W. W. Norton & Company

To Wille & Meja

THE HIDDEN CHILD

1

In the stillness of the room, the only sound came from the flies. The buzzing as their wings beat frantically. The man in the chair did not move. He hadn't moved for a long time. He wasn't actually a man anymore. Not if you defined a man as a living, breathing, sentient being. By now he was reduced to a food source, a haven for insects and maggots.

A great swarm of flies buzzed around the motionless figure. They landed occasionally, their jaws working. Then they took off again. Buzzed to and fro, searching for a fresh place to land. Edged forward. Bumped into one another. The area around the wound on the man's head was particularly interesting. The metallic smell of blood had faded long ago, replaced by a different smell that was both sweeter and mustier.

The blood had coagulated. At first it had run down the back of the man's head, down the back of the chair. Down onto the floor, where it had eventually gathered in a pool. In the beginning it had been red, full of living corpuscles. Then it had turned black. The pool was no longer recognizable as the viscous fluid that runs through the veins of a human being. Now it was only a black, sticky mass.

A few of the flies were trying to escape. They were sated. Satisfied. They had laid their eggs. Their jaws had worked hard, filling them up, appeasing their hunger. Now they wanted to get out. They banged their wings against the windowpane, trying in vain to get through the invisible barrier, hitting the glass with a faint tapping sound. Sooner or later they gave up as the hunger returned. They made their way back to the thing that had once been a man, the thing that was now merely flesh.

All summer Erica had tiptoed around the issue that constantly occupied her thoughts. She had weighed the pros and cons, decided to go up to the attic, but she had never gotten any farther than the stairs. She could blame it on the fact that there had been a lot to do over the past few months. The aftermath of the wedding, the chaos at home while Anna and the children were still living with them. But that was only part of the truth. She was quite simply afraid. Afraid of what she might find. Afraid of rooting around in something that might bring things to the surface that she would rather not know about.

Erica knew that Patrik had been on the verge of asking her several times. She could see that he was wondering why she didn't want to read the books they had found in the attic. But he hadn't asked. And she wouldn't have had an answer to give him. What frightened her most was the idea that she might have to revise her picture of reality. The picture she had of her mother, who her mother was and how she had treated her daughter, was less than positive. But it belonged to her. It was familiar. It was a picture that had stood the test of time, like an irrefutable truth, a part of her life. Perhaps it would be confirmed. Perhaps it would even be reinforced. But what if it was turned upside down? What if she had to come to terms with an entirely new reality? Until now, she had lacked the courage to take that step.

Erica placed her foot on the first stair. From downstairs in the living room she could hear Maja's joyous laughter as Patrik teased her. The sound was reassuring, and she placed her foot on the next stair. Five more and she had reached the top.

The dust whirled around in the air as she pushed open the hatch and climbed into the attic. She and Patrik had talked about remodeling it at some point in the future, perhaps as a den for Maja when she was older and wanted her own space. But at the moment it was just a storage area, with wide wooden planks on the floor and a sloping roof with exposed beams. It was half full of clutter: Christmas decorations, clothes Maja had already outgrown, various boxes crammed with things that were too ugly to put on display but too valuable or too imprinted with memories to be thrown away.

The chest was right at the far end. It was old, made of wood and metal. Erica had an idea that this kind of thing was called an American trunk. She went over and sat down on the floor. Ran her hand over the chest. She took a deep breath, then lifted the lid. A musty smell rushed toward her, and she wrinkled her nose. She wondered what it was that created that characteristic, heavy smell of age. Probably mold, she thought, and immediately her scalp began to itch.

She could still remember the feeling when she and Patrik had discovered the chest and gone through the contents. Slowly she had lifted out one object after another. Drawings she and Anna had done. Small trinkets they had made in craft lessons at school. Saved by their mother, Elsy, the mother who had never shown any interest when they came rushing up to give her the things into which they had put so much effort. Erica carefully took out one item after another and placed them on the floor beside her. The thing she really wanted was right at the bottom. She could feel the fabric with her fingers, and she gently picked it up. The child's dress had once been white, but now, when she held it up in the light, she could see that it was yellow with age. But she couldn't take her eyes off the brown marks. At first she had mistaken them for rust, but then she had realized they had to be dried blood. There was something heartrending about the contrast between the tiny dress and the spots of blood all over it. How had the dress ended up here? Who did it belong to? And why had her mother kept it?

Erica gently laid the dress down on the floor beside her. The object that had been concealed in the dress when she and Patrik first found it was no longer in the chest. It was the only thing she had removed. The soiled fabric of the child's dress had been wrapped around a Nazi medal. The feelings aroused within her when she first saw the medal had surprised her. Her heart had begun to pound, her mouth had gone dry, and images from all the newsreels and documentaries she had seen of the Second World War had flickered past her mind's eye. What was a Nazi medal doing here in Fjällbacka? In her home? Among her mother's possessions? The whole thing had seemed bizarre. She had wanted to put the medal back in the chest and close the lid, but Patrik had insisted that they should hand it over to an expert to see if they could find out more about it. Reluctantly she had agreed. It was as if she could hear whispering voices inside her, ominous warning voices. Something told her that she ought to hide the medal away and forget about it. But curiosity won the day, and at the beginning of June she had taken the medal to an expert on the history of the Second World War; with a bit of luck they would soon find out more about its origins.

However, the most interesting things that Erica had discovered in the chest were four blue notebooks right at the bottom. She recognized her mother's handwriting on the covers. That elegant, right-slanted handwriting, but in a younger, more rounded version. Erica took them out and ran a finger over the top one. "Diary" was written on each book. The word aroused mixed feelings for Erica. Curiosity, excitement, eagerness. But also fear, hesitation, and a strong sense of invading someone's private life. Did she have the right to read the diaries? Did she have the right to share her mother's innermost thoughts and feelings? By its very nature, a diary is not intended for anyone else's eyes. Her mother hadn't written them so that someone else could read the contents. Perhaps she wouldn't have wanted her daughter to see them. But Elsy was dead, and Erica couldn't ask her what she thought. She would have to make her own decision, decide what she was going to do with them.

"Erica?" Patrik's voice interrupted her thoughts, and she shouted back, "Yes?"

"Our guests are arriving!"

Erica glanced at her watch. Goodness, it was three o'clock already! Maja was celebrating her first birthday today, and their closest friends and family were coming over. Patrik must have thought she had fallen asleep up here.

"Coming!" She brushed off the dust, and after a moment's hesitation she took the notebooks and the child's dress with her as she clambered down the steep staircase. She could hear the hum of voices from below.

"Welcome!" Patrik stepped aside to let in the first guests: Johan and Elisabeth, a couple they had gotten to know through Maja, since they had a son of the same age. A son who loved Maja with a rarely seen intensity. Sometimes, however, his attentions could become a little too physical. Today, for example, William hurtled forward like a bulldozer as soon as he spotted Maja, tackling her with a skill worthy of a National Hockey League player. Strangely enough, Maja didn't really appreciate this maneuver, and William's parents had to step in quickly to remove their ecstatic little boy from his position on top of a howling Maja.

"Listen, kiddo, that's not the way we do things. You have to be gentle with girls!" Johan gazed sternly at his son as he strong-armed his offspring to prevent him from launching a fresh attack.

"He seems to have roughly the same pulling technique as you," Elisabeth said with a laugh, eliciting a wounded look in response from her husband.

"Come on, honey, you're fine. Up you get." Patrik picked up his distraught daughter and hugged her until she subsided into quiet sobs, then he put her down and gave her a gentle push in William's direction. "Look what William has brought you! A present!"

The magic word had the desired effect. With great seriousness and ceremony William held out a beautifully wrapped gift to Maja. Neither of them had completely mastered the technique of walking, and the difficulty of moving his feet in the right order while handing over the present made William land on his bottom. A well-padded diaper also contributed to his awkwardness. However, when he saw Maja's face light up at the sight of the package, he seemed to forget his own pain.

"Ooooh," Maja said excitedly, beginning to pull at the ribbon. After approximately two seconds, an expression of frustration began to appear on her face, and Patrik hurried over to offer his assistance. Together they managed to get the present open, and Maja pulled out a cuddly gray elephant, which was an instant success. She clutched it to her chest, wrapping her arms tightly around the soft body and stamping her feet up and down. Which meant that she too ended up on her bottom. William's attempts to pat the new toy were met with a downturned mouth and some very clear body language. Maja's little admirer evidently took this as a signal to redouble his efforts, and both sets of parents foresaw trouble.

"I think it might be time for a little snack," Patrik said. He picked up his daughter and carried her into the living room. William and his parents followed, and once the boy was settled in front of the big toy box, peace was restored. Temporarily, at least.

"Hi!" Erica came downstairs and greeted their guests with a hug. She gave William a pat on the head.

"Who'd like coffee?" Patrik shouted from the kitchen. "Me, please!" all three replied.

"So, how's married life?" Johan smiled and put his arm around Elisabeth.

"More or less the same as before, except that Patrik insists on calling me 'the wife' all the time. Any tips on how I can get him to stop?" Erica turned to Elisabeth and winked.

"If I were you, I'd just give up right now. Otherwise he'll start referring to you as 'the boss.' So don't complain. Where's Anna, by the way?"

"She's at Dan's place. They've already moved in together. . . ." Erica raised her eyebrows meaningfully.

"Goodness, that was quick!" Elisabeth's eyebrows also shot up. Quality gossip often had that effect.

They were interrupted by the sound of the doorbell, and Erica leapt to her feet. "That's probably them now. Or Kristina." The last name was uttered with shards of ice clinking between the syllables. Ever since the wedding, the relationship between Erica and her mother-in-law had been frostier than usual. This was largely due to Kristina's almost manic campaign to persuade Patrik that because he was a man with a career, he shouldn't even consider taking four months' paternity leave. Much to her chagrin, Patrik hadn't given an inch; in fact, he was the one who had insisted on looking after Maja during the fall.

"Hello . . . is there anyone here who happens to have a birthday today?" Erica couldn't suppress a surge of pleasure every time she heard the cheerful tone in her sister's voice. It had been missing for so many years, but now it was back. Anna sounded strong and happy and in love.

At first Anna had been worried that Erica might have something against her embarking on a relationship with Dan, but Erica had simply laughed at her concerns. It was an eternity, a whole lifetime, since Erica and Dan had been a couple. Even if she had thought it strange, she would have had no problem ignoring her feelings, just for the sheer joy of seeing Anna happy again.

"Where's my favorite girl?" Dan, tall, blond, and boisterous, was looking around for Maja. The two of them had a particularly close relationship, and she came barreling along and held up her arms as soon as she heard him. "Pesent?" she said inquiringly, having begun to grasp the concept of birthdays.

"Of course we've brought you a present, sweetheart," Dan said, nodding to Anna, who held out a big box wrapped in pink paper and silver ribbon. Maja wriggled out of Dan's arms and once again started on the bothersome process of trying to get at the contents. This time Erica helped, and together they liberated a large doll.

"Dolly," Maja said happily, clutching her gift tightly. She set off in William's direction to show him her latest treasure, repeating the word "dolly" just to be on the safe side as she held it out to him.

The doorbell rang again, and immediately Kristina walked in. Erica could feel herself beginning to grind her teeth. She really hated the way her mother-in-law gave the bell a cursory push and then walked straight in.

The present-giving ritual was repeated once more, but with rather less success this time. Maja looked rather puzzled as she held up the T-shirts that she found inside the package;

she rummaged around once more to check that there really wasn't a toy hidden away somewhere, then gazed up at her grandmother with big eyes.

"I noticed she'd more or less grown out of the top she was wearing last time I was here, so when Lindex had three for the price of two, I thought it would be a good idea to pick some up for her. They're bound to be useful." Kristina smiled with satisfaction, seemingly unmoved by Maja's disappointed expression.

Erica suppressed the urge to explain exactly how stupid she thought it was to buy clothes for a one-year-old. And not only was Maja disappointed, but Kristina had also managed to get in one of her usual digs: they were obviously incapable of dressing their daughter properly.

"Time for some birthday cake!" Patrik announced with impeccable timing; he seemed to sense that it would be a good idea to divert attention from what had just happened. Erica swallowed her annoyance and they all gathered in the living room for the big ceremony. Maja summoned up every scrap of concentration in her efforts to blow out the candle, but only managed to spray the cake with saliva. Patrik provided discreet assistance, and Maja reveled in the attention as everyone sang to her and cheered. Erica met Patrik's gaze over their daughter's blond head. She had a huge lump in her throat, and she could tell that he too was moved by the moment. One year old. Their baby was one year old. A little girl who could get around under her own steam, who clapped her hands when she heard the theme tune to *Bolibompa*, who could feed herself, gave out the wettest kisses in the whole of northern Europe, and who loved the entire world. Erica smiled at Patrik. He smiled back. At that precise moment, life was perfect.

Mellberg sighed heavily. He often did that these days. Sighed. He still found the thought of last spring's setback depressing.

But he wasn't surprised. He had allowed himself to lose control, allowed himself simply to be, to feel. You couldn't expect to do that without being punished. He should have known. Actually, you could say he deserved what he got. You could even call it a salutary reminder. Well, he had definitely learned that lesson now, and he wasn't the kind of man who made the same mistake twice, that was for sure.

"Bertil?" Annika's voice came from reception, her tone peremptory. With a swift and well-practiced gesture, Bertil Mellberg looped up the strand of hair that had tumbled down from the top of his head and reluctantly got to his feet. There weren't many women from whom he was prepared to take orders, but Annika Jansson belonged to that exclusive club. Over the years he had even developed a grudging respect for her, and he couldn't think of any other female about whom he could say the same. The ridiculous business with that woman who had come to work at the station last spring confirmed his view, if nothing else. And now they were getting another woman. He sighed again. Who would have thought it would be so difficult to get hold of a man in uniform? Instead, they insisted on sending girls to replace Ernst Lundgren. It was a disgrace.

The sound of a bark from reception made him frown. Had Annika brought one of her dogs to work? She knew what he thought about marauding hounds. He would have to have serious words with her.

But it wasn't one of Annika's Labradors. It was a scabby mutt of indeterminate color and breed, tugging on a leash held by a small, dark-haired woman.

"I found him outside," she said in a broad Stockholm accent.

"Okay, so what's he doing in here?" Bertil snapped, heading back to his office.

"This is Paula Morales," Annika said quickly, and Bertil turned back. Shit. The woman who was due to start work had some kind of Spanish-sounding name, didn't she? But she was so goddamn small. Short and skinny. However, the expression on her face was anything but weak. She held out her hand.

"Nice to meet you. And the dog was running around on his own out there. Given the state he's in, I don't think he belongs to anyone. Or at least not to anyone who's capable of looking after him."

Her tone was challenging, and Bertil wondered where she was going with this. He said, "Well, in that case, you'd better hand him in somewhere."

"Annika's already told me there isn't anywhere for stray dogs around here."

"Isn't there?"

Annika shook her head.

"Well . . . I guess you'll just have to take him home," Mellberg said, trying to wave away the mutt, which was now pressing itself against his leg. The dog ignored him and simply sat down on Mellberg's right foot.

"I can't do that. We've already got a dog, and she doesn't like company," Paula said calmly, with that same penetrating gaze.

"You take him then, Annika—surely he can hang out with your dogs?" Mellberg's tone was becoming increasingly weary. Why did he always have to concern himself with such trivial matters? He was the boss here, for God's sake!

But Annika shook her head firmly. "They're only used to each other. It just wouldn't work."

"You'll have to take him," Paula said, handing over the leash. Mellberg was so taken aback by the sheer nerve of the woman that he found himself holding the leash; the dog responded by pressing himself even closer to Mellberg's leg and letting out a small whimper.

"There you go—he likes you."

"But I can't . . . I haven't . . . ," Mellberg stammered, incapable of coming up with a suitable reply for once.

"You don't have any other pets at home, and I promise I'll ask around to see if anyone's lost him. Otherwise we'll have to try to find someone who'll look after him. We can't just let him go; he might get run over."

Against his will, Mellberg was moved by Annika's words. He looked down at the dog. It looked up at him, its eyes moist and pleading.

"Oh, all right, I'll take the goddamn dog if you're going to make such a fuss about it. But only for a couple of days. And you can give him a wash before I take him home." He wagged a finger at Annika, who looked very relieved.

"No problem, I'll give him a shower here at the station," she said eagerly, before adding, "Thank you so much, Bertil."

Mellberg grunted. "Just make sure he's spotless the next time I set eyes on him, otherwise he doesn't get through my door!"

He stomped off down the corridor and slammed the door behind him.

Annika and Paula exchanged a smile. The dog whimpered and its tail thudded up and down on the floor.

"Have a good day, you two." Erica waved to Maja, who ignored her; she was sitting on the floor, absorbed in the adventures of the Teletubbies on TV.

"We're going to have a lovely time," Patrik said, giving Erica a kiss. "Maja and I will get on just fine over the next few months."

"You make it sound as if I'm setting off across the seven seas," Erica said with a laugh. "I'll be coming down for lunch, to begin with."

"Do you think this is going to work, with you writing in your study at home?"

"Well, we can give it a go. You'll just have to try to pretend I'm not here."

"No problem. As soon as you close that study door, you no longer exist as far as I'm concerned." Patrik smiled.

"Hmm, we'll see," Erica replied, heading up the stairs. "But it's worth a try anyway; it will save me renting an office."

She went into her study and closed the door with mixed feelings. She had spent a whole year at home with Maja, and part of her had been longing for this day, longing to pass the baton to Patrik. To be able to devote herself to an adult occupation again. She was so tired of playgrounds, sandboxes, and activity sessions. Making the perfect sand pie was never going to provide enough intellectual stimulation, and however much she loved her daughter, she would soon start tearing out her hair in despair if she had to sing "The Itsy Bitsy Spider" just once more. Now it was time for Patrik to take over.

Erica sat down reverently in front of the computer, switched it on, and reveled in the familiar hum. The deadline for the new book in her series about real-life murders was in February, but she had managed to do some research over the summer, so she felt ready to start. She opened Word, clicked on the document she had called "Elias" because that was the name of the murderer's first victim, and rested her fingers on the keyboard. A gentle tap on the door interrupted her.

"Sorry to disturb you." Patrik looked slightly furtive. "I was just wondering where you put Maja's jumpsuit."

"It's in the airing cupboard."

Patrik nodded and closed the door.

Once again she placed her fingers over the keys and took a deep breath. There was another tap at the door.

"Sorry again. I promise I'll leave you in peace, but I just wanted to check—what do you think Maja should wear today?

I mean, it's quite chilly, but then she does get sweaty, and it's easy to catch a chill if. . . ." Patrik smiled sheepishly.

"Just put a thin top and pants on under her jumpsuit. And I usually go for her thin cotton hat, otherwise she gets way too hot."

"Thanks," Patrik said, closing the door once more. Erica was about to type the first line when she heard Maja yelling furiously. The sound rose to a crescendo, and, after listening to the racket for two minutes, she pushed back her chair with a sigh and went downstairs.

"I'll give you a hand. It's really hard to get her dressed at the moment."

"Thanks, I've noticed," said Patrik, whose forehead was covered in beads of sweat from the effort of wrestling with a furious and strong Maja while wrapped up in his outdoor clothes.

Five minutes later, their daughter had a face like thunder, but at least she was fully dressed. Erica gave both Maja and Patrik a kiss on the mouth before shooing them out of the house.

"Go for a nice long walk and give your mom some peace and quiet to get some work done," she said. Patrik looked worried.

"Listen, I'm sorry we . . . I suppose it'll take a few days to get into a routine, then you'll get all the peace and quiet you need, I promise."

"It's fine," Erica said, but she closed the door firmly behind them. She poured herself a big mug of coffee, then went back to her study. At last she could get started.

"Shhh . . . don't make so much fucking noise!"

"Chill—Mom says they're both away. Nobody's taken in the mail all summer, and they seem to have forgotten about it, so she's been emptying the mailbox since June. So just chill; we can make as much noise as we like." Mattias laughed, but Adam remained skeptical. There was something creepy about this old house. And there was something creepy about the old men. Mattias could say what he liked; Adam intended to sneak around as quietly as possible.

"So how do we get in, then?" He hated the fact that his anxiety was obvious from the whining note in his voice, but he couldn't help it. He often wished he was more like Mattias. Courageous, unafraid, often bordering on foolhardy. But then he was the one who got all the girls as well.

"It'll be fine. There's always a way in."

"And this is based on your vast experience of breaking into houses, is it?" Adam laughed, but was careful to be as quiet as possible.

"Listen, I've done a whole bunch of things you know nothing about," Mattias said loftily.

Yeah, right, Adam thought, but didn't dare to contradict him. Sometimes Mattias needed to pretend to be tougher than he was, which was fine. At any rate, Adam knew better than to get into an argument with him.

"What do you think he's got in there?" Mattias's eyes were shining as they slowly crept around the outside of the house, on the lookout for a window or a trapdoor, anything they could use to get past the apparently impenetrable façade.

"I don't know." Adam kept on looking around anxiously. He was liking this less and less with every passing second.

"He might have lots of cool Nazi stuff. Uniforms, that sort of thing." The excitement in Mattias's voice was unmistakable. Ever since they'd done that school project on the SS, he'd been obsessed and had read everything he could find about Nazism and the Second World War. His neighbor just down the road, who, as everyone knew, was some kind of expert on Germany and the Nazis, had proved an irresistible attraction.

"He might not have anything like that in the house," Adam ventured, but he knew his objection was doomed to failure.

"Dad said he was a history teacher before he retired, so he's bound to have a whole lot of books. There might not be any cool stuff at all."

"Well, we'll soon see." Mattias's eyes sparkled as he pointed triumphantly at a window. "Look. It's slightly ajar."

Adam miserably realized that he was right. He had been quietly hoping that it would prove impossible to get inside the house.

"We need something to push into the gap to get it open." Mattias looked around; a window catch that had fallen off and was lying on the ground provided the solution.

"Okay, let's see." With surgical precision, Mattias managed to reach up above his head with the catch and insert one end in the corner of the window. He pushed hard, but nothing moved. The window refused to budge. "Fuck, this has to work." With his tongue sticking out at one corner of his mouth, he tried again. Holding the catch above his head and exerting himself at the same time was difficult, and he was panting. Eventually he managed to push the catch a fraction farther in.

"It's going to be obvious that someone's broken in!" Adam protested faintly, but Mattias didn't seem to have heard him.

"Come on, you fucking bastard!" With beads of sweat breaking out at his temples, Mattias made one final effort and the window swung open.

"Yes!" He raised his clenched fist in a victorious gesture, then turned excitedly to Adam.

"Help me up."

"Maybe there's something to stand on, or a ladder or. . . ."

"For fuck's sake, just help me up and then I can pull you up."

Obediently, Adam stood by the wall and linked his hands to make a step for Mattias. He made a face as Mattias's shoe cut into his palm, but he bore the pain and lifted his friend as Mattias pushed off.

Mattias grabbed hold of the window ledge and managed to haul himself up, swinging first one leg and then the other inside. He wrinkled his nose. The place stank. It was fucking disgusting. He pulled aside the blind and tried to peer into the room. It looked as if he had ended up in a library, but all the blinds were closed and the room was in darkness.

"It fucking stinks in here." He half turned to Adam, holding his nose at the same time.

"Let's not bother, then," Adam said from down below, a hopeful glint in his eye.

"No chance. We're in now. This is where the fun begins. Grab my hand."

He let go of his nose and held on to the windowsill, reaching down to Adam with his right hand.

"Can you do it?"

"Of course I can. Come on." Adam took his hand and Mattias pulled as hard as he could. For a moment it looked impossible, but then Adam grabbed hold of the windowsill and Mattias jumped onto the floor to give him some space. There was a strange crunching noise under his feet as he landed. He looked down. The floor was covered in something, but the darkness made it impossible to make out what it was. Leaves and petals from a bunch of dead flowers, probably.

"What the fuck," said Adam when he had landed on the floor and failed to identify the source of the crunching sound. "Shit, it stinks," he said, looking as if he was about to throw up.

"That's what I said," Mattias said cheerfully. His nose had begun to acclimate, and the smell no longer bothered him so much. "Okay, let's see what the old man's got in here. Open the blinds."

"But what if someone sees us?"

"Who the fuck is going to see us in here? Open the fucking blinds!"

Adam did as he was told. The blinds shot up with a swishing sound, letting a harsh light into the room.

"Cool place," Mattias said, looking around with admiration. Every wall was covered with bookshelves from floor to ceiling. In one corner, two leather armchairs were arranged around a small table. The far end of the room was dominated by an enormous desk, and an old-fashioned office chair had spun around half a turn so that its back was toward them. Adam took a step forward, but the crunching noise made him look down again. This time they both saw what they were walking on.

"What the. . . ." The floor was covered in flies. Disgusting, dead, black flies. The windowsill was also thick with flies, and both Adam and Mattias instinctively wiped their hands on their pants.

"That's disgusting." Mattias grimaced.

"Where have all these flies come from?" Adam stared at the floor, and suddenly his *CSI*-indoctrinated brain made an unpleasant connection. Dead flies. Revolting smell. He pushed aside the thought, but his eyes were inevitably drawn to the office chair.

"Mattias?"

"Yes?" he answered crossly, trying to find a place to stand where he wouldn't be treading on a pile of dead flies.

Adam moved hesitantly over to the chair. Something inside was screaming at him to turn away, get out the same way he had come in, and run until he could run no more. But the curiosity was too much for him, and it was as if his feet were carrying him toward the chair of their own volition.

"Yes?" Mattias said again, but fell silent when he saw the tension in the way Adam was moving.

Adam was still a couple of feet from the chair when he stretched out his hand. He could see that it was shaking slightly. Slowly, slowly, inch by inch, he reached toward the back of the chair. The only sound was the crunch as he took one step at a time. The leather chair felt cool against his fingertips. He increased the pressure. Pushed the back of the chair to the left, so that it began to turn toward him. He took a step backward. Slowly the chair rotated, gradually revealing what was sitting in it. Behind him Adam could hear Mattias throwing up.

The eyes following his smallest movement were large and liquid. Mellberg was trying to ignore the dog, but with limited success. It was glued to his side, its expression adoring. In the end, Mellberg weakened. He opened the bottom drawer of his desk, took out a treat covered in coconut, and dropped it on the floor in front of the mutt. It was gone in two seconds, and for a moment Mellberg thought it looked as if the mutt were actually smiling. A figment of his imagination, no doubt. At least the animal was clean now. Annika had done a good job of showering and shampooing him, but Bertil had still found it rather distasteful when he'd woken up that morning to find that the dog had jumped up on the bed at some point during the night and settled down beside him. Soap probably didn't eliminate fleas and that kind of thing. What if his coat was full of horrible little creepy-crawlies just waiting to jump across to Mellberg's ample frame? But a meticulous inspection of the mutt's coat hadn't revealed any alien forms of life, and Annika had given Mellberg her word of honor that she hadn't found any fleas when she was washing him. That didn't mean the dog would be sleeping in his bed again, however. There were limits.

"So, what shall we call you?" Mellberg said, suddenly feeling stupid because he was sitting here talking to something with four legs. Then again, the mutt needed a name. He thought about it, gazing around for inspiration. All he could come up with was dumb names—Fido, Rover. . . . No, that was no good. Then he burst out laughing. He'd just had a brilliant idea. He had genuinely been missing Lundgren—not a lot, but a little bit, since he had been forced to kick him out. So why not call the mutt Ernst? There was a certain humor in the idea. He laughed again.

"Ernst—what do you think about that, eh? Sounds good, doesn't it?" He opened the drawer and took out another treat. Ernst deserved it. After all, it wasn't Mellberg's problem if the dog got fat. Annika was sure to be able to palm him off on somebody else in a day or two, so it hardly mattered if Ernst went through a few treats before then.

The shrill sound of the telephone made both Mellberg and Ernst jump.

"Bertil Mellberg." At first he couldn't make out what the voice at the other end of the line was saying; it was simply a high-pitched, hysterical babbling.

"I'm sorry, you're going to have to speak more slowly. What are you saying?" He concentrated hard, and his eyebrows shot up when he finally understood.

"A body, you say? Where?" He straightened up in his chair. The dog also sat up very straight and pricked up his ears. Mellberg scribbled down an address on the pad in front of him, ended the call with "Stay right where you are," then leapt to his feet. Ernst was right behind him.

"Stay here." Mellberg's tone was unusually authoritative, and, to his great surprise, the mutt stopped dead to await further instructions. "Basket!" Mellberg ventured, pointing to the container Annika had prepared for the dog in one corner of his office. Ernst reluctantly obeyed; he shambled over and lay down with his head resting on his paws, directing a hurt look at his temporary master. Bertil Mellberg felt strangely pleased that someone had actually obeyed him for once and, buoyed by this exertion of his authority, he hurried into the corridor, shouting to no one in particular and everyone in general: "We've had a call about a body."

Three heads appeared in three doorways: one red—Martin Molin, one gray—Gösta Flygare, and one as black as a raven's wing—Paula Morales.

"A body?" Martin said, stepping into the corridor. Annika appeared from reception.

"A teenage boy just called to report it. Apparently he and a friend were messing around and broke into a house between Fjällbacka and Hamburgsund. When they got inside, they found a body."

"The owner of the house?" Gösta asked.

Mellberg shrugged. "That's all I know. I told the boys to stay where they were; we'll get over there right away. Martin, you and Paula take one car, Gösta and I will take the other."

"Shouldn't we call Patrik?" Gösta asked tentatively.

"Who's Patrik?" Paula asked, glancing from Gösta to Mellberg.

"Patrik Hedström," Martin explained. "He works here too, but he's on paternity leave starting today."

"Of course we don't need to ring Hedström," Mellberg snorted, feeling insulted. "I'm here, after all," he added pompously, setting off toward the parking lot.

"Terrific," Martin muttered out of Mellberg's earshot; Paula raised an inquiring eyebrow. "Forget it," Martin said apologetically, but he couldn't help adding, "You'll understand in time."

Paula still looked confused, but left it at that. No doubt she would gradually come to grips with the dynamics of the workplace.

Erica sighed. The house was quiet now. Too quiet. For a year her ears had been attuned to the smallest whimper, the next scream. Now it was totally, desolately silent. The cursor was flashing on the first line in her Word document. She hadn't managed one single pathetic little character in half an hour.

Her brain simply wasn't working. She had flicked through her notes and the articles she had photocopied during the summer. After several attempts she had finally managed to arrange to see the protagonist, the murderer, but not until three weeks from now, which meant that she would have to make do with the archive material for the time being. However, the problem was that nothing was coming. The words refused to tumble out and land in the right place, and now the doubts were beginning to kick in. The doubts that always plagued a writer. Were there no more words left? Had she written her last sentence, fulfilled her quota? Were there no more books in her? Logic told her that she almost always felt like this when she was about to start work on a new project, but it didn't help. It was like torture, a process she had to go through every single time. A bit like giving birth. But today things were going unusually badly. Absentmindedly she unwrapped a chocolate caramel and pushed it into her mouth for consolation. She glanced at the blue notebooks lying on the desk next to the computer. Her mother's flowing handwriting demanded her attention. She was torn between the fear of getting close to what her mother had written and curiosity about what she might find. Hesitantly she reached out and picked up the first book. She weighed it in the palm of her hand. It was thin, very similar to the small exercise books children used in elementary school. Erica ran her fingers over the cover. The name was written in ink, but over the years the blue had faded significantly. "Elsy Moström." Her mother's maiden name; she had become Elsy Falck when she married Erica's father. Slowly she opened the book. The pages were ruled, with thin blue lines. There was a date at the top: "September 3, 1943." She read the first line:

"Will this war never end?"

2
Fjällbacka 1943

"Will this war never end?"

Elsy chewed her pen, wondering how to continue. How could she summarize her thoughts on this war that had not reached Swedish soil and yet was ever present? It felt strange to be keeping a diary. She didn't know where the idea had come from, but it was as if she needed to put down in words all the thoughts that this ordinary yet extraordinary existence brought with it. A part of her could hardly remember the time before the war. She was thirteen now, almost fourteen; she had been just nine years old when the war broke out. During the first few years it hadn't made a great deal of difference, apart from the renewed air of vigilance among the adults, the eagerness with which they suddenly began to follow the news on the wireless and in the newspapers. It was evident in their posture as they sat in the living room, completely focused on the broadcast, tense, afraid, yet at the same time strangely exhilarated. What was happening in the world was exciting, after all—menacing, but exciting. Otherwise life was more or less the same as it had always been. The boats went out to sea and returned. Sometimes the catch was good. Sometimes it was poor. At home the women went about their chores, the same chores that their mothers had done, and their mothers before them. There were children to be borne, clothes to be washed, houses to be kept clean. It was a never-ending cycle, but now the war was threatening to destroy the life and the reality they knew. That was the tension she had felt as a child, and now the war was almost here.

"Elsy?" Her mother's voice came from downstairs. Quickly Elsy closed the notebook and slipped it into the top drawer of her little desk in front of the window. She had sat here for many hours doing her homework, but now she was done with school, and she didn't really have any use for the desk these days. She got up, smoothed down her dress, and went to find her mother.

"Elsy, could you fetch some water for me?" Her mother looked gray and tired. They had spent all summer in the little room in the cellar, having rented out the rest of the house to summer visitors. The rent included cleaning, cooking, and waiting on the guests, who had been very demanding. A lawyer from Gothenburg with a wife and three feral children. Hilma, Elsy's mother, had ended up running around after them from morning till night, doing their laundry, making packed lunches for their boat trips, and tidying up indoors, while at the same time trying to look after her own family.

"Sit down for a while, Mother," Elsy said gently, hesitantly placing a hand on her mother's shoulder. Hilma gave a start. They rarely touched each other, but after a second she placed her hand on top of her daughter's and gratefully allowed herself to be guided to a chair.

"It was definitely high time they left. I've never seen the like. 'I wonder if you could possibly . . . Would you mind . . . Hilma, could you please. . . .'" Hilma mimicked their la-di-da voices, then suddenly clapped a hand to her mouth in horror. It wasn't common practice to be so disrespectful toward well-to-do folk. It was important to know one's place.

"I know you're tired, Mother. They weren't easy to deal with." Elsy poured the last of the water into a pan and put it on the cooktop. Once it was boiling, she added coffee substitute, then poured a cup for Hilma and one for herself.

"I'll fetch the water in a minute, but first of all we're going to have a little rest."

"You're such a good girl." Hilma took a sip of the woeful substitute. On special occasions she drank coffee from a saucer, with a sugar lump between her teeth. But sugar was in short supply, and this ersatz coffee didn't taste the same as the real thing anyway.

"Has Father said when he'll be home?" Elsy looked down at the table. In wartime, this question had a completely different significance. It wasn't all that long since the *Öckerö* had been torpedoed and gone down with all hands on board. Since then, every good-bye before a new voyage had been infused with a fatalistic tone. But the work must go on. There was no choice. Cargoes must be delivered, the fish must be brought ashore. That was how life worked around here, war or no war. They had to be grateful for the fact that cargo traffic to and from Norway had been allowed to continue. It was also regarded as being less dangerous than the safe-conduct traffic that went on outside the blockade. The boats from Fjällbacka were allowed to continue fishing, and even if the catches were smaller than they used to be, it was possible to top up with cargo to and from the Norwegian harbors. Elsy's father usually brought ice home from Norway, and if he was lucky he also had goods to take over there.

"I just wish . . ." Hilma fell silent, then went on: "I just wish he'd be a bit more careful. . . ."

"Who? Father?" Elsy said, although she knew perfectly well what her mother meant.

"Yes. . . ." Hilma made a face as she took another sip of her drink. "He's got the doctor's boy with him this time, and . . . it can't possibly end well, that's all I'm saying."

"Axel is courageous, he does what he can. And I expect Father wants to help out as much as possible."

"But the risks"—Hilma shook her head—"the risks he takes when that boy and his friends are with him. It just seems to me that Axel is putting your father and the others in danger."

"We have to do what we can to help the Norwegians," Elsy said quietly. "If we were in their position, wouldn't we need their help? Axel and his friends do a great deal of good."

"Let's not talk about it anymore. Are you ever going to fetch me that water?" Hilma sounded cross as she got up and went over to the sink to rinse out her cup, but Elsy didn't take it to heart. She knew that the anger had its roots in anxiety.

After a final glance at her mother's prematurely hunched back, she picked up the bucket and went to draw some water from the well.

3

To his surprise, Patrik was enjoying the walk. He hadn't had a great deal of exercise over the last few years, but if he could manage a long walk every day during his paternity leave, he might just be able to work off that incipient paunch. The fact that Erica had cut back on sugary treats at home had also had an effect on him, and he had managed to drop a few pounds for that reason alone.

He passed the gas station and continued at a brisk pace along the road leading south. He was intending to go as far as the windmill before turning back. Maja was facing forward in her stroller, babbling away happily. She loved going out, and greeted everyone they met with a cheerful "Hi" and a big smile. She really was a little ray of sunshine, although she had a mischievous streak when she set her mind to it. That must come from Erica's side of the family, Patrik thought.

As he went along, he felt increasingly happy with life. Things were going incredibly well these days. At long last he and Erica had the house to themselves. Not that he had anything against Anna and the kids, but it wasn't easy living in such close proximity day in and day out. And then there was the situation with his mother. It bothered him, and he felt as if he always ended up caught between her and Erica. He could understand Erica's irritation when his mother marched straight in and went on at great length about how they ran their home and looked after Maja, but he wished Erica could do as he did and simply turn a deaf ear. And surely they had to have some sympathy for Kristina; after all, she lived alone and didn't have much to occupy her mind apart from Patrik and his family. His sister, Lotta, lived in Gothenburg, and although that was hardly a million miles away, it was much easier for Kristina to come over to their place. She could also be a big help; he and Erica had been able to go out to dinner a couple of times while his mother babysat, and . . . he just wished Erica could appreciate the advantages a little more.

"Look, look!" Maja shouted excitedly, pointing her chubby little finger as they reached the pasture where the Rimfaxe horses were grazing. Patrik wasn't particularly fond of horses, but had to admit that Norwegian fjord horses were quite sweet, and looked relatively harmless. Patrik and Maja stopped to watch them for a while, and Patrik made a mental note to bring some apples or carrots next time. Once Maja had had her fill of gazing at the animals, they set off again toward the windmill, then headed back in the direction of Fjällbacka.

As always, he was fascinated by the church tower rising impressively over the brow of the hill, but suddenly he spotted a familiar car. No blue lights or sirens, so it didn't look as if there was an emergency, but still he felt his pulse rate increase. When the first police car came over the hill, he saw the second one right behind it, and frowned. Both cars. It must be something pretty significant. He began to wave when the first car was about a hundred yards away. It slowed down, and Patrik went over to

Martin, who was driving. Maja waved her arms excitedly. In her world it was always cool when something was happening.

"Morning, Hedström. Out for a walk, I see." Martin waved back at Maja.

"Well, yes, one has to keep in shape. What's going on?" The second car pulled in behind, and Patrik nodded to Mellberg and Gösta.

"Hello, I'm Paula Morales." Only now did Patrik notice that an unfamiliar woman in police uniform was sitting next to Martin; he shook her hand and introduced himself before Martin had time to answer his question.

"Someone's found a body. Not far from here."

"Suspicious circumstances?" Patrik frowned again.

Martin shrugged. "That's all we know at the moment. Two boys found the body and called us." The car behind sounded its horn, which made Maja jump.

"Listen," Martin said quickly. "Can't you jump in and come with us? I don't feel entirely happy with . . . you know who," he said, nodding in the direction of the other car.

"How's that going to work?" Patrik said. "I've got Maja with me and, besides, I'm actually on leave."

"Please," Martin said, tilting his head to one side. "Just come and have a look, and I promise I'll drive you home. The stroller will fit in the trunk."

"You haven't got a child seat. . . ."

"Okay, fair point. But you could walk there—it's just around the corner. First right, second house on the left. It says Frankel on the mailbox."

Patrik hesitated, but another beep from the car behind made him decide.

"All right, I'll come and have a look, but you'll have to watch Maja while I go inside. And not a word to Erica—she'd go crazy if she found out I'd taken Maja on a job."

"Promise," Martin said with a wink. He waved to Mellberg and Gösta and put the car in gear. "See you there."

"Okay," Patrik replied with the distinct feeling that this was something he was bound to regret. However, curiosity triumphed over his instinct for self-preservation, and he turned Maja's stroller around and set off briskly toward Hamburgsund.

"All this pine has to go!" Anna was standing with her hands on her hips, trying to look as fierce as possible.

"What's wrong with pine?" Dan said, scratching his head.

"It's ugly! Any more questions?" Anna said, but couldn't help laughing. "Don't look so horrified, honey. But I mean it—there's nothing uglier than pine furniture. And the bed is the ugliest thing of all. Besides which, I don't want to sleep any longer in the bed you shared with Pernilla. I can cope with living in the same house, but the same bed . . . no way."

"I get that, but buying a whole lot of new furniture is going to be expensive." He looked worried. Since he and Anna had gotten together, he had decided to keep the house, but it was still pretty tricky to make ends meet. Along with Anna's Emma and Adrian, he also had his three girls—Belinda, Malin, and Lisen—to think about.

"I've still got the money from when Erica bought me out of Mom and Dad's house. Lucas couldn't access any of that, so we can use some of it to buy new stuff. We can go together if you like, or you can give me free rein if you're brave enough."

"Believe me," Dan said, "I'm more than happy to get out of making decisions about furniture. As long as it's not too crazy, you can buy whatever the hell you like. Enough talking, come and give me a kiss." He pulled her close and kissed her long and hard. As so often happened, things quickly got steamy, and Dan had just started to unfasten Anna's bra when someone yanked open the front door and marched in. As the kitchen was in full view from the hallway, there was no doubt about what was going on.

"For God's sake, you two are so disgusting, making out in the kitchen!" Belinda stormed past them and went up to her room, her face bright red with fury. At the top of the stairs she stopped and yelled down, "I'm going back to Mom's as soon as I can! At least when I'm there I don't have to look at you shoving your tongues down each other's throats all the time! You're so embarrassing! It's disgusting! Get it? Got it? Good!"

Bang! The door of Belinda's room slammed shut, and they heard the key turn in the lock. Seconds later, music was booming out at full volume, making the plates on the drain-board jump up and down, rattling in time with the beat.

"Oops," Dan said, grimacing as he glanced at the ceiling.

"Oops indeed," Anna said, extricating herself from his embrace. "She's really struggling with all this." She picked up the dancing plates and put them in the sink.

"Yes, but she's just got to accept the fact that I've met someone new," Dan said crossly.

"Try and put yourself in her shoes. First of all, you and Pernilla split up, then"—she chose her words carefully—"a number of girls come and go, so to speak, and then I turn up and move in with two small children. Belinda is only seventeen, which is difficult enough in itself. Having to deal with three strangers moving in on top of that. . . ."

"I know you're right." Dan sighed. "But I have no idea how to handle a teenager. I mean, do I leave her alone, or will she feel neglected if I do that? Or should I go and talk to her and risk her thinking I'm interfering? I mean, where's the goddamn manual?"

Anna laughed. "I think they forgot the manual in the maternity ward. But I do think you could try talking to her. If she slams the door in your face, well, at least you've tried. And then you try again. And again. She's scared of losing you. She's scared of losing her right to be a little girl. She's scared that we'll take over everything now that we've moved in. That's hardly surprising."

"What have I done to deserve such a clever woman?" Dan said, pulling her close once more.

"I have no idea," Anna said with a smile, burying her face in his chest. "But I'm probably not all that clever. I just seem that way in comparison with your previous conquests. . . ."

"Hey!" Dan laughed and squeezed her tightly. "Don't be like that. Actually, I think we might keep that pine bed after all. . . ."

"Do you want me to stay here or not?"

"Okay, you win. It's already gone."

They laughed. And kissed. From up above, the deafening thud of pop music continued unabated.

Martin saw the boys as soon as he pulled into the drive in front of the house. They were standing slightly to one side, their arms wrapped around their bodies, shivering slightly. They both had the same pallor, and the relief on their faces when the police cars arrived was unmistakable.

"Martin Molin." He held out his hand to the closest boy, who mumbled that his name was Adam Andersson. The other boy, who was just behind him, waved his right hand in a defensive gesture as he said apologetically, and with a certain degree of embarrassment, "I threw up and wiped my mouth with. . . . It's probably best if we don't shake hands."

Martin nodded sympathetically. He had had the same reaction himself when faced with a dead body, and it was nothing to be ashamed of.

"Okay, so what happened?" He turned to Adam, who seemed more composed. He was shorter than his friend, with longish blond hair and an angry eruption of acne covering his cheeks.

"We . . . " Adam looked inquiringly at Mattias, who simply shrugged, so he went on. "We thought we'd have a look around inside the house; it seemed like both the old guys were away."

"Both the old guys?" Martin said. "Two people live here?"

Mattias replied, "Two brothers. I don't know their first names, but my mom will be able to tell you. She's been taking care of their mail ever since the beginning of June. The one guy always goes away over the summer, the other one usually stays home. But this time nobody was collecting the mail from the mailbox, so we thought. . . ." His voice died away and he stared down at his shoes. A dead fly was stuck to the top of one shoe, and with an expression of disgust he lashed out with his foot to get rid of it. "Is he the one who's dead?" he asked, glancing up.

"At this stage, you know more than we do," Martin said. "But carry on: you thought you'd take a look around inside. What happened next?"

"Mattias found a window that wasn't shut properly, and he climbed in first," Adam said. "Then he pulled me up. When we jumped down onto the floor, we noticed that something was crunching under our feet, but we couldn't see what it was because it was too dark."

"Dark?" Martin interrupted. "Why was it dark?" Out of the corner of his eye he could see Gösta, Paula, and Mellberg waiting to one side, listening to what the boys had to say.

"All the blinds were drawn," Adam explained patiently. "But we opened the blind on the window where we got in, and then we saw that the floor was covered in dead flies. And the place stank."

"It sure did," Mattias said, looking as if he might throw up again.

"And then?" Martin prompted.

"Then we moved farther into the room, and the desk chair was facing away from us so we couldn't see what was in it. And

I just got the feeling that . . . I mean, I've watched *CSI*, and dead flies plus a horrible smell . . . you don't exactly have to be Einstein to work out that somebody had died in there. So I went over to the chair and turned it around . . . and there he was!"

Evidently Mattias could see the image all too clearly; he turned away and threw up on the grass behind him. He wiped his hand across his mouth and whispered, "Sorry."

"It's okay," Martin said. "We've all done that at some point when confronted by the sight of a dead body."

"I haven't," Mellberg said superciliously.

"Me neither," Gösta put in laconically.

"No, nor me," Paula supplied.

Martin turned and gave them a dirty look.

"He looked disgusting," Adam added helpfully. In spite of the shock, he seemed to be deriving a certain amount of enjoyment from the situation. Behind him, Mattias was doubled over, retching yet again, but this time there seemed to be nothing but bile left.

"Could someone take the boys home?" Martin said, turning to his colleagues. At first no one spoke, then Gösta volunteered, "I'll take them. Come on, guys, I'll drive you home."

"We only live a couple of hundred yards away," Mattias said weakly.

"In that case, I'll walk you home." Gösta gestured to the boys to follow him, and they shambled after him like typical teenagers. Mattias looked grateful, while Adam was obviously disappointed at missing out on the next stage of the procedure.

Martin gazed after them until they had disappeared around the bend, then said in a tone of voice that was anything but optimistic: "Okay, let's see what we've got here."

Bertil Mellberg cleared his throat. "Listen, it's not that I have a problem with dead bodies and that kind of thing. . . . Definitely not. . . . I've seen plenty in my time. But I think someone ought to . . . check out the area. Might be best if I do that, since I'm the senior officer here, and the most experienced." He cleared his throat again.

Martin and Paula exchanged an amused glance, but Martin managed to rearrange his face before he replied, "Good point, Bertil. It would be best if someone with your experience checks out the garden, while Paula and I take a look inside."

"Exactly. That would be the most sensible course of action." Mellberg bounced up and down on his heels for a second, then set off across the lawn.

"Shall we?" Martin said. Paula nodded.

"Careful," Martin said before he opened the door. "We mustn't destroy any evidence in case it turns out not to be death from natural causes. We'll just have a quick look, then forensics can move in."

"I have five years' experience with the violent crimes unit, Stockholm County Police. I know how to behave at a possible crime scene," Paula pointed out, but without a trace of resentment.

"Sorry, I did actually know that," Martin apologized before focusing on the task that lay before them.

The house was eerily silent as they stepped into the hallway. There wasn't a sound, apart from their footsteps. Martin wondered if the silence would have seemed as chilling if they hadn't known that there was a body in the house; probably not, he concluded.

"In there," he whispered, then realized that there was no reason to whisper. He said it again in a normal tone of voice that bounced off the walls in the silence: "In there."

Paula followed, staying right behind him. Martin took a couple of steps closer to the room that had to be the library, and pushed the door open. The strange smell they had noticed as soon as they walked into the house was even stronger now.

The boys had been right. The floor was covered in a thick layer of flies, crunching underfoot as first he and then Paula moved into the room. The smell was sweet, cloying, but it must have been a thousand times worse at first.

"There's no doubt that someone died here a good while ago," Paula said as both she and Martin spotted what was at the far end of the room.

"No doubt at all," Martin agreed, an unpleasant taste in his mouth. He steeled himself and cautiously crossed the room, heading toward the body in the chair.

"Stay there." He held up his hand, and Paula obediently remained in the doorway. She didn't mind; the fewer feet that trampled around in the room, the better.

"This doesn't look like natural causes to me," Martin stated, bile rising and falling in his throat. He swallowed hard to quell the gag impulse, trying to concentrate on the job. In spite of the poor condition of the corpse, there wasn't much doubt. A large crush wound on the right side of the victim's head told its own story. The person in the chair had been killed with brutal force.

Martin turned and left the room. Paula followed. After a couple of deep breaths out in the fresh air, he began to feel less like throwing up. At that moment, he saw Patrik turn the corner and head toward them up the gravel path.

"It's murder," Martin said as soon as Patrik was within ear-shot. "Torbjörn and his team will have to come over and do their stuff. There's nothing else we can do right now."

"Okay," said Patrik grimly. "Can I just. . . ." He paused and looked down at Maja.

"Go in and have a look. I can take care of Maja," Martin said eagerly; he immediately went over and picked her up. "Come on, sweetheart, let's go and look at these pretty flowers."

"Fowers," Maja said happily, pointing at the colorful display.

"Have you been inside?" Patrik asked.

Paula nodded. "It's not a pretty sight. Seems as if he's been sitting there since late spring. That's my assessment, anyway."

"I imagine you've seen more than your fair share in Stockholm."

"Not many that have been dead for this long, but there were a couple."

"Okay, I'll go in and have a quick look. I'm actually on paternity leave, but. . . ."

Paula smiled. "It's hard to stay away. I can understand that. But Martin seems to have the situation under control." She nodded toward the flower bed with a smile, where Martin was crouched beside Maja, admiring the blooms.

"He's a rock. In every way," Patrik said as he set off toward the house. A few minutes later, he was back.

"I agree with Martin. Not much room for doubt; there's a severe blow to the head."

"No sign of anything suspicious," Mellberg panted as he rounded the corner of the house. "So how are things inside? Have you been in, Hedström?" He looked encouragingly at Patrik, who nodded.

"Yes, it's definitely murder, I'd say. Will you call forensics?"

"Of course," Mellberg said pompously. "I'm in charge of this madhouse, after all. What are you doing here, anyway? You were the one that insisted on taking paternity leave, and now that you've got it, you pop up like a jack-in-the-box." Mellberg turned to Paula and went on: "I don't understand these modern ideas—men staying at home changing diapers and women running around in uniform." He turned his back on them and stomped off toward the car to call forensics.

"Welcome to Tanumshede police station," Patrik said drily; Paula responded with an amused smile.

"It doesn't bother me; there are plenty of people like him. If I took any notice of the dinosaurs in the force, I'd have thrown in the towel a long time ago."

"It's just as well that you see things that way," Patrik said. "And the good thing about Mellberg is that he's consistent—he discriminates against everyone and everything."

"Well, that's some consolation," Paula laughed.

"What's so funny?" Martin asked, with Maja still in his arms.

"Mellberg," chorused Patrick and Paula.

"What's he said now?"

"Oh, just the usual," Patrik replied, reaching for Maja. "But it seems as if Paula can take it, so I'm sure things will work out. Okay, honey, time to go home. Wave good-bye like a good girl."

Maja waved and gave Martin an extra little smile; his face lit up.

"You're taking my girl away? I thought we had something going on there." He stuck out his lower lip, pretending to look sad.

"There will only ever be one man in Maja's life, and that's Daddy—isn't that right, sweetheart?" Patrik buried his nose in Maja's soft neck, and she screamed with laughter. Then he put her in the stroller and waved to his colleagues. Part of him was relieved at the thought that he could leave them and go home; another part wanted nothing more than to stay there.

She was confused. Was it Monday? Or was it Tuesday already? Britta paced nervously back and forth in the living room. It was so . . . frustrating. It was as if the harder she tried to catch something, the quicker it ran away from her. In her more lucid moments, a voice inside told her that she ought to be able to control this with willpower, that she should be able to make her brain obey her. But at the same time she knew that her brain was changing, breaking down, losing its ability to remember, to hold on to times, facts, information, faces.

Monday. It was Monday. Exactly. Yesterday her daughters and their families had been here for Sunday lunch. Yesterday. So today was Monday. Definitely. Britta stopped halfway across the room, greatly relieved. It felt like a minor triumph. She knew what day it was.

Tears sprang to her eyes, and she sat down at one end of the sofa. The Josef Frank design was reassuringly familiar. She and Herman had bought the fabric together. Which meant that she had chosen it while he made appropriate noises. Anything to make her happy. He would cheerfully have accepted an orange sofa with green polka dots if that had been what she wanted. Herman . . . where was he anyway? She started picking anxiously at the floral pattern. She knew where he was. Absolutely. She could see his mouth moving as he explained where he was going. She even remembered that he had repeated it several times. But just like the day of the week a few moments ago, the information slid away from her, mocking her, sneering at her. She gripped the arm of the sofa in frustration. She should be able to remember. If she concentrated. She started to panic. Where was Herman? Would he be gone for long? Surely he hadn't gone away? Left her here? Perhaps he'd actually left her? Was that what his mouth had been saying as it moved in her mind's eye? She had to reassure herself that it wasn't true. She had to go and look, check that his things were still there. Britta leapt to her feet and ran upstairs, the panic pounding in her ears like a tsunami. What was it that Herman had said? One glance in the closet calmed her. All his clothes were hanging in the right place. Jackets, sweaters, shirts. They were all there. But she still didn't know where he was.

Britta threw herself down on the bed, rolled into a ball like a toddler, and wept. Inside her brain, things kept on disappearing. Second by second. Minute by minute. The hard drive of her life was in the process of being wiped. And there wasn't a thing she could do about it.

"Hi, there, you two! That must have been a really long walk. You were gone for ages!" Erica came to meet Patrik and Maja, and was rewarded with a wet kiss from her daughter.

"Yes . . . I thought you were supposed to be working?" Patrik avoided looking Erica in the eye.

"I was. . . ." Erica sighed. "But I'm finding it hard to get started. I've spent most of my time staring at the screen and eating chocolate caramels. If I carry on like this, I'll weigh two hundred pounds by the time this book is finished." She helped Patrik to peel off Maja's outdoor clothes. "I couldn't help reading a few pages of Mom's diaries."

"Anything interesting?" Patrik asked, relieved that he seemed to have avoided any further questions about why their walk had taken such a long time.

"Not really—it's mostly just everyday stuff. I only read a little bit. I think I need to take my time."

Erica went into the kitchen. "Tea?" she said, mainly to change the subject.

"Please," Patrik replied, hanging up his and Maja's clothes. He followed Erica and watched as she busied herself with water, tea bags, and mugs. They could hear Maja rummaging among her toys in the living room. After a few minutes Erica placed two steaming mugs of tea on the kitchen table, and they sat down opposite each other.

"Okay, out with it," she said, gazing at Patrik. She knew him so well. That furtive expression, the fingers drumming nervously on the table. There was something he didn't want to tell her—or didn't dare.

"What?" he said, trying to look as innocent as possible.

"There's absolutely no point in opening those baby-blue eyes wide. What aren't you telling me?" She took a sip of hot tea and waited for him to stop wriggling like a worm and get to the point, her eyes dancing with amusement.

"The thing is. . . ."

"Yes?" Erica said helpfully; she couldn't deny that a small, sadistic part of her was enjoying his obvious discomfort.

"The thing is . . . something happened while Maja and I were out for our walk."

"You've both come home in one piece, so what might that have been?"

"Well. . . ." Patrik took a sip of his tea to gain some time while he tried to work out the best way to explain what had happened. "Well, we were walking down toward Lersten's mill, and my colleagues just happened to be out on a job." He ventured a glance at Erica, who raised one eyebrow and waited for the next installment.

"They'd had a call about a body in a house near Hamburg-sund, and they were on their way there."

"I see. But you're on paternity leave, so it has nothing to do with you." She stopped, the mug halfway to her mouth. "You didn't. . . ." She stared at him suspiciously.

"Er, yes," Patrik said, his voice slightly too high, his gaze fixed on the table.

"You took Maja to a place where a body had been found?" She nailed him to the spot with the look in her eyes.

"Well, yes, but Martin took Maja while I went inside for a couple of minutes. They were looking at flowers." He tried a conciliatory smile, but was met by an icy glare.

"You went inside for a couple of minutes." The shards of ice were clinking implacably. "You are on paternity leave. With the emphasis on 'leave.' And with the emphasis on 'paternity' too, for that matter! How hard can it be to say 'I'm not working at the moment'?"

"I just went inside for a couple of minutes," Patrik said feebly, but he knew that Erica was right. He was in fact on leave.

Paternity leave. His colleagues at the station could manage perfectly well. And he shouldn't have taken Maja to a crime scene.

At that moment he realized there was one tiny detail that Erica didn't know about. A muscle in his face twitched nervously as he swallowed and added, "By the way, it was a murder."

"A murder!" Erica's voice rose to a falsetto. "So, not content with taking Maja to a place where a body had been found, now you're telling me this body was the victim of a murder?" She shook her head, as if the words she was trying to get out were piling up and getting stuck in her throat.

"I'm not going to do anything else from now on." Patrik spread his hands wide. "The others will have to manage. I'm on leave until January, they know that. I'm going to devote myself to Maja, one hundred percent. Promise!"

"You'd better," Erica growled. She was so angry, she wanted to reach across the table and shake him, but then her curiosity got the better of her and she calmed down slightly.

"Where was it? Do you know who the victim was?"

"No idea. It was a big white house about a hundred yards along on the left, first right after the mill."

Erica was looking at him with an odd expression. Then she said: "A big white house with gray woodwork?"

Patrik thought for a moment, then nodded. "Yes, I think so. It said 'Frankel' on the mailbox."

"I know who lives there. Axel and Erik Frankel. You remember, I took the Nazi medal to Erik Frankel."

Patrik stared at her, lost for words. How could he have forgotten that? Frankel wasn't exactly the most common name in the world.

From the living room they could hear Maja's cheerful, wordless babble.

It was late afternoon by the time they got back to the station. Torbjörn Ruud, the chief forensic technician, and his team had arrived, done a thorough job, and left. The body was on its way to the forensic pathology unit, where it would be examined in every imaginable (and unimaginable) way.

"Hell of a Monday," Mellberg sighed as Gösta drove into the station parking lot.

"Yep," Gösta said. As usual, he had no intention of wasting words unnecessarily.

As they walked into the station, Mellberg just had time to realize that something was heading toward him at high speed when a furry form hurled itself at him, and he felt a tongue trying desperately to lick his face.

"Stop it! Stop that right now!" He waved the dog away in horror; Ernst flattened his ears and loped off in Annika's direction, radiating disappointment. At least he knew he was sure of a welcome there. Mellberg wiped off the slobber with the back of his hand, muttering darkly to himself, while Gösta struggled to keep a straight face. The fact that Mellberg's carefully arranged nest of hair had come tumbling down added to the entertainment value. Mellberg crossly adjusted his coiffure and kept muttering all the way to his office.

Gösta was chuckling as he walked into his own office, but was startled to hear a familiar bellow: "Ernst! Ernst! Come here!"

Gösta looked around in surprise. It was quite some time since his colleague Ernst Lundgren had been fired, and he hadn't heard anything to suggest that Lundgren was coming back.

But Mellberg shouted again: "Ernst! Come here! This minute!"

Gösta stepped out into the corridor, hoping to solve the mystery, and saw Mellberg pointing at something on the floor, his face bright red. A suspicion began to grow and, sure enough, the mutt came shambling along, hanging his head.

"Ernst, what is this?"

The mutt did his best to look as if he had no idea what Mellberg was talking about, but the turd in the middle of the floor of Mellberg's office told a different story.

"Annika," Mellberg roared, and a second later the station secretary came hurrying toward them.

"Oh, dear, I see we've had a little accident." She glanced sympathetically at the dog, who gratefully shuffled closer to her.

"A little accident? Ernst has crapped on my floor!"

This was all too much for Gösta, who started giggling; the effort of trying to stop himself just made things worse. Annika caught his eye, and before long they were both helpless with laughter, tears pouring down their cheeks.

"What's going on?" Martin said curiously; Paula was right behind him.

"Ernst . . ." Gösta could hardly breathe. "Ernst . . . has crapped on the floor."

Martin looked completely blank, but as he glanced from the pile on Mellberg's floor to the dog pressing itself against Annika's legs, the penny dropped.

"You're . . . you're calling the dog Ernst?" Martin said as he burst out laughing. By now only Mellberg and Paula were not cackling hysterically, but while Mellberg looked as if he was about to explode with rage, Paula hadn't a clue what was so funny.

"I'll explain later," Martin said to her, wiping his eyes. "You've got a sense of humor, Bertil, I'll say that for you," he said to Mellberg.

"Well, yes, I suppose I have," Mellberg said, reluctantly forcing a smile. "Right, Annika, could you get this cleaned up, please, so that we can get on with our work?" He grunted and went and sat behind his desk. The dog glanced uncertainly from Annika to Mellberg, but eventually decided that the worst was probably over, and followed his new master, tail wagging slowly.

The rest of them watched the odd couple in amazement, wondering what the dog saw in Bertil Mellberg that they had obviously missed.

Erica couldn't stop thinking about Erik Frankel all evening. She hadn't known him well, but he and his brother were somehow an essential part of Fjällbacka. They had always been referred to as "the doctor's sons" within the community, in spite of the fact that it was fifty years since their father had been the local physician, and over forty years since he had passed away.

Erica recalled her visit to the house the brothers had shared. Her only visit. They still lived together in the home where they had grown up, both unmarried, both with a burning interest in Germany and Nazism, albeit each in his own way. Erik had been a history teacher at the high school, but in his spare time he had collected artifacts from the Nazi period, in which he had a particular interest. Axel, the older brother, had some connection with the Simon Wiesenthal Center, if she remembered rightly, and she had a vague recollection that he had suffered during the war in some way.

She had called Erik first of all, told him what she had found, and described the medal. She had asked if he could help her research its origins, how it might have ended up among her mother's possessions. His initial reaction had been silence. She had said "Hello?" several times; she thought he had accidentally hung up. Then, in a strange tone of voice, he had said that if she brought the medal over, he would have a look at it. She had been struck by the long silence, the odd tone of voice. She hadn't mentioned it to Patrik at the time; she had convinced herself that she had imagined it. And when she went over to the brothers' house, there had been nothing untoward in his reaction to the medal. Erik had greeted her politely, shown her into the library, and asked to see the medal. He had taken it with guarded interest and examined it closely. Then he had asked if he might keep it for a while. Do a little research. Erica had nodded, grateful that someone wanted to investigate.

He had also shown her his collection. She had gazed with a mixture of fear and fascination at all the items that were so inextricably linked with a dark, evil period in history. She couldn't help asking how someone who was opposed to everything Nazism stood for could want to collect and surround himself with objects that reminded him of that very thing. Erik had hesitated before replying. Looking pensive, he had picked up a cap bearing the emblem of the SS, fingering it as he considered how to phrase his answer.

"I don't trust man's ability to remember," he had said eventually. "Without things that we can see or touch, we tend to forget whatever we do not want to remember. I collect artifacts that can remind us. And I suppose a part of me wants to keep them from those who look at them with different eyes. Admiring eyes."

Erica had nodded. She had partly understood, partly not. They had shaken hands and said good-bye.

And now he was dead. Murdered. Perhaps it had happened not long after she had been there. According to what Patrik had reluctantly divulged, he had been sitting there dead all summer.

Once again she remembered Erik's odd tone of voice when she'd told him about the medal, and she turned to Patrik, who was sitting beside her on the sofa, zapping through the TV channels.

"Do you know if the medal is still there?"

He looked at her inquiringly. "I didn't even think about it. I've no idea. But there was no sign of a robbery and, in any case, who would be interested in an old Nazi medal? I mean, they're not exactly unique. There were quite a few, as far as I know."

"Yes . . . you're right," Erica said hesitantly. She still felt uncomfortable. "But could you give your colleagues a call tomorrow and ask them to have a look for the medal?"

"Not really," Patrik said. "I think they've got other things to do at the moment. But we can speak to Erik's brother later. Ask him to find it for us. I'm sure it's still in the house somewhere."

"Oh yes, Axel. Where is he? Why didn't he find his brother all summer?"

Patrik shrugged. "I'm on paternity leave, if you recall. You could always ring Mellberg and ask him."

"Oh, very funny," Erica said with a smile. Yet she couldn't shake off the anxiety. "But don't you think it's strange that Axel didn't find him?"

"Yes, but didn't you say he was away when you went there?"

"Erik said his brother was out of the country, but that was back in June."

"Why are you wondering about this?" Patrik turned his attention back to the TV. His favorite home-improvement program was about to begin.

"Oh, I don't know," Erica said, staring blankly at the TV screen. She couldn't explain why this feeling of unease had come over her, but she could hear Erik's silence on the telephone, that slightly distorted, grating note in his voice when he asked her to come over with the medal. He had reacted to something. Something to do with the medal.

She tried to focus on Martin Timell's carpentry skills instead. With limited success.

"You shoulda been there, Gramps! That black bastard tried to cut in the line, and pow! One kick and he went down like a fucking tree. Then I kicked him in the nuts and he just lay there squealing for fifteen minutes."

"And what exactly have you achieved by doing that, Per? Apart from the fact that you could be charged with assault and sent off to a juvenile institution, you won't win any sympathy that way. The opposition will just gang up on you even more.

And, in the end, instead of assisting our cause, you will have helped to mobilize more support for those who are against us." Frans looked wearily at his grandson. Sometimes he didn't know how he was going to curb all those teenage hormones raging in the boy's body. And Per knew so little. In spite of his tough exterior, with the combat gear, heavy boots, and shaved head, he was little more than a frightened child of fifteen. He knew nothing about life. He didn't know how the world worked. He didn't know how to channel the destructive impulses so that they could be used like a spear, piercing the very structure of society.

The boy hung his head in shame, sitting there beside him on the steps. Frans knew that his harsh words had cowed the kid. He was the one his grandson wanted to impress, but he would be doing Per a disservice if he didn't show him how the world worked. It was cold and hard and unforgiving, and only the strongest would emerge victorious from the fight.

At the same time, he loved the boy, wanted to protect him from harm. Frans put his arm around his grandson's shoulders; he was struck by how skinny they still were. Per had inherited his grandfather's physique: tall and lanky, with narrow shoulders. No amount of time spent in the gym could alter their constitution.

"You just need to think," Frans said in a gentler tone of voice. "Think before you act. Use words instead of your fists. Violence should be your last resort, not your first." He gave the boy's shoulders an extra squeeze. For a second Per leaned against him, the way he used to do when he was little. Then he remembered that he wanted to be a man. That he wasn't a child anymore. But he also remembered that the most important thing in the world, both then and now, was to make his grandfather proud. Per straightened up.

"I was just so fucking mad when he pushed past me, Gramps. Because that's what they do. They push themselves forward all over the place, they think they own the world, they think they own Sweden. It made me so . . . mad."

"I know," Frans said, removing his arm from around the boy's shoulders and patting him on the knee instead. "But, please, just be careful. You're no good to me if you end up in jail."

4

Kristiansand 1943

He had battled seasickness all the way to Norway. It hadn't seemed to affect the others. They were used to it; they had grown up at sea. They had their sea legs, as his father always said. They rolled with every swell and moved steadily around the deck; they never seemed to suffer from the nausea that surged up into his throat from his stomach. Axel leaned heavily against the rail. He just wanted to bend over and throw up, but he refused to put himself through the humiliation. He knew the teasing would be good-natured, but he was too proud to put up with the fishermen's banter. They were almost there, and as soon as he stepped onto dry land, the nausea would disappear as if by magic. He knew that from experience; he had made this journey many times by now.

"Land ahoy!" shouted Elof, the skipper. "We'll be there in ten minutes." He gave Axel a long look as the boy came over to stand by him at the helm. The old man was tanned and weather-beaten, with skin like wrinkled leather, after being exposed to wind and sun since childhood.

"Everything in order?" he asked quietly, glancing around. They could see the German ships lined up in Kristiansand Harbor, a vivid reminder of reality. The Germans had invaded Norway. Sweden had been spared so far, but no one knew how long their good fortune would last. For now they would keep a watchful eye on their neighbor to the west, and on the progress of the Germans through the rest of Europe.

"You take care of your business and I'll take care of mine," Axel replied. It came out sounding rather more brusque than he had intended, but he always felt a pang of guilt at involving the crew in the risks he would have preferred to bear alone. Still, he wasn't forcing anyone to do this, he reminded himself. Elof had immediately said yes when Axel had asked if he could sail with him sometime, and transport certain . . . goods. He had never needed to explain what he was carrying, and Elof and the rest of the crew on board *Elfrida* had never asked.

They came alongside and got out the necessary papers. The Germans left nothing to chance, and there was always a rigorous examination of the relevant documents before they could even begin to unload their cargo. Once the formalities had been completed, they started to unload the machine parts that made up their official cargo. The Norwegians were there to receive the goods, while the Germans kept a close watch on the proceedings, their rifles at the ready in case the need should arise. Axel bided his time until the evening. He needed darkness to unload his special cargo. He usually carried food. Food and information. That was also the case this time.

After they had eaten dinner in oppressive silence, Axel sat down and waited impatiently for the hour on which they had agreed. A gentle tap on the glass made him and the others jump.

Axel quickly bent down, lifted up a section of the floor, and began to unload wooden crates. Silent, careful hands received the crates, which were piled up on the quayside. All this happened to the accompaniment of the Germans' loud conversations in the barracks a short distance away. By this time of night, strong drink had been consumed, which made their dangerous enterprise much easier. Drunken Germans were considerably easier to fool than sober Germans.

After a quiet "Thanks" in Norwegian, the cargo was off the boat and had disappeared into the darkness. Once again the handover had gone smoothly. With an intoxicating sense of relief, Axel went below again. Three pairs of eyes met his, but no one said a word. Elof merely nodded, then turned away and started filling his pipe. Axel felt an overwhelming gratitude toward these men. They defied both storms and Germans with the same calm approach. They had accepted long ago that the twists and turns of life and fate were not something they could control. You did the best you could, tried to live to the best of your ability. The rest was up to God's mercy.

Axel went to bed; he was exhausted. He fell asleep immediately, rocked by the gentle movement of the boat and the sound of the water lapping against the hull. Up in the barracks on the quayside, the voices of the Germans rose and fell. After a while they started singing, but by then Axel was already fast asleep.

5

"Okay, what have we got so far?" Mellberg glanced around the lunchroom. The coffee was made, the buns set out, and everyone was there.

Paula cleared her throat. "I've been in touch with Axel, the brother. Apparently he works in Paris and always spends the summer there. But he's on his way home. He sounded devastated when I told him about the death of his brother."

"Do we know when he left the country?" Martin turned to Paula, who consulted the notebook in front of her.

"June third, he says. I'll check, of course."

Martin nodded.

"Have we had a preliminary report from Torbjörn and his team yet?" Mellberg tried to move his feet a fraction. Ernst was lying on them with his full weight, but even though they were starting to go to sleep, for some reason Mellberg couldn't bring himself to push Ernst away.

"Nothing yet," Gösta said, reaching for a bun. "But I spoke to him this morning, and we might get something tomorrow."

"Good, keep at him," Mellberg said, making another attempt to shift his feet. But Ernst simply moved as well.

"Any suspects at this stage? Known enemies? Threats? Anything at all?" Mellberg looked challengingly at Martin, who shook his head.

"Nothing in our records, at any rate. But of course his area of interest was controversial. Nazism always arouses strong feelings."

"We could go over to the house and take a look. See if there are any threatening letters and so on in his drawers."

Everyone looked at Gösta in astonishment. The occasions on which he took the initiative were like volcanic eruptions—rare, but hard to ignore.

"Take Martin with you and head over there after the meeting," Mellberg said, smiling with satisfaction at Gösta, who nodded and quickly reverted to his normal lethargic expression and posture. Gösta Flygare came to life only on the golf course. His colleagues had long since realized and accepted this fact.

"Paula, can you check on when the brother—Axel, was it?—is due to land and make sure we have a chat with him? Since we don't yet know when Erik died, he could have hit his brother over the head, then fled the country. So I want you to pick him up as soon as he sets foot on Swedish soil. When does he get back?"

Paula consulted her notes once more. "He arrives at Landvetter at 9:15 tomorrow morning."

"Good, make sure he comes here before he does anything else." Mellberg really was going to have to move his feet now; he had unpleasant pins and needles, and they were beginning to feel numb. Ernst stood up, gave him a hurt look, then shambled out of the room with his tail between his legs, heading for his basket in Mellberg's office.

"Looks like true love," Annika said with a laugh as she watched him go.

"Actually," Mellberg said, clearing his throat. "I was just going to ask you—when is somebody coming to pick up that goddamn mutt?" He looked down at the table, and Annika adopted her most innocent expression.

"Well, it's not that easy. I've made plenty of calls, but it seems no one is able to take in a dog of that size, so if you could maybe take care of him for another couple of days . . . ?" Annika gazed at Mellberg with her big blue eyes.

He grunted. "I suppose I can put up with the mutt for another day or two. But that's it—after that, he's back out on the street if you can't find anywhere for him to go."

"Thank you, Bertil, that's so kind of you. I'll pull out all the stops." Annika winked at the others when Mellberg wasn't looking, and it was all they could do not to burst out laughing. They were beginning to see where this was going. Annika was a clever woman, no doubt about it.

"Excellent," Mellberg said as he got to his feet. "Let's get back to work, then." He ambled out of the kitchen.

"You heard what the boss said," Martin added. "Okay, Gösta, shall we go?"

Gösta already seemed to be regretting the fact that he had made a suggestion that was going to saddle him with more work, but he nodded wearily and followed Martin. He just had to go with it. At least he would be out on the course by seven in the morning on both Saturday and Sunday. Everything between now and then was just routine.

Erica couldn't stop thinking about Erik Frankel and the medal. She tried to focus on something else and actually succeeded for a couple of hours as she finally managed to make a start on her manuscript. But as soon as she allowed her concentration to drop, the thoughts were back. That brief meeting with Erik had given her the impression of a gentle, polite man who came to life when he had the opportunity to talk about Nazism, his great interest.

She saved what she had written so far, and after a brief hesitation she launched Internet Explorer and Googled "Erik Frankel." There were plenty of matches; some were obviously completely wrong and concerned other people. But most related to the right Erik Frankel, and she spent a good hour clicking through just part of the deluge of information. Erik had been born in Fjällbacka in 1930. He had one brother, Axel, who was four years older, but no other siblings. His father had been a doctor in Fjällbacka from 1935 to 1954, and the house in which Erik and his brother lived was the parental home. She continued searching. His name cropped up in a number of forums for those interested in Nazism, but she found nothing to suggest that he was in any way a sympathizer. Quite the contrary, although in certain posts she detected a reluctant admiration for certain aspects of Nazism. Or at least a powerful fascination, which seemed to be what drove him.

She closed down the Internet connection and linked her hands behind her head. She didn't have time for this, but her curiosity had been aroused.

A cautious tap on the door behind her made Erica jump.

"Sorry, am I disturbing you?" Patrik poked his head around the door.

"No, it's fine." She spun her chair around so that she was facing him.

"I just wanted to tell you that Maja's asleep; I really need to pop out and do some shopping. Could you take this?" He held out the baby monitor.

"Well . . . I am supposed to be working." Erica sighed to herself. "Where are you going?"

"I've got to pick up some books from the post office, then I need to go to the pharmacy for some Nezeril, then I thought I might buy a lottery ticket while I'm out. And I'll do some food shopping too, of course."

Erica suddenly felt immensely weary. She thought about all the times she had gone shopping over the past year, always with Maja in her stroller or in her arms. She had often been drenched in sweat by the time she'd finished. She hadn't had anyone to look after Maja while she'd gone swanning off to do her errands in peace and quiet. But she pushed the thought aside; she didn't want to seem petty and unaccommodating.

"Of course I'll take care of her," she said with a smile, trying to look sincere. "She's asleep anyway, so I can work at the same time."

"You're a star," Patrik said, kissing her on the cheek before he left.

"That's me, an absolute star," Erica muttered to herself, returning to her manuscript as she tried to push all thoughts of Erik Frankel to the back of her mind.

Her fingers were just hovering over the keyboard when the baby monitor crackled. Erica stiffened. It was probably nothing. Perhaps Maja was just turning over in her crib; the monitor was slightly too sensitive sometimes. She heard the sound of the car starting up, then Patrik driving off. She gazed at the screen, searching for her next sentence. Another crackle. She stared at the baby monitor as if she could cast a spell and make it stay quiet, but she was rewarded with a loud "Waaaaah." Followed by a deafening "Mommeeeee . . . Daddeeeee. . . ."

With a feeling of resignation she pushed back her chair and stood up. Typical. She opened the door to Maja's room to find her daughter on her feet, screaming the place down.

"You're supposed to be sleeping, sweetheart."

Maja shook her head.

"Come on, it's sleepy time now." Erica made an effort to speak as firmly as possible. She laid her daughter down in the crib, but Maja bounced back up as if she had rubber bands attached to her joints.

"Mommeeeee!" she screamed in a voice that could shatter glass. Erica could feel the anger bubbling up in her chest. She had done this so many times. So many days of feeding Maja, putting her to bed, carrying her around, playing with her. She loved her daughter, but she desperately needed to be able to hand over the responsibility at last. To have some respite. To have the opportunity to be an adult and do the things an adult did—just as Patrik had been able to do during the whole of the year she had spent at home with Maja.

She laid the child down again, which merely resulted in Maja's working herself up into a frenzy.

"Go to sleep!" Erica said; she backed out of the room and closed the door. Seething with rage, she picked up the phone and called Patrik's cell, hitting the buttons a fraction too hard. His phone began to ring, and she jumped when she heard a shrill sound from downstairs. Patrik's cell was on the kitchen table.

"For fuck's sake!" She slammed the portable phone down on the table, then forced herself to take a couple of deep breaths. Angry tears sprang to her eyes, but she tried to reason with her saner self. After all, it wasn't the end of the world if she had to look after Maja for a little while. At the same time, it was, because it meant she didn't feel she could let go, didn't feel that Patrik had taken the baton.

There was nothing she could do right now, though, and the most important thing was to not take it out on Maja: it wasn't her fault. Erica took another deep breath and went back into the nursery. Maja was roaring, her face bright red. And an unmistakable smell had begun to pervade the room. The mystery was solved. That was why Maja hadn't been able to sleep. With a certain level of regret, and a strong sense of inadequacy, Erica gently picked up her daughter and consoled her, cupping the downy little head against her chest. "It's all right, sweetheart, Mommy will get rid of that nasty, smelly diaper, it's all right." Maja pressed herself against her mother, snuffling quietly. Down in the kitchen, Patrik's cell began to ring again.

"Feels a bit spooky. . . ." Martin lingered in the hallway for a moment, listening to the noises that are characteristic of all old houses. Little clicks and creaks, small sounds of protest when the wind blows.

Gösta nodded. There really was something unpleasant about the atmosphere in the house, but he realized that that was probably due to the fact that they knew what had happened here, rather than anything about the house itself.

"You said Torbjörn gave us the okay to go in?" Martin turned to his colleague.

"Yes, they've done everything they need to do." Traces of fingerprint powder were clearly visible in the library—black, blurred marks that spoiled the image of what was otherwise a beautiful room

"Fine." Martin wiped his shoes on the doormat and headed in. "Shall we start in here?"

"Seems like a good idea," Gösta said with a sigh, trailing behind him.

"I'll take the desk if you make a start on the files."

"Sure." Gösta sighed again, but Martin didn't even notice. Gösta always sighed when he was given a specific job to do.

Martin cautiously approached the large desk. It was an enormous, ornate piece of furniture made of dark wood. Martin thought it would fit better in a stately English home than in this spacious, airy room. The top of the desk was almost clear, with a pen and a box of paper clips arranged in perfect symmetry. A small amount of blood had splashed onto a notepad covered in writing, and Martin leaned over to see what had been scribbled down, over and over again. *Ignoto militi*. It meant nothing to him. Gently he began to pull out one drawer at a time, methodically going through the contents. Nothing aroused his interest. He established that Erik and his brother appeared to share the workspace, and they also appeared to share a love of tidiness and order.

"Isn't this a bit weird?" Gösta held up a folder to show Martin. Every sheet of paper in it had been neatly inserted, with an index sheet at the front on which either Erik or Axel had meticulously noted what each section contained.

"Well, my paperwork certainly doesn't look like that," Martin laughed.

"I've always thought there was something wrong with people who keep things as tidy as this. I'm sure it has something to do with inadequate potty training or something like that."

"Well, that's one theory." Martin smiled. Gösta could be very funny sometimes. Although most of the time it was unintentional.

"So, have you found anything? There's nothing interesting here." Martin closed the last drawer.

"Not yet. It's mostly bills, contracts, and so on. They saved every electricity bill they ever received. In chronological order." Gösta shook his head. "Grab a folder." He pulled out a thick black folder from the bookshelf and passed it to his colleague.

Martin sat down in one of the armchairs. Gösta was right. Everything was in perfect order. He went through every section, studied every sheet of paper, but he was beginning to lose heart. Until he reached the letter *S*. A quick glance told him that *S* stood for Sweden's Friends, an organization known to have neo-Nazi sympathies. Curious, he began to leaf through the pages. Every sheet had a printed logo in the top right-hand corner: a crown set against a background of a waving Swedish flag. All the letters were from the same person—Frans Ringholm.

"Listen to this," Martin said and began to read to Gösta from one of the letters. According to the date, it was one of the most recent.

> *In spite of our shared history, I can no longer ignore the fact that you are actively working against the aims and goals of Sweden's Friends; this will inevitably have consequences. I have done my best to protect you for the sake of our past friendship, but there are stronger forces within the organization who are less than happy with this, and there will come a time when I am no longer able to offer you protection against these forces.*

Martin raised an eyebrow. "It goes on in much the same vein." He leafed through the other letters and counted a total of five.

"It seems as if Erik Frankel had trodden on the toes of a neo-Nazi organization through his activities, but paradoxically he also had a protector within that same group."

"A protector who perhaps failed in the end."

"Yes, that's possible. We'll go through the rest of the documents and see if we can find anything else. But we definitely need to chat with Frans Ringholm."

"Ringholm. . . ." Gösta stared pensively into space. "I recognize that name." He grimaced as he attempted to force his brain to produce the answer, but to no avail. He still looked thoughtful as they went through the rest of the files in silence.

After just over an hour, Martin closed the last one. "Nothing else. What about you?"

Gösta shook his head. "No, and there are no more references to Sweden's Friends."

They left the library and searched the rest of the house. There was clear evidence everywhere of the brothers' interest in Germany and World War II, but nothing that caught their attention. The house was lovely but the decor was rather dated, and the place was starting to look shabby here and there. Black-and-white photographs of Erik and Axel's parents adorned the walls and were displayed in old frames on the sideboards and chests of drawers. Their presence was strong. It didn't seem as if the brothers had made many changes to the interior of the house since the deaths of their parents, hence the old-fashioned feeling. The orderliness was disturbed only by a thin layer of dust.

"I wonder if they did their own chores, or if they had a cleaner," Martin said thoughtfully, running a finger over the chest of drawers in one of the three bedrooms.

"I can't imagine two men in their seventies or eighties doing their own housework," Gösta said, opening the closet door. "What do you think? Erik's room or Axel's?" He contemplated the row of brown jackets and white shirts hanging in the closet.

"Erik's," Martin said. He had picked up a book from the bedside table, and pointed to the first page, on which a name was written in pencil: "Erik Frankel." The book was a biography of Albert Speer. "Hitler's architect," Martin read aloud from the back cover, before replacing the book.

"He spent twenty years in Spandau after the war," Gösta mumbled, and Martin looked at him in surprise.

"How do you know that?"

"I also find the Second World War quite interesting. I've read a bit over the years. And watched documentaries on the Discovery Channel, that kind of thing."

"Right," Martin said, still looking surprised. This was the first indication in all the years they had worked together that Gösta was interested in anything besides golf.

They spent another hour looking through the house, but found nothing new. Martin felt quite satisfied as he drove back to the station; the name Frans Ringholm gave them something to go on.

The supermarket was very quiet. Patrik took his time ambling up and down the aisles. It was liberating to get out of the house for a while, to have some time to himself. It was only the third day of his paternity leave, and part of him was loving the chance to be at home with Maja. But another part of him was finding it difficult to get used to not being at work. Not that he wasn't busy all day; he had quickly noticed that there was no shortage of things to do when you were taking care of a one-year-old. The problem was that he didn't find it all that . . . stimulating, he thought guiltily. And it was incredible how restricted he was; he couldn't even go to the bathroom in peace, since Maja had now taken to standing outside yelling, "Daddy, Daddy, Daddy, Daddy" and banging on the door with her small fists until he gave up and let her in. Then she would stand there gazing at him with interest while he did what had been a rather more private activity throughout his life so far.

He felt a bit bad about asking Erica to step in while he went shopping, but, after all, Maja was asleep, so she would still be able to get some work done. Perhaps he ought to just call home and check. He reached into his pocket for his cell and realized he must have left it on the kitchen table. Damn! But everything was bound to be fine. He reached the baby-food section and started to browse among the various flavors. "Casserole in a cream sauce," "fish in dill sauce," hmm. . . . "Spaghetti Bolognese"—that sounded much better. He would take five jars of that one. Then again, perhaps he ought to start cooking for Maja himself. That was a good idea, he decided, putting back three of the jars. He could cook up a big batch of spaghetti sauce with Maja sitting beside him, and. . . .

"Let me guess—you're making the rookie's mistake of deciding to cook your own baby food."

The voice was strangely familiar but somehow in the wrong context. He turned around.

"Karin? Hi, what are you doing here?" Patrik hadn't expected to see his ex-wife in the supermarket in Fjällbacka. The last time they had seen each other was the day she left the house they shared in Tanumshede to move in with the man he had caught her in bed with. An image flickered through his mind's eye, but disappeared equally quickly. It was such a long time ago. It was all in the past.

"Leif and I have bought a house in Fjällbacka."

"Right," Patrik said, trying not to look too surprised.

"Yes, we wanted to move closer to Leif's parents now we've got Ludde." She pointed to her cart, and only then did Patrik notice a little boy sitting there, smiling from ear to ear.

"Wow," Patrik said. "We seem to have timed this perfectly. I've got a little girl the same age back at home—Maja."

"I did hear that through the grapevine," Karin laughed. "You're married to Erica Falck, aren't you? Tell her I love her books!"

"Will do," Patrik said, waggling his fingers at Ludde, who seemed hell-bent on using his charms to the maximum effect.

"So, what are you up to these days?" he asked Karin curiously. "The last I heard, you were working for an accounting firm."

"That was a while ago. I left three years ago; at the moment I'm on maternity leave from a consulting group that deals with financial matters."

"Aha—this is the third day of my paternity leave," Patrik said, not without a certain amount of pride.

"Cool! But where's . . . ?" Karin looked around, and Patrik smiled sheepishly.

"Erica's got her for a while; I had a few things to do in town."

"That sounds familiar," Karin said, smiling. "Men's inability to multitask seems to be pretty much universal."

"I suppose it is," Patrik replied, slightly embarrassed.

"Hey, why don't we meet up with the kids someday? It's not that easy to keep them occupied, and it would give each of us the chance to talk to another adult. And that's got to be a bonus!" She rolled her eyes, then looked inquiringly at Patrik.

"Sure—when and where?"

"I usually take Ludde for a long walk every day around ten o'clock. You're welcome to join us. We could meet outside the pharmacy at quarter past ten?"

"Sounds great. What time is it now, by the way? I left my cell at home, and I tend to use it to check the time."

Karin glanced at her watch. "Quarter past two."

"Shit! That means I've been out for two hours!" He jogged toward the checkout with his cart. "But I'll see you tomorrow!"

"Quarter past ten outside the pharmacy—and don't turn up fifteen minutes late as usual!" Karin shouted after him.

"I won't," Patrik called back as he began flinging his groceries onto the conveyor belt. He sincerely hoped that Maja was still asleep.

A dense morning mist lay outside the window as they began the descent into Gothenburg. Axel heard the hum as the landing gear was lowered. He leaned back against the headrest and closed his eyes. That was a mistake. Images flickered through his mind, as they had done so many times during all the years that had passed. Wearily he opened his eyes. He hadn't had much sleep the night before. He had spent most of the time just lying in his bed in the Paris apartment, tossing and turning.

The woman's voice on the phone had been cool. She had given him the information about Erik, her tone sympathetic yet detached. It was clear from her approach that this wasn't the first time she had informed someone about a death.

His head spun as he tried to imagine all the people throughout the course of history who had been told that someone close to them had died. A call from the police, a priest standing at the door, an envelope with a military seal. All those millions upon millions of people who had died. Someone must have informed the relatives. Someone always had to do that job.

Axel covered one ear with his hand; it had become an unconscious reflex action over the years. He no longer had any hearing in his left ear, and somehow the touch eased the constant low hum.

He glanced out the window, but instead caught sight of his own reflection. The gray, wrinkled countenance of a man in his eighties. Sorrowful, deep-set eyes. He touched his face. For a moment he imagined it was Erik he could see.

With a thud the wheels touched down. He had arrived.

Bearing in mind the little accident in his office, Mellberg took down the leash he had hung on a nail on the wall and clipped it to Ernst's collar.

"Come on, let's get this out of the way," he grunted. Ernst bounded happily toward the door of the station at a speed that made Mellberg break into a trot.

"I think you're supposed to take the dog out, rather than the other way around," Annika commented with amusement as they dashed past.

"You're welcome to take him out instead if you like," Mellberg growled, but he continued through the door.

Goddamn mutt. Mellberg's arms were aching from the strain of trying to hold Ernst back, but once the dog had stopped, cocked his leg against a bush, and relieved the pressure, he settled down and they were able to continue their walk at a more leisurely pace. Mellberg caught himself whistling quietly. This wasn't such a bad idea after all. A bit of fresh air and exercise might do him good. And Ernst was really obedient now. He was happily snuffling along the forest path, as calm as anything. Just like a person, he could tell that someone with a firm hand was in control. Training this mutt to behave would be no problem at all.

At that moment Ernst stopped dead. He pricked up his ears, and it looked as if every muscle in his sinewy body had tensed. Then he exploded into movement.

"Ernst? What the fuck?" Mellberg was dragged along behind him at such speed that he almost fell over, but he managed to regain his balance at the last minute and tried to keep up as the dog shot off.

"Ernst! Ernst! Stop! Sit! Here!" He was panting from the unfamiliar physical exertion, which made it difficult to shout, and the dog ignored his commands. As they more or less flew around a bend, Mellberg found out what had caused the sudden burst of speed. Ernst hurled himself at a big, pale-colored dog that looked as if it might be a similar breed; they romped around boisterously while both owners pulled at their respective leashes.

"Senorita! Sit! Bad girl! Sit!" A short, dark woman shouted at her dog in a gruff voice, and, unlike Ernst, the dog obeyed her orders and backed away from her newly found companion. She sat down, looking up at her mistress with a mixture of pleading and embarrassment.

"Bad girl, Senorita. You mustn't do that." The woman forced the dog to make eye contact as she scolded her, and Mellberg had to resist the urge to stand to attention as well.

"I'm . . . I'm really sorry," he stammered, tugging at the leash in an effort to stop Ernst from hurling himself at the dog once more; judging by the name, it must be a female.

"You don't seem to have much control over your dog." The voice was sharp and the dark eyes flashed as Senorita's mistress fixed her gaze on him. She spoke with a slight accent, which matched her southern European appearance.

"He's not my dog . . . I'm just looking after him until we. . . ." Mellberg could hear himself stammering like a teenager. He cleared his throat and tried again, attempting to sound a little more authoritative this time. "I'm not really used to dogs. And he's not mine."

"He doesn't seem to agree with you." She pointed at Ernst, who had now moved backward and was sitting pressed against Mellberg's legs, gazing up at him with adoration.

"Yes, well . . . ," Mellberg spluttered, slightly flustered.

"In that case, perhaps we can walk together. My name is Rita." She held out her hand and, after a brief hesitation, he shook it.

"I've had dogs all my life. I'm sure I can give you a few tips. And going for a walk is always more fun when you have company." She didn't wait for his response, but set off along the path. Without really understanding how it had happened, Mellberg found himself following her. It was as if his feet had a mind of their own. Ernst certainly wasn't complaining. He fell into step beside Senorita, happily wagging his tail.

6
Fjällbacka 1943

"Erik? Frans?" Britta and Elsy stepped cautiously inside. They had knocked but no one had answered. They looked around uneasily. The doctor and his wife definitely wouldn't approve of two girls coming to visit their son while they were out. They usually met down in Fjällbacka, but in a moment of daring Erik had suggested that they should come over to his house, since his parents were going to be out all day.

"Erik?" Elsy raised her voice slightly, and almost jumped out of her skin when she heard a "Sssh!" from the room straight ahead at the end of the hallway. Erik stuck his head out and waved them in.

"Axel's asleep upstairs. He got back this morning."

"He's so brave . . . ," Britta sighed, but her face lit up when she saw Frans. "Hi!"

"Hi," Frans said, but he was looking past her, at Elsy. "Hi, Elsy."

"Hi, Frans," Elsy said, but headed straight for the bookshelves.

"Wow, you've got so many books!" she said, running her fingers over the spines.

"You're welcome to borrow one if you like," Erik offered generously, but then added, "As long as you take good care of it. Dad's really particular about his books."

"Of course," Elsy said happily, devouring the titles with her eyes. She loved reading. Frans was gazing at her.

"I think books are a waste of time," Britta said. "It's much better to experience stuff yourself than to read about what someone else has done. Don't you agree, Frans?" Britta sat down in the armchair beside him and tilted her head to one side.

"One thing doesn't necessarily preclude the other," he said harshly, but without looking at her. His eyes were still fixed on Elsy. A furrow appeared between Britta's eyebrows. She bounced up from the chair.

"Are you going to the dance on Saturday?" She tried out a few dance steps across the floor.

"I don't think Mom and Dad will let me," Elsy answered quietly without turning away from the books.

"Neither will anybody else's mom and dad," Britta replied, executing a few more steps. She tried to drag Frans to his feet, but he resisted and managed to stay in his chair.

"Stop being stupid." His tone was brusque, but then he couldn't help laughing. "You're a crazy girl, Britta. . . ."

"Don't you like crazy girls? In that case, I can be serious." She adopted an earnest expression. "Or happy. . . ." She laughed so loudly that the sound bounced off the walls.

"Sssh," Erik said, looking up at the ceiling.

"Or I can be really, really quiet," Britta whispered dramatically, and Frans laughed again as he pulled her onto his knee.

"Crazy will do just fine."

A comment from the doorway interrupted them.

"You're a noisy bunch." Axel was leaning against the door-jamb, a weary smile on his face.

"Sorry, we didn't mean to wake you." Erik's voice was suffused with the adoration he felt toward his brother, and it was accompanied by a troubled expression.

"Don't worry about it. I can have a lie-down later." Axel folded his arms. "So, little brother, you're entertaining ladies while Mom and Dad are at the Axelssons.'"

"I wouldn't say that," Erik mumbled.

Frans laughed, with Britta still on his knee. "Ladies? What ladies? I can't see any ladies around here, just two snotty girls."

"Shut up, you!" Britta thumped Frans on the chest. She didn't look amused.

"And Elsy's so busy looking at the books that she hasn't even said hello."

Elsy turned around, embarrassed. "I'm so sorry. . . . Good afternoon, Axel."

"Come on, I'm just kidding. You can keep looking at the books. I'm sure Erik's told you you're welcome to borrow one if you want."

"He has." She was still blushing, and quickly turned her attention back to the bookshelves.

"How did it go yesterday?" Erik's gaze was fixed on his brother, hungry for every word he could spare.

Axel's cheerful, open face immediately shut down. "Fine," he said tersely. "It was fine." Then he turned away abruptly. "I'm going back to bed for a while. Try and keep the noise down, please."

Erik watched his brother go, his eyes filled with adoration and pride, along with a certain amount of envy.

Frans felt nothing but admiration. "He's so brave, your brother. . . . I'd like to help too. If only I was a few years older, I'd. . . ."

"You'd what?" Britta said, still sulking because he had ridiculed her in front of Axel. "You'd never have the guts. And what would your father say? From what I've heard, he'd prefer to be giving the Germans a helping hand."

"Just stop." Angrily, Frans shoved Britta off his knee. "People talk too much. And I didn't think you listened to crap."

Erik, always the peacemaker within the group, quickly got to his feet and said: "We could listen to Dad's gramophone for a while if you want. He's got some Count Basie."

He hurried over to the gramophone to put on a record. He didn't like it when people quarreled. He really didn't like it at all.

7

She had always loved airports. There was something special about standing there, watching all the planes landing and taking off. People with suitcases, their eyes full of anticipation as they set off on vacations or business trips. And all those reunions, all those good-byes. She remembered an airport long, long ago. The crowds, the smells, the colors, the noise. And the tension she could feel rather than see in her mother. The way her mother had clutched her hand so tightly. The bag that had been packed and repacked and repacked again. Nothing must go wrong. Because this was a one-way trip. She also remembered the heat, and the cold when they arrived. She hadn't believed it was possible to be so cold. And the airport where they landed had been so different. Quieter, with dull shades of gray. No one was talking loudly or waving their arms around. Everyone seemed to be enclosed inside his or her own little bubble. No one had looked her or her mother in the eye; they had just stamped their documents and, with strange voices in a strange language, had waved them on. And Mother had clutched her hand so tightly.

"Could that be him?" Martin pointed to a man who appeared to be in his eighties who was just coming through passport control. He was tall with gray hair, wearing a beige trench coat. Stylish, was Paula's first thought.

"Let's see." She took the lead. "Axel Frankel?"

He nodded. "I thought I was supposed to come to the station." He looked tired.

"We thought we might as well come and pick you up rather than sitting and waiting." Martin gave him a friendly nod.

"Oh, I see, okay. In that case, thank you for the lift. I usually have to rely on public transport, so that will be very helpful."

"Do you have to wait for your luggage?" Paula glanced over at the carousel.

"No, I've only got this." He pointed to the carry-on that he was pulling along behind him. "I travel light."

"That's an art I've never quite mastered," Paula laughed. The weariness in the man's face vanished for a moment, and he smiled back at her.

They talked about trivial matters until they were in the car and Martin had set off in the direction of Fjällbacka.

"Have you . . . have you found out anything else?" Axel's voice trembled, and he fell silent for a moment in order to compose himself.

Paula, who was sitting next to him in the back of the car, shook her head. "I'm afraid not. We were hoping you might be able to help us. For example, we need to know whether your brother had enemies you might be aware of. Anyone who you think might want to harm him?"

Axel shook his head slowly. "No, not at all. My brother was a very gentle and peaceable man, and . . . no, it's ridiculous to imagine that anyone would wish him harm."

"What do you know about his communication with a group known as Sweden's Friends?" Martin threw in the question from the driver's seat, meeting Axel's gaze in the rearview mirror.

"You've gone through Erik's correspondence with Frans Ringholm." Axel rubbed the top of his nose; he was slow to answer, but Paula and Martin waited patiently.

"It's a complicated story that goes back a long way."

"We've got plenty of time," Paula said, making it clear that she expected him to go on.

"Frans is a childhood friend of ours. We've known each other all our lives. But . . . how can I put it . . . we chose one path and Frans chose another one."

"Frans is a right-wing extremist?" Once again Martin met Axel's eyes in the mirror.

Axel nodded. "Yes. I'm not too sure what he does, or when and to what extent, but he's moved in those circles all his adult life, and he was involved in starting up this group . . . Sweden's Friends. He had a lot to deal with at home when he was growing up, but I never saw any evidence of those kinds of sympathies. Still, people change." Axel shook his head.

"And why should Sweden's Friends feel threatened by what Erik was doing? As far as I understand it, he was a historian rather than a political activist, with the Second World War as his area of expertise."

Axel sighed. "It's not so easy to make that distinction. You can't do research into Nazism and remain, or be regarded as, apolitical. For example, many neo-Nazi groups insist that the concentration camps never existed, and any attempt to write about them, to record what happened, is seen as a threat, an attack on them. As I said, it's complicated."

"And what's your involvement? Have you also received threats?" Paula studied him intently.

"Of course—to a much greater extent than Erik. My life's work has been with the Simon Wiesenthal Center."

"Which is?" Martin asked.

"You track down Nazis who fled and went underground and make sure they are brought to justice," Paula supplied.

Axel nodded. "Among other things. So, yes, I've had my fair share of threats."

"Nothing on record?" Martin's voice came from the front seat.

"The center has everything. Those of us who work there forward any letters we receive, and they're kept on file there. If you speak to them, they'll give you access to everything." He handed Paula a card that she tucked in her pocket.

"And Sweden's Friends? Have you ever gotten anything from them?"

"No . . . I'm not really sure. . . . Not as far as I can remember. But check with the center—they've got everything."

"Frans Ringholm—how does he fit in? You said he was a childhood friend?" Martin asked.

"To be accurate, he was Erik's friend. I was a few years older, so we didn't really have the same friends."

"But Erik knew Frans well?" Paula's brown eyes were still gazing intently at Axel.

"Yes, although it's been many, many years since they had anything to do with each other." Axel didn't seem entirely comfortable with the topic of conversation. He shifted in his seat. "We're talking about something that happened sixty years ago. Even without dementia, one's memories grow a little hazy." He smiled weakly and tapped his head with his forefinger.

"Not that long ago, judging by the letters. Frans has written to your brother on several occasions."

"I don't know anything about that." Axel ran a hand through his hair in a gesture of frustration. "I lived my life and my brother lived his. Each of us wasn't always aware of what the other one was doing. And it's only three years since we both took up permanent residence—well, partly permanent in my case—in Fjällbacka. Erik had an apartment in Gothenburg during the years when he was working there, and I've more or less traveled all around the world. But we've always kept the house here as a base, and if anyone asks me where I live, I always say Fjällbacka. However, I invariably spend the summer in my apartment in Paris. I can't stand all the hustle and bustle of the tourist season. Otherwise we live rather a quiet and isolated life, my brother and I. Our cleaning lady is the only person who visits us. We prefer . . . preferred it that way. . . ." Axel's voice broke.

Paula caught Martin's eye in the mirror and he shook his head slightly before turning his attention back to the highway. Neither of them could think of any more questions, and they spent the rest of the trip engaging in rather awkward small talk. Axel looked as if he might collapse at any moment, and his entire being radiated relief when they finally pulled up in front of the house.

"You don't have any problems . . . with living here now?" Paula couldn't help asking.

Axel stood in silence for a moment, gazing at the big white house with his suitcase in his hand. Eventually he said, "No. This is my home, and Erik's. We belong here. Both of us." He smiled sadly and shook hands with them before heading for the front door. Paula watched him go. He was the very picture of loneliness.

"So, did you catch it when you got back yesterday?" Karin laughed as she pushed Ludde along in his stroller. She kept up a brisk pace, and Patrik was beginning to puff and pant as he tried to keep up with her.

"You could say that." He made a face at the thought of the reception he'd received when he got home the previous day. Erica hadn't been in the best of moods. He understood her to a certain extent; after all, the plan had been that he would take responsibility for Maja during the day now, so that Erica could work. At the same time, he couldn't help thinking that she was overreacting slightly. He hadn't been on some kind of jaunt; he was actually doing the shopping for the household. And how was he supposed to know that Maja would wake up when he wasn't there? Ending up in the doghouse for the rest of the day had felt a little unfair. However, the good thing about Erica was that she never held a grudge, so that morning he had received his usual kiss and the day before seemed to have been forgotten. Then again, he hadn't dared to tell her that he would have company on his walk today. He would definitely mention it, but he was putting it off for a little while. Even if Erica wasn't particularly jealous, perhaps a walk with his ex-wife wasn't the best topic of conversation when he was already at a disadvantage.

As if Karin could read his mind, she said, "Is this okay with Erica, the two of us meeting up? I know it's years since we split, but some people are a bit more . . . sensitive."

"Hell, yes," Patrik said, unwilling to admit his cowardice. "It's cool. Erica's fine with it."

"Excellent. I mean, it's good to have company, but not if it causes problems for you at home."

"So what about Leif?" Patrik said, eager to change the subject. He leaned forward and adjusted Maja's hat, which had slipped to one side. She took no notice of him; she was fully occupied in communicating with Ludde in the stroller beside her.

"Leif. . . ." Karin snorted. "You could say it's a miracle that Ludde even recognizes him. He's always out on the road."

Patrik nodded sympathetically. Karin's new husband was a singer with the dance band Leffe's, and he could easily imagine that life as a band widow would be tricky.

"No serious problems between you, I hope?"

"We don't see each other often enough to have problems," Karin laughed, but her laughter sounded bitter and hollow. Patrik sensed that she wasn't telling the whole truth, and he wasn't quite sure what to say. It felt a bit strange to be discussing marital issues with his ex-wife. Fortunately, the sound of his cell saved him.

"Patrik Hedström."

"Pedersen here. I've got the autopsy results on Erik Frankel. I've faxed the report through as usual, but I thought you'd probably want to hear the main findings over the phone."

"Yes, of course," Patrik said slowly, with a glance at Karin, who had stopped to wait for him. "But I'm actually on paternity leave at the moment. . . ."

"Are you indeed?! Congratulations! You have a wonderful time to look forward to. I spent six months at home with both my children, and I think those were the best days of my life."

Patrik felt his jaw drop. He would never have expected this of the superefficient, reserved, and rather cold medical examiner. He suddenly pictured Pedersen, dressed in his lab coat, sitting in a sandbox, making sand pies with great precision. He laughed out loud before he could stop himself, and Pedersen barked "What's so funny?" in response.

"Nothing," Patrik said, waving his hand to indicate to Karin that he would explain later.

"Listen," he said seriously, "could you just run the results by me quickly? I was at the scene of the crime the day before yesterday, and I'm trying to keep up to speed with what's going on."

"Of course," Pedersen said, still sounding a little put out. "It's quite simple, really. Erik Frankel was struck on the head with a heavy object. Probably an object made of stone, since there are small fragments of stone in the wound, which indicates that the material in question must be quite porous. He died instantaneously when the object struck his right temple, causing a massive bleed in the brain."

"Have you any idea which direction the blow came from? Behind? In front?"

"In my opinion, the assailant was standing in front of him, and in all probability the assailant was right-handed; it's more natural for a right-handed individual to strike from the right. It would feel very awkward for a left-handed person."

"And the object? What might we be looking at?" Patrik could hear the eagerness in his voice. This was something that felt familiar and natural.

"It's your job to establish that. Something heavy, made of stone. The skull doesn't seem to have been struck by a sharp edge, however; the wound is more characteristic of a crush injury."

"Okay, that gives us something to go on."

"Us?" Pedersen said with a hint of sarcasm in his voice. "I thought you said you were on paternity leave."

"Yes, yes, that's right," Patrik said. He paused for a moment, then went on: "Will you call the station and pass on this information?"

"I suppose I'd better, under the circumstances," Pedersen said, sounding amused. "Shall I take the bull by the horns and call Mellberg, or do you have a better idea?"

"Martin," Patrik said instinctively, and Pedersen burst out laughing.

"I'd already figured that out for myself. But thanks for the tip. By the way, aren't you going to ask when the victim died?"

"Yes, of course—when did he die?" The eagerness came through in Patrik's voice again, earning him another look from Karin.

"Impossible to say exactly. He's been sitting in a warm environment for far too long. But my approximate assessment is between two and three months ago, which puts us somewhere in June."

"You can't be any more precise than that?" Patrik knew the answer to the question even before he asked it.

"We're not magicians here, you know. We don't have a crystal ball. June. That's the best I can do at the moment. I'm basing my judgment partly on the species of flies, and partly on the number of generations of flies and maggots that have been produced. Taking into account the state of decay, I have concluded that he probably died in June. It's your job to get closer to the exact date of death. Or, to be more accurate, it's your colleagues' job." Pedersen laughed.

Patrik couldn't recall ever having heard him laugh before. And now it had happened several times during one phone call. At his expense. Perhaps that was what it took to get a laugh out of Pedersen. After the usual good-byes, Patrik ended the call.

"Work?" Karin asked curiously.

"Yes, it's a case we're working on at the moment."

"The old guy who was found dead on Monday?"

"I see the grapevine is as efficient as ever," Patrik said. Karin had increased her speed once more, and he broke into a jog to catch up with her.

A red car drove past. After about a hundred yards it slowed down, and it looked as if the driver was checking her rearview mirror. Then the car reversed toward them at some speed, and Patrik swore quietly to himself. He had only just noticed that it was his mother's car.

"Hello there, you two—out for a walk together, I see!" Kristina had rolled down the window and was staring in astonishment at Patrik and Karin.

"Kristina! Lovely to see you!" Karin bent down toward the open window. "Yes, I've moved back to Fjällbacka and I happened to bump into Patrik. We realized that we're both on leave and in need of company. This is Ludvig." Karin pointed to the stroller, and Kristina leaned forward and made the obligatory cooing noises at the sight of the one-year-old.

"How delightful!" said Kristina in a tone of voice that made Patrik's stomach tie itself in knots. A thought that made the knots even bigger suddenly struck him. Without really wanting to know the answer, he asked, "And where are you off to?"

"I thought I'd stop by your place. It seems like such a long time since I was there. I've brought some homemade cakes with me." She pointed at a box of cinnamon buns and a sponge cake on the seat beside her.

"Erica's working . . . ," Patrik ventured feebly, knowing that it was a waste of time.

Kristina put the car in gear. "Excellent! In that case, I'm sure she'll be glad for a little coffee break. And you two will soon be home, won't you?" She waved to Maja, who cheerily waved back.

"Yes, we will," Patrik said, desperately trying to come up with a good way of asking his mother not to mention his companion. But his brain appeared to be completely empty, and he raised a hand in a resigned gesture of farewell. With a solid lump in his stomach he watched his mother set off toward Sälvik with a screech of tires. He was going to have some explaining to do.

The work on her book had gone well. Erica had written four pages during the morning, and she stretched contentedly on her chair. Yesterday's anger had subsided, and with hindsight she thought she had probably overreacted. She would make it up to Patrik tonight. Make something extra-special for dinner. In the lead-up to the wedding they had cut down on calories, and had both lost a few pounds, but now they were back in the old routine. And everyone deserved a treat now and again.

Pork fillet with Gorgonzola sauce, perhaps. That was one of Patrik's favorites.

Erica stopped thinking about dinner and reached for her mother's diaries. She really ought to sit down and read them in one sitting, but somehow she couldn't quite bring herself to do it. So she was taking them a little bit at a time. Small glimpses into her mother's world. She put her feet up on the desk and began the laborious task of trying to decipher the old-fashioned handwriting. So far, the content had mostly concerned everyday life at home, the chores Elsy helped with, occasional speculation about the future, the anxiety about Erica's grandfather, who was out at sea virtually all the time. Elsy's thoughts on life were expressed with the innocence and naïveté of a teenager, and Erica found it difficult to reconcile the girlish tone that came through in the diaries with her mother's harsh voice, which had never expressed a tender word or an indication of love for her or Anna; there had been nothing but a strict upbringing and a distance between them.

Partway down the second page, Erica suddenly sat up straight. She recognized a familiar name. Or two, to be precise. Elsy wrote that she had been to Erik and Axel's house while their parents were out. The entry was mainly concerned with a lyrical description of their father's enormously impressive collection of books, but Erica saw only the two names. Erik and Axel. It had to be Erik and Axel Frankel. Avidly, she read about the visit, and she began to realize that they had often hung out together: Elsy and Erik, and two other teenagers called Britta and Frans. Erica searched her memory. No, she had never heard her mother mention either of them, she was sure of it. And Axel emerged as a kind of mythical hero in Elsy's diary. Elsy described him as "incredibly brave, and almost as stylish as Errol Flynn." Had her mother been in love with Axel Frankel? No, that wasn't the impression Erica got from her description; it was more that she admired him deeply.

Erica put down the diary and thought things over. Why hadn't Erik Frankel mentioned the fact that he had known her mother when they were young? She had told him where she had found the medal, and who it had belonged to. And yet he had said nothing. Once again Erica recalled that odd silence on the phone. She had been right; he had kept something from her.

The shrill sound of the doorbell interrupted her thoughts. With a sigh, she swung down her legs and pushed back her chair. Who could it be? A "hello" from the hallway immediately supplied the answer, and Erica sighed again, even more deeply this time. Kristina. Her mother-in-law. She took a deep breath, opened the door, and headed for the stairs. "Hello?" Kristina said again, a little more insistent this time, and Erica could feel herself gritting her teeth with irritation.

"Hello," she said as cheerfully as she could manage, but she could tell it sounded false. Thank goodness Kristina wasn't particularly sensitive to nuances.

"Only me!" her mother-in-law sang out cheerfully, hanging up her jacket. "I've brought something nice to go with our coffee. Freshly baked. I thought you might appreciate it; you career girls don't have time for that kind of thing these days."

Erica could actually hear her teeth grinding by this stage. Kristina had an unbelievable knack of delivering hidden criticism. Erica often wondered if she had been born with it or had developed it through years of practice. Probably a combination of both, she usually concluded.

"Thank you, that's lovely," she said obediently, following Kristina into the kitchen, where her mother-in-law was already making coffee, as if this was her home rather than Erica's.

"You sit down," Kristina said. "I know my way around your kitchen."

"Indeed you do," Erica replied, hoping that Kristina wouldn't pick up on the sarcasm. "Patrik and Maja have gone for a walk. They probably won't be back for a while," she said, hoping this would keep the visit short.

"Oh yes," Kristina said, counting the scoops of coffee at the same time. "Two, three, four. . . ." She put the scoop back in the tin and turned her attention to Erica.

"Yes, they'll be home any minute. I passed them on the way. Isn't it great that Karin has moved here, so that Patrik can have some company during the day? It's so boring to go out walking on your own, particularly when you're used to going out to work and making a real contribution, like Patrik. They seemed to be getting on really well."

Erica stared at Kristina as she tried to process the information that had come in through her ears but was somehow refusing to make sense. Karin? Company? What Karin?

The penny dropped just as Patrik walked in through the door. Oh, *that* Karin. . . .

Patrik smiled sheepishly and, after an awkward silence, he said "Coffee, terrific!"

They had gathered in the kitchen for a meeting. It was almost lunchtime, and Mellberg's stomach was rumbling loudly.

"So, where are we?" He reached for one of the buns that Annika had set out on a plate. A little hors d'oeuvre before lunch. "Paula and Martin? You spoke to the victim's brother this morning; anything interesting?" He was chewing a mouthful of bun as he spoke, spraying crumbs all over the table.

"We picked him up at the airport this morning," Paula said. "But he doesn't seem to know much. We asked him about the letters from Sweden's Friends, but the only thing he could tell us was that Frans Ringholm was evidently a childhood friend of Erik's. However, Axel was unaware of any specific threats from the organization, although he did point out that this kind of thing wasn't unusual, given the subject matter that interested both him and Erik."

"Has Axel ever received threats?" Mellberg asked, distributing a new salvo of crumbs.

"Quite a few, apparently." Martin took over. "But they're held by the organization he works for."

"So he doesn't know whether Sweden's Friends has sent him any letters?"

Paula shook her head. "No, he doesn't seem to know much about it at all. In a way, I can understand him; he must get a whole load of crap, and why should he bother with it?"

"What was your impression of him? I've heard he was something of a hero in his youth." Annika looked curiously at Paula and Martin.

"A very stylish, distinguished elderly gentleman," Paula said. "But of course he was quite subdued because of the circumstances. I thought he seemed to be deeply affected by his brother's death—I don't know if you felt the same?" She turned to Martin, who nodded.

"Yes, I got the same impression."

"I assume you'll be questioning Axel Frankel again," Mellberg said. "Martin, I understand you've heard from Pedersen? Strange that he didn't want to speak to me."

Martin gave a little cough. "I think you might have been out with the dog at the time. I'm sure his top priority would have been to report to you."

"Hmm, perhaps you're right. Okay, what did he have to say?"

Martin summarized what Pedersen had said about the victim's injuries, and couldn't help laughing as he added, "Apparently Pedersen had called Patrik first, and said he didn't sound too happy with life as a househusband. Pedersen gave him a full report and, given that it wasn't exactly difficult to entice him to join us at the scene of the crime, I wouldn't be surprised if he and Maja turn up here before too long."

Annika laughed. "Yes, I spoke to him yesterday, and he said rather diplomatically that it was probably going to take him a while to adjust."

"I'm not surprised," Mellberg snorted. "It's a stupid idea. Grown men changing diapers and heating up baby food. That's definitely something that was better in the old days. In my day, the men weren't expected to deal with that kind of nonsense; they could do the kind of thing they were better suited to, while the womenfolk looked after the kids."

"I would have been only too happy to change diapers," Gösta said quietly, looking down at the table. Martin and Annika looked at him in surprise, then remembered something they had found out only recently. Gösta and his late wife had had a son, who died immediately after he was born. There had been no more children. They sat there in silent embarrassment, trying not to look at Gösta.

Then Annika said "Well, I think it's a good thing for men to see what hard work it is. I know I don't have any children of my own"—now it was her turn to look sad—"but all my friends have kids, and they didn't exactly spend all day lying on the couch, stuffing their faces with chocolates, when they were on maternity leave. I think this will be good for Patrik."

"You'll never convince me," Mellberg said. Then he frowned impatiently and looked at the papers on the table in front of him. He brushed off a pile of crumbs and read a few lines before addressing the group. "Okay, this is the report from Torbjörn and the boys—"

"And girls," Annika added.

Mellberg gave a loud, theatrical sigh. "And girls. . . . You're certainly on the feminist warpath today! Are we carrying out a murder investigation here, or would you rather sing 'Kumbaya' and discuss Gudrun Schyman?" He shook his head and returned to the matter at hand.

"As I said, this is the report from Torbjörn and his *technicians*. And I think we can summarize it with the words 'No surprises.' There are a number of both footprints and fingerprints, and of course we need to go through them all. Gösta, can you make sure we have prints from the two boys for elimination purposes, and we need the brother's too. Apart from that . . ." He read a little further. ". . . they seem to have established that the victim received a severe blow to the head with a heavy object."

"Just one blow, not several?" Paula asked.

"Just one, judging by the blood on the walls. I discussed the report with Torbjörn on the phone, and I asked that very question, and they can definitely establish that it was a single blow by analyzing the spatter pattern. Obviously they know what they're talking about, so the conclusion is very clear—one severe blow to the head."

"That tallies with the autopsy report," Martin said with a nod. "And the object? Pedersen thought it was something heavy and made of stone."

"Exactly!" Mellberg said triumphantly, placing his finger somewhere in the middle of the document. "There was a large stone bust under the desk with blood, hair, and brain tissue on it; I have no doubt that the fragments of stone Pedersen found in the wound will match the material the bust is made of."

"So we have the murder weapon. That's something, at least," Gösta said gloomily, taking a sip of his coffee, which had gone cold by now.

Mellberg looked around the table at his subordinates. "Okay, any suggestions as to how we move forward?" He made it sound as if he already had a long list of suitable tasks at the ready. Which was not the case.

"I think we ought to speak to Frans Ringholm. Find out more about these threats."

"And speak to people in the neighborhood, see if anyone noticed anything unusual around the time of the murder," Paula went on.

Annika looked up from her notebook. "Someone ought to interview the cleaner. Find out when she was last there, if she saw Erik that day, and why she hasn't been in to do the cleaning all summer."

"Good." Mellberg nodded. "Okay, so why are you all sitting around here? Off you go!" He fixed his gaze on the team until they had trooped out of the room. Then he reached for another bun. Delegation. That was what good leadership was all about.

They were in full agreement that attending classes was a total waste of time. Therefore, they turned up only sporadically when the spirit moved them. Which it rarely did. Today they had met up at around ten o'clock. There wasn't much to do in Tanumshede. Mostly they sat around chatting. Smoking cigarettes.

"Did you hear about that old guy in Fjällbacka?" Nicke took a deep drag and laughed. "I bet it was your grandpa and his pals that killed him."

Vanessa giggled.

"Nah," Per said sourly, but not without a certain amount of pride. "Gramps had nothing to do with it. Surely you realize they can't risk getting sent to jail just for killing some old guy. Sweden's Friends has bigger, better things in its sights."

"Have you spoken to the old man yet? Asked him if we can come to a meeting?" Nicke had stopped laughing and was now looking excited.

"Not yet . . . ," Per said reluctantly. Being the grandson of Frans Ringholm afforded him a special status within the group, and in a weak moment he had promised to see if he could get them into one of the meetings that was held in Uddevalla. But he hadn't found the right moment yet. And he knew exactly what his grandfather would say. That they were too young. That they needed a few more years to "develop to their full potential." He had no idea what was supposed to develop. They understood the issues just as well as those who were older and had already been accepted. What was there to misunderstand?

That was what he liked—the fact that it was simple. Black and white. No gray areas. Per couldn't see why people wanted to complicate life, looking at things from one side, then the other. When it was all so utterly, utterly simple. It was them and us. Nothing else. Us and them. And if *they* had just stuck to their own space, done their own thing, there wouldn't have been a problem. But they insisted on invading other people's space, insisted on constantly overstepping the boundaries that should be obvious to everyone. You could even see the difference, for fuck's sake. White or yellow. White or brown. White or that disgusting blue-black color of the Africans from the deepest, darkest jungle. So fucking simple. Although it was true that it wasn't always so easy to see the difference these days. Everything was ruined, mixed together, stirred up into one big mess. He looked at his friends, slumped on the bench beside him. Did he really know what their bloodlines looked like? Who knew what one of the whores in their families might have gotten up to? They could easily have impure blood running through their veins. Per shuddered.

Nicke looked inquiringly at him. "What the fuck is the matter with you? You look as if you'd swallowed something weird."

Per snorted. "It's nothing." But he couldn't shake off the thought and the feeling of revulsion. He stubbed out his cigarette.

"Come on, let's head for the café. It's depressing sitting around here." He nodded in the direction of the school and set off at a brisk pace without waiting to see if the others were following. He knew they would be.

For a moment he thought about the guy who had been murdered. Then he shrugged. He wasn't important.

8
Fjällbacka 1943

The cutlery clattered against their plates as they ate. All three were trying not to glance at the empty chair at the dining table. None of them was succeeding particularly well.

"Why did he have to go away again so soon?" Gertrud passed the dish of potatoes to Erik with a questioning look on her face; he added another potato to his already well-filled plate. It was simpler that way, otherwise his mother would just go on and on until in the end he had to take some more anyway. But when he looked down at everything piled high on his plate, he wondered how he was going to manage it all. Food didn't interest him. He ate only because he had to. And because his mother said she was embarrassed because he was so skinny. People would think they didn't feed him, she said.

Axel, on the other hand . . . he always had a healthy appetite. Erik stole a glance at the empty chair as he reluctantly lifted the fork to his lips. The food seemed to grow in his mouth. The sauce turned the potatoes into a soggy mess, and he began to move his jaws up and down mechanically in order to get rid of it all as soon as possible.

"He has to do what he has to do." Hugo Frankel's expression was stern as he looked at his wife, but he couldn't stop his eyes straying to Axel's empty chair opposite Erik's.

"I just thought he could have a couple of days' rest in peace and quiet at home."

"He makes up his own mind. Nobody tells Axel what to do; the decisions are his alone." Hugo's voice swelled with pride, and Erik felt that pang in his chest, the one that came sometimes when his father and mother were talking about Axel. Sometimes it almost seemed to Erik that he was invisible. As if he were only a shadow in the family, a shadow of tall, blond Axel, who always became the focus, in spite of the fact that he made no effort to do so. He made himself take another mouthful of food. Once dinner was over, he would be able to slip away to his room to read. History books were his favorite. There was something about all those facts, all those names and dates and places, that he loved. History didn't change, it was something he could absorb, something he could rely on.

Axel had never been very interested in reading, yet he had somehow managed to get through school with top grades. Erik also had good grades, but he had had to work hard for them. And no one patted him on the back or beamed with pride when they boasted about him to friends and acquaintances. Nobody boasted about Erik.

And yet he couldn't bring himself to dislike his brother. Sometimes he wished he could feel that way, wished he could hate him, loathe him, blame him for that pang in his chest. But the truth was that he loved Axel. More than anyone else. Axel was the strongest, the bravest, the one who was worth boasting about. Not Erik. That was a fact. Just like in the history books. Just like the fact that the Battle of Hastings took place in 1066. There was nothing to discuss, nothing to argue about, and it couldn't be changed. That was just the way it was.

Erik looked down at his plate; to his surprise, it was empty.

"Please, may I leave the table, Father?" His tone was hopeful.

"Have you finished already? So you have. . . . In that case, you may go. Mother and I will sit here a while longer."

As Erik went upstairs to his room, he could hear his parents' voices from the dining room.

"I hope Axel won't take too many risks, I. . . ."

"Gertrud, you have to stop mollycoddling the boy. He's seventeen years old, and the shopkeeper was saying only today that he's never had a boy like him. We should be pleased to have such a—"

The voices disappeared as he closed the door behind him. He threw himself down on the bed and picked up the book on top of the pile, the one about Alexander the Great. He had been brave too. Just like Axel.

9

"I just think you could have mentioned it. I ended up standing there like an idiot when Kristina said you were out walking with Karin."

"Yes, I know, you're right." Patrik hung his head. The hour that Kristina had spent with them had been loaded with undertones and looks, and the second the front door closed behind her, Erica had exploded.

"It's not the fact that you were out with your ex-wife that's the problem. I'm not the jealous type, as you well know. But why didn't you tell me? That's what I'm wondering. . . ."

"Yes, I realize that. . . ." Patrik avoided catching Erica's eye.

"'I realize that'! Is that all you can say? No explanation? I thought we could tell each other anything!" Erica could feel that she was verging on what could be called a major overreaction here. But the frustration of the last few days had found an outlet, and she couldn't stop herself.

"And I thought we'd sorted out the division of labor! You're supposed to be on paternity leave and I'm working. And yet you keep on disturbing me, you're in and out of my study as if it had a swing door, and yesterday you had the gall to disappear for two hours, leaving me to look after Maja! How do you think I managed when I was at home? Do you think I had a maid who stepped in to take care of her as soon as I had to go shopping, or who could tell me where Maja's gloves were?" Erica heard the shrillness of her voice; did she really sound like that? She broke off, and went on in a more measured tone: "Sorry, I didn't mean . . . I think I'll go for a walk. I need to get out of the house for a while."

"Good idea," Patrik said, looking like a tortoise who had decided to poke his head out to check if the coast was clear. "And I'm sorry I didn't say anything." His eyes pleaded with her.

"Just don't do it again." Erica managed a little smile. The white flag had been raised. She regretted flying off the handle, but they could talk later. At the moment she needed some fresh air more than anything.

She set off briskly through the town. Fjällbacka looked strangely desolate when the tourists had departed after the hectic summer months. It was like a living room the morning after a particularly riotous party that had gotten out of hand. Glasses containing the dregs of God knows what, a crumpled streamer in one corner, a comatose guest wearing a crooked party hat on the sofa. Although Erica actually preferred this time of year. The summer was so intense, so intrusive. There was now an air of calm over Ingrid Bergman Square. Maria and Mats would keep the kiosk open for a few more days, then they would close and head off to their business in Sälen as they did every year. And that was another thing she really liked about Fjällbacka: the predictability of the changes that took place. Every year the same thing, the same cycle. Same procedure as last year.

Erica nodded to the people she met as she walked past the square and headed up Galärbacken. She knew most of them, at least to say hello to. But she speeded up as soon as anyone looked as if they might want to stop for a chat. She wasn't in the mood today. As she passed the gas station and continued along Dinglevägen, she suddenly realized where she was going. No doubt her subconscious had already decided on her destination when she left Sälvik, but she had only just figured it out.

"Three cases of assault, two bank robberies, plus a few other bits and pieces. But no racial abuse," Paula said, closing the passenger door of the squad car. "I also found one or two reports on a boy called Per Ringholm, just minor stuff so far."

"That's his grandson," Martin said, locking the car. They had driven over to Grebbestad, where Frans Ringholm had an apartment next to the Gästis nightclub.

"I've cut a rug there in my time," Martin said with a smile, nodding toward the club.

"I can just imagine. But that's all over now, I assume?"

"You could say that. I haven't even seen the inside of a club for over a year." He didn't look particularly unhappy about it. To tell the truth, he was so totally in love with his Pia that he would have preferred not to leave their apartment at all, given the choice. But he'd had to kiss quite a few frogs, or rather toads, before he found his princess.

"What about you?" Martin looked curiously at Paula.

"What do you mean?" She pretended not to understand the question, and by then they had reached Frans Ringholm's door. Martin knocked loudly and was rewarded by the sound of footsteps inside the apartment.

"Yes?" A man with short, almost cropped gray hair opened the door. He was wearing jeans and a checked shirt of the type that the Swedish writer Jan Guillou always wore, with a stubborn lack of interest in fashion.

"Frans Ringholm?" Martin contemplated the man with curiosity. He was well known in the area, but his notoriety was also more widespread, as Martin had discovered from an Internet search at home. Apparently, Ringholm was a founding member of one of Sweden's fastest-growing antiforeigner organizations and, according to the gossip on various forums, Sweden's Friends was becoming a force to be reckoned with.

"That's me. What can I do for you"—he looked Martin and Paula up and down—"officers?"

"We'd like to ask you one or two questions. May we come in?"

Frans stepped to one side, his only comment a raised eyebrow. Martin gazed around in surprise. He wasn't sure what he had been expecting, but probably something grubbier, messier, less well cared for. Instead, the apartment was so neat and tidy that it made his own place look like a crack den.

"Take a seat." Frans waved in the direction of a couple of sofas in the living room to the right of the hallway. "I'm just making a pot of coffee. Milk? Sugar?" His voice was calm and polite, and Martin and Paula exchanged slightly disconcerted looks.

"Neither, thanks," Martin replied.

"Milk, no sugar," Paula said, leading the way into the living room. They sat down next to each other on a white sofa and gazed around. The room was light and airy, with big windows overlooking the water. It didn't give an excessively house-proud impression, but felt clean and welcoming.

"Coffee." Frans brought in a heavily laden tray. He placed three steaming cups on the table, along with a big plate of cookies.

"Please help yourselves." He waved a hand over the table, then picked up a cup and leaned back in a comfortable armchair. "So, how can I help?"

Paula took a sip of her coffee, then began. "I'm sure you've heard that a man was found dead just outside Fjällbacka."

"Erik Frankel, yes," Frans said, nodding sadly before sipping his coffee. "I was very sorry to hear about that. And it's dreadful for Axel. This must be a terrible blow."

"Yes, it's, er. . . ." Martin cleared his throat. He was completely taken aback by the man's affability and the fact that he was the complete opposite of what Martin had expected. He pulled himself together and said "The reason we wanted to speak to you is because we found a number of letters from you among Erik Frankel's possessions."

"Oh, so he kept the letters," Frans chuckled, reaching for a cookie. "Erik liked collecting things. I'm sure you youngsters think sending letters is pretty old-fashioned, but we old folks find it difficult to change the habits of a lifetime." He gave Paula a friendly wink. She almost smiled back, but reminded herself that the man sitting opposite had spent his entire life working against people like her, making things as difficult as possible for them. The smile disappeared.

"The letters mention a threat. . . ." She maintained a stern expression.

"Well, now . . . I'm not sure I'd call it a threat." Frans gazed at her calmly and leaned back in his chair. He crossed his legs, then went on: "I just thought I ought to let Erik know that there were certain . . . factions within the organization that didn't always act . . . how can I put this . . . sensibly."

"And you found it necessary to inform Erik of this because . . . ?"

"Erik and I were friends when we were both in short pants. I'll admit that we drifted apart, and we haven't had what you would call a conventional friendship for many years. We . . . we went in different directions in life." Frans smiled. "But I never wished Erik any harm and, yes, when I got the chance to warn him, I took it. Some people find it difficult to understand that resorting to violence isn't always the answer."

"You haven't always been so eager to shun violence," Martin said. "Three convictions for assault, a couple for bank robbery, and as I understand it, you didn't exactly serve your time like the Dalai Lama."

Frans didn't seem to be put out by Martin's comments; he simply smiled. Not unlike the Dalai Lama, in fact. "There's a time for everything. Prison has its own rules, and sometimes there's only one language that's understood. And wisdom comes with age, or so I've heard, and I've learned my lesson along the way."

"Has your grandson learned his lesson yet?" Martin reached for a cookie as he asked the question. Frans's hand shot out like lightning and seized Martin's wrist in an iron grip. With his eyes fixed on the other man, he hissed: "My grandson has nothing to do with this. Is that clear?"

Martin held his gaze for a long time, then pulled his hand away and rubbed his wrist. "Don't ever do that again," he said quietly.

Frans laughed and settled back in his chair. Once again he was his friendly, affable self. But just for a moment the façade had crumbled. There was real anger behind that calm exterior. The question was whether Erik had been the victim of that anger.

Ernst was tugging eagerly on his leash, and Mellberg was struggling to hold him back, gazing all around and trying to walk as slowly as possible. Ernst couldn't understand why his master suddenly insisted on moving at a snail's pace, and he dragged at the leash, panting like crazy as he tried to get the old man to speed up.

Mellberg had almost completed the circuit when his efforts were rewarded. He was just about to give up when he heard the sound of footsteps behind him. Ernst began to leap around in a joyful frenzy at the prospect of a playmate approaching.

"So you're out for a walk too." Rita's voice sounded just as cheerful as he remembered it, and Mellberg could feel the corners of his mouth turning up in a smile.

"Yes, we are. Out for a walk." He felt like kicking himself. What a dumb answer. He usually had such a way with the ladies, and now he was standing here sounding like an idiot. He made an effort to pull himself together and sound a bit more sensible: "Well, it's important for a dog to have plenty of exercise, so Ernst and I try to get out for at least an hour every day."

"It's not only dogs who benefit from exercise; it won't do you or me any harm either!" Rita giggled and patted her rounded tummy. Mellberg found this extremely liberating. At last a woman who realized that having a bit of meat on her bones wasn't necessarily a bad thing.

"That's true," he said, patting his own substantial belly. "We just have to be careful not to lose that certain air of authority."

"Heavens, yes." Rita laughed. The slightly old-fashioned expression sounded delightful with her accent. "That's why I always make sure I fill up afterward." She stopped outside an apartment block, and Senorita started pulling on her leash, determined to get inside. "Perhaps you'd join me for a coffee. And Danish."

With a Herculean effort, Mellberg managed to restrain himself from jumping for joy, and tried to look as if he were considering her offer. Eventually he nodded indifferently. "Maybe that's not such a bad idea. I can't stay away from work for too long, but. . . ."

"Come on in, then." She keyed in the security code and led the way. Ernst didn't seem to share his master's self-control and was leaping around with the sheer happiness of being allowed to accompany Senorita into her home.

Mellberg's first impression when he walked into Rita's apartment was "cozy." It had none of the sparse minimalism that the Swedes were so fond of; it positively crackled with warmth and color. He unclipped Ernst's leash and the dog raced after Senorita, looking as if he were politely asking permission to play with her toys. Mellberg hung up his jacket, placed his shoes neatly on the shoe rack, and followed the sound of Rita's voice into the kitchen.

"They seem to get on well."

"Who do?" Mellberg said stupidly, because his brain was fully occupied with taking in the sight of Rita's wonderfully ample behind as she stood at the sink, measuring coffee into the machine.

"Senorita and Ernst, of course." She turned around and smiled.

Mellberg gave an embarrassed laugh. "Sorry, yes. You're right, they do seem to like each other." A glance into the living room provided a rather more vivid confirmation of this fact than he would have wished. Ernst was just happily sniffing Senorita's bottom.

"Do you like Danish pastries?" Rita asked.

"Does Dolly Parton sleep on her back?" Mellberg asked rhetorically, but immediately regretted it. Rita looked puzzled.

"I don't know. Perhaps she does. I mean, with those breasts maybe she has to. . . ."

"It's just an expression," Mellberg said with another embarrassed laugh. "What I meant was, yes, I love Danish pastries."

He was surprised to see Rita setting out three cups and saucers and plates on the kitchen table. The mystery was immediately solved as she shouted into the room next door, "Coffee time, Johanna!"

"Coming!" An extremely pretty blond woman with an enormous belly appeared in the doorway.

"This is my daughter-in-law, Johanna," Rita said, pointing to the pregnant woman. "And this is Bertil, who owns Ernst. I found him in the forest," she said with a giggle. Mellberg held out his hand, and almost fell to his knees in pain a second later. He'd never felt a handshake like it, in spite of the fact that he had shaken hands with some seriously tough guys over the years.

"That's quite a grip you have there," he squeaked as he managed to extricate his hand with a sigh of relief.

Johanna looked amused as she sat down at the table with some difficulty. She shuffled until she found a position from which she could reach both her cup and the plate of Danish, and set to with a healthy appetite.

"When's it due?" Mellberg inquired politely.

"Three weeks," she answered briefly as she concentrated on pushing every last bit of the pastry into her mouth. Then she reached for another.

"I see you're eating for two," Mellberg said with a laugh, but a dirty look from Johanna shut him up. Hard work, this one.

"This is my first grandchild," Rita said proudly, tenderly patting Johanna's belly. Johanna's face lit up as she looked at her mother-in-law, and she placed her hand on top of Rita's.

"Do you have any grandchildren?" Rita asked when she had poured the coffee and sat down with Bertil and Johanna.

"Not yet," he said, shaking his head. "But I do have a son. His name is Simon, and he's seventeen." Mellberg grew several inches taller with pride. His son had come into his life comparatively recently, and at first he hadn't been all that pleased to receive the news of his existence. But they had gradually gotten to know each other, and these days he was constantly surprised by the warmth he felt whenever he thought of Simon. He was a good kid.

"Seventeen—well, you've got plenty of time in that case. But one thing I know for sure: grandchildren are life's dessert." She couldn't stop herself from patting Johanna's belly again.

They chatted happily as the dogs raced around the apartment. Mellberg was fascinated by the pure, unadulterated happiness he felt, sitting here in Rita's kitchen. After the set-backs of the last few years, he had never wanted to set eyes on a woman again. But here he was. Having a lovely time.

"So, what do you think?" Rita was looking at him with a challenging expression, and he realized he must have missed the question to which she was expecting an answer.

"Sorry?"

"I said: are you coming to my salsa class tonight? It's a beginners' group. Nothing tricky at all. Eight o'clock."

Mellberg stared at her blankly. A salsa class? Him? The idea was totally ridiculous. But then he just happened to look a little too deeply into Rita's dark eyes, and to his horror he heard his own voice saying "A salsa class? Eight o'clock? Sure thing."

Erica was already regretting her decision as she walked up the gravel path to Erik and Axel's house. It had seemed like such a good idea at first, but now she wasn't so sure, and she felt very hesitant as she raised her clenched fist and banged on the door. At first she couldn't hear anything, and thought with some relief that there was probably no one home. Then she heard footsteps, and her heart sank as the door opened.

"Yes?" Axel Frankel looked worn-out as he gazed inquiringly at her.

"Hi, my name is Erica Falck, I. . . ." She paused, unsure how to continue.

"Elsy's daughter." Axel raised his head, a strange look in his eyes. The tiredness was gone as he studied her intently. "Yes, I can see it. You're very much alike, you and your mother."

"Are we?" Erica said in surprise. No one had ever said that before.

"Yes, it's something about the eyes. And the mouth." He tilted his head to one side, apparently taking in every detail of her appearance. Then he suddenly moved aside. "Come in."

Erica stepped into the hallway.

"We'll go and sit on the veranda." He headed off down the hallway and seemed to expect Erica to follow him. She quickly hung up her coat and soon found herself in a wonderful enclosed veranda, not unlike the one she and Patrik had.

"Sit down." He didn't offer her coffee, and after they had sat in silence for a little while, Erica cleared her throat.

"The reason I . . ." She tried again. "The reason I came by is that I gave Erik a medal." She could hear how brusque she sounded, and added, "I'm very sorry for your loss, of course. I. . . ." Erica felt terribly awkward, and shifted uncomfortably as she tried to find a way to continue.

Axel waved away her obvious unease and said, pleasantly, "What's this about a medal?"

"Well," Erica said, grateful that he had taken charge. "Back in the spring I found a medal among my mother's things. A Nazi medal. I didn't know why she had it, and I was curious. And since I knew that your brother. . . ." She shrugged.

"Was he able to help you?"

"I don't know. We spoke on the phone before the summer, but then things got really busy, and . . . I'd intended to get in touch with him again, but. . . ." Her words died away.

"And now you're wondering if it's still here?"

Erica nodded. "I'm so sorry, it sounds terrible for me to be worrying about the medal when. . . . But my mother hadn't saved many things, and. . . ." She shifted again. She really should have phoned instead. This just seemed horribly cold-blooded.

"I understand. I understand completely. Believe me, if anyone knows how important our links with the past are, I do. Even if those links are based on inanimate objects. And Erik would certainly have understood. All the things he collected. All the facts. To him they weren't dead. They were alive, they told a story, they had something to teach us." He stared out of the windows, and for a moment he seemed to be somewhere far away. Then he turned back to Erica.

"Of course I'll look for the medal. But first of all, tell me a bit more about your mother. What was she like? How did her life turn out?"

Erica found his questions strange. But his expression was almost pleading, and she wanted to try to answer him.

"What was my mother like. . . . To be honest, I don't know. Mom wasn't all that young when she had me and my sister, and . . . how can I put it . . . we were never really very close. And how did her life turn out?" Erica tried to think. She was confused, partly because she didn't really understand the question, and partly because she wasn't sure how to answer it. She took a deep breath and tried. "I think she found it a bit hard. Life, I mean. She always seemed to me to be very restrained, not particularly . . . happy." Erica struggled to find a better way of describing the way things had been, but that was as close to the truth as she could get. She couldn't actually recall ever seeing her mother happy.

"I'm sorry to hear that." Axel gazed out the window once more, as if he couldn't bear to look at Erica. She wondered where these questions had come from.

"What was my mother like when you knew her?" She couldn't suppress the eagerness in her voice.

Axel's expression softened. "It was really my brother who used to hang out with Elsy; they were the same age. They were always together—Erik, Elsy, Frans, and Britta. Like a four-leaf clover." He laughed, but it was a strange, joyless sound.

"She writes about them in the diaries I found. I know about your brother, but who are Frans and Britta?"

"Diaries?" Axel gave a start, but the movement was so brief and fleeting that Erica thought she might have imagined it.

"Frans Ringholm and Britta. . . ." Axel clicked his fingers. "What was Britta's surname?" He searched the dark recesses of his memory for a moment, but failed to locate the information. "Anyway, I think she still lives here in Fjällbacka. She has two or three daughters, but I think they're quite a bit older than you. Damn, it's on the tip of my tongue, but . . . and of course she probably changed her name when she got married. Now I remember! She was called Johansson, and she married a Johansson, so she didn't need to change."

"In that case, I'm bound to be able to find her. But you didn't answer my question. What was my mother like? Back then?"

Axel sat in silence for a long time, then he said "She was a quiet, thoughtful girl. But not unhappy. Not the way you describe her. She had a kind of serene happiness about her, a happiness that came from within. Not like Britta." He snorted.

"So what was Britta like?"

"I never liked her. I couldn't understand why my brother hung out with such a . . . silly girl." Axel shook his head. "Your mother was cut from a completely different cloth. Britta was a shallow chatterbox, and she threw herself at Frans in a way that girls just didn't do in those days. Times were different then." He gave her a wry smile.

"And Frans?" Erica gazed at Axel, her mouth half open, desperate to drink in everything he could tell her about her mother. She knew such a small amount. And the more she found out, the more she realized how little she had known her mother.

"I wasn't particularly happy to see my brother spending time with Frans Ringholm either. He had a real temper, a nasty streak, and . . . no, he's not the kind of person you'd want to associate with. Neither back then nor today."

"So what does he do now?"

"He lives in Grebbestad. And you could say that our ways in life diverged completely." His tone was dry and contemptuous.

"What do you mean?"

"I mean that I have spent my life fighting against Nazism, while Frans would like to see history repeat itself, preferably on Swedish soil."

"So how does the Nazi medal I found fit into all this?" Erica leaned toward Axel, but it was as if a shutter had suddenly come down in front of his face. He got to his feet abruptly.

"The medal, of course. We'd better go and have a look for it." He led the way out of the room, and Erica followed, feeling crestfallen. She wondered what she had said to make him clam up like that, but decided this was not the time to ask. In the hallway she saw that Axel had stopped in front of a door she hadn't noticed before. It was closed, and he hesitated, his hand resting on the handle.

"It's probably best if I go in on my own," he said, his voice trembling slightly. Erica realized which room this must be: the library, where Erik had died.

"We can do this another time," she said, feeling guilty once again for bothering Axel when he was grieving.

"No, we'll do it now," he said brusquely, but then he repeated the same phrase in a gentler tone of voice to show that he hadn't meant to sound so harsh.

"I'll be back in a moment." He opened the door, went inside, and closed it behind him. Erica stayed in the hallway, listening as Axel rummaged around. It sounded as if he was opening drawers, and he must have found what he was looking for very quickly, because after a minute or two he emerged.

"Here it is." He handed over the medal, his expression inscrutable, and Erica took it in her outstretched hand.

"Thank you, I. . . ." She didn't know what to say, and simply closed her hand around the medal. "Thank you," she said again, and left it at that.

As she walked down the path away from the house with the medal in her pocket, she could feel Axel's eyes on her. She considered going back to apologize for disturbing him with her trivial concerns, but then she heard the sound of the front door closing.

10
Fjällbacka 1943

"I don't understand how Per Albin Hansson can be such a coward!" Vilgot Ringholm slammed his fist down on the table, making the cognac decanter jump. He had told Bodil to bring out the after-dinner snacks, and wondered why it was taking so long. Typical woman, dawdling about. Nothing was done properly around here unless he did it himself.

"Bodil!" he yelled in the direction of the kitchen, but to his annoyance there was no reaction. He stubbed out his cigar and bellowed again, at the top of his voice this time.

"Bodiiilll!"

"Perhaps your old lady has nipped out the back way?" Egon Rudgren chortled, and Hjalmar Bengtsson joined in the laughter, which made Vilgot even more furious. Now that damned woman was making him a laughingstock in front of his potential business partners. Enough was enough. But just as he was about to get to his feet and sort things out, his wife emerged from the kitchen carrying a fully laden tray.

"Sorry it took so long," she said, keeping her eyes downcast as she placed the tray on the table in front of them. "Frans, could you possibly—" She nodded toward the kitchen, but Vilgot interrupted her before she could finish her request.

"I'm not having Frans doing women's work in the kitchen. He's growing up fast; he can sit with us and learn a thing or two." He winked at his son, who grew visibly taller in the armchair opposite. This was the first time Frans had been allowed to stay at one of Father's business dinners for so long; usually he was expected to excuse himself straight after dessert and go to his room. But today his father had insisted that he remain. Pride swelled in his chest until he felt as if the buttons on his shirt might pop off at any moment. And a good evening was about to get even better.

"Now, what about a taste of this cognac? What do you think? The boy turned thirteen a couple of weeks ago—it's time he had his first sip, don't you agree?"

"Time?" Hjalmar laughed. "I'd say it was high time! My boys were allowed a taste at home from the age of eleven, and it certainly hasn't done them any harm, let me tell you."

"Vilgot, do you really think. . . ." Bodil looked on in despair as her husband deliberately poured a large cognac and handed it to Frans, who started coughing violently after one gulp.

"Take it easy, boy—you're supposed to sip it, not knock it back."

"Vilgot . . . ," Bodil said again, but this time her husband's eyes turned black.

"Why are you still here? Haven't you got some tidying up to do in the kitchen?"

For a moment it looked as if Bodil was going to say something. She turned to Frans, but he merely raised his glass in a triumphant gesture and said with a smile, "Cheers, Mother dear."

A burst of laughter followed her as she went back to the kitchen and closed the door behind her.

"Now, where was I?" Vilgot said, indicating that they should help themselves to the pickled-herring sandwiches on the silver tray. "Oh, yes, what's Per Albin thinking of? It's obvious that we ought to go in and support Germany!"

Egon and Hjalmar nodded. They had to agree.

"It's very sad," Hjalmar said, "to think that in these difficult times Sweden can't stand proud and uphold the Swedish ideal. It almost makes me feel ashamed to be a Swede."

All three men shook their heads in silent accord, then took a sip of cognac.

"But what am I thinking? We can't sit here drinking cognac with the herring! Frans, run downstairs and fetch some cold beers!"

Five minutes later, order was restored, and the sandwiches were washed down with gulps of cellar-chilled Tuborg. Frans had settled back in the armchair opposite his father, and he grinned from ear to ear when Vilgot opened one of the bottles and simply handed it to him.

"Well, I have to tell you I've made a decent contribution to supporting the cause. And I would recommend that you gentlemen do the same. Hitler is going to need all the good men he can get on his side."

"Business is booming," Hjalmar said, raising his bottle. "We have only just enough capacity to meet the demand for iron ore exports. Say what you like about the war, but as a business proposition it's no bad thing."

"No, and if we can make some money and get rid of these goddamn Jews at the same time, things could hardly be better." Egon reached for another sandwich. The tray was looking a little sparse by now. He took a bite, then turned to Frans, who was listening intently to every word. "You should be very proud of your father, my boy. There aren't many men like him left in Sweden."

"Mmm," Frans mumbled, suddenly embarrassed at being the center of attention.

"I hope you listen to what your father says, rather than to those who don't know what they're talking about. I'm sure you realize that most of those who condemn the Germans and the war are half-breeds. There are plenty of Gypsies and Walloons around here, and it's hardly surprising that they try to twist the facts. But your father is a man of experience. All three of us have seen the way the Jews and foreigners have tried to take over, tried to destroy what is Swedish, what is pure. No, Hitler is definitely on the right side, mark my words." Egon was really fired up by this stage, and was spraying bread crumbs everywhere. Frans was fascinated by what he had to say.

"Time to talk business, gentlemen, I think." Vilgot banged his beer bottle down on the table, and immediately all eyes were on him.

Frans sat and listened for another twenty minutes, then made his way unsteadily to bed. When he lay down fully dressed on top of the covers, he felt as if the entire room were spinning. He could hear the low hum of conversation from the other room. Eventually he fell asleep, blissfully unaware of how he would feel when he woke up.

11

Gösta sighed deeply. Summer was turning to fall, and for him that meant a rapid reduction in his rounds of golf. Admittedly the air was still warm, and in theory he had a good month left to play. But he knew from hard-won experience what usually happened. A couple of rounds would be rained out. A couple would fall victim to thunderstorms. And then from one day to the next the temperature would suddenly plummet from pleasant to unbearable. That was the disadvantage of living in Sweden. And he couldn't see any advantages to balance things out, either. Except possibly *surströmming*, the pungent tinned herring so beloved by his countrymen. Then again, if you moved overseas you could easily slip a few tins into your suit-case. That way he would have the best of both worlds.

At least things were quiet at the station. Mellberg had taken Ernst for a walk, while Martin and Paula had gone to Grebbestad to speak to Frans Ringholm. Gösta tried to think where he had heard the name before, and to his great relief the penny suddenly dropped. Ringholm. That was the name of that journalist on *Bohusläningen*. He reached for the newspaper lying on his desk and searched the pages until he was able to put his finger on the right name: Kjell Ringholm. A bad-tempered bastard who liked to have a go at local politicians and those in power. It could be a coincidence, of course, but the surname was unusual. Could he be Frans Ringholm's son? Gösta filed the information away in his brain in case it might come in handy at some point.

But for the moment he had more pressing matters to deal with. He sighed again. Over the years he had developed sighing into an art form. Perhaps he would wait until Martin got back. That would not only enable him to share the workload, but it would also give him a break of at least an hour, possibly two if Martin and Paula decided to stop off for lunch before they came back.

But what the hell, he thought. Might as well get it done rather than have it hanging over him. Gösta got to his feet and pulled on his jacket. He told Annika where he was going, took one of the cars from the underground parking lot, and set off for Fjällbacka.

It wasn't until he rang the doorbell that he realized how stupid he was. It was just after twelve; obviously the boys would be in school. He was just about to turn away when the door opened and a sniveling Adam appeared. His nose was red, his eyes glazed.

"Are you ill?" Gösta said. The boy nodded and provided further confirmation with a deafening sneeze before noisily blowing his nose.

"I'be god a code," Adam said, in a voice that demonstrated with great clarity that both nostrils were completely blocked.

"May I come in?"

Adam stepped to one side. "Id's ad your owd risk," he said, sneezing again.

Gösta's hand received a light shower of bacteria-ridden moisture, but he calmly wiped it on his sleeve. A couple of days off sick wouldn't be such a bad idea. He'd happily settle for a cold if it meant he could snuggle down on the sofa at home and watch the recording of the most recent U.S. Masters. That would give him the chance to study Tiger's swing in slow motion in peace and quiet.

"Bob's dot hobe," Adam said.

Gösta frowned as he followed the boy into the kitchen. Then it made sense. Presumably Adam was trying to say "Mom's not home." It did occur to Gösta that it was inappropriate to interview a minor without the presence of a parent or guardian, but he immediately dismissed the thought. In his opinion, rules and regulations were a damned nuisance and just made the work of the police more difficult. If Ernst had been here, he would have given Gösta his full support. His colleague Ernst, not the dog, Gösta thought with a giggle. Adam gave him an odd look.

They sat down at the kitchen table, which still showed traces of that morning's breakfast. Bread crumbs, smears of butter, spilled O'boy chocolate drink—it was all there.

"So." Gösta drummed on the table with his fingers, but instantly regretted it as they picked up a whole range of sticky remnants. He wiped them on his leg and tried again.

"So. How . . . have you handled all this?" The question sounded peculiar even to him. He wasn't particularly good at talking to either young people or to those who were "traumatized." Not that he set much store by that kind of nonsense. After all, the old guy had been dead when they found him, so how bad could it be? God knows he'd seen a few dead bodies during his time with the police, and he hadn't been left "traumatized."

Adam blew his nose, then shrugged. "Dunno. Okay, I guess. The kids at school think it's cool."

"Why did you go there in the first place?"

"It was Mattias's idea." Adam pronounced the name as "Battias," but by now Gösta's brain was attuned to it and provided a simultaneous translation of everything the boy said.

"I mean, everybody around here knows the old guys are oddballs, and that they're into the Second World War and so on, and one of the kids at school said they had a load of cool stuff at home, so Mattias thought we ought to go and take a look. . . ." The torrent was suddenly interrupted by such a violent sneeze that Gösta almost jumped out of his seat.

"So breaking into the house was Mattias's idea?" Gösta said, looking sternly at Adam.

"I don't know about breaking in," Adam said, squirming. "I mean, we weren't planning on stealing anything, we just wanted to look at the stuff. And we thought both the old guys were away, so they wouldn't even have noticed we'd been there. . . ."

"I suppose I'll have to take your word for that," Gösta said. "And you'd never been inside the house before?"

"No, honest," Adam said with an imploring look. "That was the first time."

"I need to take your fingerprints to prove what you say, and for elimination purposes. Do you have a problem with that?"

"No!" Adam said, his eyes shining. "I always watch *CSI*. I know how important it is to eliminate someone. You run all the fingerprints through the computer, and it tells you who else has been there."

"Exactly. That's just how we work," Gösta said, maintaining an expression of deadly seriousness, while inside he was laughing to himself. Run all the fingerprints through the computer. Absolutely.

He took out the necessary equipment to take Adam's fingerprints: an ink pad and a card printed with ten boxes into which he carefully pressed the boy's fingers, one after another.

"There you go," he said with satisfaction when he'd finished.

"Do you scan them in, or what?" Adam asked curiously.

"That's right, we scan them in," Gösta said, "then we run them against that database you mentioned. It contains every Swedish citizen over the age of eighteen. And some foreigners too—you know, through Interpol, that kind of thing. We have a direct link with them. Interpol. And the FBI and the CIA."

"Wow!" Adam said, gazing at Gösta with admiration.

Gösta chuckled all the way back to Tanumshede.

Herman was setting the table with care. The yellow cloth he knew Britta liked so much. The white dinner service with the raised motif. The candlesticks that had been a wedding present. And a vase of flowers. Britta had always been very particular about that. Regardless of the time of year, she always had flowers. She was a regular customer at the florist's. Or she had been. These days it was usually Herman who went there. He wanted things to be the same as usual. If everything around her was unchanged, then perhaps the downward spiral could at least be slowed down, if not halted.

The beginning had been the worst time. Before they had gotten a diagnosis. Britta had always been so well organized. Neither of them had understood why she suddenly couldn't find the car keys, how she could get the grandchildren's names wrong, why she couldn't remember the phone numbers of friends she had known for most of her life. They had blamed tiredness and stress. She had started taking multivitamins and an iron-based tonic; they thought she might have some kind of nutritional deficiency. However, in the end, they had been unable to ignore it any longer: something was seriously wrong.

When they were given the diagnosis, they had both sat in silence for a long time. Eventually Britta had let out a sob. That was all. One sob. She had squeezed Herman's hand tightly, and he had squeezed back. They both understood what it meant. The life they had shared for fifty-five years would change drastically. The illness would slowly destroy her brain, making her lose more and more of herself: her memories, her personality. The abyss yawned before them, deep and wide.

A year had passed since then. The good days were becoming more and more infrequent. Herman's hands shook as he tried to fold the napkins just as Britta always did. She usually made a fan. But in spite of the fact that he had watched her do it so often, he just couldn't get it right. After the fourth attempt, the anger and frustration got the better of him and he tore the napkin to pieces. Tiny, tiny pieces that drifted down onto the plates. He sat down and tried to pull himself together. Wiped away a tear that had forced its way out of the corner of his eye.

Fifty-five years together. Good years. Happy years. Of course they had had their ups and downs, like any married couple, but the solid foundation had always been there. They had developed together, he and Britta. Grown up together, above all when Anna-Greta came along. He had been so incredibly proud of Britta then. Before they had their daughter, he had sometimes found his wife rather shallow and silly, he had to admit. But from the moment she held Anna-Greta in her arms, she had become a different person. It was as if becoming a mother had given her a solid base that had been lacking before. They had been blessed with three daughters, and he had loved his wife more with each child.

He felt a hand on his shoulder. "Dad? How are you doing? You didn't answer when I knocked on the door, so I came in."

Herman quickly wiped his eyes and tried to force a smile when he saw his eldest daughter's worried face. But she wasn't fooled. She wrapped her arms around him and pressed her cheek against his.

"Bad day, Dad?"

He nodded and allowed himself to feel like a child in his daughter's arms for a little while. They had raised her well, he and Britta. Anna-Greta was warm and thoughtful, a loving grandmother to two of their great-grandchildren. Sometimes he couldn't figure it out. How could this gray-haired woman in her fifties be the daughter who had scampered around the house and wrapped him around her little finger?

"Where does the time go, Anna-Greta?" he said eventually, patting the arm that lay across his chest.

"I know, Dad," she said, giving him an extra hug before letting go.

"Shall we fix what's on this table? Mom won't be happy if she sees what you've done." She laughed, and he couldn't help smiling back. "I'll fold the napkins if you set out the cutlery. I think that might be best, judging by this." She pointed to the scraps of paper scattered across the table like confetti and winked at him.

"I think you're right," he said with a grateful smile. "That might be best."

"What time are they due?" Patrik shouted from the bedroom, where at Erica's insistence he was changing into something more suitable than jeans and a T-shirt. The objection "But it's only your sister and Dan coming to dinner" had had no effect. It was Friday evening and they had dinner guests, so he would just have to smarten himself up.

Erica opened the oven and peered inside. She had been feeling guilty ever since the day before when she had shouted at Patrik, and to make up for it she had made one of his favorite dishes: pork fillet wrapped in pastry, with port wine sauce and crushed new potatoes. The dish she had cooked the very first evening she'd invited him to her place. The very first evening when they. . . . She laughed quietly to herself and closed the oven door. It felt like such a long time ago, even though it was only a few years. She loved Patrik to bits, but it was remarkable how quickly everyday life and looking after a small child could kill the desire to make love five times in a row, as they had done that first night. These days the very thought of so much activity in bed made her feel exhausted. Once a week felt like a major achievement.

"They'll be here in half an hour," she yelled up to Patrik before making a start on the sauce. She had already changed into black pants and a lilac shirt that had been a favorite ever since she was living in Stockholm and still had a decent selection of boutiques to choose from. To be on the safe side, she had put on an apron, and Patrik whistled appreciatively as he came down the stairs.

"Wow, you're a sight for sore eyes! A vision! A divine, glamorous creature, but still with a touch of homemade culinarity."

"There's no such word as culinarity," Erica said with a laugh as Patrik kissed the back of her neck.

"There is now," he said. Then he took a step back and twirled around in the middle of the kitchen floor.

"So—will I do? Or do I have to go back and change?"

"You make it sound as if I'm a real nag." Erica looked him up and down, assuming a highly critical expression, but then she couldn't help laughing.

"You're a positive asset to our home. If you could just set the table as well, I might begin to understand why I married you."

"Consider it done."

Half an hour later, when the doorbell rang at exactly seven o'clock, both the table and the food were ready. Anna and Dan were on the doorstep with Adrian and Emma, who immediately raced inside and starting calling to Maja. Their little cousin was extremely popular.

"Who's this handsome guy?" Anna asked. "And what have you done with Patrik? I have to say it's high time you traded up to this luxury model."

Patrik gave Anna a hug. "Good to see you too, dear sister-in-law. . . . So, how are the turtledoves this evening? Erica and I are honored that you feel able to drag yourselves away from the bedroom for a while to visit us in our simple dwelling."

"Oh, come on!" Anna said, blushing as she pummeled Patrik's chest. But the look she gave Dan proved that Patrik undeniably had a point.

It was a very good evening for all of them. Emma and Adrian happily entertained Maja until it was time for her to go to bed, then they both crashed at opposite ends of the sofa. The meal garnered the praise it deserved, the wine was delicious and disappeared quickly, and Erica enjoyed sitting with her sister and Dan over an ordinary, pleasant dinner. Without any dark clouds on the horizon. Without even giving a thought to everything that lay behind them. Just harmless small talk and loving banter.

Suddenly the calm was disturbed by the angry sound of Dan's cell phone.

"Sorry, I'll just see who's calling at this time of night," Dan said as he went to get his phone out of his jacket pocket. He frowned as he looked at the display; he didn't appear to recognize the number.

"Hi, it's Dan," he said tentatively.

"Who did you say?

"I'm sorry, I can't quite hear what you—

"Belinda? Where?

"How?

"But I've been drinking, I can't—

"Put her in a cab and send her here. Right now! Yes, I'll pay at this end. Just make sure she gets here." He reeled off Patrik and Erica's address. The furrow in his brow had deepened and he swore as he ended the call.

"Fuck!"

"What's happened?" Anna asked anxiously.

"It's Belinda. Apparently she's been to some party and she's completely hammered. That was a friend of hers on the phone. They're putting her in a cab."

"But where is she? I thought she was supposed to be at Pernilla's in Munkedal."

"I guess that didn't happen. Her friend was calling from Grebbestad."

Dan started tapping away on his cell; it sounded as if he had waked his ex-wife. He went into the kitchen, and they could hear only fragments of the conversation. But those fragments didn't sound too friendly. A few minutes later, he came back into the dining room and sat down at the table, looking extremely frustrated.

"According to Pernilla, Belinda said she was staying over with a friend. And no doubt the friend said she was staying over with Belinda. Instead, they somehow got themselves to Grebbestad and went to this party. Goddamn it! I thought I could trust Pernilla to keep an eye on her!"

Anna stroked his arm gently to calm him down. "It's not that easy, you know. You could easily have fallen for the same story. It's the oldest trick in the book."

"No way!" Dan said furiously. "I would have called the friend's parents in the evening to check that everything was all right. I would never trust a seventeen-year-old. Just how stupid can that woman be? Can't I rely on her to look after the kids?"

"Calm down," Anna said sharply. "Let's deal with one thing at a time. The most important thing at the moment is to take care of Belinda when she gets here." She cut Dan off immediately as he opened his mouth to say something. "And we are not going to tell her off tonight. We can have that conversation tomorrow when she's sobered up. Okay?" Although her final word might have been couched as a question, everyone around the table, including Dan, realized that this was nonnegotiable. He simply nodded.

"I'll go and make up the bed in the spare room," Erica said, getting up.

"And I'll go and find a bucket or something," said Patrik, desperately hoping that this wasn't a sentence he would have to repeat when Maja became a teenager.

A few minutes later they heard the sound of a car in the drive, and Dan and Anna hurried to the door. Anna paid the cabdriver, while Dan picked up Belinda, who was sprawled on the back seat like a rag doll.

"Dad . . . ," she slurred. Then she wrapped her arms around his neck and buried her face in his chest. The smell of vomit coming off her almost made Dan throw up, but at the same time he felt an enormous compassion for his daughter, who suddenly seemed so small and fragile in his arms. It was many years since he had carried her.

A retching movement from Belinda made him instinctively turn her head to the side, away from his chest. A stinking, reddish sludge shot out over Patrik and Erica's front step. Obviously red wine had formed a large part of her overindulgence.

"Leave that and bring her inside—we'll hose down the step later," Erica said, waving Dan and Belinda inside. "Put her in the shower; Anna and I will take care of her and find her some clean clothes."

In the shower Belinda began to cry. The sound was heartrending. Anna stroked her hair while Erica gently dried her with a towel.

"Ssh, don't worry, everything will be okay," Anna said, slipping a clean T-shirt over Belinda's head.

"Kim was supposed to be there. . . . And I thought . . . but he told Linda he thought I was u-u-ugly. . . ." The words came in fits and starts, with pauses for more tears.

Anna looked at Erica over the top of Belinda's head. Neither of them would have wanted to change places with the girl for the world. There was nothing as painful as a broken teenage heart. They had both been through it and understood perfectly why she had given in to the temptation to drown her sorrows in an excess of red wine. But it was a fleeting consolation. In the morning Belinda would feel even worse, if that was possible; they knew that too, from bitter experience. The only thing they could do now was get her into bed; they would have to deal with the rest tomorrow.

Mellberg was standing with his hand on the door handle, weighing the pros and cons. There was no doubt that the cons were winning by a mile. However, two things had brought him here. First of all, he had nothing better to do on a Friday night. Second, he couldn't get Rita's dark eyes out of his mind. And yet he was still wondering whether these two factors were sufficient motivation for him to do something as utterly ridiculous as turning up at a salsa class. No doubt the place would be full of desperate women, thinking a dance class was a good way to pick up guys. Pathetic. For a moment he almost turned away; he could go to the gas station, pick up some chips, and settle down at home to watch a recorded episode of *Fill Up Your Freezer with Stefan and Christer*. He chuckled at the very thought of it. They were real funny, those two. Mellberg had just decided on Plan B when the door opened.

"Bertil! Lovely to see you! Come on in; we're just about to start." And before he had time to think, Rita had grabbed his hand and dragged him into the room. Latin American music was pumping out of a ghetto blaster on the floor, and four couples stared at him with interest as he walked in. An equal number of men and women, Mellberg noticed with surprise as the image of himself as a meaty bone being torn apart by a gang of voracious bitches in heat faded and died.

"You're dancing with me. You can help me to demonstrate," Rita said, drawing him into the middle of the floor. She positioned herself opposite him, placed one of his hands on her waist, and held the other. Mellberg struggled to restrain himself from clutching at those wonderful curves. He just didn't understand men who preferred skin and bone.

"Focus, Bertil," Rita said sternly, and he immediately stood tall. "Now watch what Bertil and I do," Rita said, turning to the other couples. "Ladies: right foot forward, transfer the weight to your left foot, right foot back. Gentlemen: the same thing but the other way around, so it's left foot forward, weight onto the right foot, left foot back. We'll practice that step until everyone has got it."

Mellberg found it difficult to understand what she meant; it was as if his brain had decided to delete even the most basic information, such as which was his left foot and which was his right. But Rita was a good teacher. With firm movements she guided his feet forward and back, and he was pleased to discover that after a while he had begun to get the hang of it.

"Okay . . . now we're going to start moving our hips as well," Rita said with an encouraging look at her pupils. "You Swedes are so stiff, but salsa is all about movement, sensuality, softness."

She demonstrated what she meant by wiggling her hips to the music in a way that made it look as if they were flowing back and forth, like a wave. Mellberg gazed at her in fascination. It looked so easy when she did it. Determined to impress her, he tried to imitate her as he moved his feet in the pattern he thought he had mastered. But now nothing worked anymore. His hips felt as if they had been somehow fused together, and any attempt to coordinate his hips and feet caused a complete short circuit in his brain. He stopped dead, utterly frustrated. To make things even worse, his hair chose this particular moment to tumble down over his left ear. He quickly adjusted it; perhaps no one had noticed. A suppressed snigger from one of the other couples immediately crushed that hope.

"I know it's hard; it takes a lot of practice," Rita said cheerfully, encouraging him to try again. "Listen to the music, Bertil, just listen. And let your body follow the beat. Don't look at your feet, look at me. When you're dancing salsa, you should always gaze into the lady's eyes. This is the dance of love, the dance of passion."

She fixed her eyes on his, and he forced himself to hold her gaze and not to look down at his feet. At first it didn't work at all. But after a while, with Rita's gentle guidance, he could feel something happening. It was as if his body suddenly began to hear the music properly. His hips started to move smoothly and sensually. He looked deeper into Rita's eyes. And as the Latin American rhythm pulsed through the air, he could feel himself falling.

12

Kristiansand 1943

It wasn't that Axel liked taking risks. Nor was he unusually courageous. He was afraid, of course he was. He would have been an idiot not to be. But this was simply something he had to do. He couldn't just sit and watch without doing anything as evil triumphed.

He stood by the rail, the wind whipping against his face. He loved the smell of the sea. He had always envied the fishermen, out from early in the morning until late at night, allowing their boats to take them wherever the fish were. Axel knew that they would laugh at him if he ever told them how he felt. He was the doctor's son, he was going to go to college and be something in life, and he was envious of them? Of the calluses on their hands, the smell of fish that impregnated their clothes, the uncertainty of not knowing whether they would come home every time they set out? They would think it both ridiculous and presumptuous of him to wish for the life they had. They would never understand. But with every fiber of his body he felt that this was the life he was meant for. Admittedly he had a good brain, but he never felt as at home with books and studying as he did here, on the deck of a boat bobbing in the waves, with the wind tearing at his hair and the smell of fish in his nostrils.

Erik, on the other hand, loved to be in the world of books. There was a glow of happiness around him as he sat in bed at night, his eyes moving back and forth across the pages of some book that was far too thick and far too old to arouse the least enthusiasm in anyone but Erik. He reveled in knowledge, wallowed in it, devoured facts, dates, names, and places like a starving man. Axel was fascinated by this, but it also made him sad. They were so different, he and Erik. Perhaps there were too many years between them. Axel was four years older. They had never played together, never shared toys. Axel was also worried about the way in which his parents differentiated between them. They praised him to the skies in a way that unbalanced the family, making Axel into something he wasn't while diminishing Erik at the same time. But how could he prevent it? He could only do what he was destined to do.

"We'll be arriving soon."

Elof's dry voice behind him made Axel jump. He hadn't heard the man approaching.

"I'll creep ashore as soon as we heave to. I'll be away for about an hour."

Elof nodded. "You take care, boy," he said with a last glance at Axel, before going astern to take over the helm.

Ten minutes later, Axel looked around carefully before clambering up onto the quay. He could see German uniforms in all directions, but most of the soldiers appeared to be busy checking the boats as they moored at the quayside. He felt his pulse rate increasing. A large number of seamen were moving around on land, either loading or unloading their cargoes, and Axel tried to look as nonchalant as those who were going about their business with no hidden agenda. He had brought nothing with him this time; he was only collecting on this trip. He had no idea what the documents he had been asked to smuggle into Sweden contained, nor did he wish to know. All he knew was the name of the person he was to deliver them to.

The instructions had been very clear. The man he was looking for would be standing at the far end of the harbor, wearing a blue cap and a brown shirt. His senses on full alert, Axel approached the area where the man was supposed to be. Everything seemed to be going well so far. No one was interested in a fisherman walking confidently along. The Germans got on with their duties and took no notice of him. Eventually he spotted the man. He was stacking crates and seemed totally focused on getting the job done. Axel made a beeline for him. The trick was to look as if he had a legitimate reason for being there. He definitely mustn't make the mistake of looking shifty, glancing around in an obvious way. He might as well stick a target on his chest.

Once he reached the man, who had ignored him completely up to now, he picked up the nearest crate and started stacking. From the corner of his eye he saw his contact drop something on the ground, hidden by some of the crates. Axel pretended to bend down to pick up another crate, but first of all he grabbed the rolled-up papers and slipped them into his pocket. The handover was complete, and he had yet to exchange a single glance with the other man.

He felt relief coursing through his veins, almost making him dizzy. The handover was always the most critical moment. Once it was done, there was a much smaller risk that someone would—

"Halt! Hände hoch!"

The German command came from nowhere. Axel stared in surprise at the man in the blue cap, and the shame-faced look he got in return made everything clear. It had been a trap. Either the whole thing had been a setup, just to get at him, or the Germans had found out what was going on and had forced those involved to help them set the trap. Whatever the truth might be, Axel knew the game was up. The Germans had probably been watching him from the moment he stepped ashore. And the papers were burning a hole in his pocket. He raised his hands in a gesture of surrender. The men facing him were from the Gestapo. The game was most definitely up.

13

A loud knocking on the door disturbed his morning ritual. Every morning, the same routine. First of all a shower. Then a shave. Then he would prepare breakfast: two eggs, one slice of rye bread with butter and cheese, a large cup of coffee. Always the same breakfast, which he would then eat in front of the TV. The years in prison had made him appreciate routine, predictability. The knocking came again, and Frans got up crossly to open the door.

"Frans." His son was standing there with the hardness in his eyes that Frans had had to get used to.

He could no longer remember the time when everything had been different, but we must accept what we cannot change, and this was one of the things he would never be able to change. It was only in his dreams that he sometimes felt a small hand in his. A vague memory from a time long, long ago.

With an almost inaudible sigh, he stepped aside to let his son in.

"Good morning, Kjell," he said. "So, what's your business with your old dad today?"

"Erik Frankel," Kjell said coldly, staring at his father as if he expected a particular reaction.

"I'm in the middle of my breakfast. You'd better come on in."

Kjell followed him into the living room. He couldn't hide a certain amount of curiosity as he looked around; he had never been inside this apartment.

Frans didn't ask if his son would like a cup of coffee; he already knew what the answer would be.

"Okay, what about Erik Frankel?"

"You know he's dead." It sounded like a statement, not a question.

Frans nodded. "Yes, I'd heard that old Erik was dead. Very sad."

"Is that what you really think? That it's very sad?" Kjell was staring at him intently, and Frans knew exactly why. He wasn't there in his capacity as a son, but as a journalist.

Frans took his time before answering. There was so much beneath the surface. So much hidden among all the memories, so much that had followed him all his life. But he could never say that to his son. Kjell would never understand. He had condemned his father long ago. They were on opposite sides of a wall so high that you couldn't even peep over it, and things had been that way for far too many years. And to a great extent, Frans had only himself to blame. Kjell hadn't seen much of his jailbird father when he was a child. His mother had brought Kjell to visit a few times, but the sight of that little face, full of questions, in the depressing, inhospitable visiting room had made Frans harden his heart and refuse any further visits. He had thought it would be better for the boy to have no father at all than the one he had. Perhaps he had been wrong. But it was too late to do anything about it now.

"Yes, I am sorry to hear of Erik's death. We knew each other when we were young, and I have fond memories of him. But we are not alike and we went in opposite directions. . . ." Frans spread his hands wide. He didn't need to explain himself to Kjell. They both knew all about opposite directions.

"But that's not true, is it? I've been reliably informed that you've been in touch with Erik recently. And that Sweden's Friends has shown an interest in the Frankel brothers. By the way, I presume you don't mind if I make a few notes?" Kjell deliberately placed a notepad on the table, his expression challenging as he put pen to paper.

Frans shrugged and waved his hand dismissively. He no longer had the energy to play this game. There was so much anger inside Kjell, and he recognized every ounce of it. It was his anger, the destructive rage that he had always carried with him. It had caused him so much trouble, destroyed so much. Kjell had used his anger differently. Frans made a point of following what his son wrote in the newspaper. A number of local big shots and industrialists had had a taste of Kjell Ringholm's anger in print in the pages of the local paper. They weren't really so different, he and Kjell, even if they had chosen different opinions. They were both driven by the rage within them. That was what had made Frans feel so at home with the pockets of Nazi sympathizers he had met during his very first spell in jail. They had shared the same hatred, the same drive. And Frans could argue, he knew how to speak; his father had schooled him well in the use of rhetoric. Being part of the Nazi gangs in jail had given him power and status; he had been someone, and his rage had been regarded as a resource, as proof of his strength. Over the years, he had grown into the role; it was no longer possible to separate Frans and his views. They had fused into a single entity. He had the feeling that the same was true of Kjell.

"Where were we?" Kjell looked down at his empty pad. "Oh, yes, apparently there had been some contact between you and Erik."

"Only because of our old friendship. Nothing in particular. And nothing that could be connected with his death."

"So you say. I expect other people will come to their own conclusions. But what was this contact about? Did it involve a threat?"

Frans snorted. "I don't know where you got your information, but I did not threaten Erik Frankel. You've written enough about my fellow travelers to know that there are always a few . . . hotheads who don't think rationally. And I simply informed Erik of that fact."

"Your fellow travelers," Kjell said with a contempt bordering on disgust. "You mean crazy reactionaries who think you can close Sweden's borders."

"Call it what you like," Frans said wearily. "But I never threatened Erik Frankel. And now I would appreciate it if you'd leave."

For a brief moment it looked as if Kjell might protest, but then he got to his feet, leaned over his father, and stared at him.

"You weren't much of a father to me. I can live with that, but I swear, if you drag my son any deeper into all this than you already have, I'll. . . ." He clenched his fists.

Frans looked up at him, calmly meeting his eyes. "I haven't dragged your son into anything. He's old enough to think for himself. He makes his own decisions."

"Just like you did," Kjell said bitterly. He stormed out as if he could no longer bear to be in the same room as his father.

Frans remained seated, his heart pounding in his chest. As he heard the front door slam, he thought about fathers and sons. And about the choices that were made for them.

"Good weekend?" Paula directed the question to both Martin and Gösta as she scooped ground coffee into the machine. They both nodded gloomily. Neither of them was particularly fond of Monday mornings, and Martin hadn't slept well all weekend.

Lately he had started lying awake at night, worrying about the child that would arrive in a couple of months. Not that it wasn't a much-longed-for baby, because it was. Very much indeed. But it was as if it had only just dawned on him what a massive responsibility he was taking on. He was going to have to protect, raise, and look after a little life, a little person, on every level imaginable. Lately, that realization had left him lying awake staring up at the ceiling every night, while Pia's huge belly rose and fell in time with her steady breathing. He pictured bullying and guns and drugs and sexual exploitation and accidents and misery. When you thought about it, there was no end to the troubles that could befall the child who was on his or her way. And for the first time he asked himself if he was up to the task. However, it was a bit late to worry about that now. In a couple of months the baby would be here, there was no getting away from it.

"My, we are cheerful this morning!" Paula sat down and rested her elbows on the table as she regarded Martin and Gösta with a smile.

"There ought to be a law against being so cheerful on a Monday morning," Gösta said, getting up to pour himself a coffee. The water hadn't finished trickling through, so when he picked up the coffee pot, the liquid started dripping onto the hot plate. He didn't even seem to notice, but simply put back the pot when he had filled his cup.

"Hey," Paula said sharply as he turned away from the mess and headed back to his chair. "You can't just leave it like that! Wipe it up."

Gösta glanced at the coffee machine; only now did he appear to notice the pools of coffee on the drainboard. "Right, yes, of course," he said glumly, picking up a cloth.

Martin laughed. "Nice to see that somebody can keep you in order!"

"Typical woman—they're always so goddamn picky."

Paula was just about to come back with a snappy retort when they all heard something in the corridor. Something rather unusual in the station. A child, babbling away happily.

Martin suddenly looked hopeful. "That must be—" he said, and before he had time to finish the sentence, Patrik appeared in the doorway with Maja in his arms.

"Morning, all!"

"Morning!" Martin said chirpily. "So, you couldn't keep away any longer!"

Patrik smiled. "Well, Maja and I thought we'd check in just to make sure you're all hard at work, didn't we, sweetheart?" Maja gurgled and waved her arms. Then she started wriggling, making it clear that she wanted to get down. Patrik obliged, and she immediately set off on wobbly legs, heading straight for Martin.

"Hi there, Maja. So you recognized Uncle Martin— remember, we looked at the pretty flowers together? You know what, Maja? Uncle Martin is going to fetch you a box of toys." He got up and went to get the toy box they kept in the station just in case someone had a child with them who might need to be distracted for a while. Maja was thrilled with the treasure chest full of wonderful and entertaining objects that appeared in the kitchen less than a minute later.

"Thanks, Martin," Patrik said. He poured coffee for himself and sat down at the table. "So, how's it going?" he said, grimacing as he took his first gulp. Obviously it had only taken a week for him to forget how disgusting the station coffee was.

"Things are a bit slow," Martin replied. "But we've got a few leads." He told Patrik about the conversations they had had with Frans Ringholm and Axel Frankel. Patrik nodded with interest.

"And Gösta went to see one of the boys to get his finger-prints and shoeprint last Friday. We just need to do the same with the other boy, then we can start eliminating their traces from the investigation."

"What did he say?" Patrik asked. "Had they seen anything interesting? Why did they decide to break into that particular house? Did you find out anything we can use?"

"Nothing helpful," Gösta said irritably. He felt as if Patrik was questioning the way he did his job, and he really didn't appreciate that at all. But at the same time, Patrik's questions had triggered something in the depths of his mind. Something was moving in there, something he felt he ought to bring to the surface. Then again, perhaps it was just his imagination. And it would only provide grist for Patrik's mill if he mentioned it.

"So to sum things up, we're kind of treading water at the moment. The only point of interest is the link to Sweden's Friends. Apart from that, Erik Frankel doesn't appear to have had any enemies, and we haven't found any other motive to suggest that someone would want him dead."

"Have you checked his bank records? There could be something there," Patrik speculated.

Martin shook his head, annoyed that he hadn't thought of it himself. "We'll do that right away," he said. "And we ought to ask Axel whether there was a woman in Erik's life. Or a man, for that matter. Someone he might have shared pillow talk with. We also need to speak to Erik and Axel's cleaner today."

"Good," Patrik said, nodding. "She should be able to explain why she hasn't been in to clean all summer, and so didn't find Erik's body."

Paula got to her feet. "I think I'll give Axel a call right now and ask whether Erik might have had a partner." She went to her office.

"Have you got those letters that Frans sent to Erik?" Patrik asked.

"Sure, I'll go and get them," Martin said. "I presume you mean you'd like to take a look at them?"

Patrik shrugged, making an effort to look indifferent. "Well, since I'm here anyway. . . ."

Martin laughed. "Once a cop, always a cop. Aren't you supposed to be on paternity leave?"

"Just wait until it's your turn. There are only so many hours you can spend in the sandbox. And Erica's working at home, so she's delighted if we stay out of her way."

"Are you sure she meant you to take refuge in the police station?" Martin's eyes twinkled.

"Maybe not. But I'm just having a quick look. Making sure you're all behaving yourselves."

"In that case, I'd better go and get those letters so that you can have a quick look. . . ."

A few minutes later, Martin returned with the five letters, now preserved in plastic sleeves. Maja looked up from the toy box and reached out for the papers in Martin's hand, but he kept them out of her reach and passed them to Patrik. "No, sweetie, you can't play with those." Maja's expression suggested that she wasn't too happy with this news, but she went back to exploring the contents of the box on the floor.

Patrik laid out the letters in a row on the table, then read them in silence, frowning deeply.

"There's nothing concrete, is there? And he keeps repeating himself. Saying Erik ought to lie low, because he can no longer protect him. That there are factions within Sweden's Friends who don't think before they act." Patrik read on. "And I get the impression that Erik answered the letters." Patrick read aloud from Frans's letter:

I think you're wrong in what you say. You talk of conse-
quences, of responsibility. I'm talking about burying the past,
looking to the future. We have different opinions, different

points of view, you and I. But we come from the same place.
The same monster lurks in the deep, and unlike you I think
it would be wrong to wake that old monster. Certain bones
should be left undisturbed. I gave you my opinion on the
past in my previous letter, and I will not mention it again.
I recommend that you do the same. At the moment I have
chosen to act in a protective capacity, but if the situation
changes, if the monster is brought out into the open, I may
well feel differently.

Patrik looked up at Martin. "Did you ask Frans what he
meant by that? What's this 'old monster' he talks about?"

"We haven't gotten around to asking him that yet. But we'll
be speaking to him again."

Paula reappeared. "I've managed to track down the woman
in Erik's life. I called Axel, as Patrik suggested, and apparently
Erik has had a 'close friend,' as he put it, for the past four years.
Her name is Viola Ellmander, and I've spoken to her as well.
She can see us this morning."

"Quick work," Patrik said, smiling appreciatively at Paula.

"Want to come along?" Martin said impulsively, but after
glancing at Maja, who was conducting a close examination of
a doll's eyes, he added, "No, of course you can't do that."

"Yes, you can—leave her with me," came a female voice
from the doorway. Annika was looking hopefully at Patrik
and gave Maja a big smile, which was immediately returned.
With no children of her own, Annika was always glad of the
opportunity to borrow someone else's.

"I'm not sure . . . ," Patrik said, gazing pensively at Maja.

"Do you think I'm not up to the job?" Annika said, folding
her arms and pretending to take offense.

"No, it's not that . . . ," Patrik said, still slightly hesitant. But
then curiosity got the better of him, and he nodded. "Okay, I'll

go along for a little while, and be back before lunch. But any problems, call me right away. And she needs something to eat at about half past ten. She still likes her food mashed up really small—actually, I think I might have a jar of meat sauce you can heat up in the microwave, and she usually gets tired after she's eaten, but all you need to do is put her in the stroller and take her for a little walk, and don't forget her pacifier and her teddy bear and she likes to have her teddy right next to her when she's falling asleep and—"

"Stop, stop!" Annika held up her hands, laughing. "Maja and I will be absolutely fine. No problem. I'll make sure she doesn't starve while she's in my care, and no doubt we can manage a little nap as well."

"Thanks, Annika," Patrik said, getting to his feet. He crouched down beside his daughter and kissed her blond head. "Daddy's just going out for a little while. You're staying here with Annika. Is that all right?" Maja looked at him with big eyes for a second, then turned her attention back to the toys and continued trying to pull out the doll's eyelashes. Slightly crestfallen, Patrik stood up and said, "There you go, that's how indispensable I am. Have a lovely time, you two."

He gave Annika a hug, then went out to the garage. He felt a surge of elation as he got into the driver's seat of the police car, with Martin in the passenger seat beside him. Paula got in the back, equipped with Viola's address on a piece of paper. Patrik reversed out of the garage and set off toward Fjällbacka, suppressing the urge to start humming with sheer joy.

Axel slowly put down the phone. Suddenly everything felt so unreal. It was as if he were still lying in bed, dreaming. The house was so empty without Erik. They had always given each other space, made sure they didn't invade each other's privacy. Sometimes days had passed without the two of them even speaking to each other. They had often eaten at different times, spent hours in their rooms at opposite ends of the house. But their habits could not be interpreted as a lack of closeness. They were very close. Or had been, Axel corrected himself. Because now there was a different kind of silence in the house. It wasn't the same silence as when Erik used to be sitting downstairs in the library, reading. Then they had always been able to break the silence by exchanging a few words if they wanted to. This silence was dense, endless.

Erik had never brought Viola here. Nor had he ever spoken of her. Axel had spoken to her only when he happened to answer the telephone when she called. Erik would usually disappear for a couple of days after that. He would pack a few essentials, say a brief good-bye, then he'd be gone. Sometimes Axel had felt jealous as he watched his brother go. Jealous because he didn't have anyone. That aspect of life had passed Axel by. There had been women, of course. But nothing that lasted beyond the first flush of love. It had always been his fault; he was in no doubt about that, yet he couldn't do anything about it. The other influence in his life had been too strong, too all-encompassing. Over the years, it had become a demanding mistress that left no room for anything else. His work had become his life, his identity, his innermost being. Exactly when it had happened, he didn't know. Actually, that was a lie.

In his silent house, Axel sat down on the upholstered chair next to the chest of drawers in the hallway. For the first time since his brother's death, he wept.

Erica was enjoying the peace and quiet at home. She could even leave her study door open without being disturbed by noise from elsewhere. She put her feet up on the desk, thinking back to her conversation with Erik Frankel's brother. It had opened some kind of floodgate within her, provoking an immense, insatiable curiosity about those aspects of her mother's personality that she clearly hadn't known about or even suspected. She also felt instinctively that she had only learned a fraction of what Axel Frankel knew about Elsy. But why would he hide anything from her? What was there in her mother's background that he didn't want to talk about? She reached for the diaries and continued reading where she had left off a couple of days earlier. But there were no clues, just thoughts and the trivia of everyday life from a teenage girl. No great revelations, nothing that could explain the strange look on Axel's face when he had talked about her mother.

Erica read on, desperately searching for something significant. Something, anything that could allay her growing uneasiness. But it wasn't until the last few pages of the third book that she found something that might possibly provide a plausible link to Axel.

Suddenly she knew what to do. She swung down her legs, picked up the diaries, and placed them carefully in her purse. She went outside to check on the weather, then put on a thin jacket and set off at a brisk pace.

She climbed the steep steps up to Badis, the old hotel, and paused at the top, perspiring from the exertion. The old restaurant looked desolate and deserted now that the summer rush was over, but, to be honest, it had been on the skids even during the summer in recent years. It was a shame. The location was unbeatable, up on the hill above the harbor with an uninterrupted view of the archipelago. But over time the building itself had begun to look very shabby, and presumably it would require a considerable investment if anyone was going to make something of it.

The house she was looking for was located a little way above the restaurant, and she was just hoping that the person she had come to see was home.

A pair of bright eyes met her as the door opened. "Yes?" said the lady who was standing in the hallway, looking at her with curiosity.

"My name is Erica Falck." Erica hesitated. "I'm Elsy Moström's daughter."

There was a glimmer of something in Britta's eyes. She stood silent and motionless for a moment, then she suddenly smiled and stepped aside.

"Of course. Elsy's daughter. I can see it now. Come on in."

Erica walked in and looked around with interest. The house was light and pleasant, with lots of photographs of children and grandchildren, and probably great-grandchildren too, on the walls.

"That's the whole tribe," Britta said with a smile, pointing to the array of pictures.

"How many children do you have, ma'am?" Erica asked politely.

"Three daughters. And please don't call me ma'am—it makes me feel so old! I am old, of course, but that doesn't mean I have to feel that way! After all, age is just a number."

"That's true," Erica agreed with a laugh. She really liked this lady.

"Come in and sit down," Britta said, gently touching Erica's elbow. After taking off her jacket and shoes, Erica followed her into the living room.

"This is a lovely house."

"We've lived here for fifty-five years," Britta said. Her face grew soft and warm when she smiled. She sat down on a big sofa with a floral pattern and patted the seat beside her. "Come and sit beside me so we can have a chat. It's so good to meet you. Elsy and I . . . we spent a lot of time together when we were young."

For a moment, Erica thought she heard the same odd tone that she had picked up during her conversation with Axel

Frankel, but a second later it was gone, and Britta was smiling her gentle smile once more.

"The thing is, I found a few of my mother's belongings when I was clearing out the attic, and . . . I was just a little curious. I didn't know very much about my mother. How did you get to know each other, for example?"

"We were classmates, Elsy and I. We sat next to each other on our very first day in school, and we just continued that way."

"And you knew Erik and Axel Frankel too?"

"Erik more than Axel. Erik's brother was a few years older than we were, and I expect he thought we were annoying brats. But he was incredibly stylish, was Axel."

"So I've heard," Erica laughed. "He still is, to tell the truth."

"I tend to agree with you, but don't tell my husband," Britta said in a theatrical whisper.

"I promise!" Erica was liking her mother's old friend more and more. "And what about Frans? As I understand it, Frans Ringholm was part of your little group, wasn't he?"

Britta stiffened. "Frans, yes. That's right. Frans was part of our group."

"It doesn't sound as if you were particularly fond of Frans."

"Not particularly fond of Frans? My dear, I was head over heels in love with Frans. But it wasn't mutual. He only had eyes for someone else."

"And who was that?" Erica said, even though she thought she already knew the answer.

"Frans was only interested in your mother. He followed her around like a puppy dog. Not that it got him anywhere. Your mother would never have looked at someone like Frans. Only a silly goose like me would fall for him; good looks were all that mattered to me back then. He was a handsome devil, with that slightly dangerous edge that's so attractive when you're a teenager, but terrifying when you're a bit more mature."

"Oh, I don't know about that," Erica said. "Even older women seem to find dangerous men attractive."

"You're probably right," Britta said. "But luckily I grew out of it. And I grew away from Frans. . . . He . . . he wasn't the kind of man you would want in your life. Not like my Herman."

"Aren't you being a bit hard on yourself? I mean, you don't seem like a silly goose to me."

"Not now, no. But I might as well admit it, until I met Herman and had my first child, well. . . . No, I wasn't a very nice girl."

Britta's honesty surprised Erica. She seemed to have a very low opinion of her younger self.

"And Erik? What was he like?"

Britta seemed to consider the question for a while, then her face softened. "Erik was a little old man even when he was a child. I don't mean that in a negative way, it's just that he seemed old for his age. And he was sensible, like an adult. He did a lot of thinking. And reading. He always had his nose stuck in a book. Frans used to tease him about it, but I think Erik got away with being a bit odd because of who his brother was."

"I gather Axel was very popular."

"Axel was a hero. And the person who admired him most of all was Erik. He worshipped the ground his brother walked on. Axel could do no wrong as far as Erik was concerned." Britta patted Erica on the leg, then suddenly got to her feet. "You know what? I'm going to make some coffee and then we can keep chatting. Elsy's daughter! This is so lovely."

Erica stayed where she was as Britta disappeared into the kitchen. She heard the clatter of china and the sound of running water. Then silence. Erica waited patiently, enjoying the view spread before her. But after a few minutes with no further sign of activity, she began to wonder. "Britta!" she shouted. No reply. She got up and went into the kitchen in search of her hostess.

Britta was sitting at the kitchen table, staring blankly into space. One of the burners on the stove was glowing bright red. An empty pan sitting on it had just begun to smoke. Erica rushed forward and grabbed the pan. "Shit!" she yelled as she burned her hand on the metal handle. She held her hand under cold running water for a while to ease the pain, then turned to Britta. It was as if a light had gone out in her eyes.

"Britta?" she said softly. For a moment, she was worried that the older woman had suffered some kind of seizure, but then Britta looked up at her.

"Imagine that—you came to see me after all this time, Elsy!"

Erica was dismayed. She began to protest: "But Britta, I'm Erica, Elsy's daughter."

Britta didn't seem to register what she had said. Instead, she continued quietly: "I've been wanting to speak to you for such a long time, Elsy. To explain. But I haven't been able to. . . ."

"What is it you haven't been able to explain? What did you want to talk to Elsy about?" Erica sat down opposite her, unable to hide her eagerness. For the first time, she felt as if she might be close to the heart of the matter, to an explanation for what she had felt during her conversations with Erik and Axel. Something that was hidden, something they had not wanted her to know

But Britta was looking at her in confusion. Part of Erica wanted to lean forward and shake her, force her to give up whatever it was that she had been on the point of saying. She repeated her question: "What is it you haven't been able to explain? Something to do with my mother? What?"

Britta waved her hand defensively, but then leaned across the table toward Erica and in a whisper that was almost a hiss, she said, "I've been wanting to talk to you. But old bones. Must. Rest. In peace. There's no point in . . . Erik said that . . . unknown soldier. . . ." Her voice died away into an unintelligible mumble as Britta stared into space.

"Bones? What bones? What are you talking about? What did Erik say?" Without realizing what she was doing, Erica had raised her voice, and in the silence of the kitchen it sounded as if she was yelling. Britta reacted by putting her hands over her ears and babbling, the way small children do when they're being scolded and don't want to listen.

"What's going on here? Who are you?" An angry male voice behind her made Erica spin around on her chair. A tall man with gray hair encircling a bald pate was staring at her, clutching two Konsum grocery bags in his hands. Erica realized that this must be Herman. She got to her feet.

"I'm sorry, I. . . . My name is Erica Falck. Britta knew my mother when she was a girl, and I just wanted to ask her a few questions. Everything seemed okay at first . . . but then . . . and she'd switched on the stove." Erica was aware that she was talking nonsense, but the whole situation felt extremely uncomfortable. Behind her, Britta's childish babble continued unabated.

"My wife suffers from Alzheimer's," Herman said, putting down the bags. Those words encompassed a bottomless grief, and Erica felt a pang of guilt. Alzheimer's. She should have realized. The rapid transition from total lucidity to bewilderment. She remembered reading that those with Alzheimer's gradually drift into a kind of no-man's land where, in the end, the fog of confusion is all that remains.

Herman went over to his wife and gently moved her hands away from her ears. "Britta, my love. I had to go and do some shopping. But I'm back now. Ssh, everything's fine. . . ." He rocked her back and forth in his arms, and gradually the babbling stopped. He looked up at Erica. "I think you'd better leave now. And I'd prefer it if you didn't come back."

"But Britta mentioned something about . . . I need to know. . . ." Erica stumbled over her words as she tried to find the right thing to say, but Herman merely stared back at her and repeated firmly: "Don't come back."

Erica crept out of the house feeling like a thief, an intruder. Behind her, she could hear Herman speaking reassuringly to his wife, but she couldn't get Britta's muddled words about old bones out of her head. What could she have meant?

The pelargoniums had been unusually good this summer. Viola did the rounds, lovingly deadheading the plants, a necessary task if they were to remain beautiful. By this stage, her cultivation of pelargoniums was quite impressive. Each year she took cuttings from the ones she already had, planted them carefully in small pots, then repotted them when they were a little bigger. Her favorite was the Mårbacka pelargonium. There was nothing to touch its beauty. There was something about the combination of delicate pink flowers and the slightly awkward, straggly stems that created an aesthetic appeal. But the rose pelargonium was lovely too.

There were a lot of pelargonium aficionados out there. Since her son had introduced her to the wonderful world of the Internet, she had joined three different forums on pelargoniums and subscribed to four newsletters. Exchanging messages with Lasse Anrell gave her more pleasure than anything. If there was one person who loved pelargoniums more than Viola did, it was Lasse. They had been exchanging e-mails ever since she had attended a talk he was giving about his book on pelargoniums. She had asked lots of questions that night; a mutual friendship had sprung up between them, and now she really looked forward to the messages that landed in her inbox at regular intervals. Erik used to tease her about it, saying that she was having a secret affair with Lasse Anrell behind his back, and that all this talk of pelargoniums was actually a code for rather more amorous activities. He had developed a particular theory about the meaning of the words "rose pelargonium," and ever since then his special name for her . . . her . . . had been rose pelargonium. Viola blushed at the thought, but her embarrassment was quickly replaced by tears as it struck her yet again that Erik was gone.

The soil in the pots quickly sucked up the water as she carefully poured a small amount into each saucer. It was important to avoid overwatering. Ideally, the soil should dry out thoroughly before watering. In many ways this was an appropriate metaphor for her relationship with Erik. They too allowed the soil to dry out between meetings, and they were careful not to overwater what they had. They continued to live apart, they each maintained their own separate lives, and they saw each other only when they wanted to. That was a promise they had made to each other at an early stage: their relationship was to be full of joy, not something that was weighed down by the petty concerns of everyday life. It was to be a mutual exchange of tenderness, love, and good conversation. When the spirit moved them.

When she heard the knock on the door, Viola put down the watering can and dried her tears on the sleeve of her blouse. She took a deep breath, glanced at her pelargoniums one more time to give her strength, and went to open the door.

14
Fjällbacka 1943

"Calm down, Britta. . . . What's happened? Is he drunk again?" Elsy stroked her friend's back reassuringly as they sat on her bed. Britta nodded. She tried to say something, but managed only a sob. Elsy drew her closer and continued stroking her back.

"Ssh, it's okay, you'll soon be able to move out. Find a job. Get away from all that misery at home."

"I'll . . . I'll never come home again once I leave," Britta sobbed into Elsy's chest. Elsy could feel the dampness on her blouse from Britta's tears, but it didn't matter.

"Was he horrible to your mom again?"

Britta nodded. "He hit her across the face. I didn't see what happened after that; I ran away. If only I was a boy—I'd beat him black and blue."

"It would be a waste of a very pretty face if you were a boy," Elsy said, laughing as she continued to rock Britta. She knew her friend well enough to realize that a little flattery could always cheer her up.

"Mmm," Britta said, her sobs beginning to subside. "But I feel sorry for the little ones."

"There's not much you can do about that," Elsy said, picturing Britta's three younger siblings. Her throat constricted with rage at the thought of the misery Britta's father, Tord, had brought upon the family. He was notorious in Fjällbacka for his inability to hold his drink, and everyone knew that he beat his wife, Rut, several times a week. She was a terrified creature who tried to hide the bruises on her face with her scarf if she had to go out before they faded. The children also suffered from time to time, but it was mostly Britta's two younger brothers who bore the brunt of their father's temper. Britta and her sister usually got off more lightly.

"I wish he'd just drop down dead. Fall in the sea and drown when he's drunk," Britta whispered.

Elsy hugged her tightly. "Ssh, you mustn't say that, Britta. You mustn't even think such a thing. With God's mercy I'm sure things will work out. Somehow. Without your committing the sin of wishing him dead."

"God?" Britta said bitterly. "I don't think God knows where we live, but still my mother sits there every Sunday saying her prayers. Much good it's done her. It's easy for you to talk about God when your parents are so lovely. And you've got no brothers and sisters to worry about and take care of." Britta's voice couldn't hide a bitterness as deep as an abyss.

Elsy loosened her grip on her friend. Kindly, but with a certain amount of sharpness, she said "Listen, things aren't always that easy here either. Mom worries so much about Dad that she's getting thinner and thinner every single day. Ever since the *Öckerö* was torpedoed, she's been convinced that every trip could be his last. Sometimes I find her standing by the window just staring out to sea, as if she's trying to put a spell on it to make it bring him home again."

"I still don't think it's the same thing," Britta said with a pathetic sniffle.

"Of course it's not the same thing, I just meant that . . . oh, forget it." Elsy knew there was no point in pursuing the conversation. She had known Britta since they were tiny, and loved her for the positive sides to her character. But there was no denying that they were sometimes hidden beneath self-obsession and an inability to see anyone else's problems besides her own.

They heard footsteps on the stairs; Britta quickly sat up straight and started frantically drying her eyes.

"You've got visitors." Hilma's voice was guarded. Frans and Erik appeared behind her.

"Hi!"

Elsy could tell from her mother's face that she didn't appreciate the visit, but still she left them alone after adding, "Elsy, don't forget you have to take back the Östermans' laundry soon. Ten minutes. And you know Dad will be home shortly."

She disappeared down the stairs, and Frans and Erik settled down on the floor in Elsy's room since there was nowhere else to sit.

"I don't think your mom is very pleased to see us," Frans said.

"My mother doesn't think different kinds of people should mix," Elsy said. "She sees you as upper class, for some unknown reason." She smiled mischievously, and Frans stuck out his tongue at her. Meanwhile Erik was gazing at Britta.

"Are you all right, Britta?" he said quietly. "You look a bit upset."

"Nothing for you to worry about," she snapped, proudly tilting up her chin.

"Girls' stuff, no doubt," Frans said with a laugh.

Britta gazed at him adoringly and gave him a big smile, even though her eyes were still red.

"Why do you always have to tease us, Frans?" Elsy said, clasping her hands in her lap. "There are actually people who have a difficult time, you know. Not everyone is as lucky as you and Erik. The war has taken its toll on too many families. You two ought to bear that in mind."

"You two? How did I get dragged into this?" Erik said, sounding hurt. "I mean, we all know that Frans is a brainless idiot, but accusing me of not having an awareness of how people suffer. . . ." Erik was obviously offended, but gave a start and yelled "Ow!" when Frans delivered a sharp blow to his upper arm.

"Who are you calling a brainless idiot? In my opinion, only an idiot would use language like 'not having an awareness of how people suffer.' It makes you sound about eighty. At least. I don't think reading all those books does you any good at all. I think you've gone a bit wrong up here." Frans demonstrated what he meant by tapping his temple with his forefinger.

"Just ignore him," Elsy said wearily. Sometimes she got so tired of the boys and their constant bickering. They were incredibly childish.

A sound from downstairs made her face light up. "Dad's home!" She smiled happily at her three friends and got up to go downstairs. But something in her parents' tone of voice made her stop. Something had happened. Agitated voices rose and sank, and there was no trace of the cheerful chatter that usually accompanied her father's return. Then she heard heavy footsteps approach the stairs and begin to climb. As soon as she saw her father's face, she knew something was wrong. He was ashen, and he was running a hand over his hair; he only did that when he was seriously worried.

"Dad?" she said tentatively, her heart pounding. What could have happened? She tried to catch his eye, but saw that he was looking straight at Erik. He opened his mouth to speak several times, but closed it again when the words wouldn't come out. But eventually he managed to say, "Erik, I think you'd better go home. Your mother and father . . . are going to need you."

"What's happened? Why . . . ?" Erik's hand flew to his mouth as he realized what kind of bad news Elsy's father was likely to be bringing him. "Axel? Is he . . . ?" He couldn't finish the sentence, and swallowed over and over again to try to get rid of the lump that had formed in his throat. The thoughts were whirling around in his head, and he suddenly pictured Axel's dead body. How could he face his mother and father? How could he?

"He's not dead," Elof said, waving his hand defensively when he realized what the boy was thinking. "He's not dead," he repeated. "But the Germans have captured him."

There was total confusion on Erik's face as he tried to process this new information. Relief and joy that at least Axel wasn't dead were quickly replaced by anxiety and horror at the knowledge that his brother was now in the hands of the enemy.

"I'll walk home with you," Elof said. His whole body seemed to be weighed down by the difficult task that lay before him: having to tell Axel's parents that their son would not be coming back from his trip this time.

15

Paula was perfectly happy in the back seat of the car. There was something pleasant and reassuring about Patrik and Martin's banter in the front. At the moment, Martin was in the middle of a long explanation as to why Patrik's driving wasn't one of the things he missed, but it was clear that the colleagues were good friends, and she had already developed a considerable measure of respect for Patrik.

So far, Tanumshede had proven to be a stroke of luck. She didn't quite know what it was, but ever since they had moved here, she had had the feeling of coming home. She had spent so many years in Stockholm that she had forgotten what it was like to live in a small community. Perhaps Tanumshede reminded her in many ways of the little village in Chile where she had spent the first few years of her life, before the family fled to Sweden. She couldn't come up with any other explanation for why she had fit in with the tempo and atmosphere of

Tanumshede so quickly. There was nothing she missed about Stockholm. Perhaps that was because as a police officer she had seen the worst of the worst, which colored her view of the city. But she had never really fit in there, either as a child or as an adult. She and her mother had been allocated a small apartment on the outskirts of Stockholm. They had been part of an early influx of immigrants; in school, she was the only one in her class from a non-Swedish background, and she had paid dearly for that. Every minute of every day she had paid for the fact that she had been born in a different country. Even her ability to speak perfect Swedish without a trace of an accent after only twelve months didn't help: her dark eyes and black hair betrayed her.

On the other hand, in contrast to what many outsiders believed, she hadn't encountered any racism whatsoever when she joined the police. By that time, the Swedes had grown used to people from other countries, and she was hardly regarded as an immigrant any longer—partly because she had lived in Sweden for so long and partly because her South American origins made her seem much less "foreign" than immigrants from the Arab world and Africa. She had often thought it bizarre that her own escape from immigrant status had been due to the fact that she seemed less unusual than the current wave of refugees.

That was why she found men like Frans Ringholm so frightening. They didn't see the nuances, the variations; they simply looked at the surface for a second, then attached thousands of years of prejudice to that surface. It was the same kind of discrimination that had forced her and her mother to flee. Someone had decided that nothing but one way, one type, was acceptable. An autocratic power decreed that everything else was incorrect. People like Frans Ringholm had always existed. People who thought they had the intelligence, or the strength or the power, to be the ones who determined the norm.

"What number did you say it was?" Martin turned to Paula, interrupting her thoughts. She looked down at the piece of paper in her hand.

"Number seven."

"Over there," Martin said, pointing out the house to Patrik, who pulled over and parked the car. They were in Kullenområdet, an apartment complex just above the playing field in Fjällbacka.

The usual nameplate on the door had been replaced by a significantly more personal one made of wood, with VIOLA ELLMANDER in ornate writing, entwined with hand-painted flowers. The woman who opened the door matched the nameplate perfectly. Viola was round but shapely, and her expression was kind and friendly. When Paula saw her romantic floral dress, she pictured a straw hat balancing on top of the gray hair that was caught up in a bun.

"Please come in," Viola said, stepping to one side. Paula gazed appreciatively around the hallway. Viola's home was very different from her own, but she liked it. She had never been to Provence, but this was how she imagined it would look. Rustic furniture combined with floral fabrics and pictures featuring plants and flowers. She craned her neck to look into the living room and saw that the style was consistent.

"I've made coffee," Viola said, leading the way into the living room. Delicate rose-patterned china was set out on the coffee table, along with a plate of cakes and cookies.

"That's very kind," Patrik said, lowering himself gently onto the sofa. Once the introductions were out of the way, Viola poured them all coffee from a pretty pot, then seemed to be waiting for them to take the initiative.

"Your pelargoniums are beautiful—how do you do it?" Paula heard herself ask as she sipped her coffee. Patrik and Martin looked at her in surprise. "Mine always shrivel up or rot," she said by way of explanation. Patrik and Martin were even more taken aback.

Viola clearly appreciated the compliment. "Oh, it's not that difficult, really. You just have to let the soil dry out before you water the plant and make sure you don't drown it. And I got an excellent tip from Lasse Anrell: you can use a small amount of urine as a fertilizer occasionally! It does the trick if they're a bit slow to flower."

"Lasse Anrell?" Martin echoed. "The sports correspondent on *Aftonbladet*? And on Channel 4? What has he got to do with pelargoniums?"

Viola looked as if she couldn't even bring herself to answer such a stupid question. As far as she was concerned, Lasse was first and foremost an expert on pelargoniums; the fact that he also happened to be a sports journalist was on the extreme periphery of her awareness.

Patrik cleared his throat. "As we understand it, you and Erik Frankel used to see each other on a regular basis." He hesitated, then added "I'm . . . I'm very sorry for your loss."

"Thank you," said Viola, looking down into her coffee cup. "Yes, we used to see each other. Erik stayed over sometimes, maybe twice a month."

"How did you meet?" Paula asked. It was hard to imagine how these two had gotten together, now that she had seen how different their homes were.

Viola smiled, and Paula noticed that two enchanting dimples appeared.

"Erik gave a talk at the library a few years ago. Let me think . . . four years, perhaps? He was speaking about Bohuslän and the Second World War, and I went to hear him. We got chatting afterward, and . . . well, one thing led to another." She smiled at the memory.

"You never met at his place?" Martin reached for a cookie.

"No, Erik thought it was better to meet here. He shares . . . shared the house with his brother, and even though Axel was away a lot, he . . . he preferred to come here."

"Did he ever mention anything about receiving threats?" Patrik asked.

Viola shook her head decisively. "No, never. I can't even imagine . . . I mean, why would anyone want to threaten Erik, a retired history teacher? The very idea is ridiculous."

"But he had actually received threats—indirectly, anyway, because of his interest in Nazism and the Second World War. Certain organizations don't like it when someone paints a picture of history that they don't agree with."

"Erik didn't paint a picture, as you so sloppily put it," Viola said, a sudden flash of anger in her eyes. "He was a true historian, meticulous when it came to facts, and very particular about showing the truth exactly as it was, not as he or anyone else might have wished it to be. Erik didn't paint. He put together a puzzle. Slowly, slowly, piece by piece, he worked out what reality looked like. A little bit of blue sky here, a fragment of a green meadow there, until eventually he could show the results to everyone else. Not that he would ever have finished," she said, the softness returning to her expression. "A historian's work is never done. There are always a few more facts, a little more reality to dig out."

"Why was he so passionate about the Second World War?" Paula asked.

"Why does anyone develop an interest? Why do I love pelargoniums? Why not roses?" Viola shrugged, but at the same time she looked thoughtful. "Although in Erik's case perhaps you don't have to be a genius to figure out the reason. His brother's experiences during the war affected him more than anything else, I think. He never spoke of them to me, but I could read between the lines sometimes. He mentioned what

160

happened to his brother just once, and that was the only occasion on which I ever saw Erik drink too much. It was the last time we saw each other." Her voice broke, and Viola took a few seconds to compose herself before she went on. "Erik came by unannounced, which was unusual in itself, and he'd obviously been drinking. That was even more unusual; I'd never seen him like that. And he went straight to my drinks cupboard and poured himself a large whiskey. Then he sat down on the sofa and started talking as he knocked back the whiskey. I couldn't understand most of what he said; it was incoherent and seemed like drunken rambling. But it was about Axel, that much I did figure out. What had happened to him while he was a prisoner. How it had affected the family."

"You said that was the last time you saw Erik—how come? Why didn't you meet up over the summer? Why didn't you wonder where he was?"

Viola's face contorted as she struggled to hold back the tears. Eventually she said in a thick voice, "Because Erik said goodbye to me. He left here at around midnight—well, staggered away is probably a more accurate description—and the last thing he said was that this had to be our farewell. He thanked me for our time together, and kissed me on the cheek. Then he left. I just thought he was talking nonsense because he was drunk. I behaved like a complete idiot the following day; I sat here staring at the phone all day, waiting for him to call me and explain, or apologize, or . . . anything at all. . . . But I didn't hear from him. And because of my stupid, stupid pride, I refused to call him, of course. If I'd called him instead of just giving up, perhaps he wouldn't have had to sit there. . . ." The tears got the better of her, and she was unable to finish the sentence.

But Paula understood what she meant. She placed her hand on top of Viola's and said gently, "It wasn't your fault. How were you supposed to know?"

Viola nodded reluctantly and wiped away the tears with the back of her hand.

"Do you remember what day he was here?" Patrik said hopefully.

"I can check my diary," Viola said, getting to her feet; she was obviously relieved at the prospect of a break. "I always make a little note each day, so it should be easy to find." She left the room and was gone for a short while.

"It was the fifteenth of June," she said when she came back. "I remember because I'd been to the dentist that afternoon, so I'm absolutely certain."

"Okay, thanks," Patrik said as he got up.

When they had taken their leave of Viola and were back out in the street, they were all preoccupied with the same thought: what had happened on the fifteenth of June to make Erik do something so out of character as to get drunk, then end his relationship with Viola so abruptly? What could have happened?

"It's obvious Pernilla has no control over her!"

"Come on, Dan, that's hardly fair! How can you be so sure you wouldn't have fallen for the same story?" Anna was leaning against the drainboard with her arms folded, glaring at Dan.

"No chance!" Dan's blond hair was standing on end because he kept running a hand through it in frustration.

"Oh, really. . . . Weren't you the one who was seriously considering the possibility that someone had broken in during the night and eaten all the chocolate in the pantry? If I hadn't found the wrappers under Malin's pillow, you would still have been out there searching for a burglar with chocolate smeared around his mouth. . . ." Anna suppressed a laugh as her anger began to subside. Dan looked at her and couldn't help smiling.

"You have to admit she was very convincing when she swore she was innocent."

"Absolutely. That kid is a shoo-in for an Oscar when she grows up. But remember that Belinda can be equally convincing, so perhaps it's not so surprising that Pernilla believed her. And you can't swear that you wouldn't have done the same."

"I suppose you're right," Dan said sulkily. "But Pernilla should have called the other girl's mother to double-check. I would have."

"I'm sure you would. And from now on, so will Pernilla."

"Why are you talking about my mom?" Belinda came down the stairs, still wearing her nightdress and with her hair sticking out in all directions. She had refused to get out of bed since they picked her up from Erica and Patrik's on Saturday morning, hung over and obviously remorseful. However, most of the remorse seemed to have dissipated, only to be replaced by even more of the anger that appeared to be her default position these days.

"We're not really talking about your mom," Dan said wearily, fully aware that a row was inevitably brewing.

"So you're bad-mouthing my mom again, are you?" Belinda snapped at Anna, who cast a resigned glance at Dan.

Anna turned to Belinda and said calmly, "I have never bad-mouthed your mother. As you well know. So don't speak to me in that tone of voice."

"I'll speak in whatever fucking tone of voice I like!" Belinda yelled. "This is my house, not yours! So why don't you take your fucking kids and move out!"

Dan took a step forward, his eyes dark with anger.

"Don't speak to Anna like that! She lives here now, and so do Adrian and Emma. And if that doesn't suit you, then—" As soon as he started the sentence, he realized it was the stupidest thing he could have said at that moment.

"No, it doesn't suit me! I'm going to pack my bags and go home to Mom! And I'm going to stay there until that bitch and her brats have moved out!" Belinda turned on her heel and ran back upstairs. Both Dan and Anna gave a start when they heard the door of her bedroom slam shut.

"She might be right, Dan," Anna said faintly. "Maybe all this happened too fast. After all, she didn't have much time to get used to the idea before we came along and invaded her space and her life."

"She's seventeen years old, for God's sake. But she behaves like a five-year-old."

"You have to try to see this from Belinda's point of view. It can't have been easy for her. She was at a sensitive age when you and Pernilla split up, and—"

"Thank you, I don't need you guilt-tripping me right now. I know it was my fault we split up, and you don't have to throw that in my face."

Dan marched past Anna and out the front door. For the second time in one minute, a door slammed so loudly that the windowpanes rattled. Anna stood motionless by the sink for a few seconds, then she slid down onto the floor and wept.

16
Fjällbacka 1943

"I heard the Germans finally got their hands on Axel Frankel." Vilgot chuckled with satisfaction as he hung up his coat in the hallway. He handed his briefcase to Frans, who took it and placed it in its usual spot, leaning against the chair.

"About time, too," he continued. "Treason, that's what I call the things he was up to. I know there aren't many here in Fjällbacka who would agree with me, but people are like sheep, they just follow the flock and bleat on command. It's people like me who are capable of thinking for themselves who see reality as it is. And, believe me, that boy was a traitor. Let's hope they make short work of him."

Vilgot had gone into the living room and settled down in his favorite armchair. Frans was right behind him, and Vilgot looked up at him sternly.

"So, where's my drink? You're running late today!" The tone of voice was dissatisfied, and Frans hurried over to the cupboard and poured his father a stiff drink. This was a routine they had observed ever since he was a little boy. His mother had been unhappy that Frans was allowed to handle spirits at such a young age, but as usual she hadn't had much say in the matter.

"Sit down, boy, sit down." With the glass firmly clutched in his hand, Vilgot waved expansively at the armchair beside him. The familiar smell of alcohol drifted toward Frans as he sat down; the drink he had poured his father definitely wasn't his first of the day.

"Your old dad has had an excellent day, Frans." Vilgot leaned forward, and the alcohol fumes made the boy's nostrils prickle. "I've signed a contract with a German company. An exclusive contract. I'm going to be their sole supplier in Sweden. They said it's been difficult to find good working partners. . . . I can well believe it." Vilgot laughed and his big belly wobbled. He swallowed his drink in one gulp and held out the glass to Frans. "Same again." His eyes were glazed. Frans's hand was shaking slightly as he took the glass and poured the clear liquid with the acrid smell; he spilled a few drops.

"Have one yourself," Vilgot said. It sounded more like an order than an invitation. Which it was. Frans put down his father's full glass and reached for an empty one for himself. His hand was no longer shaking as he filled it to the brim. Concentrating hard, he carried both glasses over to his father. Vilgot waited until he had sat down, then raised his glass. "Bottoms up!"

Frans felt the liquid searing his chest, all the way down into his belly, where it settled in a warm lump. His father was smiling. A trickle of schnapps dribbled down his chin.

"Where's your mother?" Vilgot asked quietly.

Frans stared at a point on the wall beyond his father. "She's gone to see Grandma. She won't be back until late." His voice sounded muffled and metallic, as if it belonged to someone else. Someone from outside.

"Excellent. So we can have a good chat, man-to-man. Go on, son—have another!"

Frans could feel his father's eyes on his back as he got up and went to fill his glass. This time he brought the bottle back with him. Vilgot smiled appreciatively; he was ready for a refill.

"You're such a good boy!"

Once again Frans felt the alcohol burning his throat before it was transformed into a warm glow somewhere around his midriff. The contours of everything around him began to dissolve. He felt as if he were floating in a kind of limbo, somewhere between reality and unreality.

Vilgot's voice softened. "I'll make thousands on this deal, and that's just over the next few years. And if the Germans keep increasing their demand for arms, it could be significantly more. We could be talking millions here. And they also promised to put me in touch with other companies who are in need of our services. Once I've got my foot in the door. . . ." Vilgot's eyes were shining in the twilight. He licked his lips. "You'll be taking over a very successful business one day, Frans." He leaned forward and placed a hand on his son's leg. "A very successful business indeed. The day will come when you can tell everyone in Fjällbacka to take a running jump. When the Germans have seized power, when we're in charge, we'll have more money than people here have ever dreamt of. So drink a toast with your dad to the good times to come." Vilgot raised his glass and clinked it against his son's, which Frans had once again filled to the brim.

The feeling of well-being spread through Frans's chest as he drank a toast with his father.

17

Gösta had just started a round of golf on the computer when he heard Mellberg's footsteps out in the corridor. He quickly shut down the game, picked up a report, and tried to look as if he were lost in concentration. Mellberg's footsteps were coming closer, but there was something different about them. And why was the chief making that strange whimpering noise? Overcome with curiosity, Gösta rolled his desk chair backward so that he could stick his head out into the corridor. The first thing he saw was Ernst, ambling in front of Mellberg with his tongue lolling out of his mouth as usual. Then he saw a strange, hunched creature shuffling laboriously along. It looked a lot like Mellberg. And yet it didn't.

"What the hell are you gawking at?"

Yes, the voice and the tone definitely belonged to the chief.

"What's happened to you?" Gösta asked. By now Annika was peering out from the kitchen, where she was busy feeding Maja.

Mellberg mumbled something inaudible.

"Sorry?" Annika said. "What did you say? We didn't quite get that."

Mellberg glared furiously at her, then said "I've been salsa dancing. Any questions?"

Gösta and Annika stared at each other, lost for words. They had to make a real effort to keep their faces straight.

"Well?" Mellberg bellowed. "Any smart remarks? Anyone? Because there's plenty of room for reductions in salary in this station!" Then he slammed the door of his office.

Annika and Gösta stared at the closed door for a few seconds, then it all got too much for them. They laughed until the tears poured down their cheeks, but they tried to be as quiet as possible. Gösta tiptoed across to Annika in the kitchen and, after checking that Mellberg's door was still shut, he whispered "Did he really say he'd been salsa dancing? Did he?"

"I'm afraid so," Annika said, wiping away the tears with her sleeve. Maja gazed at them in fascination from her place at the table with a bowl in front of her.

"But how? Why?" Gösta said dubiously as pictures of the phenomenon began to appear in his mind.

"It's the first I've heard of it." Annika shook her head, still laughing, and sat down to continue feeding Maja.

"Did you see the state he was in? He looked like that creature from *Lord of the Rings*—Gollum, that was it." Gösta did his best to imitate the way Mellberg had been moving, and Annika covered her mouth with her hand to stop herself laughing out loud.

"It must have been a terrible shock for Mellberg's body. I don't think he's exercised since . . . well, ever."

"I'm sure you're right. I've always wondered how he passed the physical during training."

"Then again, he could have been a real athlete in his youth for all we know." Annika thought about what she had just said, then shook her head. "No, I guess not. That was certainly the highlight of the day—Mellberg at a salsa class. Who'd have thought it." She tried to slide a spoon into Maja's mouth, but the child was having none of it. "This little minx is refusing to eat. If I don't get something down her, Patrik will never trust me with her again," she sighed, trying one more time. But Maja's mouth was as unassailable as Fort Knox.

"Can I try?" Gösta said, reaching for the spoon. Annika looked at him in astonishment.

"You? Be my guest. But don't get your hopes up."

Gösta didn't reply; he simply changed places with Annika and sat down next to Maja. He knocked off half the enormous amount of food Annika had scooped up, then raised the spoon in the air. "Vroom, vroom, vroom, here comes the airplane. . . ." He waved the spoon around like a plane and was rewarded with Maja's undivided attention. "Vroom, vroom, vroom, here comes the airplane and IN she goes. . . ." Maja's mouth opened as if by magic, and the plane flew straight in with its cargo of spaghetti Bolognese.

"Mmm, wasn't that yummy?" Gösta said as he scooped up another spoonful. "Choo, choo, choo, there's a train coming this time. . . . Choo, choo, choo and INTO the tunnel." Maja's mouth opened once again, and the spaghetti disappeared into the tunnel.

"Well, I'll be . . . ! Where did you learn to do that?" Annika said in amazement.

"Oh, it was nothing," Gösta said shyly, but he beamed with pride as a racing car zoomed in with spoonful number three.

Annika sat down at the kitchen table and watched as Gösta slowly emptied the bowl in front of Maja, and every last bit disappeared.

"Life is very unfair sometimes, Gösta," she said softly.

"Have you never thought of adoption?" he asked without looking at her. "In my day it wasn't so common, but now I wouldn't hesitate. Practically every other kid is adopted these days."

"We have talked about it," Annika replied, drawing circles on the tablecloth with her index finger. "But somehow we never got around to it. We've tried to make sure our life is filled with other things, but. . . ."

"Well, it's not too late," Gösta said. "If you start now, it might not take very long. And the color of the child's skin is irrelevant, so go for the country with the shortest waiting list. There are so many kids in need of a home. And if I were a child, I would thank my lucky stars if I ended up with you and Lennart."

Annika swallowed and looked down at the movement of her finger against the cloth. Gösta's words had awoken something within her, something she and Lennart had suppressed over the past few years. Perhaps they had been afraid. All those miscarriages, the hopes that had been dashed over and over, had somehow made her heart fragile, delicate. They hadn't dared to hope again, hadn't dared to risk yet another failure. But perhaps they were stronger now. Perhaps they could, perhaps they were brave enough. Because the yearning was still there, every bit as strong, every bit as powerful. They had never managed to eliminate that longing for a child to hold in their arms, a child to love.

"I'd better go and get some work done." Gösta got to his feet without looking at Annika; he simply patted Maja clumsily on the head. "At least she's had her lunch, so Patrik doesn't need to worry about her starving to death when she's here with us."

He was almost out the door when Annika spoke quietly: "Thanks, Gösta."

He nodded, embarrassed. Then he disappeared into his office and closed the door behind him. He sat down at the computer but stared unseeing at the screen. All he could see was Maj-Britt. And the boy. He had lived for just a few days. It was all so long ago. An eternity. Almost a lifetime. But he could still feel that tiny hand gripping his finger.

Gösta sighed and opened up the golf game once more.

For three hours she managed to push aside the thought of that dreadful visit to Britta. During that time, she wrote five pages of the new book, then thoughts of Britta resurfaced and she gave up any further attempt at writing.

She had felt so ashamed when she left Britta's house. She had found it difficult to shake off the recollection of the look on Herman's face when he saw her sitting at the kitchen table next to his wife, who was falling apart. Erica understood perfectly. It had been incredibly insensitive of her not to pick up the signals. But at the same time, she wasn't really sorry she had gone to see Britta. She was slowly acquiring more and more pieces of the puzzle surrounding her mother. Admittedly they were diffuse and vague, but it was significantly more than she had had up till now.

It was very strange. She had never even heard the names Erik, Britta, and Frans, and yet they must have been very important during a certain period of her mother's life. None of them seemed to have been in touch with any of the others when they were adults. In spite of the fact that they had all remained in the small community of Fjällbacka, it was as if they had existed in parallel worlds. And the picture of Elsy that Axel and Britta had begun to paint was remarkably similar, while at the same time it was a million miles from the mother Erica remembered. She had never thought of her mother as warm or considerate, or having any of the positive qualities they had attributed to Elsy. She couldn't say that her mother had been an unpleasant person, but she had been distant, closed off. The warmth she had once possessed had somehow disappeared along the way, well before Erica and Anna were born, and Erica suddenly felt a paralyzing sense of grief for all that she had lost. All the things she could never have again. Her mother was gone; she had died four years ago in the car accident that had also killed Tore, Erica and Anna's father. There was nothing she could revive, nothing she could demand compensation for, nothing she could beg or plead for, nothing she could accuse her mother of. The only thing she could hope to find was understanding. What had happened to the Elsy her friends described? What had happened to that kind, softhearted Elsy?

A knock on the door interrupted her thoughts, and she went to open it.

"Anna? Come on in." With the perceptiveness of a big sister, she immediately noticed that Anna's eyes were red-rimmed.

"What's happened?" she said, sounding more anxious than she had intended. Anna had been through so much in recent years, and Erica had never quite been able to let go of the maternal role she had adopted toward her sister while they were growing up.

"Just the problems that go with trying to blend two families," Anna said with a weak attempt at a smile. "Nothing I can't handle, but it would be good to talk."

"Talk away," Erica said. "I'll make us a cup of coffee, and if I dig around in the cupboard I'm sure I can find something suitable for comfort eating."

"So you've given up on the diet now that you're a married woman?" Anna said.

"Oh, don't," Erica sighed, heading for the kitchen. "After spending a week sitting in front of the computer, I'll need to buy new pants before long. These are as tight as a sausage skin around my waist."

"I know exactly what you mean," Anna said, sitting down at the table. "I feel like I've put on at least five pounds since I moved in with Dan, and it doesn't help that he seems to be able to eat whatever he likes without gaining an ounce."

"How annoying is that?" Erica said, arranging Danish pastries on a plate. "Does he still eat cinnamon buns for breakfast?"

"Oh, was he already doing that when you were together?" Anna shook her head, laughing. "You can imagine how easy it is to persuade the children that a good breakfast is essential when Dan is sitting there dipping cinnamon buns in hot chocolate."

"Listen, Patrik's lumpfish caviar and cheese sandwiches dipped in hot chocolate don't exactly brighten my day either. . . . Anyway, what's happened? Is Belinda making trouble again?"

"I think that's what's behind it all, but everything has gone wrong, and today Dan and I had a fight because of it and. . . ." Anna looked upset as she reached for a pastry. "The thing is, it's not really Belinda's fault, and that's what I keep trying to explain to Dan. She's reacting to a new situation in which she's been given no choice. And she's right when she says that she didn't ask to be saddled with me and two kids."

"That may be true, but you still have the right to insist that she behave in a civilized manner. And that's Dan's responsibility. Dr. Phil says that a stepparent should never have to discipline a child of that age. . . ."

"Dr. Phil?" Anna laughed so much, she swallowed some pastry crumbs the wrong way and ended up having a coughing fit. "It's definitely time your maternity leave was over, Erica! Dr. Phil?"

"I'll have you know I've learned a great deal from Dr. Phil," Erica said huffily. No one got away with joking about her idol. Watching Dr. Phil was the highlight of her day, and she intended to continue taking her lunch break in time for his show.

"He might have a point," Anna admitted reluctantly. "I feel as if Dan either doesn't take the situation seriously enough, or else he takes it too seriously. I've had a hell of a time since last Friday, trying to persuade him not to start arguing with Pernilla about the way the children are brought up. But he started ranting and raving, saying he couldn't trust her to look after the kids, and . . . he flew into such a rage. And in the middle of all that, Belinda came downstairs, and the whole thing fell apart. Now she says she doesn't want to live with us anymore, so Dan has put her on the bus to Munkedal."

"What do Emma and Adrian think about all this?" Erica took another pastry. She would tackle her diet next week. Definitely. If she could just get into a routine with her writing this week, then. . . .

"So far, so good, knock on wood—they think it's great." Anna knocked on the kitchen table. "They adore Dan and the girls, and they love having older sisters. So up to now, it's all quiet on that front."

"And what about Malin and Lisen—how are they handling things?" Belinda's younger sisters were eleven and eight.

"They're fine too; they like messing around with Emma and Adrian, and they at least seem to tolerate me. No, it's mostly Belinda who's being difficult. But then I guess she's at that age—she's supposed to be difficult." Anna sighed before she too reached for another pastry. "Anyway, what about you? How's it going? Are you getting on well with the book?"

"Okay, I think. It's always a bit slow at first, but I've got plenty of written material to work on, and I've also got a few interviews arranged. It's all starting to take shape. But . . ." Erica hesitated. The instinct to protect her sister in every situation was deep-rooted, but she decided that Anna had the right to know what she was doing. She quickly went over everything, starting with the medal and the other items she had found in Elsy's trunk. She told Anna about the diaries, and about the fact that she had spoken to a couple of people from their mother's past.

"Why haven't you told me any of this before?"

Erica shifted uncomfortably. "Yes, well, I know. . . . But I'm telling you now, aren't I?"

Anna seemed to be considering whether to criticize her sister, but then decided to let it pass.

"I'd like to see the things you found," she said curtly.

Erica quickly got to her feet, relieved that her sister wasn't going to start an argument over Erica's failure to keep her informed. "Of course, I'll go and get them." Erica ran upstairs and got the items she kept in her study. Back in the kitchen, she placed them on the table: the diaries, the child's dress, and the medal.

Anna stared at them. "Where the hell did she get this from?" she said, laying the medal on her palm. She turned it this way and that, studying it intently. "And this? Whose is this?" She held the dress up to her eyes so that she could examine the marks that covered most of the garment.

"Patrik thinks it's blood," Erica said, which made Anna lower the dress in horror.

"Blood? Why would Mom have kept a child's dress covered in blood in a chest?" With a look of disgust she put it down on the table and picked up the diaries instead.

"Anything questionable in here?" Anna asked, waving the blue books at her sister. "No sexual revelations that will leave me traumatized for life if I read them?"

"No," Erica laughed. "You're seriously disturbed, Sis. No, there's nothing questionable in there. To be honest, there isn't much of anything, just very ordinary, everyday stuff. But I have been wondering about one thing. . . ." For the first time, Erica put into words the thought that had been lurking at the back of her mind for a while.

"What's that?" Anna said curiously as she leafed through the diaries.

"Well, I'm wondering if there are any more of these somewhere. They end in May 1944, when the fourth book is full. And I know Mom could have gotten tired of keeping a diary, but would that have coincided with her getting to the end of the fourth book? It just seems a bit odd."

"So you think there are more? Even if there are, what else would they tell you, apart from what's in here? I mean, it doesn't seem as if Mom had a very exciting life. She was born and raised here, met Dad, had us, and . . . well, that's about it, isn't it?"

"Maybe," Erica said thoughtfully. She wondered how much to tell her sister. She had nothing concrete, after all—just her intuition. She knew that what she had found out so far revealed the contours of something bigger, something that had cast a shadow over her life and Anna's. Above all, the medal and the dress must have played a role in their mother's life, and yet they had never even been mentioned.

She took a deep breath and told Anna in detail about her conversations with Erik, Axel, and Britta.

"So you went to see Axel Frankel a couple of days after his brother had been found dead, and asked for Mom's medal? Wow, he must have thought you were a real vulture, Sis!" Anna said with the brutal honesty only a younger sibling can get away with.

"Do you want to know what he said, or not?" Erica said indignantly. However, she had to admit that Anna had a point. The visit hadn't been the most sensitive course of action.

By the time Erica had finished her account, Anna was frowning. "It sounds as if they knew a completely different person. What did Britta say about the medal? Did she have any idea why Mom had a Nazi medal?"

Erica shook her head. "I didn't get around to asking her. She has Alzheimer's; she got confused after a while and then her husband came home and he got very upset and"—Erica cleared her throat—"he asked me to leave."

"Erica!" Anna exclaimed. "You went and interrogated an old lady with dementia! And her husband threw you out! I must say I have some sympathy with him. . . . This whole thing has tipped you over the edge." Anna shook her head in disbelief.

"Yes, but aren't you curious too? Why did Mom have all this stuff hidden away? And why is it that people who knew her when she was young describe a total stranger? The Elsy they talk about is not the one we grew up with. Something happened somewhere along the way. . . . Britta was just getting to it when she started to get mixed up, she said something about old bones and . . . I can't remember exactly, but it sounded as if she was using that as a metaphor for something that was hidden and . . . I might be imagining things, but there's something odd about all this, and I mean to get to the bottom of it." The telephone rang, and Erica broke off in the middle of her ramblings and went to answer it.

"Hello? Oh, hi, Karin." Erica turned to Anna, raising her eyebrows. "Everything's fine, thanks. Yes, it's good to talk to you after all this time too." She made a face at Anna, who looked as if she hadn't a clue what was going on. "Patrik? No, he's not here at the moment. He and Maja were going to the station, and I don't know where they are now. Oh, okay . . . yes, I'm sure they'd like to go for a walk with you and Ludde tomorrow. Ten o'clock. Outside the pharmacy. Sure, I'll tell him, then he can give you a call if he has other plans, but as far as I know that should be fine. Thanks, Karin. Speak soon. Thanks. Bye, now."

"What was all that about?" Anna said, looking puzzled. "Who's Karin? And why is Patrik meeting her outside the pharmacy tomorrow?"

Erica sat down at the kitchen table. After a long pause, she said: "Karin is Patrik's ex-wife. She and dance-band Leif have actually moved to Fjällbacka. It just so happens that she and

Patrik are on maternity/paternity leave at the same time, so they're going for a walk together in the morning."

Anna burst out laughing. "You just fixed up a meeting between Patrik and his ex-wife? OMG, this is fantastic. Does he have any ex-girlfriends? You could give them a call and see if they want to join in. We don't want him getting bored while he's on paternity leave, do we?"

Erica glared at her sister. "Could I remind you that Karin was the one who called here? And there's nothing odd about that, is there? They're divorced, and have been for several years. And they're both on leave at the same time. Nothing odd about it at all. I don't have any problem with their meeting up. Absolutely not."

"Right," Anna laughed, clutching her stomach. "I can tell from your tone of voice that you definitely don't have a problem with it. By the way, your nose is growing longer by the second!"

Erica wondered whether to throw a pastry at her sister but decided against it. Anna could think what she liked; Erica was *not* jealous.

"Shall we go and have a chat with the cleaner right away?" Martin suggested. Patrik hesitated briefly, then took out his cell.

"I'll just check that Maja's okay."

After speaking to Annika, he put his cell away and nodded. "All right, no problem. She just got Maja to sleep in her stroller. Do you have the address?" He turned to Paula.

"Yup." Paula leafed through her notebook and read the address out loud. "Her name is Laila Valthers. She said she'd be home all day. Do you know where she lives?"

"Yes, it's one of the houses by the rotary as you come into Fjällbacka from the south."

"The yellow ones?" Martin asked.

"Exactly—you know how to get there, don't you? You just take a right up ahead by the school."

It took them less than two minutes to reach the right address, and Laila Valthers was indeed at home. She looked a little scared as she opened the door. She seemed very reluctant to let them in, so they remained standing in the hallway. As they didn't have many questions to ask her, they saw no reason to push the issue.

"I believe you work as a cleaner for the Frankel brothers?" Patrik's voice was calm and reassuring; he was doing his best to make their presence as unthreatening as possible.

"Yes, but I hope I'm not going to get into trouble because of that . . . ," Laila said quietly, almost whispering. She was small and seemed to be dressed for a day at home; she was wearing brown clothes in some kind of fleecy fabric. Her hair was a nondescript mousy color, and was cut in a short and doubtless practical style that was less than flattering. She was shifting uneasily from one foot to the other, her arms folded across her chest, and she seemed very eager to hear what they had to say in response. Patrik thought he knew what the problem was.

"You mean they paid you in cash for the work you did? I can assure you we have no interest in that side of things, nor would we report you to the IRS. We're conducting a murder inquiry, so our focus is on other matters entirely." He ventured a consoling smile, and was pleased to see that Laila stopped moving around.

"They used to leave my money in an envelope on the chest of drawers in the hallway every other week. We'd agreed that I would go there on a Wednesday, every two weeks."

"Did you have your own key?"

Laila shook her head. "No, they always left me the key under the doormat, then I put it back when I'd finished."

"So why weren't you in to do any cleaning over the summer?" Paula asked the question they really wanted an answer to, the mystery that had to be cleared up.

"I'd expected to be going in as usual; they hadn't said anything different. But when I turned up, there was no key. I knocked on the door, but no one came. Then I tried phoning to see if there had been some kind of misunderstanding, but no one answered. I mean, I knew that Axel, the older brother, would be away over the summer; he always has been, all the years I've worked there. And when no one was home I just assumed that the younger one was away as well. I did think it was a bit much that they hadn't bothered to tell me, but now of course I understand why. . . ." She looked down at the floor.

"And you didn't notice anything out of the ordinary?" Martin asked.

Laila shook her head decisively. "No, I can't say I did. I can't think of anything."

"Do you happen to know what date it was when you turned up and couldn't get in?" Patrik wondered.

"Yes, because it was my birthday. And I thought it was just typical of my bad luck; I'd intended to go and buy myself something with the money I earned."

She fell silent, and Patrik asked, gently, "So, what date was it? Your birthday?"

"Of course, silly me," she said, looking upset. "It was June 17. Definitely. June 17. And I went there twice more, but there was still no one there, and still no key under the mat. So then I just assumed they'd forgotten to tell me they were both away all summer." She shrugged, a gesture that made it clear she was used to people forgetting to tell her things.

"Thanks, you've been really helpful." Patrik held out his hand to say good-bye, and almost shuddered at the limp handshake. It felt as if someone had placed a dead fish in his hand.

"So, what do you think?" Patrik said once they were back in the car and heading toward the station.

"I think we can be pretty sure that Erik Frankel was murdered sometime between June 15 and 17," Paula said.

"I'm inclined to agree," Patrik said, nodding as he took the sharp bend just before Anrås much too fast, missing a garbage truck by a hairbreadth. The truck driver shook his fist at Patrik as Martin grabbed the handle above the door in terror.

"Did you get your driver's license for Christmas?" Paula asked from the back seat, apparently unmoved by their near-death experience.

"What do you mean? I'm an excellent driver!" Patrik said, feeling insulted as he looked to Martin for support.

"Sure you are," Martin said with a scornful laugh. He turned to Paula: "I tried signing Patrik up for that TV program *Sweden's Worst Drivers*, but I think they thought he was overqualified. I mean, it wouldn't be much of a competition if Patrik was on."

Paula snickered, and Patrik responded in a hurt tone of voice: "I don't know what you're talking about. All those hours we've spent together in a car—have I ever had a collision or any other kind of incident? No, exactly. My driving record is unblemished, so this is pure slander." He snorted and glared at Martin; as a result, he almost crashed into the Saab in front of them and had to stomp on the brakes.

"I rest my case," Martin said, holding up his hands as Paula burst out laughing in the back seat.

Patrik sulked all the way back to the station, but at least he stuck to the speed limit.

Kjell was still angry following the encounter with his father. Frans had always had that effect on him. Actually, that wasn't true. Not always. When he was little, disappointment had been the dominant feeling. Disappointment mixed with love, which over the years had metamorphosed into a hard core of hatred and anger. He was aware that he had allowed those emotions to determine the choices he had made, which in practical terms meant he had allowed his father to determine the course of his life. But that was something he could do nothing about. All he had to do was remember the feeling he'd had when his mother dragged him along on one of those visits to see Frans in jail. The cold, gray visitors' room. Completely impersonal, devoid of emotion. His father's clumsy attempts to talk to him, pretending he was a part of Kjell's life rather than someone observing from a distance. Behind bars.

It had been many years since his father's last stint in jail, which didn't mean he had become a better man. Just that he'd gotten smarter. He had chosen another way. And as a consequence, Kjell had chosen the way that was diametrically opposite. He had written about antiforeigner organizations with a frenzy and a passion that resulted in his name and reputation stretching far beyond the walls of *Bohusläningen*'s offices. He had often flown from Trollhättan to Stockholm in order to sit on some TV sofa and talk about the destructive forces within neo-Nazism and how society should deal with these forces. Unlike many others who, in the namby-pamby spirit of the age, were willing to engage in open discussion with neo-Nazi groups, Kjell preferred to maintain a hard line. They simply should not be tolerated. They should be opposed at every juncture, face counterarguments wherever they chose to speak, and should in fact be shown the door, like the unwelcome vermin they were.

He parked outside his ex-wife's house. This time he hadn't bothered to call in advance. When he did, she sometimes made a point of going out before he got there, but today he had made sure she was home. He had sat in the car a short distance away, waiting for her. After an hour, she had driven up and parked in the driveway. She had obviously been shopping, because she lifted a couple of Konsum paper bags out of the trunk. Kjell had waited until she got inside before driving the last hundred yards to the house. He got out and knocked loudly on the front door. A weariness came over Carina's face when she saw who was standing there.

"Oh, it's you. What do you want?" Her tone was curt. Kjell felt a surge of irritation. Why couldn't she understand how serious this was? Why couldn't she see that it was time to take off the gloves? The feelings of guilt burned in his breast, further fueling his irritation. Did she have to look so . . . crushed all the time? Still? After ten years?

"We need to talk. About Per." He pushed past her and began to remove his jacket and shoes. For a moment, Carina looked as if she was about to object, but then she shrugged and went into the kitchen, where she positioned herself with her back to the sink, arms folded as if she was preparing for battle. They had executed this particular dance many times before.

"So what is it this time?" She shook her head, the dark bob falling in her eyes so that she had to push back her fringe with her index finger. He had seen that gesture so many times. It was one of the things he had loved about her during those first few years. Before the everyday tedium had taken over, before love had faded, leading him to change their lives. He still didn't know whether he had made the right choice.

Kjell pulled out one of the kitchen chairs and sat down. "We have to tackle this situation. You have to understand that this is not something that will solve itself. Once you get into this pattern, you—"

Carina interrupted him by holding up her hand. "Who says I think this will solve itself? It's just that I happen to have a different view of how things should be solved. And sending Per away is not a solution—you should realize that as well."

"What you don't realize is that he needs to get away from this environment!" He ran a hand angrily through his hair.

"By 'this environment,' you mean your father." Carina's voice was dripping with contempt. "I think you need to sort out your own problems with your father before you drag Per into this."

"Problems? What problems?" Kjell could hear his voice getting louder and forced himself to take a few deep breaths in order to calm down. "First of all, I don't just mean my father when I say that Per needs to get away from here. Do you think I can't see what's going on? Do you think I don't know you've got bottles hidden all over the place?" Kjell motioned toward the kitchen cabinets. Carina was about to protest, but he held up his hand and stopped her. "And there is nothing to resolve between Frans and me," he said through gritted teeth. "As far as I'm concerned, I would prefer to have nothing more to do with him, and I certainly don't intend to let him have any influence over Per. But since we can't monitor the kid 24/7, and since you don't seem particularly interested in keeping an eye on him, the only solution I can see is to find a residential school where there are people who can deal with that kind of thing."

"And how exactly do you think that's going to work?" Carina yelled at him, and her fringe flopped over her eyes once more. "They don't just pack teenagers off to schools like that for no reason; they have to have done something first. But maybe you're just rubbing your hands and waiting for him to step out of line so you can—"

"Breaking and entering," Kjell interrupted her. "He broke into a house."

"What the fuck are you talking about?"

"At the beginning of June. The owner of the house caught him red-handed and called me. I went over and picked Per up. He'd gotten in through a cellar window and was busy gathering up all kinds of stuff when the owner caught him and simply locked him in. Threatened to call the cops if Per didn't give him his parents' number. And, yes, Per gave him my number." He couldn't help feeling a certain satisfaction at the disappointment and devastation on Carina's face.

"Per gave him your number? Why not mine?"

Kjell shrugged. "Who knows? I guess your dad is always your dad."

"Whose house did he break into?" Carina looked as if she was still finding it difficult to swallow the idea that Per had chosen to give Kjell's number.

He hesitated for a few seconds before answering, then said "It was that old man who was found dead in Fjällbacka last week. Erik Frankel. It was his house."

"But why?" She shook her head.

"That's what I'm trying to tell you, for God's sake! Erik Frankel was an expert on the Second World War; he had lots and lots of artifacts from those days, and I guess Per wanted to impress his pals by showing them some genuine Nazi memorabilia."

"Do the police know about this?"

"Not yet," he said coldly. "But of course that depends on whether. . . ."

"You'd do that to your own son? Report him for breaking and entering?" Carina whispered, staring at him.

Suddenly a hard knot formed in his stomach. He pictured her as she had looked the first time they met, at a party at the journalism school. She had gone with a friend who was a student there, but the friend had disappeared with some guy as soon as they arrived, and Carina had ended up sitting on a sofa feeling lost and lonely. He had fallen in love with her the moment he saw her. She had been wearing a yellow dress and a yellow hair band; her hair was longer back then, just as dark as now, but without the gray strands that had started to appear. There was something about her that had made him want to take care of her, protect her, love her. He remembered the wedding, the dress she had thought was so very beautiful at the time; these days it would be regarded as an eighties relic, with far too many frills and big puffed sleeves. In any case, he had thought she was a vision. And the first time he saw her with Per. Tired, not a scrap of makeup, and wearing an ugly hospital gown. But she had looked up at him and smiled with their son in her arms, and he had felt as if he could fight dragons, or take on an entire army and win.

As they stood there in Carina's kitchen like two combatants facing one another, each of them saw a fleeting glimpse of the way things used to be. For a moment they remembered the times when they had laughed together, made love together, before love was forgotten and turned into something fragile and brittle. Making him vulnerable. The knot in his stomach hardened even more.

He tried to dismiss the memories. "If I have to, I will make sure the cops get hold of this information," he said. "Either we fix things so that Per gets away from here, or I will let the police do the job instead."

"You bastard!" Carina said in a voice that was thick with tears and disappointment over all the promises that had been broken.

Kjell stood up. Although it was a real effort, his eyes were cold as he said "Well, that's what's going to happen. I have a few suggestions as to where we can send Per; I'll e-mail them to you so that you can have a look. And he is to have no contact whatsoever with my father—not under any circumstances. Do you understand?"

Carina didn't answer him, but bowed her head as a sign of capitulation. It had been a long time since she had had the strength to fight Kjell. The day he'd given up on her, on them, was the day she had given up on herself.

Kjell got in the car, drove a few hundred yards, then parked again. He rested his head on the steering wheel and closed his eyes. Pictures of Erik Frankel flickered through his mind, along with what he had learned from Erik. The question was, what should he do with the information?

18
Grini, outside Oslo, 1943

The cold was the worst thing of all. Never feeling warm. The dampness absorbed what little warmth there was, wrapping itself around his body like a cold, wet blanket. Axel curled up in a ball on his bunk. The days were so long here in solitary confinement. But he preferred this tedium to the interruptions. The interrogations, the blows, the endless questions raining down on him. How could he give them any answers? He knew so little, and he would never tell what little he did know. They could kill him before he would do that.

Axel ran a hand over his head. There was only stubble left, and the short hairs felt rough against his palm. They had showered the captives and shaved their heads as soon as they arrived, and put them in Norwegian uniforms. As soon as they caught him, he had realized where he was going to end up: in the prison about eight miles outside Oslo. But nothing could have prepared him for the reality of this place, for the bottomless fear that filled every hour of every day, for the tedium and the pain.

"Food." There was a clattering noise outside the cell, and the young guard placed a tray in front of the bars.

"What day is it?" Axel asked in Norwegian. He and Erik had spent virtually every summer vacation with their maternal grandparents in Norway, and he spoke the language fluently. He saw the same guard every day and always tried to talk to him because he was desperate for human contact. Usually he received only the briefest of answers, and the same thing happened today.

"Wednesday."

"Thanks." Axel tried to force a smile. The boy turned to leave. The thought of being left abandoned in the cold and isolation suddenly seemed unbearable, so Axel attempted to get him to stay by asking another question.

"What's the weather like?"

The boy stopped. Hesitated. He glanced around, then walked back toward Axel.

"It's cloudy. Pretty cold too." Axel was struck by how young he looked. He was probably about the same age as Axel, perhaps a couple of years younger, but the way Axel felt at the moment he probably looked significantly older; just as old on the outside as on the inside.

The boy began to move away again.

"Cold for the time of year, isn't it?" His voice broke, and he could hear how peculiar the comment sounded. Once upon a time, such meaningless chitchat had felt superficial, but now it was a lifeline, a reminder of the world that seemed more and more like a faded memory.

"You could say that. But it's often cold in Oslo at this time of year."

"Are you from around here?" Axel quickly threw in before the guard had time to turn away.

The boy hesitated; he seemed reluctant to answer. He glanced around again, but there was no sign of anyone nearby.

"We've been here for a couple of years, that's all."

Axel decided to continue: "How long have I been here? It feels like forever." He laughed but was alarmed by how harsh and unfamiliar it sounded. It had been a long time since he had had a reason to laugh.

"I'm not sure if I'm allowed to. . . ." The guard tugged at his collar; he didn't look altogether comfortable in the restrictive uniform. But he would get used to it in time, Axel thought. He would grow accustomed to the uniform, and to the way he had to deal with people. That was human nature, after all.

"What does it matter if you tell me how long I've been here?" Axel said persuasively. There was something very disturbing about existing in a timeless vacuum, with no clocks, dates, or weekdays by which to measure his life.

"About two months. I'm not sure."

"About two months. And it's Wednesday, and it's cloudy. That'll do me." Axel smiled at the boy, and was rewarded with a tentative smile in return.

When the guard had gone, Axel sank down on his bunk with the tray on his knee. The food left a great deal to be desired. They were given the same thing every day: potatoes fit only for pigs, and disgusting stews. But no doubt it was one aspect of the attempt to break them down. He dipped his spoon unenthusiastically into the gray sludge in the bowl, but eventually hunger made him lift it to his mouth. He tried to pretend he was eating his mother's beef stew, but it didn't really work. It just made everything worse because it allowed his thoughts to stray to the places where he had forbidden them to go: his home and his family, his mother and father and Erik. Suddenly even hunger was not enough; nothing could make him eat. He put down the spoon and leaned back against the rough wall. Suddenly he could picture them all so clearly. Father with the big gray mustache that he combed meticulously every night before he went to bed. Mother with her long hair caught up in a bun at the nape of her neck and her glasses on the end of her nose as she worked on her crochet by the lamplight in the evenings. And Erik. In his room with his nose in a book, no doubt. What were they doing? Were they thinking of him right now? How had his parents coped with the news that he had been captured? And Erik? He was a quiet boy who often kept himself to himself. His sharp intellect processed texts and information with impressive speed, but he found it difficult to show his feelings. Sometimes Axel would give his brother a really long bear hug, just to wind him up and to feel his body go rigid with discomfort at such close physical contact. But after a while Erik would soften and relax, allowing himself to give in to the intimacy for a few seconds before he eventually snapped "Let go of me!" and pulled away. Axel knew his brother so well. Much better than Erik could ever imagine. He knew that Erik sometimes felt like a bit of a misfit in the family, felt that he couldn't match up to Axel. And now things would be more difficult than ever for him. Axel wasn't stupid; he realized that the anxiety about his fate would affect Erik's everyday life, and that the space available for his brother in the family would diminish even further. He didn't even dare think about what life would be like for Erik if he died.

19

"Hi, we're home!" Patrik closed the door and put Maja down on the floor in the hallway. She immediately set off toward the living room, and he had to grab hold of her jacket to stop her.

"Hang on a second, honey. Let's take off your shoes and jacket before you go and find Mommy." He took off her outdoor clothes and let her go.

"Erica? Are you home?" he shouted. No reply, but when he listened carefully he could hear the tapping of a keyboard from upstairs. He carried Maja up to Erica's study.

"So this is where you're hiding!"

"Yes, I've done quite a few pages today. And Anna came over for coffee." Erica smiled at Maja and held out her arms. Maja toddled over and placed a big wet kiss on Erica's lips.

"Hi, sweetheart—so what have you and Daddy been up to today?" She rubbed noses with her daughter, and Maja laughed delightedly; Eskimo kisses were their specialty. "You were gone a long time," Erica said, switching her attention to Patrik.

"Yes, I pitched in and did a bit of work," Patrik said enthusiastically. "The new girl seems very good, but they hadn't really considered every angle, so I went to Fjällbacka with them and did a couple of home visits, which meant we were able to establish a two-day window during which Erik Frankel must have been murdered, and. . . ." He stopped in midsentence when he saw the expression on Erica's face. He realized immediately that he should probably have thought before he opened his mouth.

"And where was Maja when you 'pitched in and did a bit of work'?" Erica asked icily.

Patrik shifted uncomfortably. If he was really lucky, perhaps the fire alarm would go off . . . no, obviously not. He took a deep breath and went for it.

"Annika looked after her for a while. At the station." He couldn't understand how it could possibly sound so bad when he said it out loud, when it hadn't even crossed his mind earlier on that it might not be appropriate.

"So Annika looked after our daughter at the police station while you went out on a job for a couple of hours. Have I understood you correctly?"

"Er . . . yes . . . ," Patrik said, frantically searching for a way to turn the situation to his advantage. "She had a lovely time. Apparently she ate really well, then Annika took her for a little walk and she fell asleep in the stroller."

"I have no doubt that Annika did an excellent job as a babysitter. That's not the issue. What upsets me is that we agreed you would take care of Maja while I got back to work. And it's not as if I'm insisting that you spend every single minute with her from now until January; I have no doubt that we'll use a babysitter from time to time. But I think it's a bit early to start handing her over to the station secretary and taking off on some job when you've only been on paternity leave for a week. Or perhaps you don't agree?"

Patrik wondered briefly whether Erica's question was rhetorical, but as she seemed to be expecting an answer, he realized that that probably wasn't the case.

"Well, when you put it like that, I suppose. . . . Okay, it was stupid of me. But they hadn't even checked whether Erik was seeing someone, and I just got so carried away . . . I'm sorry, it was a really dumb thing to do!" He ran a hand through his brown hair, making it stand on end. "From now on: no work. Promise. Just me and Maja. Honest." He stuck both thumbs up in the air, attempting to look as trustworthy as possible. Erica looked as if she had more to say, but then she sighed deeply and got up from her desk.

"Well, you don't look as if you've come to any harm, sweetie. Shall we say that Daddy is forgiven, and go and fix something to eat?" Maja nodded enthusiastically. "Daddy can make us a carbonara by way of compensation," Erica said, heading downstairs with Maja on her hip. Maja nodded again with equal enthusiasm; Daddy's carbonara was one of her absolute favorites.

"So what conclusion did you reach?" Erica asked a little while later, as she sat at the kitchen table watching Patrik. He had put on the water for the spaghetti and was frying bacon. Maja was settled in front of *Bolibompa* on TV, and they had some time to themselves.

"We think he died sometime between June 15 and 17." He stirred the contents of the frying pan. "Ouch!" Some of the melted fat had splashed up and burned his arm. "Hell, that hurts! Good thing I'm not frying this bacon in the nude."

"I couldn't agree more, darling. . . ." Erica winked at him and he walked over and kissed her on the mouth.

"So I'm 'darling' again—does that mean I'm back in your good books?"

Erica pretended to consider the matter. "I wouldn't go quite that far, but let's say you're not in my bad books. If the carbonara is good enough, then maybe. . . ."

"So, how was your day?" Patrik went back to his cooking. He lifted out the pieces of meat and placed them on paper towels to drain. The secret of a good carbonara was to get the bacon really crispy; there was nothing worse than slimy bacon.

"Where do I start?" Erica sighed. First of all she told him about Anna's visit and the problems of being stepmother to a teenager. Then she took a deep breath and told him about her visit to Britta. Patrik put down the spatula and stared at her in disbelief.

"You went to her house to question her? And she's got Alzheimer's? It's hardly surprising that her husband was furious with you; I would have felt the same."

"Thank you, that's exactly what Anna said, so I've had enough criticism already." Erica scowled. "Anyway, I didn't know that when I went there."

"So, what did she say?" Patrik asked as he lowered the spaghetti into the boiling water.

"You do realize you've got enough there to feed a small army," Erica said as two thirds of the package of pasta disappeared into the saucepan.

"Who's in charge here?" Patrik asked, threatening her with the spatula. "So what did Britta say?"

"Well, she and my mom seem to have spent a lot of time together when they were young. Apparently they were pretty close, the two of them and Erik Frankel and somebody called Frans."

"Frans Ringholm?" Patrik said with interest as he stirred the spaghetti.

"Yes, I think that was his name. Frans Ringholm. Do you know who he is?" Erica gazed at him with curiosity, but Patrik shrugged dismissively.

"Did she say anything else? Had she kept in touch with Erik or Frans? Or Axel, for that matter?"

"I don't think so. It didn't sound as if any of them had had any contact with the others, but I could be wrong." Erica frowned as she went over the conversation in her mind.

"There was one thing . . . ," she said hesitantly. Patrik stopped stirring and waited for her to go on.

"She said something . . . it was something about Erik and 'old bones.' Old bones being allowed to rest in peace. And Erik had said. . . . Then she disappeared into the mist and I couldn't find out any more. She was very confused by that time, so I'm not sure how much credence you can give to what she said. It was probably just nonsense."

"Not necessarily," Patrik said slowly. "Not necessarily. That's the second time I've heard a reference to bones in connection with Erik Frankel. I wonder what the hell it means."

And while Patrik pondered, the pasta took the opportunity to boil over.

Frans had prepared himself carefully for the meeting. The board met once a month, and there were many issues to be discussed. It would soon be election year, and their greatest challenge lay ahead.

"Are we all here?" He looked around the table, silently counting the other five board members. They were all men. The idea of equal rights for women had yet to reach the neo-Nazi organizations. And it probably never would.

The premises in Uddevalla had been leased from Bertolf Svensson, and they were now in the basement of the apartment house he owned. The place was normally used for social events, and there were still visible traces of a party thrown by one of the tenants over the weekend. The group also had access to an office in the same building, but it was small and not really suitable for board meetings.

"I don't think much of their attempts at cleaning up," Bertolf muttered, kicking an empty beer bottle and sending it rolling across the floor. "I'll have to have a word with them later."

"Let's get down to business," Frans said firmly. They didn't have time for idle chat.

"How far have we gotten with the preparations?" He turned to Peter Lindgren, the youngest board member. He had been chosen to coordinate the campaign, in spite of loudly voiced objections from Frans, who simply didn't trust him. As recently as last summer he had been arrested for assaulting a Somali in the square in Grebbestad, and Frans just didn't believe Lindgren was capable of remaining calm to the extent that was now necessary.

As if to confirm Frans's suspicions, Peter Lindgren avoided the question and said, "Have you heard what happened in Fjäll-backa?" He laughed. "Obviously someone has made short work of Erik Frankel—that fucking traitor to his race!"

"I trust that none of our people had anything to do with the matter, so I suggest that we return to the agenda," Frans said, fixing his eyes on Peter. For a moment the two men engaged in a silent power struggle, then Peter looked away.

"We're well on the way. Recruitment of new members has been going well lately, and we have made sure that everyone, both old and new, is prepared to do the footwork in order to spread our message far and wide between now and the election."

"Good," Frans said curtly. "And the party registration, has that been done? Ballots?"

"All under control." Peter drummed his fingers on the table, clearly annoyed at being interrogated like a schoolboy. He couldn't resist having a go at Frans.

"So you failed to protect your old pal. What was so impor-tant about that guy that made you think it was worth sticking your neck out for him? People have been talking, you know. Questioning where your loyalties lie. . . ."

Frans got to his feet and stared at Peter. Werner Hermansson, who was sitting beside him, grabbed his arm. "Don't listen to him, Frans. And Peter, shut the fuck up. This is ridiculous. We're supposed to be talking about how to move forward, not sitting here slinging crap at one another. Come on, guys, shake hands." Werner looked appealingly at Peter and Frans. Apart from Frans, he was the longest-serving member of Sweden's Friends, and he had also known Frans longer than anyone. It was Peter's safety that concerned him; he had seen what Frans was capable of.

For a moment, the situation hung in the balance. Then Frans sat down.

"At the risk of repeating myself, may I suggest that we get back to the business of the meeting. Any objections? Anything else we need to waste time on? Well?" He stared down every single member of the board in turn, then went on. "It seems as if most of the practical matters are well in hand, so perhaps we should discuss which issues we should bring to the fore in the party manifesto? I've spoken to quite a few people here in town, and I really think we can win a seat on the council this time. People have realized how careless the government and the local authorities have been when it comes to immigration; they can see their jobs going to non-Swedes. They see the local budget being eaten up by benefit payments to that same group. There's widespread discontent with the way things have been handled at a local level, and we can exploit that mood."

Frans's cell rang loudly in his pocket. "Damn. Sorry, I forgot to switch it off. I'll do it right away." He took out his phone and looked at the display. He recognized the number: Axel's landline. He refused the call and turned off the phone.

"Sorry about that; now where were we? As I said, we're in an ideal position to exploit the ignorance the council has shown when it comes to the problems arising from immigration, and. . . ."

He continued talking; everyone's attention was focused on him, but his thoughts were racing away in a completely different direction.

The decision to skip math was a no-brainer. If there was one class he would never dream of attending, it was math. There was something about numbers and all that stuff that made his flesh creep. He just didn't get it. His brain turned to mush as soon as he tried to add or subtract. What was the point of it all, anyway? He was never going to be something boring like an accountant, so it was a waste of time sitting there sweating.

Per lit a cigarette and gazed out across the school yard. The others had gone off to Hedemyr's for a bit of shoplifting, but he hadn't the energy to go with them. He had stayed over with Tomas last night, and they had played *Tomb Raider* until five o'clock in the morning. His mother had called his cell several times, so in the end he had simply turned it off. He would have preferred to stay in bed all day, but Tomas's mom had thrown him out when she left for work. They couldn't think of anything else to do, so they'd wandered down to school.

But now he was getting seriously bored. Perhaps he should have gone with the gang after all. He got up to follow them, but sat down again when he saw Mattias emerge through the main doors with that stupid girl in tow, the one all the boys were always running after for some reason. He'd never understood why they thought Mia was so hot. That blonde Lucite type had never done it for him.

He pricked up his ears and tried to listen in on their conversation. Mattias was doing most of the talking, and apparently whatever he was saying was very interesting, because Mia's baby-blue eyes were wide with fascination. As they came closer, Per was able to pick up fragments here and there. He kept very still. Mattias was so busy trying to get inside Mia's pants that he didn't even notice Per sitting a short distance away.

"You should have seen how fucking pale Adam went when he saw him. But I realized right away what had to be done, and I told Adam to back away slowly so we wouldn't destroy any evidence."

"Wow," Mia said admiringly.

Per laughed to himself. Mattias was certainly laying it on thick to get her in the sack. She must be dripping wet down there.

He kept listening. "And the coolest thing of all is that none of the others had the balls to go there, apart from us. The others kept on talking about it but, let's face it, talking is one thing, doing something about it is another."

Per had heard enough. He jumped up from the bench and caught up with Mattias. Before Mattias realized what was happening, Per jumped on him from behind and brought him crashing to the ground. He sat on Mattias's back and bent one arm upward until Mattias was screaming with pain, then Per grabbed hold of his hair. That ridiculous surfer style was just perfect. He deliberately pulled back Mattias's head, then slammed it down on the asphalt. He ignored the fact that Mia was standing there screaming just a few yards away. She turned and ran back to the school for help, but Per kept on banging Mattias's head on the hard ground as he hissed "I've never heard such crap in my entire fucking life! You little bastard, I'm not letting you get away with this, you fucking . . . shit. . . ." Per was so angry that everything went black, and the rest of the world disappeared. The only thing he could feel was Mattias's hair in his hand, the jolt that ran up his arm every time the other boy's head hit the asphalt. The only thing he could see was the blood beginning to seep out onto the black path. The sight of those patches of red filled him with a sense of well-being. It reached a place deep inside him, caressed it, nurtured it, filled him with a calmness he had rarely felt before. He made no attempt to fight the rage, but allowed it to suffuse his body; he willingly surrendered to it, reveling in the awareness of something primitive, something that pushed everything else aside, all of life's miserable little complications. He didn't want to stop, couldn't stop. He continued yelling and slamming Mattias's head down, kept on seeing the red stickiness every time he lifted the boy's head, until someone grabbed hold of him from behind and pulled him away.

"What the hell do you think you're doing?" Per turned around and was almost surprised to see the math teacher's furious and horrified expression. Up in the school building, faces were staring out of every window, and a small group of curious onlookers had gathered in the yard. Per looked down at Mattias's lifeless body with no emotion whatsoever, and allowed himself to be dragged a few yards away from his victim.

"Are you out of your mind?" The teacher's face was only inches from Per's. He was yelling at the top of his voice, but Per turned his head away, the very picture of apathy.

He had felt so good for a while there. Now there was nothing but emptiness.

He stood in the hallway for a long time, looking at the photographs on the wall. So many happy times. So much love. Their black-and-white wedding photo, he and Britta looking much more austere than they had actually felt. Anna-Greta in Britta's arms, Herman behind the camera. If he remembered correctly, he had put down the camera immediately after taking that photograph in order to hold his daughter in his arms for the first time. Britta had anxiously reminded him to support the baby's head, but it was as if he instinctively knew what to do. From then on, he had been very much a hands-on dad, far more than what was expected of a man in those days. His mother-in-law had often scolded him, saying a man shouldn't be changing diapers or bathing a baby. But he hadn't been able to help himself. It had come so naturally to him, and in any case it didn't seem right for Britta to carry the load all by herself when they had their three girls one after the other. They really wanted more, but after the third delivery, which had been ten times more complicated than the first two added together, the doctor had drawn him aside and explained that Britta's body would be unable to cope with another pregnancy. And Britta had wept. Bowed her head without looking at him, the tears pouring down her cheeks, and begged him to forgive her because she had been unable to provide him with a son. He had looked at her in astonishment. It had never occurred to Herman to wish for anything other than what he already had. Surrounded by his four girls, he felt richer than any man had a right to be. It had taken him a while to convince her, but when she realized that he meant it, she had dried her tears and they had focused on the girls they had brought into the world.

Now there were so many more to love. The girls had children of their own; Herman and Britta had taken their grandchildren into their hearts, and he had once again been able to demonstrate his skill with a diaper when they stepped in to help out. It was so difficult to get the balance right these days when it came to family, home, and work. But he and Britta had been so happy and grateful that there was a place for them, someone to help, someone to love. And now some of the grandchildren had little ones too. His fingers were a little stiffer these days, but with these fancy new diapers he could still manage to help out now and again. He shook his head. Where had all those years gone?

He went upstairs and sat down on the edge of the bed. Britta was having her afternoon nap. Today had been a bad day. Sometimes she was unable to recognize him and thought she was back in her childhood home. She had asked about her mother, and then, with fear in her voice, about her father. He had gently stroked her hair, reassuring her over and over again that her father had passed away many years ago. That he could no longer hurt her.

He caressed her hand as it lay on top of the crocheted coverlet. The skin was wrinkled, marked with the same age spots he had on his own hands. But she still had those long, elegant fingers. He smiled to himself as he noticed her pink nail polish. She had always been a little vain; that had never left her. But he hadn't complained. She had always been a beautiful wife, and during fifty-five years of marriage he had never even looked at another woman.

Her eyelids flickered. She was dreaming. He wished he could get into her dreams, live within them with her, pretend that everything was just the way it had always been.

In her confusion today she had talked about the thing they had agreed never to mention again. But as her brain deteriorated and withered away, the walls that had been built up around the secret over the years had begun to crumble. They had shared the secret for so long that it had somehow become an invisible component in the tapestry of their lives. He had allowed himself to relax, to forget.

Erik's visit had not been a good thing. Not in any way. It had created that ever-widening crack in the wall. If it couldn't be sealed up, then a deluge could burst through, carrying them all with it.

But he didn't need to worry about Erik anymore. *They* didn't need to worry about Erik anymore. He continued patting Britta's hand.

"Oh, I forgot to tell you yesterday: Karin called. You have a date outside the pharmacy at ten o'clock to go for a walk."

Patrik stopped in midmovement. "Karin? Today? In"—he looked at his watch—"thirty minutes?"

"Sorry," Erica said in a tone of voice that made it perfectly clear she wasn't sorry at all. Then she relented. "I was going to drive down to the library to do some research, so if you and Maja can be ready in twenty minutes, I can give you a ride."

"Is that . . . ," Patrik hesitated, "okay with you?"

Erica walked over and kissed him on the lips. "Compared with the fact that you've been using the police station as a nursery for our daughter, a date to go for a walk with your ex-wife is nothing."

"Ha ha, very funny," Patrik said sullenly, mainly because he knew Erica was right. What he had done yesterday was anything but smart.

"Don't just stand there—go and get dressed! I would definitely have something to say if you went off to meet your ex-wife looking like that!" Erica laughed and looked her husband up and down as he stood there in the bedroom wearing nothing but his underpants and a pair of socks.

"I think it makes me look like a bit of a hunk," Patrik said, striking a series of exaggerated bodybuilder's poses. Erica laughed so hard, she had to sit down on the bed.

"Stop, please stop!"

"But why?" Patrik said, pretending to be upset. "I'm incredibly fit, you know. This is just to fool the bad guys, to give them a false sense of security." He patted his stomach, which wobbled rather more than it would have if it had been pure muscle. Marriage hadn't done much for his waistline.

"Enough!" Erica howled. "I'll never be able to have sex with you again if you keep on like that!" Patrik's response was to leap on her with a roar and start tickling her.

"Take that back! Take it back right now!"

"Okay, okay, I take it back, get off!" yelled Erica, who was extremely ticklish.

"Mommy! Daddy!" came a delighted cry from the doorway as Maja clapped her hands in delight at the unexpected performance. She had been enticed by the interesting noises coming from her parents' room.

"Come over here and Daddy will tickle you too," Patrik said, lifting her onto the bed. A second later, both mother and daughter were helpless with laughter. Afterward they lay on the bed exhausted and snuggled together, until Erica sat up abruptly. "Right, you two, time to get a move on. Patrik, you sort yourself out and I'll get Maja ready."

In twenty minutes, Erica was heading toward the town center and the municipal building that housed the pharmacy and the library. She was a little curious. She had never met Karin before, although of course she had heard quite a lot about her, in spite of the fact that Patrik hadn't said a great deal about his previous marriage.

She parked the car, helped Patrik lift the stroller out of the trunk, then went along with him to say hi to Karin. She took a deep breath and held out her hand.

"I'm Erica," she said. "We spoke on the phone yesterday."

"How lovely to meet you!" Karin said, and Erica realized to her surprise that she spontaneously liked the woman standing in front of her. Out of the corner of her eye she could see Patrik shifting uncomfortably, and she couldn't help enjoying the situation to a certain extent. It was actually quite funny.

She studied his ex-wife with interest and quickly established that Karin was slimmer than she was, slightly shorter, and had dark hair caught up in a simple ponytail. She wasn't wearing any makeup, she had delicate features, but appeared a little . . . tired. No doubt that was thanks to looking after a toddler, Erica thought, and realized that she wouldn't have stood up to a close inspection either before Maja started sleeping through the night.

They chatted for a while, then Erica waved good-bye and went into the library. In a way it had been a relief to finally put a face to the woman who had been a big part of Patrik's life for eight years. She hadn't even seen a picture of her before. Given the circumstances that had led to their divorce, Patrik had understandably chosen not to keep any pictorial evidence of their time together.

The library was as quiet as usual. She had spent many hours here, and there was something about the place that gave her a feeling of immense satisfaction.

"Morning, Christian!"

The librarian looked up and beamed when he saw Erica.

"Morning, Erica—good to see you again! So, how can I help you today?" As always, his Småland accent sounded delightful. Erica wondered why people from Småland seemed so nice as soon as they opened their mouths. In Christian's case, that first impression was entirely accurate. He was pleasant and helpful and very good at his job. He had often helped Erica find information she had thought would be virtually impossible to track down.

"Is it the same case as last time?" he asked hopefully. Erica's research projects always provided a welcome diversion from his otherwise monotonous work; he spent most of his time looking up information on fishing, sailing boats, and the native fauna of Bohuslän.

"No, not today," she said, sitting down in front of his desk. "I'm looking for some facts about certain people from Fjäll-backa. People and events."

"Could you perhaps be a little more specific?" he replied with a wink.

"I'll try." Erica reeled off the names: "Britta Johansson, Frans Ringholm, Axel Frankel, Elsy Falck—sorry, Moström—and . . . ," she hesitated for a couple of seconds, then added, "Erik Frankel."

Christian was taken aback. "Isn't he the man who was found dead?"

"Yes," Erica said.

"And Elsy—is she your . . . ?"

"My mother, yes. I need some information about these people, around the time of the Second World War. Actually, let's just say the war years themselves."

"1939 to 1945, in other words."

Erica nodded and waited expectantly as Christian tapped away on his keyboard.

"How's your own project going, by the way?"

A dark shadow passed over the librarian's face. Then it was gone, and he answered her question. "Not too bad, thanks; I think I'm about halfway. And it's mainly thanks to your tips that I've gotten this far."

"Oh, it was nothing," Erica said, waving away his praise with a certain amount of embarrassment. "You only have to say if you need any more help or if you want me to read through the manuscript when it's finished. Have you got a working title, by the way?"

"*The Mermaid*," Christian said, without looking her in the eye. "It's going to be called *The Mermaid*."

"What a good title. Where does it—" Erica began, but Christian interrupted her brusquely. She looked at him in surprise; this wasn't like him at all. She wondered if she had said something to upset him, but couldn't figure out what it might be.

"I've found some articles that might be of interest," he said. "Would you like me to print them out for you?"

"Yes, please," Erica replied, still a little puzzled. But when Christian returned from the printer a few minutes later with a pile of copies for her, he was back to his usual friendly self.

"This should keep you busy for a while. Just let me know if you need anything else."

Erica thanked him and left the library. She was in luck: the café next door had just opened, and she bought herself a coffee, then sat down and began to read. However, what she found was so interesting that she left her cup untouched, and the coffee grew cold.

"So, where are we now?" Mellberg grimaced as he stretched his legs. Who would have thought his aches and pains after a bit of exercise would last so long? At this rate, he would just about have recovered by Friday, in time to put his body through the wringer yet again at the salsa class. But strangely enough, the thought wasn't as off-putting as he had expected. There had been something about the combination of the catchy music, the closeness of Rita's body, and the fact that, toward the end of last week's class, his feet had actually begun to pick up the steps. No, he definitely wasn't going to give up yet. If anyone had the potential to become the salsa king of Tanumshede, it was Mellberg.

"Sorry, what did you say?" He gave a start, having completely missed what Paula said while he was lost in daydreams of the Latin beat.

"We think we've established a time frame for Erik Frankel's murder," Gösta said. "He was with his . . . girlfriend, or whatever you call someone of that age, on June 15. He told her he was through with her, and he was noticeably drunk, which was completely out of character, according to her."

"And the cleaner went to the house on June 17 and couldn't get in," Martin added. "That doesn't necessarily mean he was dead at that stage, of course, but it suggests that he probably was. She had never been unable to get in before. If the brothers weren't home, they always used to leave her a key."

"Okay, for the time being we'll work on the assumption that he died between June 15 and 17. Check where his brother was at the time." Mellberg bent down and scratched Ernst behind the ears; he was in his usual place under the kitchen table, lying on Mellberg's feet.

"Do you really think Axel Frankel had anything to do with . . . ?" Paula broke off in midsentence when she saw Mellberg's irritated expression.

"I don't think anything right now. But you know as well as I do that most murders are committed by a family member. So check on the brother. Got it?"

She nodded. For once, Mellberg was right. She couldn't allow the fact that she had found Axel Frankel so likable to prevent her from doing her job properly.

"And the boys who broke into the house? Have we done what's necessary as far as they're concerned?" Mellberg looked around the table, clearly expecting a response. Everyone's eyes turned to Gösta, who looked extremely uncomfortable.

"Yes and no. . . . The thing is . . . I've taken fingerprints and shoe prints from one of the boys, Adam, but I haven't quite gotten around to . . . the other one . . ."

Mellberg stared at him. "So you've had several days to carry out this one simple little task, but—and I quote— you 'haven't quite gotten around to' it? Have I understood you correctly?"

Gösta nodded, looking miserable. "Kind of . . . yes, I guess so. But I'll take care of it today." Another glare from Mellberg. "Right away," Gösta said, hanging his head.

"You'd better," Mellberg said, switching his attention to Martin and Paula.

"Anything else? What about Frans Ringholm? Anything of interest there? Personally, I think that seems like the most promising lead; we ought to turn Sweden's Friends, or whatever the hell they call themselves, inside out."

"We spoke to Frans at home, but didn't really get anything more to go on. According to him, certain elements inside the organization had sent threatening letters to Erik Frankel, and Frans was doing his best to intervene and protect Erik because of their friendship in the past."

"And these 'elements'"—Mellberg drew quotation marks in the air—"have we spoken to them?"

"Not yet," Martin said calmly, "but it's on the agenda for today."

"Excellent," Mellberg said as he tried to nudge Ernst off his feet, which were beginning to feel numb. This merely resulted in Ernst producing a loud doggy fart before settling back down in exactly the same place.

"Okay, that leaves just one more thing to discuss, which is that this station is not a day-care center! Is that perfectly clear?" He fixed his gaze on Annika, who had sat in silence, taking the minutes all through the meeting. She looked back at him over the top of her reading glasses. After a lengthy silence, during which Mellberg had begun to feel very uncomfortable, wondering whether perhaps his tone of voice had been a little too sharp, she spoke.

"I did my work yesterday even when I was taking care of Maja for a while, and that's the only thing that need concern you, Bertil."

A silent battle of wills ensued as Annika calmly stared back at Mellberg. Eventually he looked away and mumbled "Yes, well, you probably know best. . . ."

"Besides which, it was thanks to Patrik's dropping by that we realized we'd forgotten to check on Erik's bank records." Paula smiled at Annika to show her support.

"I'm sure we'd have thought of it ourselves sooner or later, but because of Patrik, it ended up being sooner . . . rather than later," Gösta said, glancing at Annika before looking down again and studying the table with great interest.

"Hmm. I just thought if a person was on paternity leave, then he was on paternity leave," Mellberg said sourly, well aware that he had lost the battle. "Anyway, we've all got work to do." Everyone got to their feet and put their coffee cups in the dishwasher.

At that moment, the telephone rang.

20
Fjällbacka 1944

"I thought I'd probably find you here." Elsy sat down beside Erik, who was sheltered in the cleft of a rock.

"At least I have more chance of being left in peace here," Erik said crossly, but then his face softened and he closed the book in his lap. "Sorry," he said. "I didn't mean to take out my bad mood on you."

"Is Axel the reason for your bad mood?" Elsy asked gently. "How are things at home?"

"It's as if he's already dead," Erik said, gazing out across the choppy waters of the inlet. "Mom is definitely behaving as if Axel were already dead, while Dad just mutters to himself and refuses to talk about it."

"And how do you feel?" Elsy asked, looking intently at her friend. She knew Erik so well. Better than he realized. They had spent so many hours playing together, she and Erik, Britta, and Frans. But they would soon be adults, and the time for games was almost over. However, at this moment, she could see no difference between fourteen-year-old Erik and the five-year-old who had already been an old man in the body of a child. It was as if Erik had been born with a maturity beyond his years, and had gradually grown into the person he was meant to be—as if the child, the boy, and the youth were merely stages he had to pass through before he reached the point at which his skin fit him perfectly.

"I don't know how I feel," Erik said flatly, turning away. But not before Elsy had seen something glittering in the corner of his eye.

"Yes, you do," she said, without taking her eyes off his profile. "Talk to me."

"I feel so . . . divided. On the one hand, I'm so sorry about what's happened to Axel, so afraid of what he might be going through. The very thought that he might die makes me . . ." he searched for the right word, but it wouldn't come. Elsy understood exactly what he meant, and waited quietly for him to continue.

"But the other side of me feels such . . . rage." His voice deepened, giving a hint of what Erik would sound like as an adult.

"I'm so angry because I've become invisible—now more than ever. I don't exist. As long as Axel was at home, it was as if he could divert a little of the light that shone on him onto me—just a little ray of light, now and again. A little glimmer of light, of attention, that would come my way. And that was enough. I've never asked for any more than that. Axel deserved to be in the spotlight, to be the center of attention. He's always been better than me. I would never have the courage to do what he's done. I'm not brave. I don't stand out from the crowd. And

I don't have Axel's talent for making people around me feel good. Because that's where I think his secret lay . . . lies. . . . He always makes everyone around him feel good. I don't have that ability. I make people nervous, uneasy. They don't quite know what to do with me. I know too much. I don't laugh enough. I. . . ." He had to pause for breath after what was probably his longest coherent speech ever.

Elsy couldn't help laughing. "Be careful you don't use up all your words, Erik. You're usually so careful with them!" She smiled, but Erik clenched his jaw.

"That's exactly what I mean. Right now I feel as if I could start walking and just keep on walking and walking and walking, and never come back again. And nobody at home would even notice I'd gone. To my mom and dad I'm nothing more than a shadow on the periphery of their vision, and in a way I think it would almost be a relief if that shadow disappeared, so that they could focus entirely on Axel." His voice broke, and he turned away in embarrassment.

Elsy put her arm around him and rested her head on his shoulder, bringing him back from the dark place where he found himself.

"Erik, of course they would notice if you disappeared. They're just . . . preoccupied with trying to deal with what's happened to Axel."

"It's been four months since the Germans took him," Erik said dully. "How long are they going to be preoccupied? Six months? A year? Two years? A lifetime? I'm here right now. I'm still here. Why doesn't that matter? And yet at the same time I feel like a terrible person because I'm jealous of my brother, who's probably stuck in prison somewhere and might well be executed before we ever set eyes on him again. What a wonderful brother I am."

"Nobody doubts the fact that you love Axel." Elsy patted his back. "But it's hardly surprising that you want to be seen, to be acknowledged. I'm absolutely sure that your parents love you, but you need to tell them how you're feeling; you have to make them see you."

"I don't dare." Erik shook his head. "What if they think I'm a terrible person?"

Elsy took his head between her hands, forcing him to look at her. "Now you listen to me, Erik Frankel. You are not a terrible person. You love your brother and your parents. But you're grieving too. You have to tell them that; you have to demand a little space for yourself. Understand?"

He tried to turn away, but she held his head firmly between her palms and looked him straight in the eye. Eventually he nodded. "You're right. I'll talk to them. . . ."

Impulsively, Elsy threw her arms around him and hugged him tightly. She felt him relax as she stroked his back.

"What the hell is going on here?" A voice behind them made them pull apart. Elsy turned around and saw Frans staring at them, his face white, his hands clenched into fists.

"What the hell?!" he repeated. He seemed unable to find any other words. Elsy realized how things must have looked, and spoke calmly in an effort to make Frans understand what had actually been going on before he lost his temper completely. She had seen him flare up many times in the past; it was just as if someone had struck a match. There was something about Frans—as if he were permanently ready to fly into a rage, constantly looking for reasons to express his anger. And she was smart enough to know that he was sweet on her. In this situation, that could lead to disaster unless she managed to explain to him. . . .

"Erik and I were just having a chat." Her tone was calm and matter-of-fact.

"Yes, I noticed the two of you just having a chat," Frans said; there was something in his eyes that made Elsy shudder.

"We were talking about Axel, how hard it is to cope with the thought of his being taken by the Germans," she said, holding Frans's gaze. The cold, savage look in his eyes faded slightly. She kept going. "I was comforting Erik. That's all. Come and sit here and talk to us." She patted the rock beside her. Frans hesitated, but his fists had begun to unclench, and that look in his eyes had gone. He sighed deeply and sat down.

"Sorry. . . ," he said, without looking at her.

"It's fine," she said, "but try not to jump to conclusions."

Frans didn't say anything for a while. Then he turned to face Elsy. The emotional intensity she saw in his eyes frightened her more than the cold anger of a few moments earlier. She suddenly had a premonition that this wasn't going to end well.

She also thought about Britta, and the lovesick way she always looked at Frans.

This definitely wasn't going to end well.

21

"Erica seems really nice." Karin smiled as she pushed Ludde along in his stroller.

"She's the best," Patrik said, unable to stop himself from smiling. Admittedly they'd had a few problems lately, but nothing serious. He felt incredibly lucky to wake up next to Erica every morning.

"I wish I could say the same about Leif," Karin said. "But I really am getting sick of life as the wife of a musician in a dance band. Then again, I knew what I was getting into, so I suppose I can't really complain."

"Things change when you have kids," Patrik said, partly as a statement, partly a question.

"You don't say," Karin said sarcastically. "I was probably naïve, but I had no idea how much hard work was involved, and how demanding it is when you have a small child, and. . . . It's not so easy to carry everything alone. Sometimes I feel as if I'm the one who does all the hard work. I deal with the sleepless nights, change his diapers, play with him, feed him, take him to the doctor when he gets sick. Then Leif turns up and you'd think he was Santa Claus himself, judging by the reception he gets from Ludde. It just feels so goddamn unfair."

"But who does Ludde turn to if he hurts himself?" Patrik said.

Karin smiled. "You're right, it's me he wants. So the fact that I'm the one who's carried him around night after night must mean something. But I don't know . . . I just feel kind of cheated. It wasn't supposed to be like this." She sighed and adjusted Ludde's hat, which had slipped to one side, leaving an ear exposed.

"I have to say it's been much more fun than I could have imagined," Patrik said. A penetrating look from Karin soon made him realize that he had said something dumb.

"Does Erica feel the same?" she said sharply, and Patrik could see where she was coming from.

"No, she doesn't. Or she didn't, at least." He felt a pang of guilt as he remembered how pale and somehow joyless Erica had looked during Maja's first months.

"Could that be because Erica was torn away from her adult life to stay home with Maja, while you went off to work every day?"

"I helped out as much as I could," Patrik protested.

"Helped out, yes," Karin said, moving ahead of him with her stroller as they reached the narrow stretch of road leading to Badholmen. "There's a hell of a difference between 'helping out' and being the person who has to carry the ultimate responsibility. It's not that easy to figure out how to calm a crying baby, what and when they're supposed to eat, and how to keep yourself and a baby occupied for at least five days a week, usually with no access to the company of other adults. Being CEO of Baby Inc. is a completely different matter from being a mere assistant, standing on the sidelines waiting for orders."

"But you can't blame everything on fathers," Patrik said, pushing Maja's stroller up the steep incline. "As far as I can see, it's often the mother who doesn't want to relinquish control to the father; if you change a diaper, you do it wrong; if you feed the baby, you're not holding the bottle in the right way, and so on. I don't think it's always that easy for a father to share that CEO role."

Karin remained silent for a little while, then she looked at Patrik and said "Is that what Erica was like when she was at home with Maja? Was she reluctant to let you in?" She waited calmly for his response.

Patrik considered the question carefully and eventually had to admit, "No, she wasn't. It was more that I thought it was nice to avoid taking on the main responsibility. When Maja was upset and I was trying to console her, it was good to know that however much she cried, I could always hand her over to Erica if she didn't settle down, and Erica would fix it. And of course it was nice to go off to work in the morning, because that meant it was always fun to come home to Maja in the evening."

"Because you'd had your dose of adult company," Karin said drily. "So how's it going now that you're in charge? Is it working?"

Patrik thought for a moment, then shook his head. "No. I haven't exactly earned top marks as a stay-at-home dad so far. But it's not that easy. I mean, Erica works from home, and she knows where everything is, so. . . ." He shook his head again.

"Sounds familiar. Every time Leif comes home, he stands in the middle of the floor and yells, 'Kaaarin! Where are the diapers?' Sometimes I wonder how you guys manage at work when you can't even remember where the diapers are kept at home."

"Hey, come on!" Patrik said, giving Karin a poke in the side. "We're not that useless! Give us some credit. It's only a generation ago that a man would hardly ever change a baby's diaper, and I actually think we've come a long way since then. It's not so easy to make that kind of transformation overnight.

Our fathers were our role models, after all, and yes, it takes time to change things. But we're doing our best."

"*You* might be," Karin said, with a hint of bitterness in her tone once more. "But Leif definitely isn't doing his best."

Patrik said nothing, because there wasn't really anything to say. As they went their separate ways in Sälvik at the intersection by the Norderviken Sailing Club, he felt both sad and reflective. For a long time he had resented Karin because of the way she had deceived him, but now he just felt incredibly sorry for her.

The phone call had sent them racing to the car. As usual, Mellberg mumbled some excuse and scuttled back to his office, but Martin, Paula, and Gösta set off along Affärsgatan, heading for Tanumshede High School. They had been told to go to the principal's office, and since it wasn't their first visit to the school, Martin had no problem leading them straight there.

"So, what exactly has happened?" He looked around the room, in which a sullen teenager was sitting on a chair, flanked by the principal and two men whom Martin assumed were teachers.

"Per attacked another student," the principal said grimly, perching on the desk. "Thank you for coming so quickly."

"How's the student?" Paula asked.

"In pretty bad shape. The school nurse is with him, and an ambulance is on its way. I've called Per's mother—she should be here soon." The principal glared at the boy, who responded with an indifferent yawn.

"You're coming down to the station with us," Martin said, signaling to Per to stand up. He turned to the principal. "See if you can get hold of his mother before she gets here; if not, ask her to follow us to the station. My colleague Paula Morales will stay here to interview the witnesses who saw the assault."

Paula nodded. "I'll make a start right away," she said.

෴

Per still looked indifferent a short while later as he slouched along the corridor behind Martin and Gösta. A large number of curious students had gathered there, and Per reacted to the attention by grinning and giving them the finger.

"Fucking idiots," he muttered.

Gösta looked at him sharply. "Keep it shut until we get to the station."

Per shrugged and did as he was told. As they drove the short distance from the school back to the low building that housed both the police station and the fire department, he sat and stared out of the car window without saying a word.

When they arrived, they put him in an interview room and waited for his mother to arrive. Suddenly Martin's phone rang. He listened with interest to what the caller had to say, then turned to Gösta with a thoughtful look in his eyes.

"That was Paula. Guess who the victim was."

"No idea—is it someone we know?"

"It certainly is. Mattias Larsson, the boy who found Erik Frankel's body. He's on his way to the hospital right now, so we'll have to speak to him later."

Gösta absorbed the information without saying anything, but Martin noticed that the color had drained from his face.

Ten minutes later, Carina rushed into the station and breathlessly asked about her son. Annika calmly showed her into Martin's office.

"Where's Per? What's happened?" She was obviously fighting back tears and was extremely upset. Martin held out his hand and introduced himself. Formality and familiar rituals often had a reassuring effect, and it seemed to work on this occasion. Carina repeated her question, but in a more subdued tone of voice, then sat down on the chair that Martin offered her. He grimaced slightly as he sat down behind his desk and recognized the familiar smell drifting across from the woman opposite him. Stale booze, distinctive and easy to identify. Perhaps she'd been to a party the previous day. But he didn't think so. There was something bloated and slightly puffy about her features, the telltale signs of an alcoholic.

"Per has been brought in because he allegedly assaulted a fellow student in the school yard."

"Oh, my God," she said, clutching the arms of the chair. "How . . . ? The person he. . . ." She couldn't finish the sentence.

"He's on his way to the hospital at the moment. Apparently he was very badly beaten."

"But why?" She swallowed hard, shaking her head at the same time.

"That's what we're hoping to find out. Per is in one of our interview rooms, and with your permission we would like to ask him a few questions."

Carina nodded. "Of course." She swallowed again.

"Okay, let's go and talk to Per." Martin led the way. He stopped in the corridor and tapped on the doorjamb of Gösta's office. "Come on—we're going to speak to the boy."

Carina and Gösta politely shook hands, then the three of them went into the room where Per was waiting, trying to look as if he were bored to death. But the mask slipped for a second when his mother walked in. It wasn't much—a slight twitch at the corner of one eye, a faint tremble in his hands. Then he forced himself to adopt an unconcerned expression once more and fixed his gaze on the wall.

"Oh, Per, what have you done now?" Carina's voice faltered as she sat down next to her son and tried to put her arm around him. He shook her off and didn't answer the question.

Martin and Gösta sat down opposite Per and Carina, and Martin switched on a tape recorder. As a matter of course, he also had a notebook and pen, and he arranged these on the table. Then he quickly stated the date and time, for the benefit of the tape, and cleared his throat.

"So, Per, can you tell us what happened? Mattias is on his way to the hospital in an ambulance, by the way. Just in case you were wondering."

Per simply smiled, and his mother nudged him in the ribs with her elbow.

"Per! Answer the question! And of course you were wondering about Mattias. Weren't you?" Her voice betrayed her again, and her son still refused to look at her.

"Let Per answer for himself," Gösta said with a reassuring nod at Carina.

There was a lengthy silence as they waited for the boy. Eventually his head came up.

"Mattias was talking a load of crap, that's all."

"What do you mean by 'crap'?" Martin said pleasantly. "Could you be a little more specific?"

Another long silence. Then: "He was coming on to Mia, she's supposed to be like the school prom queen or something, and I heard him boasting about how brave he'd been when he and Adam went to that old guy's house and found him. He said nobody else had the nerve to go there! I mean, what the fuck was he talking about? They only got the idea because I'd already been there at the beginning of June. Their ears were like satellite dishes when I was telling them about all the cool stuff in the house; it's obvious they would never have dared go in first. Fucking geeks."

Per laughed, and Carina looked down at the table in embarrassment. It took a few seconds before Martin registered what Per had said. He said slowly, "Are you talking about Erik Frankel's house? In Fjällbacka?"

"Yes, that old guy Mattias and Adam found dead. The one who had all that cool Nazi stuff," Per said, his eyes shining. "I was going to go back with the gang to pick up a few things, but then the old guy turned up and locked me in and called my dad and—"

"Just hang on a minute," Martin said, holding up his hands. "Let's just slow down, shall we? Are you telling me that you broke into Erik Frankel's house and he caught you? And locked you in?"

Per nodded. "I didn't think he was home; I got in through a cellar window. But he came downstairs while I was in that room with all those books and crap like that, and he closed the door and locked it. Then he made me give him my dad's number, and he called him."

"Did you know about this?" Martin glanced sharply at Carina.

She nodded feebly. "Yes, but Kjell, my ex-husband, only told me the other day. I had no idea until then. And I don't understand why you didn't give my number, Per, instead of dragging your father into all this!"

"I don't expect you to understand," Per said, looking at his mother for the first time. "All you do is lie around drinking; you don't give a shit about anything else. You stink of stale booze right now, by the way—did you know that?" Per's hands were shaking again, just as they had been when Carina, Martin, and Gösta first came into the room and he had lost control for a moment.

Tears welled up in Carina's eyes as she stared at her son, then she said, quietly, "Is that all you have to say to me, after everything I've done for you? I've fed you and clothed you and been there for you all these years, when your father went away and ignored us." She turned to Martin and Gösta. "He just left one day. Packed his bags and took off. I found out he'd hooked up with some twenty-five-year-old and gotten her pregnant, so he left me and Per without so much as a backward glance. He simply started a new family and left us behind like garbage."

"It's ten years since Dad left," Per said wearily, suddenly looking considerably older than his fifteen years.

"What's your father's name?" Gösta asked.

"My ex-husband is Kjell Ringholm," Carina replied shortly. "I can give you his number."

Martin and Gösta exchanged a glance.

"Kjell Ringholm who works for *Bohusläningen*?" said Gösta as the pieces began to fall into place. "Frans Ringholm's son?"

"Frans is my grandfather," Per said proudly. "He's the coolest guy I know. He's even been in jail, but now he's in politics. They're going to win the next election and kick out all the blacks."

"Per!" Carina looked horrified as she turned to the police officers. "He's at the age when he's searching, trying out different roles. And his grandfather isn't a good influence on him. Kjell has banned Per from seeing Frans."

"Good luck with that," Per muttered. "And that old guy with the Nazi stuff—he got what he deserved. I heard him talking to Dad when he came to pick me up; he said he could give Dad some good material for the articles he was writing about Sweden's Friends and about Frans in particular. They thought I couldn't hear them, but they arranged to meet up again before too long. Fucking traitors—I can understand why my granddad is ashamed of Dad," Per said, his voice full of loathing.

Smack! Carina slapped him across the face and, in the silence that followed, mother and son stared at one another with equal measures of surprise and hatred. Then Carina's face softened. "Sorry, sorry, sweetheart. I didn't mean to . . . I . . . sorry." She tried to put her arms around him, but Per pushed her away immediately.

"Get off me, you drunken bitch! Don't touch me! Leave me alone!"

"Okay, let's all calm down." Gösta got to his feet and glared at Carina and Per. "I don't think we're going to get much further today. You're free to go for the time being, Per. But. . . ." He looked inquiringly at Martin, who gave an almost imperceptible nod. "But we will be contacting social services on this matter. We've seen a number of things that concern us, and we think it would be best if social services took a closer look. And of course the investigation into the attack on Mattias will continue."

"Is that really necessary?" Carina said, her voice trembling, but there was no real energy behind the question. Gösta got the impression that part of her was relieved at the thought of someone tackling her situation.

When Per and Carina had left the station, side by side but without looking at each other, Gösta followed Martin into his office.

"Plenty of food for thought there," Martin said as he sat down.

"Absolutely," Gösta said, biting his lip and rocking slightly on his heels.

"You look as if you've got something to say."

"Ah, well, yes, maybe there is just one small matter." Gösta braced himself. Something had been nagging away at his subconscious for a couple of days, and during the interview he had suddenly realized what it was. Now he was wondering exactly how to put it. Martin wasn't going to be very happy.

He stood on the top step for a long time, hesitating. Eventually he knocked; Herman opened the door almost immediately.

"You came."

Axel nodded but stayed exactly where he was.

"Come in. I didn't tell her you were coming; I wasn't sure if she would remember."

"Are things really that bad?" Axel's expression was sympathetic; Herman looked tired. It couldn't be easy.

"Is this the whole tribe?" Axel said, nodding toward the photographs in the hallway. Herman's face lit up.

"Yes, that's everyone."

Axel studied the photographs, his hands clasped behind his back. Midsummer celebrations and birthdays, Christmases and everyday life. A whole panoply of people, children, grandchildren. For a moment he allowed himself to reflect on what his own wall of pictures would have looked like, if he had put one together. Days at the office. Endless piles of paper. Countless dinners with political highfliers and other influential individuals. Few, if any, friends. Not many people could cope with him, with the constant pursuit, the drive to track down just one more out there. One more criminal living a pleasant life that he didn't deserve. One more who had blood on his hands but still enjoyed the privilege of being able to pat his grandchildren on the head with those very hands. How could family, friends, a normal life compete with that obsession? For most of his life he hadn't even allowed himself to consider whether he might have missed out on something. And the reward was so great when his work bore fruit. When the years of searching through archives, years of interviewing people who forgot more and more quickly, finally resulted in the past catching up with those who were guilty, in bringing them to justice. That reward was so great that it pushed aside the longing for a normal life. Or at least that was what he had always thought. But now, standing here in front of Herman and Britta's photographs, he wondered for a brief moment if he had been wrong to prioritize death over life.

"They're lovely," Axel said, turning away. He followed Herman into the living room and stopped dead when he saw Britta. In spite of the fact that he and Erik had been based in Fjällbacka for all these years, it had been decades since he had last seen her. There had been no reason for their paths to cross.

Now the years fell away with brutal force, and he swayed unsteadily. She was still lovely. She had always been more beautiful than Elsy, who could best be described as a pretty girl. But Elsy had been blessed with an inner glow, a kindness that far outweighed Britta's superficial beauty. And yet something had changed over the years. There was no trace now of Britta's former brittle spikiness; she exuded nothing but maternal warmth, a maturity that must have come with age.

"Axel?" she said, getting up from the sofa. "Axel, is that really you?" She held out both her hands and he took them in his own.

So many years had passed. So very many years. Sixty. A lifetime. When he was younger, he could never have imagined that time could pass so quickly. The hands he held in his were wrinkled and covered in tiny liver spots. Her hair was no longer dark, but a lovely silver-gray. Britta gazed calmly into his eyes.

"It's good to see you again, Axel. You've aged well."

"That's funny, I was just thinking the same about you," Axel said with a smile.

"Come and sit down and we'll have a chat. Herman, could you fix us some coffee?"

Herman nodded; he left the room and busied himself in the kitchen. Britta sat down on the sofa, still holding Axel's hand as he sat down beside her.

"To think that we got old too, Axel. Who would have thought it?" she said, tilting her head to one side. Some of her youthful coquettishness still lingered, Axel thought with amusement.

"You've done a lot of good over the years, or so I've heard," Britta said, looking searchingly at him. He avoided her gaze.

"I don't know about that. I've done what had to be done. There are certain things that can't be swept under the carpet," he said, then stopped speaking abruptly.

"You're right there, Axel," Britta said seriously. "You're right there."

They sat side by side in silence looking out across the bay until Herman arrived with coffee on a floral-patterned tray.

"There you go."

"Thanks, darling," Britta said. Axel felt his heart contract when he saw the looks they exchanged. He reminded himself that through his work he had been able to help give many people a sense of peace. They had had the satisfaction of seeing their tormentors brought to justice. That was also a kind of love. Not personal or physical, perhaps, but it was love all the same.

As if she could read his thoughts, Britta asked, as she passed him a cup of coffee, "Have you had a good life, Axel?"

The question contained so many dimensions, so many layers, that he didn't know how to answer. He pictured Erik and his friends back home in the library, lighthearted and carefree. Elsy with her lovely smile and her gentle ways. Frans, who made everyone around him feel as if they were constantly tiptoeing around the crater of a volcano, but who also had something fragile and vulnerable about him. Britta, who had seemed so different from the way she was now. She had worn her beauty like a shield, and he had written her off as an empty shell, with nothing inside that was worth bothering about. And perhaps that had been true at the time, but the years had filled up the shell, and now she seemed to glow from within. And Erik. The thought of Erik was so painful that his brain wanted to reject it but, sitting there in Britta's living room, Axel forced himself to see his brother as he had been back then, before the bad times came along. Sitting at Father's desk, with his feet up. The brown hair always slightly messy, the distracted expression that always made him look significantly older than he was. Erik. Dear, beloved Erik.

Axel realized that Britta was waiting for a response. He forced himself back to the present and tried to find the answer. But as always, past and present were inextricably entwined, and in his memory the sixty years that had passed became a confusion of people, places, and events. His hand holding the coffee cup trembled, and eventually he said, "I don't know. I think so. As good as I deserve."

"I've had a good life, Axel. And I decided long, long ago that I deserved it. You should do the same."

His hand shook even more, and coffee splashed onto the sofa. "Oh, I'm so sorry . . . I. . . ."

Herman leapt to his feet. "Don't worry, I'll fetch a cloth." He disappeared into the kitchen and quickly returned with a blue-checked dish towel soaked in water, which he gently dabbed at the sofa.

Britta let out a loud groan, and Axel gave a start. "Oh, no, Mother will be furious. Her best sofa! This isn't good."

Axel looked inquiringly at Herman, who responded by rubbing furiously at the stain.

"Do you think it will come off? Mother's going to be so angry with me!" Britta was rocking back and forth, anxiously watching Herman's efforts to get rid of the coffee. He got up and put his arm around his wife. "It's fine, darling. It will come off, I promise."

"Are you sure? Because if Mother gets cross, she might tell Father and. . . ." Britta clenched one hand into a fist and nibbled nervously at her knuckles.

"I promise I'll get it off. She'll never know anything about it."

"Good. Good. That's good," Britta said, beginning to relax. Then she stiffened once more and stared at Axel. "Who are you? What do you want?"

He glanced at Herman for guidance.

"It comes and goes," Herman said, sitting down beside Britta and patting her hand reassuringly. She stared intently at Axel as if his face were something irritating, mocking, which kept slipping away from her. Then she gripped Axel's hand tightly and brought her face very close to his.

"He calls to me, you know."

"Who does?" Axel said, fighting the urge to pull back his face, his hand, his body.

Britta didn't reply. Instead he heard the echo of his own words on her lips.

"There are certain things that can't be swept under the carpet," she whispered slowly, her face no more than an inch from his.

He jerked his hand away and looked at Herman over Britta's silver-gray head.

"You can see how things are," Herman said wearily. "What are we going to do now?"

∞

"Adrian! Will you cut that out?!" The sweat was pouring off Anna as she tried to get him dressed, but recently he had developed wriggling into such an art form that it was impossible to get as much as one sock on one foot. She tried to hold him while pulling on a pair of underpants, but he slid out of her grasp and ran around the house laughing.

"Adrian! Stop that right now! Please, darling, Mommy doesn't have time. We're supposed to be going to Tanumshede with Dan. We're going shopping. You can check out the toys in Hedemyr's," she promised, well aware that bribery might not be the best way to handle the getting-dressed crisis. But what else could she do?

"Aren't you two ready yet?" Dan said as he came downstairs to find Anna sitting on the floor next to a pile of clothes, while Adrian ricocheted around the room. "My lecture starts in half an hour; I need to leave soon."

"Right, you take care of this then," Anna snapped, throwing Adrian's clothes at him. Dan looked at her in surprise. She'd been a bit volatile lately, but perhaps that was hardly surprising. Bringing two families together was more stressful than either of them had expected.

"Come here, Adrian," Dan said, grabbing the naked savage as he shot past. "Let's see if I've still got the knack." He managed to get Adrian into his underpants and socks with unexpected ease, but that was the end of it. Adrian tried out his wriggling technique on Dan, and flatly refused to have his pants put on. Dan made a couple of attempts while keeping admirably calm, then his patience snapped. "Adrian, keep STILL!"

An astonished Adrian stopped in midmovement. Then his face went bright red. "YOU'RE not my daddy! Go AWAY! I want my daddy! Daddeeee!"

It was all too much for Anna. The memories of Lucas, of that terrible time when she had been like a prisoner in her own home, came rushing to the surface and she burst into tears.

She ran upstairs and threw herself on the bed, overcome with heartrending sobs.

Then she felt a gentle hand on her back. "Darling, what's the matter? That was nothing to worry about. It's just that this is all still new to Adrian, and he's testing the boundaries. And let me tell you, it's nothing compared with the way Belinda used to behave when she was little. He's just an amateur compared to her. I once got so tired of the way she always carried on when I was trying to get her dressed that I dumped her outside the front door in nothing but her underpants. Although I have to say that Pernilla was furious with me. It was December, after all. She was only out there for a minute or so before I changed my mind."

Anna didn't laugh. Instead, the sobbing merely increased, until her entire body was shaking.

"Darling, what's wrong? I'm getting really worried now. I know you've been through a lot, but we can fix this. We all just need a little bit of time to calm down. You and I . . . we can fix this together."

She looked up at him, her face red and swollen with tears, and sat halfway up on the bed.

"I . . . I . . . know," she gulped as she tried to control the crying. "I . . . I . . . know . . . and . . . I . . . don't . . . understand . . . why I'm . . . so upset." Dan stroked her back reassuringly, and the weeping gradually subsided.

"I'm . . . just a bit . . . oversensitive. I don't . . . know why. . . . I usually . . . only get . . . like this . . . when—" Anna stopped abruptly in midsentence and stared openmouthed at Dan.

"What?" he said, looking bewildered. "You usually only get like this when . . . ?"

At first Anna couldn't bring herself to speak, and then after a little while she nodded slowly, wide-eyed. "I usually only get like this when I'm . . . pregnant."

There was total silence in the bedroom. Then a little voice came from the doorway: "I got dressed. All by myself. I'm a big boy. Are we going to the toy shop now?"

Dan and Anna looked at Adrian, standing in the doorway positively bursting with pride. No doubt about it. His pants were on backward, and his top was inside out. But he had gotten dressed. All by himself.

A delicious smell had wafted as far as the hallway. Filled with anticipation, Mellberg went into the kitchen. Rita had called just before eleven to ask if he would like to come to lunch, since Senorita had expressed a wish to play with Ernst. He hadn't asked how the dog had communicated this wish to her mistress; there were certain things you just accepted, like manna from heaven.

"Hello again." Johanna was standing next to Rita, helping to chop vegetables—with a certain amount of difficulty since her belly forced her to stand some distance away from the countertop.

"Hi there. Something smells good," Mellberg said, sniffing the air.

"Chili con carne," Rita said, coming over and giving him a kiss on the cheek. Mellberg resisted the urge to raise his hand and touch the spot where her lips had made contact, and sat down at the table instead. It was set for four. "Are we having company?" he asked.

"My partner is coming home for lunch," Johanna said, rubbing her lower back.

"Shouldn't you be sitting down?" Mellberg said, pulling out a chair. "That must be pretty heavy to carry around."

Johanna did as he suggested and sat down beside him, puffing and blowing. "You have no idea. But hopefully it will soon be over. I'll be so glad when the time comes." She stroked her belly.

"Would you like to feel?" she said to Mellberg when she saw the look on his face.

"Is that allowed?" he said inanely. He hadn't found out about the existence of his own son until Simon was a teenager, so this aspect of parenthood was a mystery to him.

"Here, it's kicking." Johanna took his hand and placed it on the left side of her belly.

Mellberg jumped as he felt a powerful kick against his palm. "Oh, my God! That was something else! Doesn't it hurt?" He stared at her bump, feeling one strong kick after another beneath his hand.

"Not really. It's a bit unpleasant when I'm trying to get to sleep, that's all. My partner thinks we've got a football player in there."

"I'd have to agree," Mellberg said, reluctant to take his hand away. The experience had aroused strange feelings, and he found it difficult to define them. Longing, fascination, a sense of loss. . . . He didn't really know.

"Does his father have any talents in that direction that the baby might inherit?" he asked with a laugh. To his surprise, his question was met with total silence. He looked up and met Rita's astonished gaze.

"But, Bertil, don't you know that—"

At that moment the front door opened.

"That smells great, Mom," a female voice came from the hallway. "What are we having? Your fantastic chili?"

Paula walked into the kitchen, and the stunned look on her face was reflected on Mellberg's.

"Paula?"

"Chief?"

There was a rattling sound inside Mellberg's head as the pieces fell into place. Paula had moved here with her mother. Rita had recently arrived. And those dark eyes. Why hadn't he noticed it before? They had exactly the same eyes. There was just one thing he didn't quite—

"So you've already met my partner," said Paula, putting her arms around Johanna. She stared at him warily, daring him to say the wrong thing, do the wrong thing.

Out of the corner of his eye he could see Rita watching him, radiating tension. She had a wooden spoon in her hand, but had stopped stirring the chili as she waited for his reaction. A thousand thoughts whirled through his mind. A thousand prejudices. A thousand comments he had made over the years, comments that might not always have been thought through. But suddenly he realized that this was the one moment in his life when he had to say the right thing, do the right thing. There was far too much at stake. With Rita's dark eyes fixed on him, he said calmly, "I didn't know you were going to be a mom. And so soon. Congratulations! Johanna has been kind enough to let me feel that little bundle of energy in there, and I tend to agree with your theory that she's about to give birth to a footballer."

Paula didn't move a muscle for a few more seconds; she kept her arms around Johanna and her eyes locked on Mellberg's, trying to figure out if there was any hint of sarcasm, anything hidden beneath the surface of his words. When she relaxed and smiled, saying "It's amazing to feel those kicks, that's for sure," it was as if the entire room had imploded with relief.

Rita went back to her stirring and said, with a laugh, "That's nothing compared with how you used to kick, Paula. I remember your dad used to joke that it seemed as if you wanted to come out by a different route from the usual one!"

Paula kissed Johanna on the cheek and sat down at the table. She couldn't help staring at Mellberg, who was in fact feeling enormously pleased with himself. He still thought the idea of two women living together was bizarre, and he couldn't get his head around this business of the baby at all. Sooner or later he was going to have to satisfy his curiosity on that particular point. . . . But still. He had said the right thing, and to his surprise he had actually meant it.

Rita placed a big bowl of chili on the table, telling everyone to help themselves. The look she gave Mellberg was the final proof that he had done the right thing.

He could still feel the taut skin of Johanna's belly beneath his hand, and that little foot kicking against his palm.

"You're just in time for lunch. I was about to call you." Patrik tasted the tomato soup with a teaspoon, then set the pan on the table.

"Wow—what have I done to deserve this?" Erica came up behind him and kissed the back of his neck.

"You think this is it? You mean all I had to do to impress you was to make lunch? Damn, that means I've done the laundry, cleaned the living room, and changed the light bulb in the bathroom for nothing!" Patrik turned around and kissed her on the mouth.

"Whatever you're on, I want some," Erica said, looking at him in surprise. "And where's Maja?"

"She's been asleep for the last fifteen minutes, so we should be able to have our lunch in peace, just the two of us. And then you can go upstairs and do some work while I take care of the dishes."

"Okaaay . . . now you're freaking me out. Either you've spent all our money, or you're going to tell me you have a mistress, or you've been accepted into NASA's latest space program and you're about to announce that you'll be orbiting the earth for the next twelve months. . . . Or else my husband has been abducted by aliens, and you're some kind of humanoid robot. . . ."

"How did you guess I was going into space?" Patrik said with a wink. He sliced some bread, put it in a basket, then sat down opposite Erica. "No, to tell you the truth, Karin said something when we were out walking today that made me think, and . . . well, I just think I ought to do a bit more than I have been doing. But don't count on getting this treatment all the time; I can't guarantee that I won't have a relapse!"

"So all a woman has to do to get her husband to help more around the house is to send him out on a date with his ex-wife. I must pass that on to my girlfriends. . . ."

"Absolutely," Patrik said, blowing on a spoonful of soup. "Although it wasn't actually a date. And I don't think Karin's having a particularly easy time at the moment." He summarized what she had said, and Erica nodded. Even if Karin seemed to be getting considerably less support at home than Erica had, the situation still sounded very familiar.

"So, how did you get on at the library?" Patrik asked, slurping down his soup.

Erica's face brightened. "I found lots of really useful material. You have no idea how many exciting things happened in and around Fjällbacka during the Second World War. Food, information, arms, and people were smuggled both to and from Norway, and both German deserters and Norwegian resistance fighters came here. And then there was the danger from mines, several fishing boats and cargo ships went down with everyone on board when they hit mines. And did you know that a German plane was shot down outside Dingle? The Swedish air force shot down a plane there in 1940, and all three crew members died. And I've never even heard about it. I thought the war had passed without having much effect here, apart from the difficulties with rationing and so on."

"It sounds as if you've really gotten into this," Patrik laughed, serving Erica more soup.

"Yes, and there's more! I asked Christian to look for possible references to my mother and her friends. I wasn't really expecting to find anything; they were so young back then. But look at this. . . ." Erica's voice shook as she went to get her brief-case. She put it on the table and took out a thick wad of papers.

"Wow—that's quite a pile you have there!"

"I've been sitting in the library reading for three hours," Erica said, flicking through the pages with trembling fingers. Eventually she found what she was looking for.

"There! Look at that!" She pointed to an article featuring a large black-and-white photograph.

Patrik carefully scrutinized the piece. The photograph was the first thing that drew his gaze. Five people, standing side by side. He screwed up his eyes to read the caption, and recognized four of the names: Elsy Moström, Frans Ringholm, Erik Frankel, and Britta Johansson. But the fifth name was one he hadn't heard before. A boy, probably about the same age as the others: Hans Olavsen. He read the rest of the article in silence as Erica kept her eyes fixed on his face.

"So? What do you think? I don't know what it means, but it can't be a coincidence. Look at the date. He came to Fjäll-backa just when my mother appears to have stopped writing her diary—almost to the day. Do you see? It can't be a coincidence! This has to mean something!" Erica was pacing excitedly up and down the kitchen.

Patrik bent his head over the photograph again, studying the five young people. One of them dead, murdered, sixty years later. His gut feeling told him that Erica was right. This had to mean something.

Paula's head was spinning as she made her way back to the sta-tion. Her mother had mentioned that she had met a nice man who kept her company while she was walking the dog, and that she had managed to entice him along to her salsa class. But Paula could never have imagined that he would turn out to be her chief. And it wasn't overstating the case to say that she wasn't exactly thrilled. Mellberg was more or less the last man on earth she would want her mother to hook up with. On the other hand, she had to admit that he had handled the information about her and Johanna really well. Surprisingly well. Her fear of narrow-mindedness had been her strongest argument against moving to Tanumshede. It had been difficult enough for her and Johanna to be accepted as a family in Stockholm. And in a small town . . . it could easily turn out to be a disaster. But she had talked things through with Johanna and her mother, and the three of them had decided that if it didn't work out, they would simply have to move back to Stockholm. So far, everything had gone much better than they'd expected. She was very happy in her job, her mother had found her footing with her salsa class and a part-time job at the Konsum supermarket, and even though Johanna would be on maternity leave for some time, she had already spoken to a local company that was definitely interested in recruiting someone with her financial skills. When Paula had seen Mellberg's expression as she walked in and put her arm around Johanna, she had felt as if everything was about to collapse like a house of cards. At that precise moment, their whole existence could have fallen apart, but Mellberg had surprised her. Perhaps he wasn't quite as hopeless as she had thought.

Paula exchanged a few words with Annika at the reception desk, then tapped on the doorjamb of Martin's office and walked in.

"How did it go?"

"With the assault? He confessed—he didn't really have much choice. His mother has taken him home, but Gösta is informing social services. It doesn't seem to be a particularly good situation."

"As is so often the case," Paula said, taking a seat.

"The really interesting thing is that it turns out the reason behind this attack was that Per broke into Erik Frankel's house back in the spring."

Paula raised an eyebrow but allowed Martin to continue. When he had told her the full story, they both sat in silence for a little while.

"I wonder what Erik had that might have been of interest to Kjell?" Paula said eventually. "Could it have been something to do with his father?"

Martin shrugged. "I have no idea. But I think we ought to have a word with him and find out. We have to go to Uddevalla anyway to speak to some of the members of Sweden's Friends, and the newspaper is based there. And we can see Axel on the way."

"Sounds like a plan," Paula said, getting to her feet.

Twenty minutes later, they were standing outside Erik and Axel's house once more. Axel looked older than the last time she had seen him, Paula thought. Grayer, thinner, almost transparent somehow. He smiled politely as he let them in; he didn't ask why they were there but simply showed them to the veranda.

"Have you made any progress?" he asked as they were sitting down. "With the investigation," he added unnecessarily.

Martin glanced at Paula, then said "We are following up a number of leads. The most important thing is that we have managed to figure out approximately when your brother must have died."

"That's a big step forward," Axel said with a smile that failed to touch the sadness and weariness in his eyes. "When do you think it happened?"

"He saw his . . . lady friend, Viola Ellmander, on June 15, so we're absolutely certain he was alive then. The second date is a little more uncertain, but we think he was already dead on June 17, when your cleaner. . . ."

"Laila," Axel supplied when he noticed that Martin was struggling to recall her name.

"Laila, that's it. She came over on June 17 intending to do the cleaning as usual, but no one answered the door when she arrived, nor had the key been left for her; apparently this is what normally happens if you're not home."

"Yes, Erik was extremely conscientious about leaving the key for Laila, and as far as I'm aware, he's never forgotten. So if he didn't open the door and there was no key, then. . . ." Axel fell silent and quickly ran a hand over his eyes as if he could see images of his brother and wanted to wipe them away immediately.

"I'm very sorry," Paula said gently, "but we do have to ask where you were between the fifteenth and seventeenth of June. I promise you it's just a formality."

Axel waved away her assurances. "There's no need to apologize. I realize it's all part of your job. And, besides, don't the statistics show that most murders are committed by someone in the family?"

Martin nodded. "Yes, but we'd like the information so that we can eliminate you from our inquiries, if possible."

"Of course. I'll just go and get my diary."

Axel was gone for a few moments, and returned with a thick diary. He sat down and began to leaf through the pages.

"Okay . . . I traveled from Sweden on a direct flight to Paris on June 3, and I didn't come back until you . . . were kind enough to pick me up at the airport. But the fifteenth to the seventeenth . . . let's see . . . I had a meeting in Brussels on the fifteenth, traveled to Frankfurt on the sixteenth, then went back to the main office in Paris on the seventeenth. I can provide you with copies of my tickets if necessary." He handed Paula the diary.

She studied it carefully, but after a questioning glance at Martin, who shook his head, she pushed it back across the table.

"I don't think that will be necessary, thank you. Do you remember anything about those dates with regard to Erik? Anything at all? Any phone calls? Something he might have mentioned?"

Axel shook his head. "No, unfortunately. As I said, my brother and I weren't in the habit of calling each other frequently when I was out of the country. Erik probably wouldn't have called me unless the house was on fire." He laughed for a second, then abruptly fell silent and ran his hand over his eyes once more.

"Is there anything else I can help you with?" he said, carefully closing the diary.

"Actually, there was one thing," Martin said, gazing intently at Axel. "We questioned a boy named Per Ringholm earlier today; he was involved in an assault down at the school. He told us that he had broken into this house at the beginning of June and that Erik had caught him, locked him in the library, and called his father, Kjell Ringholm."

"Frans's son," Axel stated.

Martin nodded. "Exactly. Per overheard part of a conversation between Erik and Kjell during which they arranged to meet at a later date, because Erik had some kind of information that he thought would interest Kjell. Does that sound familiar?"

"I don't know what you're talking about," Axel replied firmly.

"And you have no idea what Erik might have wanted to tell Kjell?"

Axel sat in silence for a long time, as if he was considering the question. Then he shook his head slowly. "No, I can't imagine what it might have been. Although Erik did spend a lot of time researching the period around the Second World War, and of course he came into contact with Nazism from that time, while Kjell has a keen interest in combating neo-Nazism in Sweden today. So there might well have been some link there, something of historical interest that could provide Kjell with background material. I'm sure if you ask Kjell, he'll be able to tell you what it was about."

"We're on our way to Uddevalla to speak to him now. Here's my cell number, just in case anything occurs to you." Martin jotted down his number on a piece of paper and passed it to Axel, who carefully tucked it away inside his diary.

Paula and Martin drove back to the station in silence, but their thoughts were running along the same lines. What were they missing? Which questions should they have asked? They both wished they knew.

"We can't put it off anymore. She can't stay at home for much longer." Herman gazed at his daughters with such bottomless despair that they could hardly bring themselves to look him in the eye.

"We know, Dad. You're doing the right thing; there's no alternative. You've taken care of Mom for as long as possible, but now it's time for someone else to step in. We'll find a fantastic place for her." Anna-Greta came and stood behind her father and put her arms around him. She shuddered as she felt how thin he was beneath his shirt. Britta's illness had taken its toll on him, perhaps more than they had realized. Or wanted to realize. She leaned forward and rested her cheek against his.

"We're here, Dad. Me, Birgitta, Margareta, and our families. We're here for you, you know that. You'll never have to feel alone."

"I'll feel alone without your mother. Nobody can do anything about that," Herman said sadly, quickly wiping a tear from the corner of his eye with his shirtsleeve. "But I know this is the best thing for Britta. I know it is."

The three daughters exchanged glances. Herman and Britta had been at the heart of all their lives, something solid, something permanent to lean on. Now the very foundation of their existence was shaking, and they reached out to each other to try to regain some semblance of stability. It was terrifying to see a parent shrink, be diminished, become smaller than his or her offspring. To have to be the adult in a relationship with someone who had always seemed infallible, indestructible. Even though they no longer regarded their parents as god-like beings with the answers to everything, it was still painful to watch them lose the strength they had once had.

Anna-Greta gave Herman's thin shoulders a couple of extra squeezes, then she sat down at the kitchen table again.

"Will she be okay while you're here?" Margareta said anxiously. "Maybe I should pop over and check on her."

"She fell asleep just before I left," Herman said. "But she doesn't usually sleep for more than an hour, so I'd better be going." He got laboriously to his feet.

"Why don't we go over and sit with her for a couple of hours? Then you could lie down and have a rest," Birgitta suggested. "Dad could use the guest room for a while, couldn't he?" she said to Margareta, since they had gathered at her house for a cup of coffee and a discussion about their mother.

"That's a really good idea," Margareta said, smiling encouragingly at her father. "You have a rest and we'll go over and see Mom."

"Thanks, girls," Herman said, heading for the hallway. "But your mother and I have looked after each other for over fifty years, so I'd like to keep on taking care of her for the few hours we have left. Once she's in the home, then. . . ." He didn't finish the sentence but hurried out of the front door before his daughters saw the tears.

Britta smiled. The lucid moments that her brain denied her during her waking hours were more frequent when she was asleep. She could see everything so clearly. Some of the memories weren't welcome but forced their way to the surface anyway. Like the sound of her father's belt on a child's bare behind. Or her mother's tearstained cheeks. Or the lack of space in the little house on the hill, where the shrill cries of the younger children reverberated through the rooms and made her want to put her hands over her ears and scream. But other memories were more pleasant. Like summer days running across the warm rocks, playing without a care in the world. Elsy in the floral dresses her mother made with such skill. Erik in his short pants, that serious expression on his face. Frans with his curly blond hair; she had always wanted to run her hand through it, even when they were so small that the difference between boys and girls had no real meaning.

A voice penetrated those memories in her sleep. A voice she recognized all too well. A voice that had spoken to her with increasing frequency, allowing her no peace, whether she was awake, asleep, or lost in the fog. It cut through everything, wanted everything, insisted on its place in her world. It denied her any respite, refused to allow her to forget. She had thought she would never hear that voice again, and yet it was here. It was very strange. And very frightening.

She rolled her head from side to side on the pillow, trying to shake off the voice, shake off the memories that were disturbing her slumber. Eventually she succeeded. Happy memories floated to the surface. The first time she had seen Herman. The day she knew that he was the one for her, that they would be together. A wedding. Britta herself in a beautiful white dress, dizzy with happiness. The pain and then the love when Anna-Greta was born. And Birgitta and Margareta, whom she loved just as much. Herman changing diapers and looking after the children in spite of her mother's loud protests. He had done it out of love. Not out of duty or because of her demands. She smiled. Her eyelids flickered. She wanted to stay right here among these memories. If she had to choose just one memory to fill her mind for the rest of her life, it would be the image of Herman bathing their youngest daughter in the little tub especially made for new babies. He was humming away to himself as he gently supported her small head with his hand, moving a washcloth over her tiny body with immense solicitousness. He met his daughter's gaze as she followed every movement with wide eyes. Britta saw herself standing in the doorway; she had crept there to watch them. If she forgot everything else, she would fight to hold on to that memory. Herman and Margareta, his hand beneath her head, the tenderness, the closeness.

A noise jerked her out of the dream. She tried to find her way back. Back to the sound of the water splashing as Herman wet the washcloth. The sound of Margareta's contented babbling as the warm water enveloped her body. But a new sound forced her even closer to the surface, even closer to the fog that she wanted to avoid at all costs. Waking carried with it the risk of being swallowed up by the fuzzy grayness that filled her head and occupied more and more of her time.

Reluctantly she opened her eyes. A figure was looking down at her. Britta smiled. Perhaps she wasn't awake after all. Perhaps she was still keeping the fog at bay with the memories that came while she slept.

"Is that you?" she said, gazing up at the person leaning over her. Her body was limp and heavy with the sleep that had not yet left her completely, and she couldn't move. For a minute or so, neither of them said a word. There wasn't much to say. Then a sense of certainty began to seep into Britta's damaged brain. Memories rose to the surface. Long-forgotten feelings sparked into life. And she felt the fear take hold, the fear from which her increasing confusion had liberated her. Now she saw Death standing by the side of her bed, and her entire being protested at having to leave this life now, leave everything she had. She gripped the sheet with both hands, but only guttural noises emerged from her parched lips. Fear flooded her body, and her head thrashed from side to side. Desperately she tried to send a message, call to Herman for help, as if he could hear her through the thought waves she was sending into the ether. But she already knew that it was in vain. Death had come to collect her, his scythe would soon fall, and there was no one who could help her. She would die alone here in her bed. Without Herman. Without the girls. Without saying good-bye. At that moment the fog was gone, and her brain was clearer than it had been for a long time. With fear racing like a wild animal in her chest, she eventually managed to take a deep breath and let out a scream. Death didn't move. He simply looked down at her in the bed, looked and smiled. It wasn't an unpleasant smile, which made it all the more frightening.

Then Death leaned forward and picked up the pillow on Herman's side of the bed. Britta watched in terror as the whiteness came closer. The final fog.

Her body protested briefly, panicking because of the lack of air. She tried to take a breath, get some oxygen into her lungs. Her hands let go of the sheet, scrabbling wildly in the air. Met with resistance, with skin. Tore and scratched, fighting to live for just a little while longer.

Then there was only darkness.

22
Grini, outside Oslo, 1944

"Time to get up!" The voice of the guard echoed through the barracks. "Fall in for inspection in five minutes!"

With a huge effort Axel opened one eye at a time. For a second he was completely disoriented. The barracks was in darkness, and it was so early that virtually no light penetrated from outside. But it was still an improvement compared with the cell in which he had spent his solitary confinement during the first few months. He preferred the stench and the cramped conditions of the barracks to the long days of loneliness. There were thirty-five hundred prisoners in Grini, or so he had heard. That didn't surprise him. There were people wherever he turned, with a resigned expression on their faces that no doubt matched his own.

Axel sat up and rubbed the sleep from his eyes. The order to fall in for inspection came several times a day, whenever the guards felt like it, and God help anyone who was slow to comply. But today he found it difficult to drag himself out of bed. He had dreamed of Fjällbacka, dreamed of sitting up on Veddeberget, gazing out across the water and watching the fishing boats as they came in, laden with herring. He had almost heard the sound of the gulls screeching as they greedily circled the masts of the incoming boats. It was actually a pretty ugly noise, but it had somehow become a part of the town's soul. He had dreamed of the breeze blowing around him, warm and gentle on a summer's day. And the smell of seaweed, carried on the breeze all the way to the top of the hill where he would greedily breathe it in.

But it was impossible to cling to the dream; reality was much too cold and raw. Instead, he felt the coarse fabric of the blanket against his skin as he pushed it aside and swung his legs over the side of the rickety bunk. The hunger tore at his belly. They were given food, but far too little and far too infrequently.

"Out you go," the youngest of the guards said as he walked through the barracks. He stopped in front of Axel.

"It's cold today," he said in a friendly tone of voice.

Axel avoided meeting his eye. This was the same boy he had questioned when he first arrived; he had seemed friendlier than the others, and this had indeed turned out to be the case. He had never seen the boy abuse or humiliate anyone, as most of the other guards did. But the months in jail had drawn a clear boundary between them. Prisoner and guard. They were like two completely different creatures. Their lives were so disparate that Axel could hardly bring himself to look at the guards when they came into view. His own Norwegian Guards uniform was the main thing that marked him as an inferior human being. He had learned from the other prisoners that the uniform had been introduced after one of their number had escaped in 1941. He wondered how anyone could possibly have the strength to get away. He felt weak, completely lacking in energy, thanks to a combination of hard work, insufficient food, too little sleep, and too much anxiety about those back home. And too much misery.

"Better get a move on," the young guard said, giving him a gentle push.

Axel did as he was told and hurried. The consequences could be harsh for those who arrived late for morning inspection.

As he was walking down the steps to the yard, he suddenly stumbled. He lost his footing and felt himself falling forward, toward the guard, who was just in front of him. His arms flailed as he tried to regain his balance, but instead of air he felt the guard's uniform and body. With a heavy thud, Axel abruptly landed, and the air left his lungs as he took the impact on his chest. There was a brief silence, then he felt hands dragging him roughly to his feet.

"He attacked you," said another guard, who was clutching Axel's collar. He was called Jensen, and he was known for his cruelty toward the prisoners.

"I don't think . . . ," the young guard said hesitantly as he got up and brushed the dirt off his uniform.

"I said he attacked you!" Jensen's face was bright red. He seized every chance to make life difficult for those in his power. When he walked through the camp, the mass of men parted like the Red Sea before Moses.

"No, he—"

"I saw him go for you," the older man yelled, taking a menacing step forward. "Are you going to teach him a lesson, or am I?"

"But he—" The guard, who was no more than a boy, looked desperately at Axel and then at his colleague.

Axel gazed at him with indifference. He had long ago stopped reacting, stopped feeling. Whatever happened happened. If you resisted, you didn't survive.

"Right, in that case, I'll—" The older guard moved toward Axel, raising his rifle.

"No! I'll do it! It's my job," the boy said, his face pale as he stepped between them. He looked Axel in the eye, almost as if he were asking for forgiveness. Then he raised his hand and slapped Axel across the face.

"Is that your idea of punishment?" Jensen bellowed. A small crowd had gathered around them by now, and some of the other guards were laughing expectantly. Any interruption to the daily grind of prison life was welcome.

"Hit him harder!" Jensen insisted, his face growing even redder.

The boy looked at Axel once more, but still Axel refused to meet his gaze. A clenched fist shot out and hit Axel on the jaw. His head jerked back, but he was still on his feet.

"Harder!" Several of the guards had joined in, and beads of sweat glistened on the young guard's forehead. He gave up the attempt to make eye contact with Axel. His eyes were glassy now, and he bent down, picked up his rifle from the ground, and raised it, ready to strike.

Axel turned away out of pure reflex, and the blow struck him just above the left ear. It felt as if something inside had burst, and the pain was indescribable. When the next blow came, he took it full in the face. After that, he remembered nothing more. He was aware of nothing but the pain.

23

There was no sign on the door to indicate that these premises were occupied by Sweden's Friends—just a note above the mailbox stating NO JUNK MAIL, and a nameplate that said SVENSSON. Martin and Paula had been given the address by their colleagues in Uddevalla, who kept a watchful eye on the organization's activities.

They hadn't called in advance but had taken a chance on finding someone there during office hours. Martin rang the bell. A shrill tone could be heard inside, but at first nothing happened. He was about to try again when the door opened.

"Yes?" A man in his thirties gave them an inquiring look, frowning as he noticed their uniforms. The frown deepened when he saw Paula. For a few seconds he looked her up and down in silence in a way that made her want to knee him in the groin.

"So. How can I help the forces of law and order?" he asked nastily.

"We'd like a few words with someone from Sweden's Friends. Are we in the right place?"

"Sure. Come in." The man, who was tall, blond, and big in a kind of muscle-bound way, stepped back to let them in.

"I'm Martin Molin, and this is Paula Morales. Tanumshede police."

"You've come a long way," the man said, leading the way into a small office. "I'm Peter Lindgren." He sat down at the desk and pointed to two visitors' chairs.

Martin made a mental note of the name; he would check on Lindgren in the system as soon as he got back to the station. Something told him that the records would contain some very useful information about the man sitting opposite them.

"What can I do for you?" Peter leaned back and clasped his hands in his lap.

"We're investigating the murder of a man named Erik Frankel. Does the name sound familiar?" Paula made an effort to keep her voice steady. There was something about men like this that made her flesh creep. Ironically, that was probably exactly the way Peter Lindgren felt when he saw someone like her.

"Any reason why it should?" Peter said, addressing Martin rather than Paula.

"Yes," Martin said. "You've had a certain amount of . . . contact with him. Threats, to put it more accurately. But you know nothing about this?" His tone was skeptical.

Peter Lindgren shook his head. "No, that doesn't ring any bells. Do you have any proof of these . . . threats?" he asked with a smile.

Martin felt as if he was being scrutinized inside and out. After some hesitation, he said "What we do or don't have at this stage is irrelevant. But we know that your organization has threatened Erik Frankel. We also know that a man who is part of Sweden's Friends, Frans Ringholm, knew the victim and warned him about these threats."

"I wouldn't take Frans too seriously," Lindgren said with a dangerous glint in his eye. "He's well respected within our . . . organization, but Frans is no longer a young man, and there's a new generation ready to take over. Different times, different rules—and people like Frans don't always understand those rules."

"But you do?" Martin said.

Peter spread his hands wide. "You have to know when to follow the rules and when to break them. The important thing is to do whatever serves our cause in the long run."

"And your cause in this case would be what, exactly?" Paula could hear the hostility in her voice, which earned her a warning glance from Martin.

"A better society," Peter said calmly. "Those who have led this country have not governed it well. They have allowed . . . foreign elements to take up far too much space. Allowed what is Swedish, what is pure, to be pushed out." He gave Paula a challenging look; she swallowed hard several times, forcing herself to keep quiet. This was neither the time nor the place, and she was well aware that he was trying to provoke her.

"But we can sense that a wind of change is blowing. People have become more and more aware that we are heading for the edge of an abyss if we continue like this, if we permit those in power to keep on tearing down what our forefathers built. We can offer a better society."

"And in what way—theoretically, of course—would an elderly, retired history teacher constitute a threat to a . . . better society?"

"Theoretically"—Peter clasped his hands in his lap once more—"theoretically he wouldn't constitute much of a threat, of course. But he contributed to the propagation of a false narrative, a narrative that the victors in the Second World War have worked hard to put forward. And needless to say, that could not be tolerated. Theoretically."

Martin started to say something, but Peter interrupted him. Clearly he hadn't finished.

"All those images, all those accounts from concentration camps and the like are nothing more than pure fabrication, exaggerated lies that have been hammered into our consciousness over the years as the truth. And do you know why? In order to totally suppress the original message, the right message. It is those who were victorious in the war who write its history, and they decided to drown the reality of what had happened in blood, to distort the image that was presented to the world, so that no one would dare to stand up and ask if the right side had won. And Erik Frankel was a part of that obfuscation, that propaganda. And that is why—theoretically—someone like Erik Frankel would be an obstacle to the society we want to create."

"But as far as you are aware, your organization has not threatened him in any way whatsoever?" Martin gazed at Lindgren, knowing exactly what answer he was going to get.

"Absolutely not. We operate within the rules of democracy. Ballots. An election manifesto. Gaining power through the voice of the people. Anything else would be utterly alien to us." He looked at Paula, who clenched her fists in her lap. In her mind's eye, she could see the soldiers who had come and taken away her father. They had had that same look in their eyes.

"In that case, we won't take up any more of your time." Martin got to his feet. "The police in Uddevalla have passed on the names of the other board members, so naturally we will be speaking to them on this matter as well."

Peter stood up and nodded. "Of course. But none of them will say anything different. And as far as Frans is concerned

. . . I wouldn't pay too much attention to an old man who lives in the past."

Erica was finding it difficult to concentrate on her writing. She kept on thinking about her mother. She turned to the pile of articles and placed the picture on the top. It was so frustrating, staring at the faces of these young people without being able to find any answers. She bent over the picture, studying each of them in turn. Erik Frankel first of all. A serious expression. Stiff bearing. There was something sorrowful about him, and, without knowing if she was right or wrong, she drew the conclusion that the capture of his brother by the Germans had taken its toll. But he had had the same aura of seriousness and sorrow when she went to see him in June to ask about her mother's medal.

Erica moved along to the person standing next to Erik. Frans Ringholm. He looked good. Very good. Blond hair down past his collar, probably slightly longer than his parents would have wished. His smile was broad and charming. His arms were draped casually around the shoulders of those standing on either side of him; neither of them seemed to appreciate the gesture.

Erica studied the person to the right of Frans intently. Her mother. Elsy Moström. Admittedly, the expression on her face was slightly softer than Erica had ever seen, but there was a certain tension in her wistful smile, suggesting that she wasn't pleased about the placement of Frans's arm. Erica couldn't help thinking how pretty her mother was. She looked so nice. The Elsy she had grown up with had been cold, inaccessible. Nothing about the girl in the picture gave any hint of the unapproachable woman she would become. Slowly Erica ran one finger gently over Elsy's face. Everything could have been so different if this had been the mother she had gotten to know. What happened to this girl? What took away all the gentleness?

Why had that wistfulness been replaced by indifference? Why was she never able to put those soft arms, visible in the short sleeves of her floral dress, around her daughters? Why was she never able to give them a hug?

Erica sadly moved on to the next person in the picture. Britta wasn't looking at the camera; her attention was focused on Elsy. Or Frans. It was impossible to tell. Erica reached for a magnifying glass and held it over Britta's face, screwing up her eyes in order to see the image as clearly as possible. She still couldn't be sure, but her first impression was that Britta looked angry. The corners of her mouth were turned down. There was a tension in her jawline. And the look in her eyes . . . Erica was almost certain: Britta was staring at Elsy or Frans, or perhaps both of them.

And so to the last person in the picture. Roughly the same age as the others. Also blond, like Frans, but with shorter, curly hair. Tall but slender, with a pensive expression on his face. Not happy, not sad. Pensive was the best description Erica could come up with.

She read the article again. Hans Olavsen was a Norwegian resistance fighter who had escaped from Norway on board the *Elfrida*, a fishing boat from Fjällbacka. He had been given a safe passage by the boat's skipper, Elof Moström, and according to the article he was now celebrating the end of the war with his friends in Fjällbacka.

Erica returned the sheet of paper to the pile. There was something about the dynamic between the young people in that picture, something that felt . . . damn, she couldn't put her finger on it. Call it what you like—gut feeling, intuition. She just knew that the answers to all her questions were here somewhere, and the more she found out, the more questions she had. She knew she had to learn more about this picture, about the relationship between the friends and about Hans Olavsen, the Norwegian resistance fighter. And there were only two people left to ask: Axel Frankel and Britta Johansson. Britta was the closest; Erica had to find an explanation for the anger in her eyes. She was reluctant to bother the confused old lady again, but if she could just explain to Britta's husband why she needed to speak to his wife, perhaps he would understand. Perhaps he would allow her to talk to Britta again, hopefully in a period of lucidity. Tomorrow, Erica decided. Tomorrow she would take the bull by the horns and go there again.

Something told her that Britta had the answers she needed.

24
Fjällbacka 1944

The war had taken its toll on Elof Moström. All those trips across the water, which was no longer his friend but his enemy. He had always loved the sea off Bohuslän. He loved the way it moved, the way it smelled, the way it sounded as it surged against the bow of his boat. But since the war had begun, his friendly relationship with the sea had changed. The sea was now his enemy. Danger lurked beneath its surface, mines that could blow him and his crew sky-high at any moment. And the Germans patrolling the waters weren't much better. You never knew what they were going to come up with next. The sea had become unpredictable, in a way that was completely different from what the Swedes had been used to, what they had come to expect. Storms, the risk of running aground—those were things the Swedes had learned to deal with, things they could cope with because of generations of experience. And if nature got the upper hand, they accepted it with composure, with equanimity.

This new unpredictability was much worse. And if they survived the trips across the water, further dangers awaited them once they had anchored in the harbors where they were to load and unload their cargoes. The occasion on which they had lost Axel Frankel to the Germans had provided a clear reminder of that. Elof stared out toward the horizon, allowing himself to think of the boy for a few moments. So courageous. So apparently untouchable. Now no one knew where he was. Elof had heard rumors suggesting that he had been taken to Grini, but he had no way of knowing whether they were true, or if Axel was still there. It was said that a number of the prisoners held in Norway had begun to be transported to Germany. Perhaps that was where the boy was. Perhaps he was no longer alive. After all, a whole year had elapsed since the Germans took him, and no one had heard a thing. He couldn't help but fear the worst. Elof took a deep breath. He bumped into the boys' parents from time to time. Dr. Frankel and his wife—she was a doctor too. But he couldn't bring himself to look them in the eye. Whenever possible, he would cross the street and hurry past, his eyes fixed on the sidewalk. Somehow he felt as if he ought to have been able to do more. He had no idea what that might have been. But something. Perhaps he should have refused to take the boy with him.

It broke his heart to see the boy's brother. Erik, with his serious little face. Not that he had ever been the life and soul of the party, but since Axel disappeared he had become even quieter. Elof had been intending to have a word with Elsy; he didn't like her spending time with those boys, Erik and Frans. Not that he had anything against Erik; there was a kindness in his eyes. But Frans . . . hooligan was the word that came to mind there. Neither of them was a suitable companion for Elsy.

They came from two different classes. Two completely different groups of people. He and Hilma might as well have been born on a different planet from the Frankels and the Ringholms, and their worlds should never meet. Nothing good could ever come of it. It was probably okay when they were little, playing tag and hide-and-seek. But they were older now. Nothing good could come of it.

Hilma had mentioned it to him several times. Asked him to have a word with the girl. But so far he hadn't had the heart to do it. Things were difficult enough with the war. Friends were perhaps the only luxury young people had these days, and who was he to deprive Elsy of her friends? But sooner or later he would have to do something about it. Boys would be boys, after all. Childhood games would soon turn into secret embraces; he knew that from his own experience. He too had once been young, although these days it felt like a lifetime ago. It would soon be time for the two worlds to separate. That was how things were, and how they must remain. It was impossible to change the natural order of things.

"Captain! You'd better come and have a look at this."

Elof was startled out of his musings and looked in the direction from which the voice had come. One of the crew was urgently waving him over. Elof frowned and headed in his direction. They were out on the open water, and it would be several hours before they reached Fjällbacka.

"We have a stowaway," Calle Ingvarsson said drily, pointing to the hold. Elof looked on openmouthed as a boy who had been curled up behind a sack came creeping out.

"I found him when I heard something from down below. He was coughing so much, it's a wonder we didn't hear him on deck," Calle said, tucking a plug of snuff under his top lip. He made a face. Wartime snuff was nothing more than an unsatisfactory substitute.

"Who are you, and what are you doing on my boat?" Elof said harshly. He wondered if he should call for reinforcements from one of the crew members up above.

"My name is Hans Olavsen and I came aboard in Kristiansand," the boy said in a lilting Norwegian accent. He held out his hand, and after a brief hesitation Elof shook it. The boy looked him straight in the eye. "I was hoping to get to Sweden. The Germans have . . . well, let's just say I can't remain on Norwegian soil if I value my life."

Elof stood in silence for a long time, thinking things over. He didn't like to be deceived in this way, but on the other hand . . . what else could the boy have done? Walked up to him in front of all the Germans patrolling the harbor and politely asked if he might travel to Sweden?

"Where are you from?" he said eventually, looking the boy up and down.

"Oslo."

"And what have you done that makes it impossible for you to stay in Norway?"

"People don't talk about what they have been forced to do during the war," Hans said as a shadow passed across his face. "But let's just say that I can no longer be of any use to the resistance movement."

He must have been taking people across the border, Elof thought. It was a dangerous job, and if the Germans were on to you it was best to get away while you still could. He felt himself beginning to relent. He thought of Axel, who had made the trip to Norway so often without considering what the consequences might be when it came to his own safety; he had paid the price. Was Elof a lesser man than the doctor's eighteen-year-old son? He made up his mind on the spot.

"Very well, you can stay. We're heading for Fjällbacka. Have you had anything to eat?"

Hans shook his head and swallowed. "Not since the day before yesterday. The journey from Oslo was . . . difficult. I couldn't take a direct route."

"Calle, see that the boy gets some food inside him. I need to go and make sure we get home in one piece. The Germans insist on scattering those goddamn mines all over the place." He shook his head and set off up the steps. When he turned around, he met the boy's gaze; he was overwhelmed by the sympathy he felt. How old could he be? Eighteen, no more. And yet there was so much in those eyes that shouldn't be there. Lost youth, and a loss of the innocence that should be a part of that youth. The war had undeniably claimed many victims. Not only those who were dead.

25

Gösta was feeling slightly guilty. If he had done his job properly, perhaps Mattias Larsson wouldn't be lying in the hospital now. Then again, he didn't actually know if it would have made a difference. But he might have found out that Per had broken into the Frankel house back in the spring, which might have altered the course of events. When Gösta had been at Adam's house taking his fingerprints, the boy had actually mentioned that someone in school had said that there was "a load of cool stuff" in the house. That was what had been nagging away at the back of his mind, irritating him, mocking him. If only he had been a little more attentive. A little more conscientious. To put it briefly, done his job properly. He sighed—that special Gösta sigh, honed to perfection through years of practice. He knew exactly what he had to do now. He had to try and make things right, as far as possible.

He went down to the garage and took the remaining squad car; Martin and Paula had gone to Uddevalla in the other one. Forty minutes later, he parked outside the hospital in Strömstad. The receptionist informed him that Mattias's condition had stabilized, and told Gösta how to get to his room.

He took a deep breath before he pushed open the door. There were bound to be members of the family there. Gösta didn't like meeting relatives. Things always got so emotional, making it hard to maintain a professional distance. And yet he had sometimes surprised both his colleagues and himself by showing a certain sensitivity in his dealings with people in difficult situations. If he had been able to summon up the energy and the enthusiasm, he might have been able to use that skill in his job, turn it into an asset. Instead, it was a rare and not particularly welcome visitor.

"Have you got him?" A big man in a suit with his tie askew leapt to his feet when Gösta walked in. He had had his arm around a woman in tears; judging by the resemblance to the boy in the bed, she was Mattias's mother. Although to be fair, any similarity Gösta noticed came from his memories of the encounter with Mattias outside the Frankel house. The boy in the bed didn't look like anyone. His face was one swollen, red-raw wound, with bruises beginning to form. His lips were twice the normal size, and it looked as if he could just about see through one eye; the other was completely closed.

"When I get hold of that . . . bastard," Mattias's father swore, clenching his fists. There were tears in his eyes, and once again Gösta acknowledged that this business of relatives and their emotions was something he could easily do without.

But he was here now. Might as well get it over and done with. Especially since the longer he looked at Mattias's damaged face, the more guilty he felt.

"Let us do our job," Gösta said, sitting down on a chair beside them. He introduced himself, then looked Mattias's parents in the eye in order to be certain that they were listening.

"We've brought Per Ringholm in for questioning. He's admitted the assault, and there will be consequences for him. At this stage I can't say what those consequences will be; that's up to the prosecutor to decide."

"But he is locked up?" Mattias's mother said, her lips trembling.

"Not at the moment. It's only in exceptional cases that the prosecutor would recommend that a minor should be arrested. In practice it's highly unusual. Per has therefore been sent home with his mother while we continue our inquiries. We've also contacted social services."

"So he gets to go home with his mom, while my son is lying here and—" Mattias's father's voice broke as he looked in disbelief from Gösta to his son.

"For the moment, yes. But as I said, there will be consequences; I can promise you that. I would like to have a few words with Mattias, if possible, just to make sure we've covered everything."

The boy's parents looked at one another, then nodded.

"Okay, but only if he's up to it. He's been conscious just occasionally; they've got him on medication for the pain."

"We'll let Mattias call the shots," Gösta said reassuringly as he moved his chair closer to the bed. Initially he had some difficulty in understanding the slurred speech, but eventually he had confirmation of what had taken place, and it matched Per's account.

When he had finished asking questions, he turned to the parents again. "Could I possibly take his fingerprints while I'm here?"

Once again they exchanged glances, and Mattias's father spoke for them both. "I guess so. If it's necessary in order to. . . ." He couldn't finish the sentence; his eyes filled with tears as he looked at his son.

"It'll only take a minute," Gösta said, getting out his fingerprint kit.

A short while later, he was sitting in the car looking at the box containing the set of prints. They might have no significance whatsoever in the case. But he had done his job. Eventually. It was small consolation.

"Last stop for today, okay?" Martin said as they got out of the car at the newspaper's main office.

"Yes, time we were heading home soon," Paula said, looking at her watch. She hadn't said a word since they'd left the headquarters of Sweden's Friends, and Martin had left her to her thoughts. He understood that it must be difficult for her to be confronted with a person like that, someone who judged her before she had even said hello, who saw only the color of her skin and nothing else. He found that sort of thinking deeply unpleasant, but with his pale, freckled skin and his bright red hair, he had never been subjected to the kind of looks that Paula got. There had been the odd spate of teasing in the school yard because of his hair color, but that was a long time ago, and it wasn't the same thing at all.

"We'd like to speak to Kjell Ringholm," Paula said, leaning on the reception desk.

"One moment, please." The receptionist picked up the phone and informed Kjell that he had visitors.

"Please take a seat; he'll be with you shortly."

"Thank you." They sat down in the armchairs arranged around a low table and waited. After a few moments, a slightly rotund man with dark hair and a bushy beard came toward them. It occurred to Paula that he looked a lot like Björn. Or Benny. She could never tell them apart.

"Kjell Ringholm," he said, holding out his hand. His handshake was firm, almost painfully so, and Martin couldn't help wincing.

"Let's go to my office," Kjell said, leading the way. "Please sit down. I thought I knew all the police officers in Uddevalla,

but I haven't seen you two before. Whom do you work for?"
He sat down at his desk, which was cluttered with papers.

"We're not based in Uddevalla. We're from Tanumshede."

"Really?" Kjell looked surprised, but for a second Paula
thought she had glimpsed something else. "So what's on your
mind?" He leaned back, folding his hands over his stomach.

"First of all, we have to tell you that we picked up your son
earlier today; he had assaulted a classmate."

The man behind the desk sat up straight. "What the hell are
you saying? You picked up Per? Who did he . . . ? How is . . . ?"
He stumbled over the words that came pouring out of his mouth,
and Paula waited calmly for him to pause so that they could answer
his questions.

"He attacked a schoolmate by the name of Mattias Larsson
in the school yard. Mattias has been taken to Strömstad hospital and, according to the latest reports, his condition is stable,
although he has sustained a number of serious injuries."

"What. . . ." Kjell seemed to be finding it difficult to take
in what they were saying. "But why did nobody call me? It
sounds as if all this happened hours ago."

"His mother came to the station and sat with Per while we
questioned him, then he was allowed to go home with her."

"It's not an ideal situation, as you no doubt noticed."

"We realized during the interview that there were certain
. . . problems." Martin hesitated. "Which is why we've asked
social services to check things out."

Kjell sighed. "Yes, I should have dealt with it earlier. But
something always got in the way . . . I don't know. . . ." He
stared at a photograph on his desk; it showed a blond woman
and two children about nine or ten. There was a brief silence.

"So what happens now?"

"The prosecutor will review the incident and decide how
to proceed. But this is a serious matter."

Kjell waved his hand. "I know, I understand. Believe me, I'm not taking this lightly. I fully appreciate the gravity of the situation. But I'd just like a firmer idea of what you think. . . ." He looked at the photograph again, then turned his attention back to the two officers.

"Hard to say," Paula replied. "But my guess would be a juvenile treatment center."

Kjell nodded wearily. "Perhaps that would be for the best, in a way. Per has been . . . difficult for a long time, and maybe this will bring him to his senses. But life hasn't been easy for him. I haven't been around as much as I should have been, and his mother . . . well, I'm sure you could see what was going on there. But she hasn't always been that way. It was the divorce that. . . ." His voice died away, and his eyes drifted to the photograph once more. "She took it very hard."

"There was something else," Martin said, leaning forward and gazing intently at Kjell.

"Yes?"

"During the interview, it emerged that Per had broken into a house back in June. And that he was caught by the owner of the house, Erik Frankel. We understand that you are already aware of this incident?"

For a moment Kjell didn't say a word, then he slowly nodded. "That's true. Erik Frankel called me after he'd locked Per in the library, and I went over there." He gave a wry smile. "It was quite amusing, actually, seeing Per locked in among all those volumes. That was probably the closest contact he's ever had with books."

"Breaking into someone's house isn't particularly amusing," Paula said acidly. "It could have ended very badly."

"You're right, I know, I'm sorry. Bad joke." Kjell smiled apologetically. "But both Erik and I agreed that it was best not to make a big thing out of it; Erik thought it would teach Per a lesson, and that he was unlikely to do something like that again. That's all. I picked Per up, gave him a scolding, and. . . ." He shrugged, a resigned expression on his face.

"Apparently you and Erik Frankel discussed something else while you were in the house. Per heard Erik say that he had some information that might interest you in your capacity as a journalist, and he claims that you agreed to meet at a later date. Does that ring any bells?"

After a short silence, Kjell shook his head. "No, I have to say I don't remember that at all. Per either made it up or misunderstood. Erik just said that I was welcome to contact him if I needed any help with background information on the Nazis."

Martin and Paula regarded him with considerable skepticism. Neither of them believed a single word he said. It was obvious that he was lying, but they had no way of proving it.

"Do you know if there was any contact between Erik Frankel and your father?" Martin said eventually.

Kjell's shoulders dropped slightly, as if he was relieved at the change of subject.

"Not as far as I know. But then again, I have no idea what my father gets up to, nor am I interested. Except insofar as it affects what I write."

"Doesn't it feel odd?" Paula asked. "Hanging your father out to dry like that?"

"You of all people ought to understand the importance of actively opposing antiforeigner feeling," Kjell replied. "It's like a cancerous growth on our society, and we must fight it with every means we have at our disposal. And if my father happens to be a part of that cancerous growth, well, that's his choice." Kjell spread his hands wide. "In any case, the only bond between me and my father is that he happened to get my mother pregnant. All through my childhood I only saw him in the visitors' rooms at various prisons, and as soon as I was old enough to think for myself and make my own decisions, I said he wasn't a person I wanted in my life."

"So you have no contact with Frans? What about Per?" Martin asked, more out of curiosity than because it had any relevance to the investigation.

"I have no contact whatsoever with my father. Unfortunately, he has managed to fill Per's head with a lot of foolish nonsense. When Per was small we could make sure they didn't have anything to do with one another, but now he's older and is free to move around . . . let's just say we haven't been able to prevent it as we would have wished."

"Well, I think that's about it. For now," Martin added as he got to his feet. Paula followed his example.

On the way out the door, Martin stopped and turned around. "You're absolutely certain you have no information about or from Erik Frankel that might be of use to us?"

Their eyes met, and for a second it looked as if Kjell might be wavering. Then he shook his head and said, firmly, "No, nothing. Nothing at all."

They didn't believe him that time either.

Margareta was concerned. No one had answered the phone at her parents' house since Herman had been over the previous day. That was unusual, and worrying. They always made a point of letting the girls know if they were going anywhere, but these days they hardly ever went away. She rang home every evening for a chat; it was a ritual they had observed for many years, and she couldn't recall an occasion when her parents hadn't picked up. But this time when she called the number that was second nature to her, the phone just rang and rang into the emptiness, and no one answered. She had wanted to go over and check on them the previous evening, but her husband, Owe, had persuaded her to leave it until the next day. They had probably just gone to bed early. But now it was morning, and there was still no answer. Margareta could feel herself getting more and more anxious, until she was almost certain that something had happened. It was the only explanation she could come up with.

She pulled on her shoes and jacket and headed resolutely for her parents' house. It was a ten-minute walk, and she spent every second cursing herself for having listened to Owe rather than going over there the night before. Something was wrong, she could feel it.

When she was only a hundred yards away, she saw someone standing at the front door. She tried to see who it was, but didn't recognize Erica Falck, the writer, until she got closer.

"Can I help you?" she said pleasantly, but she could hear the anxiety permeating her voice.

"I . . . I was looking for Britta. But there's no answer. . . ." The blond woman seemed to be at something of a loss.

"I've been calling them since yesterday and no one has picked up the phone, so I've just come to make sure they're all right," Margareta said. "You can come in and wait in the hall." She reached up to one of the beams holding up the little roof above the door and removed a key. Her hand was shaking slightly as she inserted it in the lock.

"Come in, I'll go and take a look around," she said, suddenly feeling grateful that there was someone else there. She should really have called one or both of her sisters before she came over, but then she wouldn't have been able to hide how serious she thought the situation might be, how the worry was eating her up inside.

She went through the ground floor; everything was neat and tidy, just as it always was.

"Mom? Dad?" she called, but got no reply. By now the fear was beginning to tear at her, and she was finding it difficult to breathe. She should have called her sisters, she should have called her sisters.

"Stay here while I go and look upstairs," she said to Erica. She didn't rush up the stairs; she walked slowly, terrified of what she might find. Everything was so unnaturally quiet.

But when she reached the top step, she heard a faint noise. It sounded like a sob. Almost like a small child crying. She stopped for a moment to figure out where it was coming from, and soon realized it was her parents' bedroom. With her heart pounding, she hurried over and slowly pushed open the door. It took a few seconds to process what she was seeing. Then she heard, as if from far away, her own voice screaming for help.

It was Per who answered the door.

"Grandpa," he said, looking like a puppy hoping for a pat on the head.

"What have you done now?" Frans said brusquely, pushing past him into the hall.

"But I . . . he . . . he was talking a load of crap. Was I just supposed to take it?" Per sounded hurt. He had thought that his grandfather would understand, even if no one else did. "Besides, it was nothing compared to the stuff you've done," he said sullenly, even though he couldn't look Frans in the eye.

"And that's exactly why I know what I'm talking about." Frans took hold of Per's shoulders and shook him, forcing his grandson to look at him. "We'll sit down and have a chat, and maybe I can get some sense into that stubborn head of yours. Where's your mom, anyway?" Frans looked around for Carina, ready to defend his right to be there and speak to his grandchild.

"She's probably sleeping it off," Per said, slouching into the kitchen. "She hit the bottle as soon as we got home yesterday, and she was still at it when I went to bed. I haven't heard anything from her in a while."

"I'll go and see if she's okay. You make some coffee," Frans said.

"But I don't know how to . . . ," Per began to object in a whining tone of voice.

"In that case, it's high time you learned," Frans snapped, heading for Carina's bedroom.

"Carina," he said briskly as he walked in. The only sound was a loud snore. She was about to fall out of bed, and one arm was trailing on the floor. The room stank of vomit and stale booze.

"For fuck's sake," Frans said. Then he took a deep breath and went over to the bed. He put one hand on her shoulder and shook her.

"Time to wake up, Carina." Still no reaction. He looked around. The bathroom opened off her bedroom, and he went in and began to run a bath. As the water poured into the tub, he began to undress her, a look of disgust on his face. It didn't take long; she was only wearing a bra and pants. He wrapped the sheet around her, carried her next door, and simply dropped her into the water.

"What the hell," his ex-daughter-in-law spluttered, suddenly wide awake. "What the hell are you doing?"

Frans didn't reply. Instead he went over to her closet, opened the door, and pulled out some clean clothes. He placed them on the toilet seat next to the bath.

"Per's making coffee. Get yourself washed and dressed and come to the kitchen."

For a moment it looked as if she was thinking of objecting, but then she nodded submissively.

"So, have you mastered the art of using the coffee machine?" Frans asked Per, who was sitting at the kitchen table picking at his cuticles.

"It'll probably taste like shit," Per mumbled sourly, "but at least I tried."

Frans studied the pitch-black liquid that had begun to trickle down into the glass pot. "Well, it sure looks strong enough."

They sat in silence opposite one another for a long time, Frans and his grandson. It was such a strange feeling to see his own history in somebody else—some of his father's traits were definitely noticeable in the boy. The father he still wished he had killed. Perhaps everything would have been different if he had. Used all the anger boiling away inside him, directed it at the person who actually deserved it. Instead, it had come hissing out in all directions, with no clear target. It was still there, he knew that, but he no longer allowed it to rule him, as it had when he was younger. Now he was the one who controlled his rage, not vice versa. And that was what he had to make his grandson understand. There was nothing wrong with the anger itself, it was just a matter of ensuring that you were the one who decided when it was the right moment to release it. Anger was a carefully aimed arrow, not an ax to be swung wildly around your head. He had tried that before. The only thing it had brought him was a life mainly spent in prison, and a son who could barely bring himself to look at him. There was no one else. The members of the organization were not his friends. He had never made the mistake of thinking they were, or of trying to make them his friends. They were all too full of their own personal anger to be able to make that kind of connection with other people. They shared a goal. Nothing more.

He looked at Per and saw his father. But he also saw himself. And Kjell. The son he had tried to get to know during those short prison visits, and during the brief periods when he was out. An undertaking that was doomed to failure. To be honest, he didn't even know whether he loved his son. Perhaps he had loved him once. Perhaps his heart had leapt when Rakel turned up at the prison with their son. He could no longer remember.

As he sat there at the table with his grandson, the strange thing was that the only love he could really recall was the love he had felt for Elsy. It was sixty years ago, but it had etched itself in his memory. Elsy and his grandson. They were the only people he had ever really cared about, the only people who had ever managed to evoke any emotions in him. There was nothing else. His father had killed everything. Frans hadn't thought about his father for a long time, or the rest of it. But suddenly the past had been brought to life. And now it was time to think about it.

"Kjell will go crazy if he finds out you came here." Carina was standing in the doorway. She was swaying slightly, though she was clean and dressed. Her hair was dripping wet, but she had draped a towel around her shoulders to protect her shirt.

"I don't care what Kjell thinks," Frans said firmly. He got up to pour coffee for himself and Carina.

"That looks disgusting," she said as she sat down and stared into the cup, which was filled to the brim with pitch-black liquid.

"Just drink it." Frans started opening cupboards and drawers.

"What are you doing?" Carina took a mouthful of coffee and made a face. "Keep your fucking nose out of my cupboards!"

He didn't say a word but began removing bottles, one after another, and methodically poured the contents into the sink.

"You've got no right to interfere!" she yelled. Per got up to leave the room.

"Stay exactly where you are," Frans said, pointing a commanding finger at him. "We are going to sort this out right now."

Per immediately obeyed, sinking back into his chair.

An hour later, when all the booze was gone, only the truth remained.

Kjell stared at the computer screen, his guilty conscience nagging away at him. Ever since the visit from the police the day before, he had been trying to pluck up the courage to go and see Per and Carina, but he just couldn't do it. He didn't know where to start. What frightened him was the fact that he was beginning to give up. He could fight any number of external enemies. He could attack those in power or the neo-Nazis, he could tilt at the most enormous windmills without ever feeling tired; but when it came to his former family, when it came to Per and Carina, it was as if he no longer had any strength left. His guilty conscience had consumed it all.

He looked at the photograph of Beata and the children. Of course he loved Magda and Loke, and he wouldn't want to be without them . . . but at the same time everything had moved so fast, gone so wrong. He had ended up in a situation that simply carried him along with it, and he still wondered sometimes whether it had brought more bad than good. Perhaps the timing had been unfortunate. Perhaps he had been in the middle of some kind of midlife crisis, and Beata had turned up at exactly the wrong moment. At first he hadn't believed it could be true—that a pretty young girl like her could be interested in someone like him; after all, she really should have regarded him as an old man. But it had been true, and he had been unable to resist it. Going to bed with her, touching her firm, naked body, seeing the admiration shining from her eyes; it had all been so intoxicating. He hadn't been able to think straight, to take a step back and make rational decisions. Instead, he had allowed himself to be swept along. Ironically, he had just begun to show the first signs of coming to his senses when the situation had slipped from his grasp. He had begun to tire of never meeting with any counterarguments in their discussions, of the fact that she knew nothing about the moon landings or the revolt in Hungary. He had even begun to tire of her smooth skin beneath his fingers.

He could still remember the moment when everything collapsed. He remembered as if it were yesterday. The meeting in the café. Her big blue eyes shining with joy as she told him that he was going to be a father, that they were going to have a child together, and now he would have to tell Carina, as he had promised to do for so long.

He had understood in that moment what a huge mistake he had made. He remembered the heavy feeling in his chest, the realization that this mistake couldn't be fixed. He had briefly considered leaving her there at the table. Walking away, going home and settling down on the sofa next to

Carina, watching the news while five-year-old Per slept safely in his bed.

But his male instinct told him that that option was not available to him. There were mistresses who didn't tell the wife, and there were those who did. He knew instinctively which category Beata fell into. She wouldn't care whom or what she destroyed, if he destroyed her first. She would trample all over his life, ruin everything without so much as a backward glance. And he would be left sitting there among the wreckage.

And so he had chosen the coward's way out. He couldn't bear the thought of being alone, sitting in some disgusting bachelor pad, staring at the walls and wondering where the hell his life had gone. So he had chosen the only way that was left: Beata's way. She had won. He had walked out on Carina and Per, dumped them like trash by the roadside as if they weren't good enough for him. He had humiliated and crushed Carina, and he had lost Per. That was the price he had paid for the feeling of young skin beneath his fingers.

Perhaps he could have held on to Per, if only he had had the strength to get over the guilt that settled on his chest like a block of stone every time he thought about the family he had left behind. But he just couldn't do it. He had made sporadic efforts, played the authority figure, played dad on rare occasions, with woeful results.

And now he no longer knew his son. Per was a stranger to him. And Kjell just didn't have the energy to try anymore. He had turned into his father. That was the bitterest truth of all: after a lifetime of hating the father who had discarded Kjell and his mother and chosen a life they had no part of, Kjell had done exactly the same thing with his own family.

Kjell slammed his fist down on the desk, trying to replace the pain in his heart with a physical pain. It didn't help, so instead he opened the bottom drawer to look at the only thing that could divert his thoughts from the place that was so painful to visit.

He stared at the folder. For a moment he had been tempted to hand over the material to the police, but the professional journalist in him had put the brakes on at the last minute. He hadn't gotten much from Erik. When he came to Kjell's office, he had spent most of the time talking in circles and had seemed unsure of what he wanted to say, how much he was prepared to reveal. At one point, Kjell had thought he was about to leave without having revealed anything at all.

He opened the folder. He wished he had had time to ask Erik more, find out what he wanted Kjell to do, where he should start searching. All he had was a few newspaper articles that Erik had given him, without comment or explanation.

"What am I supposed to do with these?" Kjell had asked.

"That's your job," Erik had replied. "I realize it might seem strange, but I can't give you all the answers. I just don't have the strength. But I'm giving you the tools; the rest is up to you."

And then he had walked away. Left Kjell at his desk, gazing at a folder containing three newspaper articles.

Kjell scratched his beard and opened the folder. He had already read the material several times, but things kept getting in the way, and he hadn't had time to focus on it. To be honest, he had also wondered whether there was any point in spending a lot of time on it. The old man could have been senile, and if the story really was as explosive as he had hinted, why hadn't he just come out with it? But now things were completely different. Erik Frankel had been murdered. And suddenly the folder was burning Kjell's fingers.

It was time to roll up his sleeves and get down to work, and he knew exactly where to begin. The only common denominator in all three articles: a Norwegian resistance fighter by the name of Hans Olavsen.

26
Fjällbacka 1944

"Hilma!" Something in Elof's tone of voice brought both his wife and daughter rushing to meet him.

"What's all the shouting about?" Hilma said, but stopped dead when she saw that Elof had company.

"Have we got a guest?" she said, nervously drying her hands on her apron. "And here I am in the middle of doing the dishes. . . ."

"It's fine," Elof said reassuringly. "This young man doesn't care about all that. He came in on the boat with us today. He's on the run from the Germans."

The boy held out his hand to Hilma and, as she shook it, bowed his head.

"Hans Olavsen," he said in his musical Norwegian accent; he extended his hand to Elsy, who shook it awkwardly and gave a little curtsy.

"He's had a difficult journey to Sweden, so perhaps we could offer him some refreshments," Elof said. He hung up his sailor's cap and gave his coat to Elsy, who stood there clutching it.

"Don't just stand there, girl; hang my coat up," he said sternly, but he couldn't help gently stroking his daughter's cheek. Given the dangers that every voyage now involved, it always felt like a gift when he was able to return home to Elsy and Hilma. He cleared his throat, disconcerted at having revealed such emotion in front of a stranger, and gestured toward the other room.

"Come in, come in. I'm sure Hilma will find us something to eat and drink," he said, sitting down at the kitchen table.

"We haven't much to offer," Hilma said, her eyes downcast. "But you are very welcome to share what little we do have."

"I'm very grateful," the boy said, sitting opposite Elof as he hungrily eyed the sandwiches Hilma had laid out on the table.

"Come along, help yourself," she said, and went over to the cupboard to pour each of the men a little drop of the hard stuff. It was expensive, but entirely appropriate for an occasion such as this.

They ate in silence for a while. When there was only one sandwich left, Elof pushed the plate across to the Norwegian, urging him with a glance to take it. Elsy watched surreptitiously as she helped her mother with the dishes. This was so exciting! To think that someone who had fled from the Germans was sitting in their kitchen, and had come all the way from Norway! She couldn't wait to tell the others. A thought struck her, and she almost blurted it out. But her father must have had the same idea, because he asked the question at that very moment.

"By the way, the Germans captured a boy from our village. It's over a year ago now, but I wonder if you . . . ?" Elof looked hopefully at the boy.

"It's very unlikely that I would know anything about him. There are so many people coming and going. What's his name?"

"Axel Frankel," Elof said, still hopeful. But the disappointment showed in his eyes when the boy thought for a while and then slowly shook his head.

"No, I'm sorry. We haven't come across anyone of that name. I don't think so, anyway. You haven't heard anything about what's happened to him? Has no one been able to supply a little more information?"

"I'm afraid not," Elof replied. "The Germans picked him up in Kristiansand, and we've heard nothing since. For all we know, he could be—"

"No, Father, that's not possible!" The tears welled up in Elsy's eyes, and she ran upstairs to her room feeling terribly embarrassed. She couldn't believe she had humiliated herself and her parents in that way, crying like a baby in front of a total stranger.

"Does your daughter know this . . . Axel?" the Norwegian boy said, sounding concerned as he stared after her.

"His younger brother is a friend of hers. He's taken it very badly, and so has the rest of Axel's family, of course," Elof said with a sigh.

A dark shadow passed across Hans Olavsen's face. "Yes, many people have suffered because of this war," he said. Elof could tell that he had witnessed things no boy of his age should have to see.

"What about your own family?" Elof said gently. Hilma, who was busy drying a plate by the sink, stopped to listen.

"I don't know where they are," Hans said eventually, looking down at the table. "When the war is over, if it ever ends, I'll start looking for them. I can't go back to Norway until then."

Hilma looked at Elof and, after a silent conversation conducted entirely through an exchange of glances, they were agreed. Elof cleared his throat.

"During the summer we usually rent out the house to visitors while we live in a room down in the basement. But for the

rest of the year, that room is empty. Perhaps you would like to
. . . stay here for a while and rest up, decide what you're going
to do next? And I can probably find a job for you as well; not
full-time, perhaps, but at least you'd have some money in your
pocket. I would of course have to inform the local police that
I've taken you in, but as long as I promise to take responsibility
for you, that shouldn't be a problem."

"Only if you will allow me to pay for the room with the
money I earn," said Hans, looking at them with a mixture of
gratitude and guilt.

Elof exchanged another glance with Hilma, then nodded.
"That's fine. Any contribution is welcome during wartime."

"I'll go and get the room ready," Hilma said, putting on
her coat.

"I really do appreciate this," the boy said, bowing his head—
but not before Elof had seen the tears shining in his eyes.

"Don't mention it," he said awkwardly. "Don't mention it."

27

"Help!"

Erica gave a start as she heard the cry from upstairs. She rushed toward the sound and took the stairs in just a few strides.

"What is it?" she said, but stopped dead when she saw Margareta's face. She was standing in the doorway of one of the bedrooms; Erica moved toward her and inhaled sharply when a large double bed came into view.

"Daddy," Margareta whimpered as she went back into the room. Erica remained in the doorway, unable to understand what she was seeing and what she ought to do now.

"Daddy . . . ," Margareta said again.

Herman was lying on the bed. He was staring blankly into space, and he didn't react when Margareta spoke to him. Britta was lying beside him. Her face was white and stiff, and there was no doubt that she was dead. Herman was close beside her, his arms wrapped around her rigid body.

"I killed her," he said quietly. Margareta gasped.

"What are you saying, Dad? Of course you didn't kill Mom!"

"I killed her," he repeated in a monotone, clutching his dead wife even more tightly.

His daughter walked around the bed and sat down next to him. Gently she tried to loosen his vise-like grip, and after a few attempts she succeeded. She stroked his forehead and spoke to him in a low voice.

"Dad, it wasn't your fault. Mom wasn't very well. Her heart probably gave up. It's not your fault, you must realize that."

"It was me, I killed her," he said, staring at a mark on the wall.

Margareta turned to Erica. "Could you call an ambulance, please?"

Erica hesitated. "Shall I call the police too?"

"My father is in shock. He doesn't know what he's talking about. There's no need for the police," Margareta said sharply. Then she turned back to her father and took his hand.

"Let me take care of this now, Dad. I'll call Anna-Greta and Birgitta and we'll help you. We're here for you."

Herman didn't reply; he simply lay there motionless, letting her hold his hand, but he didn't return her squeeze.

Erica went downstairs and took out her cell. She stood there thinking for a long time before she punched in a number.

"Hi, Martin, it's Erica—Patrik's wife. There's a bit of a situation here. I'm at the house of a woman named Britta Johansson; she's died and her husband is saying he killed her. It looks like natural causes, but. . . . Okay, I'll wait here. Will you call an ambulance, or shall I? Okay."

Erica ended the call, hoping she hadn't done something stupid. Admittedly, it looked as if Margareta was right, and Britta had simply died in her sleep, but in that case why was

Herman saying he had killed her? And it was a remarkable coincidence that yet another person in her mother's immediate circle had died, just two months after Erik's death. No, she had definitely done the right thing.

She went back upstairs.

"I've called for help," she said. "Is there anything else I can . . . ?"

"If you could make some coffee, I'll try and get Dad downstairs."

Gently she moved Herman into a sitting position. "Come on, Dad, let's go downstairs and wait for the ambulance."

Erica went down to the kitchen. She rummaged around until she had found everything she needed, then made a big pot of coffee. A few minutes later she heard footsteps on the stairs, and saw Margareta slowly and carefully leading Herman down. She helped him over to one of the kitchen chairs, and he slumped down heavily.

"I hope they'll be able to give him something," Margareta said anxiously. "He must have been lying next to her since yesterday. I don't understand why he didn't call us. . . ."

"I've . . . ," Erica hesitated, then tried again. "I've called the police too. I'm sure you're right, but I had to . . . I couldn't. . . ." The right words just wouldn't come, and Margareta was staring at her as if she had taken leave of her senses.

"You've called the police? You think my father was serious? Are you out of your mind? He's in shock because he found his wife dead, and now he's supposed to answer a whole load of questions from the police? How dare you?!" Margareta took a step toward Erica, who was holding the coffeepot, but the doorbell rang before she could get any farther.

"That must be them. I'll go and open the door," Erica said, keeping her eyes lowered as she put down the coffeepot and hurried into the hall.

She was right; when she opened the door, Martin was the first person she saw.

He nodded grimly. "Erica."

"Hi, Martin," she said quietly, stepping to one side. What if she was wrong? What if she was subjecting a broken man to an unnecessary ordeal? But it was too late now.

"Britta is up in the bedroom," she said, then nodded toward the kitchen. "Her husband is in there, with her daughter. She was the one who found. . . . It seems as if Britta's been dead for a while."

"Okay, we'll take a look," Martin said, beckoning to Paula and the ambulance crew. He introduced Paula and Erica to each other and then went into the kitchen where Margareta was standing behind her father, stroking his shoulders.

"This is absolutely ridiculous," she said, staring at Martin. "My mother died in her sleep, and my father is in shock. Is this really necessary?"

Martin held up his hands. "I'm sure you're right. But since we're here, why not let us take a look? We'll soon be out of your way. And I'm very sorry for your loss." He met her gaze steadily, and eventually she nodded reluctantly.

"She's upstairs. Is it okay if I call my sisters and my husband?"

"Of course," Martin said, heading for the stairs

Erica hesitated, then followed him and the medics. She stood slightly to one side and spoke quietly to Martin. "I came here to speak to Britta about Erik Frankel, among other things. Her death might be a coincidence, but don't you think it's a bit odd?"

Martin looked at her as he let the duty doctor go in first. "You mean there's some kind of link? In what way?"

"I don't know," Erica said, shaking her head. "But I'm doing some research on my mother at the moment, and both Erik Frankel and Britta were childhood friends of hers. There was a Frans Ringholm in the group too."

"Frans Ringholm?" Martin said, looking sharply at her.

"Yes, do you know him?"

"We've . . . come across him in connection with Erik's murder," he said thoughtfully as the wheels began to turn in his brain.

"So isn't it a bit strange that Britta is dead as well? Two months after Erik Frankel?" Erica persisted.

Martin still looked unsure. "We're not talking about young people here, though. I mean, things happen at their age: strokes, heart attacks, all kinds of stuff."

"Well, I can tell you right now that this was neither a stroke nor a heart attack," the doctor said from the bedroom. Both Martin and Erica were taken aback.

"So what was it?" Martin went and stood right behind the doctor next to Britta's bed; Erica chose to stay in the doorway, but craned her neck so that she could see.

"This lady was suffocated," the doctor said, pointing at Britta's eyes with one hand as he lifted her eyelid with the other. "You see? Petechiae."

"Petechiae?" said Martin uncomprehendingly.

"Little red dots on the white of the eye, caused by tiny blood vessels bursting as a result of increased pressure in the blood system. Characteristic in cases of suffocation, strangulation, and the like."

"But couldn't she have suffered some kind of attack that made it hard for her to breathe?" Erica asked. "Wouldn't that produce the same symptoms?"

"That's certainly a possibility," the doctor said. "But as I've already seen a feather in her throat from my initial inspection, I would put money on this being your murder weapon." He pointed to a white pillow next to Britta's head. "However, the petechiae also indicate that there must have been direct pressure on the throat as well; for example, if someone used a hand to choke her. But the autopsy will provide definite answers to all these questions. One thing is for sure: I won't be signing this death off as due to natural causes until the medical examiner proves me wrong. This is now a crime scene." He got to his feet and left the room, moving cautiously.

Martin did the same and took out his cell to call the technicians, who would go over the room in minute detail.

After ushering everyone downstairs, he went into the kitchen and sat down opposite Herman. Margareta looked at him, frowning as she realized that something was wrong.

"What's your father's name?" Martin asked her.

"Herman." Her frown deepened.

"Herman," Martin said, "can you tell me what's happened here?"

At first there was no response. The only sound was the ambulance crew, talking quietly in the living room. Then Herman looked up and said, clearly, "I killed her."

Friday brought glorious late summer weather. Mellberg strode out with Ernst trotting along beside him; even the dog seemed to appreciate the warm, sunny day.

"Guess what, Ernst?" Mellberg said, waiting for the dog to cock his leg against a bush. "Daddy's going to bust a few moves on the dance floor again tonight."

Ernst tilted his head to one side and looked inquiringly at his master, then went back to his more pressing concerns.

Mellberg caught himself whistling as he thought about that evening's class, and about the feeling of Rita's body against his. He could really get into this salsa dancing, no doubt about it.

His mood darkened as the Latin beat drifted away, only to be replaced by thoughts of the investigation. Or, rather, investigations. Why couldn't a person get a bit of peace and quiet in this town? Why were people so hell-bent on killing one another?

Oh, well, at least one case seemed pretty much open-and-shut. The woman's husband had confessed, after all. They were just waiting for the report from the ME confirming that it was homicide, and that would wrap it up. Martin Molin was going around muttering that it was a bit strange that someone with a connection to Erik Frankel had also been murdered, but Mellberg wasn't taking much notice of him. For God's sake, as he understood it they had been childhood friends. Sixty years ago. That was a lifetime and had nothing whatsoever to do with this case. It was a ridiculous idea, but just to be on the safe side he had given Molin permission to check it out, go through phone calls and so on just to see if he could find a link. He wouldn't find anything, but at least it would keep him quiet.

Suddenly Mellberg realized that his feet had brought him to Rita's apartment while he was lost in thought. Ernst positioned himself in front of the door, eagerly wagging his tail. Mellberg glanced at his watch. Eleven o'clock. The perfect time for a coffee break, if she was home. He hesitated for a moment, then pressed the button on the intercom. No reply.

"Hi there." A woman's voice behind him made him jump. He turned and saw Johanna waddling toward them. She was swaying slightly, one hand pressed against the bottom of her back.

"Hard to believe it could be so damned difficult just to go for a little walk," she said, sounding frustrated as she leaned back to stretch her spine, grimacing. "Sitting at home waiting is driving me crazy, but I guess my body doesn't want the same thing as my head." She sighed and stroked her huge belly. "I presume you're looking for Rita?" she said, looking at him with a knowing smile.

"Er, well, yes . . . ," Mellberg said, suddenly feeling embarrassed. "We . . . Ernst and I . . . we were just out for a little walk, and Ernst wanted to come and see Senorita . . . so we. . . ."

"Rita isn't home," Johanna said, still with that knowing smile. She obviously found his confusion highly amusing. "She's spending the morning with a girlfriend. But if you'd like to come up for coffee anyway—that is, if Ernst still wants to come up even though Senorita isn't home—then you're very welcome to keep me company. I'm going stir-crazy," she said with a wink.

"That . . . that would be nice," Mellberg said, following her into the building.

Once inside the apartment, Johanna sank down on one of the kitchen chairs, puffing and blowing.

"I'll make some coffee in a minute—I just need to catch my breath first."

"You stay there," Mellberg said. "I saw where everything was the other day—I can make the coffee. It's better if you rest."

Johanna looked at him in amazement as he started opening cupboards and drawers, but gratefully remained where she was.

"That must be really heavy," Mellberg said, glancing at her belly as he filled the machine with water.

"You don't know the half of it. Being pregnant is totally overrated, I have to say. First of all, you feel like shit for three or four months, and you have to make sure you're never far from the bathroom in case you need to throw up. Then you're okay for a couple of months, and in fact it's all quite nice. Then you turn into Barbapapa overnight. Or maybe that should be Barbamama."

"Yes, and then. . . ."

"Don't even go there," Johanna said sternly, wagging her finger at him. "I don't dare even think about that yet. If I start contemplating the fact that there's only one way out for this baby, I begin to panic. And if you say 'Yes, but women have been giving birth to children since time began and have survived and gone on to have more, so it can't be that bad,' then I'm afraid I'll have to punch you."

Mellberg held up his hands defensively. "You're talking to someone who's never been anywhere near a maternity unit."

He poured the coffee and sat down at the table with her.

"Being able to eat for two must be nice, though," he said with a grin as she pushed a third cookie into her mouth.

"And I'm taking full advantage," Johanna said with a laugh, reaching for another cookie. "You seem to have adopted the same philosophy, although you can't blame pregnancy," she teased, prodding Mellberg's substantial belly.

"The salsa classes will get rid of this in no time." He patted his stomach.

"I'll have to come and watch you two one of these days," Johanna said with a warm smile.

For a moment, Mellberg was both intrigued and surprised at the idea that someone actually seemed to appreciate his company, and he realized that he felt very comfortable with Rita's daughter-in-law. He took a deep breath and ventured to ask the question that had been nagging away at him ever since lunch the other day, when all the pieces fell into place.

"How . . . the father . . . who . . . ?" Perhaps it wasn't the most well-formulated question he had ever come out with, but Johanna understood what he meant. She looked at him intently for a few seconds and seemed to be wondering whether or not to answer. Eventually her face softened, and she appeared to have decided that nothing more than curiosity lay behind his words.

"A clinic. In Denmark. We've never met the father. I didn't pick some guy up in a bar one night, if that's what you were thinking."

"No . . . no, of course not," Mellberg said, although he had to admit that the thought had crossed his mind.

He looked at his watch. He needed to be heading back to the station. It was almost lunchtime, and he couldn't miss that.

He carried the cups and plates over to the sink, then stood there hesitating for a few seconds before taking out his wallet from his back pocket. He handed Johanna his business card and said, "If you . . . if there's a problem, or if you need . . . I mean, I assume Paula and Rita will be on standby until . . . but anyway, just in case. . . ."

Johanna accepted the card with a surprised expression, and Mellberg hurried out into the hallway. He didn't know where the impulse to give Johanna his card had come from; perhaps it was because he could still remember the feeling of that tiny foot kicking against his palm when she had placed his hand on her belly.

"Come along, Ernst," he said brusquely, nudging the dog out of the apartment. He closed the door behind him without saying good-bye.

Martin was staring at the lists of telephone calls. They didn't prove that his gut feeling had been correct, nor did they provide any evidence to the contrary. Just before Erik Frankel had been murdered, someone from Britta and Herman's house had called the number he shared with Axel. Two calls had been registered then, along with one more just a couple of days ago, when Britta or Herman must have contacted Axel. There was also one call to Frans Ringholm.

Martin gazed out of the window, then pushed back his chair and put his feet up on the desk. He had spent the morning going through all the papers, all the photographs, and everything else they had come up with during the investigation into Erik Frankel's death. He was determined not to give up until he had found a possible link between the two murders, but so far there was nothing. Except for the phone calls.

He threw down the lists in frustration. He felt as if he had reached a dead end. He knew that Mellberg had only given him permission to look into the circumstances surrounding Britta's death in order to keep him quiet. Like everyone else, Mellberg seemed convinced that her husband was the guilty party. However, so far they had been unable to question Herman; according to the doctors, he was in a state of deep shock and had been hospitalized. They would just have to wait until the medics decided he was strong enough to cope with an interview.

The whole thing was such a goddamn mess, and he didn't know what to do next. He stared at the case file, as if he could somehow make it talk, then suddenly he had an idea. Of course. Why hadn't he thought of it before?

Twenty-five minutes later, he pulled into Patrik and Erica's drive. He had spoken to Patrik on the way to check that he was home, and the door opened as soon as he rang the bell. Maja was in Patrik's arms, and she started waving her hands as soon as she saw their visitor.

"Hi, sweetie," Martin said, waggling his fingers. She reached out her arms to him, and since she refused to let go, he found himself sitting on the sofa in the living room a little while later with Maja on his knee. Patrik was in the armchair, studying the papers and photographs and pensively stroking his chin.

"Where's Erica?" Martin said, looking around.

"Sorry?" Patrik glanced up in confusion. "Oh, she's gone to the library for a couple of hours to do some more research for her new book."

"I see," Martin said. He concentrated on entertaining Maja so that Patrik could read through everything in peace.

"So you think Erica's right?" Patrik said eventually. "You agree that there might be a link between the murders of Erik Frankel and Britta Johansson?"

Martin pondered for a few moments, then nodded. "Yes, I do. I don't have any concrete proof at the moment, but if you're asking me what I think, then the answer is that I'm almost certain there's a connection."

Patrik nodded. "Well, it's undeniably a remarkable coincidence otherwise." He stretched out his legs. "Have you asked Axel Frankel and Frans Ringholm what the phone calls from Britta and Herman's house were about?"

"Not yet." Martin shook his head. "I wanted to speak to you first, check that it's not just me who has no idea what's going on, searching for something else when we've already got a confession."

"Her husband, right . . . ," Patrik said thoughtfully. "The question is, why is he saying he killed her if he's not the one who did it?"

"How should I know? To protect someone, maybe?" Martin shrugged.

"Hmm. . . ." Patrik leafed through the papers on the table. "And have you made any progress with the investigation into Erik Frankel's death?"

"I wouldn't exactly call it progress," Martin said dispiritedly, bouncing Maja up and down on his knee. "Paula's looking a little more closely into Sweden's Friends, and we've spoken to the neighbors, but nobody can remember seeing anything out of the ordinary. The Frankel brothers' house is in a pretty secluded location, so we didn't have much hope that anyone would have noticed anything, and unfortunately those fears were justified. Apart from that, you've got everything there." He pointed to the papers spread out in front of Patrik.

"What about Erik's finances?" Patrik pulled out some sheets from the bottom of the pile. "Anything there that seemed odd?"

"Not really. It's mostly the usual stuff—bills, the odd small cash withdrawal."

"No transfer of larger sums, nothing like that?" Patrik was studying the columns of figures intently.

"The only thing that caught our eye was a monthly transfer from Erik's account. According to the bank, it's been a regular payment for almost fifty years."

Patrik stopped dead and looked up at Martin. "Fifty years? And where has this money been going?"

"To a private individual in Gothenburg, apparently. The name is in there somewhere. The amounts have never been very large; they have increased over the years, but at the moment the monthly payment is around two thousand kronor, which didn't seem very . . . I mean, it's hardly likely to be blackmail or something like that—who would keep paying up for fifty years?"

Martin could hear how lame that sounded, and felt like slapping his own forehead. He should have followed up on that transfer. Oh, well, better late than never.

"I'll give him a call today and find out what it's about," Martin said, shifting Maja across to the other knee, because the leg she had been sitting on was going to sleep.

Patrik sat in silence for a little while, then said, "Listen, I could do with getting out and about." He opened the folder and found the piece of paper. "The money has been transferred to someone by the name of Wilhelm Fridén. I can go to his home and speak to him personally. I've got the address here." He waved the piece of paper. "I presume this is current?"

"Yes, that's the address we got from the bank, so it should be."

"Good. In that case I'll go tomorrow. It could be a sensitive matter, so I think that would be better than a phone call."

"Okay, if you're happy to do that, I'd be very grateful," Martin said. "But what about . . . ?" He pointed to Maja.

"She can come with me," Patrik said, beaming at his daughter. "We can call on Aunt Lotta and your cousins too, can't we, sweetheart? You'll have fun with your cousins."

Maja gurgled in agreement and clapped her hands.

"Could I hang on to this for a couple of days?" Patrik said, picking up the folder. Martin thought about it. He had copies of most things, so it shouldn't be a problem.

"Sure, you keep it. And let me know if you find anything else you think we should take a closer look at. If you check out the Gothenburg angle, we'll speak to Frans and Axel about why Britta or Herman called them."

"In that case, don't mention the bank transfer just yet, until I dig up more information."

"Of course."

"Don't lose heart," Patrik said comfortingly as he and Maja showed Martin out. "You know how it goes. Sooner or later that one little piece falls into place, and everything makes sense."

"I know," Martin said, but he didn't sound convinced. "I just think it's really bad timing that you're on leave right now; we need you." He smiled to take the sting out of his words.

"Believe me, you'll end up in this position one day. And when you're sitting at home surrounded by dirty diapers, I'll be back at the station, firing on all cylinders." Patrik winked at Martin, then closed the door behind him.

"Hey, we're off to Gothenburg tomorrow, you and I," he said, dancing around the hallway with Maja in his arms. "Now all we have to do is sell it to Mommy."

Maja nodded in agreement.

Paula felt incredibly tired. Tired and disgusted. She had spent several hours surfing the net, looking for information on neo-Nazi organizations in Sweden, and Sweden's Friends in particular. It still seemed likely that the group was behind Erik Frankel's death, but the problem was that they didn't have anything concrete to go on. They hadn't found any threatening letters, only hints in the missives from Frans Ringholm, who had written that certain elements inside Sweden's Friends were not happy with Erik's activities, and that he could no longer guarantee protection against these forces. Nor was there any forensic evidence linking any of them to the scene of the crime. All the members of the board had voluntarily, and scornfully, provided fingerprints, thanks to the assistance of the police in Uddevalla, but SKL, the National Forensics Laboratory, had established that none of them matched the prints found in Erik and Axel's library. The issue of alibis had left the police equally frustrated. None of them had a completely watertight alibi, but most had one that was good enough until the police had evidence pointing in a particular direction. Several of them had also confirmed that Frans had been with them on a trip to visit a sister organization in Denmark during the period in question, thus providing him with an alibi. The problem was that the organization was so large, much bigger than Paula had imagined, and they couldn't possibly check alibis and take fingerprints from everyone connected to Sweden's Friends. That was why they had decided to limit their questions to the members of the board for the time being, but they were getting nowhere fast.

Paula kept surfing, growing increasingly frustrated. Where did all these people come from? Where did all that hatred come from? She could understand hatred that was directed against a specific individual, against someone who might have done you an injustice. But to hate people indiscriminately because they came from a different country, or because their skin was a particular color? No, she just didn't get it at all.

Paula herself hated the thugs who had killed her father. She hated them so much that she would have killed them without hesitation if she had had the chance, if they were still alive. But her hatred stopped there, even if it could have continued to expand upward, outward. She had refused to allow herself to be filled with so much hatred. Instead, she had restricted her animosity to the men who had fired the bullets straight into her father's body. Otherwise she would have ended up hating the country she came from, and how could she do that? How could she have carried the burden of hating the country where she was born, had taken her first steps, played with friends, sat on her grandmother's knee, heard the songs that were sung in the evenings, danced at the parties that were full of such joy? How could she have hated all that?

But these people. . . . She scrolled down the page, reading one article after another about how people like her should be eradicated or at least chased back to wherever they came from. And there were pictures. Quite a lot from Nazi Germany, of course: the black-and-white images she had seen so many times before, the piles of naked, emaciated bodies that had been tossed aside like rubbish after the people had died in the concentration camps. Auschwitz, Buchenwald, Dachau . . . all the names that were so terrifyingly familiar, forever linked to the ultimate evil. But here, on these websites, they were lauded and celebrated. Or denied. For there were also the Holocaust deniers, like Peter Lindgren, who claimed that it had never happened. That six million Jews had not been driven from their homes, persecuted, tortured, killed, gassed to death in the concentration camps during the Second World War. How could anyone deny such things, when there was so much evidence, so many witnesses? How did the warped minds of these people work?

She jumped as a knock on the door interrupted her thoughts.

"Hi, what are you up to?" Martin stuck his head around the door.

"I'm looking up all the background information I can find on Sweden's Friends," she said with a sigh. "But it's scary stuff. Did you know that there are around twenty neo-Nazi organizations in Sweden? And that the Sweden Democrats won a total of 281 seats in 144 municipalities? Where the hell is this country going?"

"I have no idea, but it certainly makes you wonder," Martin said.

"It's a fucking disgrace," Paula said, angrily throwing down her pen, which skidded across the desk and landed on the floor.

"Sounds as if you could do with a break from all that," Martin said. "I thought we might go and have another chat with Axel."

"About anything in particular?" Paula said curiously as she got up and followed Martin to the garage.

"I just thought it might be a good idea to speak to him again; after all, he was the person who was closest to Erik and knew him better than anyone. But there was one thing I wanted to check on. . . ." He hesitated. "Look, I know I'm the only person who thinks there's some connection with the murder of Britta Johansson, but someone called Axel from the Johanssons' place only the other day, and there was another call back in June, although of course it's impossible to say whether that one was to Erik or Axel. I've just gone through the Frankels' phone records, and someone from their house called Britta or Herman in June. Twice. Before they'd called the Frankels."

"It's certainly worth looking into," Paula said as she fastened her seat belt. "And as long as it means I can avoid reading about those goddamn Nazis for a while, I'm prepared to go along with any theory, however much of a long shot it might be!"

Martin nodded and drove out of the garage. He understood Paula completely, but something told him that his idea wasn't such a long shot after all.

Anna had been in a daze all week, and it wasn't until Friday that she began to feel she could deal with the information. Dan had taken it much better; after the initial shock, he had been going around humming to himself. He had brushed aside all her objections with a cheery "It'll be fine! This is going to be so cool! Having a baby together—it's going to be fantastic!"

But Anna hadn't quite reached "fantastic" yet. She caught herself stroking her stomach, trying to imagine the tiny, tiny lump inside. Something unidentifiable so far, a microscopic embryo that would become a child in just a few months. In spite of the fact that she had done this twice before, it still seemed incomprehensible. Perhaps even more so this time. She barely remembered her pregnancies with Emma and Adrian; they had vanished into a fog, where the fear of being beaten dominated every hour, whether she was awake or asleep. All her energy had gone into protecting her belly, protecting the life inside from Lucas.

This time there was no need for that and, for some bizarre reason, it scared her. This time she could be happy. Was allowed to be happy, would be happy. She loved Dan; she felt safe with him. She knew that it would never occur to him to hurt her or anyone else. How could that possibly be frightening? She had spent the last few days trying to understand and deal with her emotions.

"So, what do you think? Is it a boy or a girl? Any feelings one way or the other?" Dan had crept up behind her and slipped his arms around her; he was now stroking her still-flat stomach.

Anna laughed and tried to continue stirring what she was cooking, in spite of the fact that Dan's arms were in the way.

"I'm only seven weeks along! Don't you think that's a bit early to start getting an idea of what it might be? Anyway, why are you asking?" She turned to face him, looking concerned. "I hope you're not pinning your hopes on having a son, because it's the father who determines the sex, you know, and given that you've already got three girls, the statistical probability is that—"

"Ssh." Dan laughed and placed his finger on Anna's lips. "I'll be just as thrilled whatever we have. If it's a boy, great. If it's a girl, terrific. And besides. . . ." His face grew serious. "As far as I'm concerned, I already have a son—Adrian. I hope you know that. I thought you did. When I asked the three of you to move in here, I didn't just mean into the house. I meant here too." He placed his fist on his chest just above his heart, and Anna had to swallow the lump in her throat. She didn't quite manage to stop a single tear running down her cheek, and her lower lip began to tremble. Dan wiped away the tear, then held her face between his palms. He looked into her eyes, forcing her to meet his gaze.

"If it's a girl, then I guess Adrian and I will have to join forces against all you ladies. But always remember that I think of you, Emma, and Adrian as a package. And I love all three of you. And you in there—I love you too!" he shouted at her stomach.

Anna laughed. "I don't think the ears develop until some-where around the twentieth week."

"Oh, my children develop really, really early," Dan said with a wink.

"I see," Anna said, but she couldn't help laughing again. They kissed for a while, but jumped as the front door was yanked open, then banged shut.

"Hello? Who's that?" Dan said, heading for the hallway.

"Me!" came a surly voice. Belinda was gazing at them from beneath her fringe.

"How did you get here?" Dan said, looking annoyed.

"How the fuck do you think? Same fucking way as I left. On the bus, obviously."

"If you can't speak to me in a civil manner, then I'd rather you didn't speak to me at all," Dan said grimly.

"Oh, well, in that case. . . ." Belinda placed her forefinger on her cheek and pretended to consider the matter. "Yes,

I've decided. In that case, I'd prefer NOT TO SPEAK TO YOU AT ALL!" With that, she stormed upstairs to her room, slammed the door so hard that it nearly came off its hinges, then put her music on so loud that they could feel the floor vibrating beneath their feet.

Dan slumped down on the bottom step, pulled Anna close, and spoke to her stomach, which was now level with his mouth.

"I hope you're covering your ears in there. Because your dad is going to be way too old for vocabulary like that when you're her age."

Anna stroked his hair sympathetically as the music continued to pound above them.

28
Fjällbacka 1944

"Did he have any news about Axel?" Erik couldn't hide his excitement. All four of them had gathered in the usual place on Rabekullen, the hill above the churchyard. They were all curious to hear what Elsy had to tell them about the news that had spread like wildfire through the village—Elof had brought home a Norwegian resistance fighter who had fled from the Germans.

Elsy shook her head. "No. Dad asked him, but he said he didn't know anything about Axel."

Disappointed, Erik looked down at the granite, kicking at a patch of gray lichen with his boot.

"Maybe he doesn't know him by name, but if we described Axel, then perhaps he might remember something?" Erik said with a fresh spark of hope in his eyes. If only there was some indication that his brother was still alive. Yesterday his mother had put into words for the first time what they all feared. She had wept, her tears more heartrending than ever, and said that they should light a candle in church for Axel on Sunday, because he was probably no longer alive. His father had gotten angry and shouted at her, but Erik had seen the resignation in his eyes. He too believed that Axel was dead.

"We'll go and talk to him," Britta said eagerly, getting up and brushing down her skirt. She ran a hand over her hair to make sure that her braids were smooth, provoking a spiteful comment from Frans.

"I'm sure you're primping and preening out of concern for Erik. I didn't know you were fond of Norwegians, Britta. Aren't there enough Swedish boys for you?" He laughed, and Britta's face flushed with anger.

"Shut up, Frans—you're just making yourself look ridiculous. Of course I'm concerned about Erik, and I want to find out about Axel. And there's no harm in looking respectable."

"In that case, you're going to have to try much harder. If you want to look respectable," Frans said, tugging at Britta's skirt. She turned even redder and looked as if she was about to burst into tears when Elsy said, sharply, "Cut it out, Frans! You say such stupid things sometimes. Enough!"

He stared at her, and all the color drained from his face. He jumped to his feet and ran off, his expression thunderous.

Erik was poking at a few loose stones with his fingers. Without looking at Elsy he said, quietly, "Just be careful what you say to Frans. There's something about him, something bubbling away under the surface. I can feel it."

Elsy stared at him in astonishment, wondering where that peculiar comment had come from. But she knew instinctively that he was right. She had known Frans since they were little, but something was growing inside him, something uncontrollable, untamable.

"Don't be ridiculous," Britta snorted. "There's nothing the matter with Frans. We were just . . . messing around."

"You're blind because you're in love with him," Erik stated. Britta thumped him on the shoulder.

"Ouch—what did you do that for?" he said, clutching his shoulder.

"Because you're talking such nonsense. Now, are we going to go and speak to this Norwegian boy about your brother or not?"

Britta marched off, and Erik exchanged a look with Elsy.

"He was in his room when I left. I don't suppose it can do any harm to have a chat with him," she said.

A short while later, Elsy tapped on the basement door. Hans looked slightly taken aback when he opened it and saw the little gathering outside. "Hi?" he said inquiringly.

Elsy glanced at the others before she spoke. Out of the corner of her eye she could see Frans sauntering toward them, looking considerably calmer and with his hands nonchalantly shoved in his pockets.

"We wondered if we could come in for a chat?"

"Of course," Hans said, stepping to one side. Britta winked coquettishly at him as she walked past, and the boys shook hands. There wasn't much furniture in the small room. Britta and Elsy sat down on the only two chairs, Hans sat on the neatly made bed, and Frans and Erik settled down on the floor.

"It's about my brother," Erik said, looking up at Hans. There was still that faint glimmer of hope in his eyes. "My brother has been helping your countrymen ever since the war began. He's traveled on Elsy's father's boat, the one that brought you here, transporting various things back and forth to your side. But a year ago the Germans picked him up in Kristiansand, and," he blinked, "we've heard nothing since then."

"Elsy's father asked me about him," Hans said, meeting Erik's gaze. "But unfortunately I don't recognize the name.

And I don't remember hearing anything about a Swede who was captured in Kristiansand. But there are many of us, and a considerable number of Swedes have helped us too."

"Perhaps you don't know the name, but you might have seen him?" Erik's voice was eager, and his hands were clasped tightly in his lap.

"I doubt it, but you're welcome to try. Tell me what he looks like."

Erik described Axel to the best of his ability. It wasn't difficult; in spite of the fact that his brother had been gone for a whole year, he could still picture him with total clarity. Then again, there were plenty of others who looked like Axel, and it was difficult to come up with any distinguishing features that would set him apart from other Swedish boys of his age.

Hans listened, then shook his head. "No, that doesn't ring any bells. I really am sorry."

Erik slumped down, clearly disappointed. They all sat in silence for a while, then Frans said "Why don't you tell us about your adventures during the war? You must have seen some pretty exciting stuff!" His eyes were shining.

"There's not much to say, really," Hans said reluctantly, but Britta protested. She didn't take her eyes off him as she begged him to tell them something, anything, about what he had been involved in. Eventually the Norwegian gave in and started to tell them about how things had been in Norway. He talked about the German occupation, about the suffering of his countrymen, about the things they had done to fight back. The four young people sat there openmouthed as they listened to him. It was all so thrilling. Admittedly they could see a hint of sorrow in the Norwegian's eyes, and they realized that he must have seen some terrible things. But still—there was no getting away from the fact that it was exciting.

"I think you're incredibly brave," Britta said, blushing prettily. "Most boys wouldn't have the courage; it's only people like Axel, and you, who are brave enough to fight for what they believe in."

"What do you mean—we wouldn't have the courage?" Frans snapped. He was even more annoyed by the fact that the admiring looks Britta usually directed at him now seemed to be focused on the Norwegian. "Erik and I are every bit as brave, and when we're as old as Axel and . . . how old are you, by the way?" he asked Hans.

"I've just turned seventeen," Hans replied. He seemed uncomfortable with the level of interest in both himself and his exploits. He caught Elsy's eye. She had been sitting quietly, just listening to the others, but she immediately picked up on his signal.

"I think we should let Hans rest now; he's been through a lot," she said gently but firmly. Her friends reluctantly got to their feet, thanking Hans as they backed out of the room. Elsy was the last to leave, and she turned around just before she closed the door.

"Thanks," Hans said with a faint smile. "It was nice to have some company; you're all welcome to come again. But right now I'm just a bit. . . ."

Elsy smiled back. "I understand perfectly. We'll come back another time, and we must show you around Fjällbacka too. Now get some rest."

She closed the door; but strangely enough, the image of him lingered in her mind and refused to go away.

29

Erica wasn't at the library as Patrik had thought. She had been on her way there, but just as she was parking the car, an idea had struck her. There was someone else who had been close to her mother, and who had been her friend considerably more recently than sixty years ago. She was actually the only friend of her mother's that Erica could think of during the years while she and Anna had been growing up. Why hadn't it occurred to her before? Of course, she tended to think of Kristina only as her mother-in-law these days, and she had somehow managed to forget that Kristina had also been Elsy's friend.

Resolutely she started the car again and set off toward Tanumshede. This was the first time she had made a spontaneous visit to Kristina's home, and she glanced at her cell, wondering if she ought to call first. No, why the hell should she? If Kristina could come marching into their place unannounced and whenever she felt like it, then surely Erica could do the same.

She was still feeling vaguely irritated when she arrived, and just to make the point she pressed the bell for a second, then walked straight in. "Hello?" she called out.

"Who's that?" Kristina's voice came from the kitchen, sounding slightly worried. A moment later, she appeared in the hallway.

"Erica?" she said in amazement, staring at her daughter-in-law. "What are you doing here? Is Maja with you?" She looked all around but didn't see her grandchild anywhere.

"No, she's at home with Patrik," Erica said. She took off her shoes and placed them neatly on the rack.

"Come on in," Kristina said, sounding puzzled. "I'll make us a cup of coffee."

Erica followed her into the kitchen, looking at her mother-in-law in surprise. She almost didn't recognize her. Kristina was always beautifully made up and impeccably dressed, and when she came to visit them she always came across as a bundle of energy, talking nonstop and constantly on the move. This woman was a completely different person. She was still in a faded old nightgown, in spite of the fact that it was late morning, and she wasn't wearing a scrap of makeup. This made her look much older, with visible lines and wrinkles. Nor had she done anything with her hair; it was still flat from lying on the pillow.

"Look at the state I'm in," Kristina said as if she could read Erica's mind; she ran a hand distractedly through her hair. "There just doesn't seem much point in getting all dressed up if you don't have anything in particular to do, or somewhere to be."

"But you always sound as if you have plenty to do," Erica said, sitting down at the table.

Kristina didn't say anything at first; she simply placed two mugs and a package of cookies on the table.

"Retirement isn't easy when you've worked all your life," she said finally, pouring the coffee. "And everybody else is busy. I suppose there are things I could do, but I just haven't had the energy to. . . ." She reached for a cookie and avoided looking at Erica.

"So why did you tell us you had such a lot going on all the time?"

"Oh, you young people have your own lives. I didn't want you to feel you had to look after me. God knows, I don't want to be a burden. And sometimes when I come to see you, I get the feeling that you don't really want me there, so I thought it was best to. . . ." She fell silent, and Erica stared at her, lost for words. Kristina looked up and went on. "You should know that I live for the time I spend with you and Patrik and Maja. Lotta has her own life in Gothenburg, and it's not always easy for her to come here or for me to go there, for that matter—they have so little room. And, as I said, I get the impression you're not always pleased to see me when I turn up at your house. . . ." She looked away again, and Erica felt ashamed of herself.

"That's largely my fault, I have to confess," Erica said gently. "But you're always welcome. You and Maja have so much fun together. The only thing we ask is that you respect our privacy. It's our home, and you are very welcome as our guest. So we, or I, would appreciate it if you could call and check if it's okay before you come, rather than walking straight in, and, for God's sake, please don't try to tell us how to run our home and raise our children. If you can respect those rules, we will be very happy to see you, and I'm sure Patrik will jump at the chance of some help during his paternity leave."

"I'm sure he will," Kristina said with a laugh that reached her eyes this time. "How's he doing?"

"Things were a bit tricky for the first few days," Erica said, telling the story of Maja's visits to a crime scene and the police station. "But I think we've established the ground rules now."

"Men!" Kristina said. "I remember when Lars was home alone with Lotta for the first time. She must have been about a year old, and I was going out shopping on my own. After just twenty minutes, the manager of the shop came to tell me that Lars had phoned; there was a crisis and I had to go home. So I left all my shopping and rushed back, and there certainly was a crisis!"

"What had happened?" Erica asked, wide-eyed.

"Wait till you hear this—he couldn't find the diapers; he thought my sanitary pads were Lotta's diapers. Then he couldn't work out how to put the damn thing on, so when I walked in he was standing there trying to fasten it with duct tape."

"You're kidding me!" Erica said, joining in with Kristina's laughter.

"He soon learned. Lars was a good father to Patrik and Lotta when they grew up, I can't deny that. But times were different back then."

"Speaking of different times," Erica said, taking the opportunity to change the subject to the real purpose of her visit. "I'm trying to find out a bit more about my mother, about her childhood and so on. I came across some things in the attic, including some old diaries, and . . . well, they've made me think."

"Diaries?" Kristina said, staring at Erica. "What was in them?" Her tone was sharp, and Erica looked at her mother-in-law in surprise.

"They weren't particularly interesting, unfortunately. Mostly just teenage thoughts. But she does write about the friends she used to hang out with in those days: Erik Frankel, Britta Johansson, and Frans Ringholm. And now two of them, Erik and Britta, have been murdered within just a few months. It could be a coincidence, but it seems a bit strange."

Kristina was still staring. "Britta's dead?" she said, and it was obvious that she was having difficulty taking in the news.

"Yes, didn't you know? I thought you would have heard it through the grapevine by now. Her daughter found her dead two days ago, and it looks as if she was suffocated. But her husband keeps saying he killed her."

"So both Erik and Britta are dead?" Kristina said. She looked as if the thoughts were churning around in her head.

"Did you know them?" Erica asked curiously.

"No." Kristina shook her head decisively. "I only knew of them through what Elsy told me."

"And what was that?" Erica asked, leaning eagerly across the table. "That's exactly why I came here, because you were Mom's friend for so many years. I thought that if anyone knows stuff about Mom, it's you. So what did she tell you about those years? And why did she suddenly stop keeping a diary in 1944? Or are there more somewhere? Did Mom ever say anything about that? And in the last diary she mentions that a Norwegian resistance fighter had come to stay with them, a boy called Hans Olavsen. I've found newspaper clippings that seem to suggest the four of them spent quite a lot of time with him. Where did he go?" The questions came spilling out so fast that Erica could barely keep up herself. Kristina remained silent, her face closed.

"I can't answer your questions, Erica," she said slowly. "The only thing I can tell you is where Hans Olavsen went. Elsy told me he disappeared back to Norway as soon as the war was over. She never saw him again."

"Were they . . ." Erica hesitated, unsure how to put it. "Did she love him?"

Kristina didn't say anything for a long time. She fiddled with the pattern on the wax cloth and seemed to be considering her answer very carefully. Eventually she met Erica's gaze.

"Yes," she said. "She loved him."

It was a beautiful day. Axel hadn't thought about that kind of thing for a long time: the idea that some days could be nicer than others. But today really was something else. Halfway between summer and fall. A warm, gentle breeze. The light had lost the harshness of summer and begun to acquire the glow of fall. A really lovely day.

He went over and stood by the bay window and looked out, his hands clasped behind his back. But he didn't see the trees beyond the yard or the grass that had been allowed to grow rather too long and was now beginning to wither as the seasons changed. Instead, he saw Britta. Lovely, lively Britta; he had never thought of her as anything other than a silly girl back in those days, during the war. One of Erik's friends, pretty but rather vain. She hadn't interested him. She had been too young, and he had been too preoccupied with what had to be done, what he could do. She had been nothing more than a presence on the periphery of his world.

But he was thinking about her now. What she had been like when he saw her the other day. Sixty years on. Still pretty. Still slightly vain. But the years had changed her, made her a different person. He wondered whether he had changed as much. Maybe. Maybe not. Maybe the years in German captivity had changed him enough for a lifetime so that he was incapable of further change. He had seen everything, faced every horror. Perhaps that had damaged something deep inside him that could never be healed or restored.

Axel saw other faces before him. The faces of the people they had hunted down, those he had helped to catch. Not through exciting chases like some Hollywood movie, but through methodical work, discipline, and administration. Through sitting in his office doggedly following a fifty-year paper trail. Through querying identities, payments, travel, and possible places of refuge. They had caught them, one by one. Made sure they were punished for the transgressions that were slipping further and further back in time. They would never catch up, he knew that. There were still so many of them out there, and more and more were dying these days. And instead of dying in prison, in degradation, they were dying of old age in peace, without ever being forced to face up to what they had done. That was what drove him, that was why he could never rest but had to keep on searching, hunting, going from one meeting to the next, going through archive after archive. If there was one left out there who he could help catch, then he couldn't rest.

Axel stared unseeing out of the window. He knew it had become an obsession. He had allowed his work to swallow up everything else. It had turned into a lifeline, something he could cling to when he doubted himself or his humanity. As long as he was hunting them down, he didn't have to question who he was. As long as he was working for the cause, he was slowly but surely atoning for his guilt. Only by refusing to stand still could he push aside everything he couldn't bear to think about.

He turned around. Someone was ringing the doorbell. For a moment he couldn't tear himself away from all those faces flickering before his eyes, then he blinked and went to open the door.

"Oh, it's you two," he said when he saw Paula and Martin. The weariness took over for a second. Sometimes he felt as if it would never end.

"Could we come in for a chat?" Martin said pleasantly.

"Of course," Axel said, showing them to the same spot on the veranda where he'd brought them on their previous visit.

"Any news? I heard about Britta, by the way. Terrible. I saw her and Herman only a few days ago, and I find it so difficult to believe that he. . . ." Axel shook his head.

"It really is a tragedy," Paula said. "But we're trying not to jump to conclusions."

"I thought Herman had confessed." Axel said.

"Well, yes, but. . . ." Martin paused. "Until we're able to question him, then. . . ." He opened his hands. "Actually, that's why we wanted to speak to you."

"Of course, although I don't understand how I can help."

"We've checked the phone calls made from Britta and Herman's line, and your number comes up on three occasions."

"I can certainly tell you about one of those. Herman called me a couple of days ago and asked me to come over and see Britta. We hadn't been in touch for many, many years, so it was something of a surprise. But as I understood it, she was unfortunately suffering from Alzheimer's, and I think Herman just wanted her to meet up with someone from the old days, in the hope that it might help in some way."

"So that was why you went over there?" Paula said, watching him closely. "Because Britta wanted to see someone from the old days?"

"That's what Herman said, anyway. Admittedly we weren't particularly close back then. She was really Erik's friend, but I thought it couldn't do any harm. And at my age it's always nice to share memories, of course."

"So, what happened when you were there?" Martin asked, leaning forward slightly.

"She was quite lucid for a while, and we chatted about the good old days. But then she got very confused, and there wasn't much point in staying, so I made my excuses and left. Such a tragedy. It's a cruel illness."

"And the calls at the beginning of June?" Martin consulted his notes. "A call from this number on the second, then one from Britta or Herman on the third, and finally another from them on the fourth."

Axel shook his head. "I don't know anything about those. They must have spoken to Erik. But it was probably about the same thing, and actually it was more natural for Britta to want to see Erik, if she'd started harking back to the old days. It was those two who were friends, as I said earlier."

"The thing is, the first call came from your phone," Martin persisted. "Do you have any idea why Erik might have called them?"

"As I told you in our previous conversation, my brother and I may have lived under the same roof, but we didn't get involved in each other's affairs. I have no idea why Erik might have decided to contact Britta. Perhaps he simply wanted to renew their friendship. That kind of thing happens as we get older. The past suddenly seems to move closer and becomes more important to us."

Axel realized how true that was as soon as he said it. In his mind's eye he could see people from the past rushing toward him, laughing and jeering. He clutched the arm of the chair. This was no time to let himself be caught out.

"So you think Erik might have instigated a meeting, for the sake of their old friendship?" Martin said skeptically.

"As I said," Axel relaxed his grip on the arm of the chair, "I have absolutely no idea, but that seems like the most plausible explanation."

Martin and Paula exchanged glances. It didn't look as if they were going to get any further, even though Martin had an annoying feeling that he was being given tiny fragments of something much bigger.

When they left, Axel went and stood by the window once more, the faces from the past dancing before him.

"Hi, how did you do at the library?" Patrik's face lit up as Erica walked in.

"Oh . . . I didn't go to the library," Erica replied with an odd expression on her face.

"So where did you go, then?" Maja was having her afternoon nap, and Patrik was cleaning up after their lunch.

"I went to see Kristina," she said, joining him in the kitchen.

"Kristina who? Oh, you mean Mom?" Patrik said, clearly taken aback. "Why did you do that? I'd better make sure you're not getting sick!" He went over and placed one hand on her forehead. Erica waved him away.

"Come on, it's not that strange. I mean, she is my mother-in-law after all. I can call and see her if I want. On the spur of the moment."

"Sure you can," Patrik said with a laugh. "Okay, out with it—why did you go to see my mother?"

Erica told him about her sudden realization just outside the library that there was in fact someone else who had known Elsy when she was young. She also told him about Kristina's strange reaction, and about the revelation that Elsy had had a relationship with the young Norwegian who had fled from the Germans. "But then she refused to say any more," Erica said, thoroughly frustrated. "Or perhaps she didn't know any more. I'm not sure. Anyway, it seemed as if Hans Olavsen somehow abandoned my mother. He left Fjällbacka and, according to Kristina, Elsy said he'd gone back to Norway."

"So what's your next move?" Patrik asked as he put the leftovers from lunch in the refrigerator.

"I'm going to try to track him down, of course," Erica said, heading for the living room. "By the way, I think we should invite Kristina over on Sunday so that she can spend some time with Maja."

"Now I'm positive you've got a temperature," Patrik laughed. "But, sure, I'll give Mom a call and see if she wants to come over on Sunday. She might not have time, of course—she's always so busy."

"Mmm," Erica said in a strange tone of voice. Patrik shook his head. Women. He would never understand them. Then again, maybe that was the point.

"What's this?" Erica shouted from the living room. Patrik went to see what she was talking about. She was pointing at the folder on the coffee table, and Patrik could have kicked himself for not putting it away before she got home. He knew her well enough to realize that it was too late to keep her away from it now.

"It's the case file on the murder of Erik Frankel," he said, wagging a warning finger at her. "And anything you read in there is absolutely confidential, okay?"

"Yeah, yeah," Erica said distractedly, waving him away like an annoying fly. She sat down on the sofa and started leafing through the documents and photographs.

An hour later, she had gone through the entire contents of the folder, and started from the beginning again. Patrik had looked in on her a few times but had eventually abandoned any attempt at communication, and settled down with the morning paper, which he hadn't yet had time to read.

"You don't have much physical evidence to go on," Erica said, running her finger down the report from forensics.

"No, it does seem a bit thin," Patrik said, putting aside the newspaper. "No fingerprints in the library apart from Erik and Axel's and those of the two boys who found the body. Nothing appears to be missing, and the footprints have also been traced back to the same people. The murder weapon was lying under the desk, and it was a weapon that was already on the scene, so to speak."

"Not a premeditated murder, in other words—more of a sudden impulse," Erica mused.

"Yes, unless someone knew that the stone bust was kept on the windowsill, of course." Patrik remembered something that had occurred to him a couple of days earlier. "By the way, when did you take that medal to Erik Frankel?"

"Why?" Erica still sounded as if she were miles away.

"I'm not sure; it might be totally irrelevant, but it would be useful to know."

"It was the day before we went to the zoo with Maja," Erica said as she continued to leaf through the papers. "Wasn't that June 3? In which case I went to see Erik on the second."

"Did you get any information about the medal? Did he say anything while you were there?"

"If he had, I would have told you when I got home. No, he just said he wanted to do a little more research before he told me anything."

"So you still don't know what kind of Nazi medal it is?"

"No," Erica said, looking thoughtfully at Patrik. "But it's definitely something I ought to get on to. I'll look it up tomorrow, although I'm not sure where to start." She bent over the folder again, closely scrutinizing the photographs from the scene of the crime. She picked up the top picture and peered at it.

"I can't see . . . ," she muttered, then got to her feet and went upstairs.

"What is it?" Patrik asked, but got no reply. He picked up his newspaper again and a moment later Erica came back down, waving a magnifying glass.

"What are you doing?" he said, gazing at his wife over the top of the paper.

"I'm not sure. . . . It's probably nothing, but . . . it looks as if something has been scribbled on the notepad on Erik's desk. But I can't quite make it out. . . ." She bent her head over the picture and placed the magnifying glass over the small white patch that was the notepad.

"I think it says . . ." she narrowed her eyes. "I think it says '*Ignoto militi.*'"

"Right, and what the hell does that mean?" Patrik said

"I don't know. I imagine there's some military connection. But it's probably nothing; just a scribble," she said, sounding disappointed.

"By the way. . . ." Patrik lowered the newspaper and tilted his head to one side. "I had a chat with Martin when he brought the folder over, and he asked if I could do him a favor in return." That wasn't quite what had happened, of course; Patrik had jumped in right away and offered to help, but that wasn't something he felt the need to share with Erica. He cleared his throat and went on. "Erik Frankel has been making regular payments to someone in Gothenburg once a month for fifty years; Martin wants me to check it out."

"Fifty years?" Erica said, raising her eyebrows. "He's been giving money to someone for fifty years? What's that all about? Blackmail?" She couldn't hide her excitement.

"No one has any idea. And it's probably nothing, but. . . . Anyway, Martin was wondering if I might have time to go over there."

"Great, I'll go with you," Erica said enthusiastically.

Patrik stared at her. That wasn't quite the reaction he had been expecting.

"Right, well, yes, maybe," he said, wondering if there was any reason he shouldn't take her with him. But it was only a routine errand, checking up on a money transfer, so he couldn't see that it would be a problem.

"Okay, we'll all go. We could call and see Lotta afterward, so Maja can say hello to her cousins."

"Excellent," Erica said; she liked Patrik's sister. "And I might be able to find someone I can ask about the medal while we're in Gothenburg."

"Good idea. Make a few calls this afternoon and see if you can track down someone who knows about that kind of thing."

He looked down at his newspaper and began to read again, making the most of the opportunity before Maja woke up.

Erica went back to examining the little notepad on Erik's desk. *Ignoto militi.* Something was stirring in the back of her mind.

This time it took only half an hour or so before he got the hang of it.

"Well done, Bertil," Rita said appreciatively, giving his hand an extra squeeze. "You're really getting into the rhythm now, I can feel it."

"I guess so," Mellberg said modestly. "I've always been a good dancer."

"Have you really?" she said, smiling. "I heard that you had coffee with Johanna today." She looked up at him. That was something else he found appealing about Rita. He wasn't particularly tall, but the fact that she was so petite made him feel like a giant.

"I just happened to be passing," he said, unable to hide his embarrassment. "And Johanna came along and asked if I wanted to come up for a coffee."

"Oh, so you just happened to be passing?" Rita laughed as they moved in time to the salsa beat. "What a pity I wasn't home when you just happened to be passing. But Johanna said you had a really nice time together."

"Yes, she's a lovely girl," Mellberg said, once again feeling the sensation of the baby's foot kicking against the palm of his hand. "A really lovely girl."

"It hasn't always been easy for them," Rita sighed. "And I don't mind admitting that I found it a bit difficult to get my head around it at first. But I guess I knew before Paula brought Johanna home. They've been together for nearly ten years now, and I can honestly say that there's no one I would rather see as

Paula's partner. They're perfect for each other, and when that happens, gender is irrelevant."

"But surely things must have been easier in Stockholm? People must have accepted their relationship more readily?" Mellberg said tentatively, then swore as he accidentally trod on Rita's toes. "I mean, it's so common there. If you watch TV, you sometimes get the impression that virtually everybody in Stockholm is inclined that way."

"I wouldn't agree with that," Rita said, laughing. "We were a bit nervous about moving here, but I have to say I've been pleasantly surprised. I don't think the girls have come up against any problems so far. Then again, perhaps people haven't realized. We'll cross that bridge when we come to it. What are they supposed to do? Stop living? Not move to where they want to be? Sometimes you just have to be brave and venture into the unknown." She suddenly looked sad, gazing off into the distance over Mellberg's shoulder. He thought he knew what she was thinking about.

"Was it difficult? Having to flee from your own country?" he said gently, realizing to his surprise that he actually wanted to hear the answer. He usually made a point of avoiding asking sensitive questions, or else he would ask because it was expected of him but didn't really care about the response. This time he really wanted to know.

"It was both difficult and easy," Rita said, and in her dark eyes he could see that she had experienced things he couldn't even begin to imagine.

"It was easy to leave the place that my country had become, but difficult to leave the country that it had once been." For a moment she lost the rhythm of the dance and stopped, her hands still in Mellberg's. Then her eyes flashed; she pulled away and clapped loudly.

"Okay, everyone, time to learn the next step, which is a spin. Bertil, you're going to help me demonstrate." She grabbed his hands again and slowly showed him the steps that would allow him to spin her around once under his arm. It wasn't easy, and he got in a mess with both his hands and feet, but Rita didn't lose patience. She went through it over and over, until Bertil and the other couples had gotten the hang of it.

"This is going to go really well," she said, looking up at him. He wondered if she was just talking about the dance. Or something else. He hoped it was the latter.

Darkness was falling. The hospital sheets rustled slightly whenever he moved, so he was trying to keep still. He would have preferred total silence. He couldn't do anything about the noises from outside, the sound of voices, people walking up and down the corridor, the clatter of trays. But in here he could make sure it was as quiet as possible. That the silence was not disturbed by rustling sheets.

Herman stared out the window. His reflection had begun to appear on the glass as the sky grew darker outside, and he thought how pitiful the figure in the bed looked. A shrunken, gray old man in a white hospital gown, with sparse hair and wrinkled cheeks. It was as if Britta had somehow given him an air of authority, a dignity that had filled him, made him more than he was. As if she had been the one who gave his life meaning. And now it was his fault that she was gone.

The girls had been to visit him today. Held him, hugged him, gazed at him with anxious eyes and talked to him in worried voices. But he hadn't even been able to bring himself to look at them. He was afraid they would see the guilt in his eyes. See what he had done. What he had brought about.

They had carried the secret for such a long time, he and Britta. Shared it, hidden it away, atoned for it. At least that was what he had thought. But when her illness came and her defenses began to crumble, he had realized in a moment of clarity that nothing could ever be atoned for. Sooner or later, time and destiny would catch up with a person. It was impossible to hide. It was impossible to run. They had naïvely believed that it was enough to live a good life, to be good people. To love their children and raise them as people who could pass on that love. And eventually they had foolishly imagined that the good they had created had overshadowed the evil.

He had killed Britta. Why couldn't they understand that? He knew they wanted to talk to him, ask him questions, cast doubt on what he had said. If only they would accept the way things were.

He had killed Britta. And now he had nothing left.

"Have you any idea who this person is, and why Erik has been transferring money all these years?" Erica asked as they approached Gothenburg. Maja had behaved impeccably in the back seat, and as they had managed to get away shortly before eight-thirty, it was still only ten o'clock when they drove into the city.

"No, the only information we have is what's in front of you," Patrik said, nodding at the piece of paper in a plastic folder on Erica's knee.

"Wilhelm Fridén, Vasagatan 38, Gothenburg. Date of birth October 3, 1924," she read aloud.

"There you go—that's all we know. I spoke briefly to Martin last night; he hasn't found any links to Fjällbacka, and there's no criminal record. Nothing. So this is a shot in the dark. Speaking of which, what time is your appointment with that guy about the medal?"

"Twelve o'clock in his antique shop," Erica said, patting the pocket where the medal lay safely wrapped in a soft cloth.

"Are you staying in the car with Maja, or are you going to take her for a walk while I speak to Wilhelm Fridén?" Patrik asked as he pulled into a parking space on Vasagatan.

"What?" Erica said, sounding offended. "I'm coming with you, obviously."

"But you can't do that . . . what about Maja?" Patrik said feebly. As soon as he spoke, he realized where that particular discussion was going. And where it would end.

"If she can visit crime scenes and the police station, then I'm sure she can come and see an old man of eighty," Erica said. Her tone made it perfectly clear that there was no room for discussion.

"Okay," Patrik said with a sigh. He knew when he was beaten.

They made their way up to the third floor of the turn-of-the-century apartment block and rang the doorbell. A man in his sixties answered, looking at them questioningly.

"Yes? How can I help you?"

Patrik held up his police ID. "My name is Patrik Hedström and I'm with the Tanumshede police. I have some questions relating to a Wilhelm Fridén."

"Who's that?" came a faint female voice from inside the apartment. The man turned and shouted "It's a police officer wanting to ask questions about Dad!"

He turned back to Patrik. "I can't for the life of me imagine why the police would be interested in my father, but please come in." He stepped aside and raised his eyebrows in surprise when Erica walked in with Maja in her arms.

"I see police officers are getting even younger these days," he said, clearly amused.

Patrik gave an embarrassed smile. "This is my wife, Erica Falck, and our daughter, Maja. They . . . my wife has a personal interest in the case we're currently investigating, and. . . ." He broke off. There wasn't really any satisfactory explanation for a police officer turning up to question someone with his wife and a one-year-old in tow.

"I'm sorry, I haven't introduced myself. My name is Göran Fridén, and the person you're asking about is my father."

Patrik looked at him with curiosity. He was of medium height with gray, slightly curly hair and blue eyes.

"Is your father home?" Patrik asked as they followed Göran Fridén down a long hallway.

"Unfortunately, you're too late if you have any questions for my father. He died two weeks ago."

"Oh." Patrik was taken aback. That wasn't the answer he had been expecting. He had been sure the man was still alive, in spite of his advanced age, because his death wasn't registered in the public records. It was probably because he had passed away so recently; it was no surprise that it took time for information to appear in the records. He felt a deep sense of disappointment. His intuition told him this was an important lead; was he too late?

"You can speak to my mother if you like," Göran said, showing them into the living room. "I mean, I don't know what it's about, but she might be able to help."

A small, frail old lady with snow-white hair got up from the sofa. She was still pretty. She came toward them with her hand outstretched.

"Märta Fridén." She looked at them inquisitively, and broke into a smile as soon as she saw Maja. "Well, hi there! What a sweetie! What's her name?"

"Maja," Erica said proudly, taking an immediate liking to Märta Fridén.

"Hello, Maja," Märta said, patting her on the cheek. Maja beamed with delight at the attention and started wriggling like crazy when she spotted an old doll sitting at one end of the sofa.

"No, Maja," Erica said firmly, trying to restrain her daughter.

"Oh, let her have a look at it," Märta said, waving her hand. "There's nothing here too precious for her to touch. Since

Wilhelm passed away, I've realized more and more that we can't take it with us when we go." Her eyes grew sad, and her son came and put his arm around her.

"Sit down, Mom, and I'll make some coffee for our guests and give you the chance to have a little chat."

Märta's eyes followed him as he went into the kitchen. "He's a good boy," she said. "I try not to be a burden; children have their own lives to live. He's too nice for his own good some-times, but Wilhelm was so proud of him." She seemed to lose herself in her memories for a moment, then she turned to Patrik.

"Now, what did the police want to talk to my Wilhelm about?"

Patrik cleared his throat, aware that he was on thin ice. He might end up exposing a whole lot of things that this lovely little lady would have preferred not to know about, but he had no choice. Tentatively, he said "Well, the thing is, we're investigating a murder up north, in Fjällbacka. I'm based in Tanumshede, and Fjällbacka comes under the jurisdiction of Tanumshede," he explained.

"Goodness, a murder," Märta said with a frown.

"Yes, a man named Erik Frankel has been murdered," Patrik said, pausing to see if there was any reaction. As far as he could tell, Märta didn't appear to recognize the name. She soon confirmed this.

"Erik Frankel? That doesn't sound familiar at all. What has led you to Wilhelm?" She leaned forward, looking interested.

"Well . . . ," Patrik hesitated. "It appears that this Erik Frankel has been making a monthly payment to a Wilhelm Fridén—your husband—for almost fifty years. And naturally we are wondering why this payment has been made, and what the connection between them might have been."

"Wilhelm has been receiving money from . . . from a man in Fjällbacka called Erik Frankel?" Märta looked genuinely astonished. Göran walked in with a tray of coffee, a quizzical expression on his face.

"So what's all this about?" he asked.

His mother answered him. "This police officer says that a man called Erik Frankel, who has been murdered, has been paying money to your father every month for fifty years."

"What?" Göran exclaimed, sitting down next to his mother. "To Dad? But why?"

"That's exactly what we're wondering," Patrik said. "We were hoping that Wilhelm himself would be able to tell us."

"Dolly," Maja said happily, holding up the old doll to show Märta.

"That's right," Märta said, smiling at Maja. "She was my dolly when I was a little girl."

Maja clasped the doll gently and gave her a hug. Märta could hardly take her eyes off the child.

"What an adorable little girl," she said, and Erica nodded enthusiastically.

"How much money are we talking about?" Göran said, staring at Patrik.

"Not huge sums: two thousand kronor a month over the last few years. But the amount has gradually increased over the years, seemingly in line with inflation. So even though the actual figure has changed, the approximate value has remained constant."

"Why didn't Dad ever mention this?" Göran said, looking at his mother.

She shook her head slowly. "I have no idea. But, to be honest, Wilhelm and I never discussed financial matters. He took care of that side of things while I ran the home, as was common practice for our generation. That was how we shared the responsibilities. If it wasn't for Göran, I'd be completely lost now, trying to deal with bills and loans and so on." She placed her hand on her son's, and he patted it gently.

"I'm happy to help, Mom, you know that."

"Do you have any documentation concerning the family finances that we could take a look at?" Patrik said, feeling rather dispirited. He had hoped to find answers to all his questions regarding this strange monthly payment, but instead he seemed to have hit a dead end.

"Everything is with our lawyer at the moment," Göran said apologetically, "but I'll ask them to copy it all and send it over to you."

"We'd really appreciate that," Patrik replied, feeling slightly more optimistic. Perhaps they would be able to get to the bottom of this after all.

"Sorry, I forgot to pour the coffee," Göran said, jumping to his feet.

"We really need to get going," Patrik said, glancing at his watch. "Please don't go to any trouble on our behalf."

"I'm sorry we couldn't be of more use." Märta tilted her head to the side and smiled at Patrik.

"No problem, it can't be helped. And I'm sorry for your loss," Patrik said. "I hope it hasn't been an imposition, our coming here and asking questions so soon after . . . I mean, we didn't know, but. . . ."

"It's fine, my dear," she said, waving away his apologies. "I knew my Wilhelm inside out, so whatever that payment is about, I'm absolutely certain it doesn't involve anything criminal or unethical. So you're welcome to ask whatever you like, and, as Göran said, we're happy to make sure any financial information is passed on to you. I'm just sorry I wasn't able to help."

Everyone got up and headed for the hallway. Maja toddled after them, still clutching the doll.

"Okay, honey, we have to give the doll back now." Erica steeled herself for the inevitable outburst.

"Oh, let the child keep it," Märta said, stroking Maja's hair as she passed by. "As I said, I can't take anything with me when I go, and I'm too old to play with dolls."

"Are you sure?" Erica stammered. "It's so old, and I'm sure it brings back happy memories, and. . . ."

"The memories are in here," Märta said, tapping her forehead. "Not in our possessions. Nothing would give me more pleasure than to know that someone will play with Greta again. I'm sure she's been terribly bored, sitting here on the sofa with an old lady!"

"Thank you. Thank you so much," Erica said. To her annoyance, she found she was so moved that she had to blink fiercely to hold back the tears.

"Don't mention it." Märta stroked Maja's head once more, then both she and her son came to the door to see them off.

The last thing Erica and Patrik saw before the door closed behind them was Göran, tenderly putting his arm around his mother's shoulders and kissing the top of her white head.

Martin was wandering around restlessly at home. Pia was working, and when he was alone in the apartment he found it impossible to stop thinking about the case. It was as if his sense of responsibility for the investigation had increased tenfold because Patrik was on leave, and he wasn't completely certain that he was up to the task. In a way, asking Patrik for help had felt like weakness, but he relied heavily on his colleague's judgment, perhaps less so on his own. Sometimes he wondered if he would ever feel completely confident in his professional role. There was always that lurking doubt, the insecurity that had been there ever since the Police Academy. Was he really suited to this job? Could he reach the level of achievement that was expected of him?

He paced up and down as he brooded. He realized that his current uncertainty about the job was due to the fact that he was facing the biggest challenge of his life, and he didn't know if he would be able to deliver. What if he didn't measure up? What if he couldn't give Pia the support she needed? What if he couldn't live up to what was expected of a father? What if, what if. . . . His head was spinning, and eventually he realized he would have to do something concrete to stop himself going crazy. He grabbed his jacket, got in his car, and headed south. At first he didn't know where he was going, but as he approached Grebbestad, everything became clear. He had been thinking about that call from Britta and Herman's house to Frans Ringholm ever since the previous day. The same people kept on popping up in both investigations, and even though the cases appeared to be running parallel, Martin had a gut feeling that there was a crossover somewhere. Why had Herman or Britta called Frans in June before Erik died? There was only one call in the phone records, on June fourth. It hadn't lasted very long; two minutes and thirty-three seconds, as Martin recalled. But why had they wanted to speak to Frans? Was it as simple as Axel had suggested: that because of Britta's illness, she had wanted to rekindle old friendships? With people who, by all accounts, she hadn't spoken to in sixty years? Admittedly, the human brain could play some odd tricks, but . . . no. There was something else going on here. Something that eluded him. And he had no intention of giving up until he found out what it was.

Frans was on his way out when Martin met him in the doorway of his apartment.

"How can I help you today?" Frans asked politely.

"Just one or two more questions."

"I was just heading out for my daily walk. If you want to talk to me, you're welcome to come along; I don't change my schedule for anyone. That's how I keep in shape." He set off toward the water, and Martin joined him.

"You don't mind being seen with a cop, then?" Martin said with a wry smile.

"Listen, I've spent so much time with you guys over the years, I'm used to your company," Frans said, a glint of amusement in his eye. "Okay, so what can I do for you?" All trace of humor was gone. Martin had to break into a jog to keep up; the old man set an impressive pace.

"I don't know if you've heard, but there has been another murder in Fjällbacka."

Frans slowed down briefly, then increased his speed once more. "No, I hadn't heard. Who was it?"

"Britta Johansson." Martin studied Frans intently.

"Britta?" Frans turned to look at Martin. "But how? Who?"

"Her husband claims he did it. But I'm not so sure. . . ."

Frans gave a start. "Herman? But why? I can't believe. . . ."

"Did you know Herman?" Martin made an effort to hide how important the answer to this question was.

"No, I can't say I did," Frans said, shaking his head. "Actually, I've only met him once. He called me in June and told me Britta was sick, and that she'd said she wanted to see me."

"Didn't you find that a little strange? Bearing in mind that you hadn't seen each other for sixty years?" Martin made no attempt to hide his skepticism.

"Of course I found it a little strange. But Herman explained that she had Alzheimer's, and apparently it's not unusual for sufferers to go back to memories of the past and people who were important to them. After all, we did grow up together, the whole gang."

"And the whole gang consisted of . . . ?"

"There was me, Britta, Erik, and Elsy Moström."

"Of whom two are dead, murdered within the space of two months," Martin said, panting slightly as he jogged along next to Frans. "Don't you think that's a remarkable coincidence?"

Frans kept his eyes fixed on the horizon. "When you get to my age, you've experienced enough coincidences to know that they're not all that unusual. Besides, you said Britta's husband had confessed to her murder. Do you think he killed Erik too?" Frans looked across at Martin.

"We don't think anything at the moment. But it does give me pause for thought when two people who were part of a group of four are murdered within such a short period of time."

"As I said, there's nothing strange about strange coincidences. It's just chance. And fate."

"That sounds very philosophical for a man who's spent most of his life in jail. Was that due to chance and fate as well?" Martin's tone was slightly acidic, and he had to remind himself to keep his personal feelings out of it. But he had seen the effect on Paula during the last week of what Frans Ringholm stood for, and he found it difficult to hide his disgust.

"Chance and fate had nothing to do with it. I was an adult and perfectly capable of making my own decisions when I embarked on that particular course. And of course with hindsight I can say that I shouldn't have done that, or that, or that. . . . And that I should have taken that path instead. Or that one. . . . Or that one. . . ." Frans stopped and turned to Martin. "But we don't have that advantage when we are living our lives, do we?" he said, setting off again. "The advantage of knowing how things are going to turn out. I made my own choices. I lived the life I lived. And I've paid the price."

"And what about your opinions? Did you choose those too?" Martin realized that he was genuinely curious about the answer. He didn't understand these people at all, those who condemned whole sections of humanity. He had no idea how they could justify that to themselves. And while a part of him was full of loathing for them, he was also curious about what made them tick, just as a small child wants to take a radio apart to see how it works.

Frans didn't say anything for a long time. He seemed to realize that Martin's question was genuine, and was considering how best to answer it.

"I stand by my opinions. I think there is something wrong with society, and this is my interpretation of what the problem is. And therefore I regard it as my duty to try to help make things right."

"But putting the blame on entire ethnic groups. . . ." Martin shook his head. He just didn't get it at all.

"You are making the mistake of regarding people as individuals," Frans said drily. "Man has never been an individual. We are one element of a group. One part of a collective. And these groups have fought against one another throughout history, fought for their place within the hierarchy, the world order. You might wish that things were different. But they're not. And even if I don't use violence to secure my place in the world, I am a survivor. The one who will eventually emerge victorious in that world order. And it is always the victors who write the historical narrative."

When he had finished speaking, he looked at Martin, who felt a shiver run down his spine in spite of the fact that he was pouring with sweat from the fast pace Frans had set. There was something deeply frightening about being faced with such fanatical conviction. The realization that there was no logic on earth that could convince Frans and his like that their view of the world was distorted chilled Martin to the bone. It was just a matter of keeping them restrained, minimizing their influence, decimating their numbers. Martin had always believed that if you could just reason with a person, you would eventually be able to reach a core that could be changed. But in Frans's eyes he saw a core so fiercely protected by rage and hatred that it would never be possible to penetrate its defenses.

30
Fjällbacka 1944

"This is good," Vilgot said, helping himself to more fried mackerel. "This is very tasty, Bodil."

She didn't answer, but simply bowed her head with relief. She always felt as if she had been given a breathing space when her husband was temporarily in a good mood and pleased with her.

"That's something for you to remember, boy—when you get married, you need to make sure first that the girl is talented both in the kitchen and in bed!" Vilgot guffawed, his mouth wide open, showing the food inside, and pointed his fork at Frans.

"Vilgot!" Bodil said, not daring to go beyond a faint note of protest in her tone of voice.

"The boy might as well learn," he said, shoveling down another huge forkful of mashed potato. "And by the way, you should be proud of your father today. I just had a call from

Gothenburg about that Jew named Rosenberg: his firm has gone bust, thanks to the fact that I've taken so much business from him this past year. That's definitely something to celebrate! And that's the way to treat them; we need to force them to their knees one by one, both financially and with the whip!" He laughed until his belly wobbled. The butter from the mackerel had trickled down his chin, which shone with grease.

"It won't be easy for him to make a living, with the way things are these days," Bodil said. But as soon as she had spoken, she realized her mistake.

"Do go on, my dear," Vilgot said in a deceptively gentle voice, putting down his knife and fork. "If you're feeling sympathetic toward one of his sort, I'd very much like to hear your further thoughts on the matter."

"I didn't mean anything by it," she said, her eyes downcast, hoping that this sign of capitulation might enable her to get away with it. But a familiar glint had already appeared in Vilgot's eye, and now his full attention was focused on his wife.

"But I'm interested in what you have to say. Do please go on."

Frans glanced from one parent to the other as a hard knot formed in his stomach, growing bigger all the time. He could see his mother beginning to tremble under Vilgot's gaze. And there was a glazed look in Vilgot's eyes, a look that Frans had seen many times before. He wondered whether he should ask to be excused from the table, but then he realized it was already too late.

Bodil's voice was unsteady, and she swallowed hard several times before she spoke. "I was just thinking about his family. It might be hard to find another job these days."

"This is a Jew we are talking about, Bodil." Vilgot's tone was admonitory, and he spoke slowly, as if to a child. And that particular tone seemed to rouse something within his wife.

She lifted her head and said, with a hint of stubbornness, "But surely Jews are people too? They have to feed their children, just as we do."

Frans felt the knot in his stomach grow to gigantic proportions. He wanted to yell at his mother, tell her to shut up, not to speak to his father like that. What had gotten into her? How could she say that to him? And sticking up for a Jew? How could that possibly be worth the price he knew she would have to pay? Suddenly he felt an unreasonable hatred toward his mother. How could she be so stupid? Didn't she know there was never any point in challenging his father? The best thing to do was to bow your head and do as he said, never to oppose him. If you did that, you could escape his wrath for a while. Stupid, stupid woman. She had just shown the one thing you must never let Vilgot Ringholm see: a flicker of revolt. A little spark of defiance. Frans shuddered at the thought of the powder keg this spark was bound to ignite.

The room went completely silent. Vilgot stared at his wife, apparently unable to take in what she had just said. A vein started throbbing in his neck, and Frans watched as he clenched his fists. He wanted to get out of here. To run away from the table and keep on running until he could run no more. Instead he felt as if he were glued to the chair, incapable of movement.

Then came the explosion. Vilgot's clenched fist shot out and hit Bodil right on the chin, sending her flying. The chair fell over and she crashed to the floor. She groaned with pain, a sound that Frans could feel in his very bones, but instead of arousing sympathy, he felt even angrier with her. Why couldn't she have kept her mouth shut? Why did she have to make him witness this?

"So you're a lover of the Jews, are you?" Vilgot said, getting to his feet. "Well? Are you?"

Bodil had managed to turn over and was on all fours, trying to catch her breath.

Vilgot drew back his foot and kicked her hard in the midriff. "ARE YOU? Answer me! Do I have a Jew lover in this house? Here in my own home? Do I?"

She didn't answer, but began laboriously trying to crawl away. Vilgot followed her and delivered another kick, which landed in exactly the same spot. She jerked and collapsed on the floor, but managed to drag herself onto all fours again and made another attempt to crawl away.

"You're a fucking bitch, that's what you are! A fucking disgusting, Jew-loving bitch!" Vilgot spat out the words and when Frans glanced at his father's face, he could see a greedy pleasure in his eyes. Vilgot kicked Bodil yet again as he continued to shower her with abuse. Then he looked at Frans. His face was glowing with excitement, an expression Frans recognized all too well.

"I'm going to teach you how to deal with bitches, my boy. It's the only language they understand. Watch and learn, my boy, watch and learn." He was breathing heavily, his eyes fixed on Frans, as he slowly unfastened his belt and his pants. Then he took a few steps over to Bodil, who had managed to crawl a short distance away. He grabbed her hair with one hand and pulled up her skirt with the other.

"No, please, no . . . think of . . . Frans," she begged.

Vilgot merely laughed and yanked her head back as he pushed into her with a loud groan.

The knot inside Frans's stomach hardened into a cold, solid lump of hatred. And when his mother turned her head and met his eyes, down on her knees on the floor, as his father thrust into her over and over again, he knew that his only hope of survival was to hold on to that hatred.

31

Kjell spent Saturday morning at the office. Beata had taken the children to see her parents, and it seemed like an excellent opportunity to do some research on Hans Olavsen. So far he had drawn a blank. There were far too many Norwegians with the same name at that time, and unless he could find something that would enable him to start eliminating some of them, he would get nowhere.

He had read the articles Erik had given him several times without finding anything concrete to go on, and without being able to work out what Erik had wanted him to get from all this. That was what surprised him the most. If Erik Frankel had wanted him to find something out, then why hadn't he just said what it was? Why this cryptic approach with the newspaper articles? Kjell sighed. The only thing he knew about Hans Olavsen was that he had been a Norwegian resistance fighter during the Second World War. The question was how he could use this information in order to make progress. For a second, he considered speaking to his father, asking him if he knew anything more about the Norwegian, but he immediately dismissed the idea. He would rather spend a hundred hours in some dusty archive than ask his father for help with anything.

An archive. That was a thought. Was there some kind of register of resistance fighters in Norway? A great deal must have been written about the subject, and there was bound to be someone who had researched the resistance movement and attempted to chart its history. There always was.

He made several searches on the Internet, trying search terms in various combinations until he eventually found what he was looking for. Someone called Eskil Halvorsen had written several books on Norway during the Second World War, with a particular emphasis on the resistance movement. This was the man he needed to talk to. Kjell found the Norwegian telephone directory on the Internet and quickly located Eskil Halvorsen's number. He reached for the phone and punched in the digits, but had to start again because he had forgotten to use the international dialing code for Norway. The fact that he was disturbing the man on a Saturday morning didn't bother him at all; as a journalist, he couldn't afford to have scruples like that.

After Kjell had waited impatiently for a few seconds, Eskil Halvorsen answered the phone. Kjell explained why he was calling, and said that he was trying to locate a man by the name of Hans Olavsen, who had been a part of the Norwegian resistance movement and had fled to Sweden during the last years of the war.

"So it's not a name you recognize off the top of your head?" Kjell couldn't help feeling disappointed as he doodled on a notepad. A part of him had been hoping for immediate success.

"Yes, I realize we're talking about thousands of individuals who were active within the resistance movement, but is there any possibility that . . . ?"

He was treated to a lengthy discourse on the organizational structure of the resistance movement, and feverishly made notes as he listened. It was undeniably a fascinating topic, particularly as neo-Nazism was one of his special interests, but he must remember what he was actually trying to find out.

"Is there an archive anywhere with the names of those who were part of the resistance movement?

"Okay, so there is a certain amount of documentation. . . .

"Could you possibly help me to check if there's any information on Hans Olavsen, and where he is now?

"Thank you, I really appreciate that. And he came to Sweden in 1944, to Fjällbacka, if that's of any assistance in your research."

Kjell ended the call with a satisfied expression on his face. He might not have found out anything right away as he had hoped, but he had the feeling that if anyone could dig out information about Hans Olavsen, it was the man he had just spoken to.

And there was one thing he could do himself in the meantime. The library in Fjällbacka might well have something on the Norwegian. It was worth a try, in any case. He looked at his watch. If he left now, he could get there before it closed. He picked up his jacket, shut down the computer, and left the office.

Many miles away, Eskil Halvorsen had already begun to search for information on Hans Olavsen.

Maja was sitting in the car, still clutching the doll. Erica had been genuinely moved by the old lady's gesture, and was delighted that Maja had fallen in love with the doll at first sight.

"Wasn't Märta lovely?" she said to Patrik, who merely nodded as he focused on navigating through the Gothenburg traffic, with one-way streets all over the place and streetcars appearing out of nowhere, frantically ringing their bells.

"Where shall we park?" he said, looking around.

"There's a space." Erica pointed, and Patrik pulled in.

"It's probably best if you and Maja don't come in with me," she said as she lifted the stroller out of the trunk. "I don't think an antique shop is the best environment for our light-fingered daughter."

"You could be right," Patrik said, settling Maja in the stroller. "We'll go for a walk, shall we, sweetheart? You can tell me all about it afterward."

"Promise." Erica waved good-bye to Maja and headed for the address she had been given over the telephone. The antique shop was on Guldheden, and she found it right away. The bell over the door tinkled as she walked in, and a short, thin man with a white beard emerged from behind a curtain.

"Can I help you?" he said politely and expectantly.

"Hi, my name is Erica Falck. We spoke on the phone." She went over and held out her hand.

"*Enchanté,*" he said, kissing the back of her hand, much to Erica's surprise. She couldn't remember the last time someone had kissed her hand. If they ever had.

"Ah, yes, you had a medal and you wanted to find out more about it? Come through and we can sit down while I take a look at it." He held up the curtain for her and she had to duck slightly to get through an unusually low doorway. Once inside, she stopped dead in amazement. Every inch of the walls in the dark cubbyhole was covered in Russian icons, leaving room for just a small table and two chairs.

"My passion," said the man who had introduced himself as Åke Grundén during the previous day's telephone conversation.

"I own Sweden's foremost collection of Russian icons," he said proudly as they sat down.

"They're very beautiful," Erica said, looking around with interest.

"Far more than that, my dear, far more than that," he said, positively glowing with pride as he gazed at his collection. "They are the bearers of a history and a tradition that is . . . magnificent." He broke off and put on a pair of glasses. "I'm afraid I have a tendency to become rather long-winded on this subject, so it's probably best if we turn to what you came for. I must say it sounds intriguing."

"I understand that medals from the Second World War are one of your areas of expertise."

He looked at her over the top of his glasses. "It's easy to become rather isolated when one has missed the opportunity to surround oneself with people, prioritizing old artifacts instead. I'm not completely convinced that I've got my priorities right, but it's easy to be wise after the event." He smiled, and Erica smiled back. He had a quiet, ironic sense of humor that appealed to her.

As she reached into her pocket and took out the medal wrapped in its soft cloth, Åke switched on a powerful lamp on the table. He watched with reverence as she opened up the cloth and revealed the medal.

"Ah . . . ," he said, placing it in the palm of his hand. He studied it intently, turning it this way and that beneath the bright light, screwing up his eyes to make sure he didn't miss any of the smaller details.

"Where did you find it?" he asked eventually, peering over the top of his glasses once more.

Erica told him how she had discovered the medal at the bottom of her mother's trunk.

"And your mother had no links to Germany, as far as you know?"

Erica shook her head. "Not that I've ever heard of, anyway. But I've been doing some research lately, and Fjällbacka, where my mother grew up, is quite close to the Norwegian border, and during the war there were many people who wanted to help the Norwegian resistance movement in its struggle against the Germans. For example, I know that my maternal grandfather allowed his boat to be used to smuggle things over to Norway. Toward the end of the war he actually brought back a Norwegian resistance fighter, who then lodged with the family."

"Yes, there was certainly a great deal of contact between the coastal towns and occupied Norway. The province of Dalsland also had a lot to do with the Germans and Norwegians during the war." He sounded as if he was thinking aloud, as he continued to study the medal.

"Of course I have no idea how this came into your mother's possession," he said. "But I can tell you that it's a medal called the Iron Cross, which was awarded for particular valor during the war."

"Is there any kind of register of those who received it?" Erica asked hopefully. "I mean, the Germans were good administrators during the war, whatever else you might say about them, so surely there must be some kind of record. . . ."

Åke shook his head. "No, I'm afraid not. And I have to tell you that this medal wasn't all that rare. This particular example was known as the Iron Cross First Class. Approximately four hundred and fifty thousand were handed out during the war, so it's impossible to trace the person who received this one."

Erica was disheartened. She had hoped that the medal would provide more information than this, but it had turned out to be yet another dead end.

"Oh, well, it can't be helped," she said, unable to hide the disappointment in her voice. She got up and thanked Åke, and once again he planted a kiss on the back of her hand.

"I'm very sorry," he said, showing her out. "I wish I could have been more helpful. . . ."

"That's okay," she said, opening the door. "I'll just have to find another way, because I really do want to find out why my mother had this medal."

But as the door closed behind her, she felt a sense of hopelessness. She would probably never get to the bottom of the mystery of the medal.

32

Sachsenhausen 1945

He had survived the transport in a daze. What he remembered most was that his ear had ached and festered. He had been herded onto the train to Germany with a crowd of other prisoners from Grini, unable to focus on anything but the pain in his head, which felt as if it were about to explode. Even the news that they were being moved to Germany had evoked nothing but a dull indifference. In a way it felt like a liberation. He understood what it meant, of course. Germany meant death. It wasn't a fact; nobody really knew what was waiting for them. But there were whispers. And hints. And rumors about the death that awaited them there. They knew that they were referred to as NN prisoners. *Nacht und Nebel.* Night and fog. The plan was for them to disappear, to die, without a trial or a verdict. They would simply slip away into the night and the fog. They had all heard the stories, prepared themselves for what they might find at their destination.

But nothing could have prepared them for the reality. They had arrived in hell itself. A hell without flames licking at their feet, but a hell nonetheless. He had been there for a few weeks now, and what he had seen so far haunted his dreams in his uneasy sleep each night and filled him with terror each morning when they were forced out of bed at three o'clock to start work, which went on without a break until nine o'clock in the evening.

It wasn't easy for the NN prisoners. They were regarded as already dead and were near the bottom of the pecking order. So that there would be no doubt as to who they were, they wore a red *N* on their backs. The red indicated that they were political prisoners. Criminals wore green symbols, and there was a constant battle between red and green over supremacy within the camp. The only consolation was that the Scandinavian prisoners had formed an alliance. They were spread throughout the camp, but every evening after work they would meet up and talk about what was happening. Those who could spare a little would slice off a piece of their daily bread ration, then they would gather up all the scraps of bread and give them to their fellow countrymen in the infirmary. They were determined that as many Scandinavian prisoners as possible would make it home, but for many of them it was too late. Axel had already lost count of those who had died.

He looked down at his hand, holding the shovel. It was nothing more than skin stretched over bone; there was no flesh. Exhausted, he leaned on the shovel for a moment while the nearest guard was looking the other way, but hurriedly started trying to dig again when the guard glanced in his direction. Every shovelful made him pant with exertion. Axel forced himself to ignore the reason he and his fellow prisoners were digging. He had made that mistake the first time; never again. The sight was still there every time he closed his eyes. Piles of human beings. Corpses. Emaciated skeletons that had been thrown onto the scrap heap and were now to be tossed into a hole, one on top of the other. It was easier not to look. He could see the pile only in his peripheral vision, as he laboriously struggled to shift enough earth to avoid attracting the unwelcome attention of the guards.

Beside him a prisoner sank to the ground. Every bit as gaunt and malnourished as Axel, he collapsed in a heap and was unable to drag himself to his feet again. Axel briefly considered going over to help him, but such thoughts no longer took root in his mind; they never led to any action. Because now the only thing that mattered was survival. The minimal reserves of energy Axel had were not enough for anything else. It was every man for himself, surviving as best he could. He had listened to the advice of the German political prisoners: *Nie auffallen.* Don't stand out from the crowd, don't draw attention to yourself. Instead, the important thing was to move discreetly toward the center of the group and keep your head down if trouble broke out. And so Axel watched with indifference as the guard went over to the man who had collapsed, grabbed his arm, and dragged him down to the deepest section of the grave where they had finished digging. The guard then clambered calmly out of the pit, leaving the prisoner there. He didn't waste a bullet on him. These were hard times, and it would be foolish to shoot someone who was virtually dead already. The corpses would simply be piled on top of him. If he wasn't dead by then, the weight of the bodies would suffocate him. Axel turned away from the sight of the prisoner in the grave and continued digging. He no longer thought about everyone back home. There was no room for that kind of thing if he was going to survive.

33

Two days later, Erica was still feeling dispirited at the lack of information on the medal. She knew that Patrik felt the same after his failed attempt to find out about the payments to Wilhelm Fridén. But neither of them had given up. Patrik was still hoping that the documents from Fridén's lawyer would help, while Erica was determined to carry on researching into the origins of the medal.

She had gone into her study to do some writing, but found it impossible to focus on her book. There was too much going on inside her head. She reached for the bag of chocolate caramels, enjoying the taste as the chocolate began to melt in her mouth. She would have to put a stop to this soon. It was just that there had been so much going on lately, and she couldn't deny herself the pleasure of eating a few candies. She would tackle it before long. After all, she had managed to lose weight before her wedding last spring, through sheer willpower. If she'd done it once, she could do it again. But not today.

"Erica!" Patrik called from downstairs. She went out onto the landing to see what he wanted.

"Karin just called; Maja and I are going for a walk with her and Ludde."

"Okay," Erica said, rather indistinctly because she was still chewing the caramel. She went back into her study and sat down at the computer. She hadn't really made her mind up what she thought about this business of Patrik going for walks with Karin. Admittedly, she had seemed very nice, and it was a long time since she and Patrik had split up. Erica was absolutely certain that their relationship was all in the past as far as Patrik was concerned. But even so, it felt a bit odd watching him go off with his ex-wife. After all, they had once shared a bed. Erica shook her head to push away the images that came into it and consoled herself with another chocolate caramel. She really must pull herself together. She wasn't usually the jealous type.

In order to distract herself, she spent a little while surfing the Internet. Something occurred to her, and, full of anticipation, she typed *Ignoto militi* into the search engine. A number of hits immediately appeared. She chose the top one and read the item with interest. Now she remembered why the expression had seemed familiar. On a school trip many years ago, the entire group of moderately interested pupils had been taken to the Arc de Triomphe. And the grave of the Unknown Soldier. *Ignoto militi* simply meant "To the Unknown Soldier."

Erica frowned as she read on. Thoughts were whirling through her mind, turning into questions. Was it just chance that Erik Frankel had scribbled those words on the notepad on his desk? Or did it have some significance? If so, what? She continued reading, but found nothing more of interest and minimized the window. With a third caramel in her mouth, she put her feet up on the desk and wondered what her next step should be. She had an idea just before she swallowed the last bit of the candy. There was one person who might know something. It was a long shot, but. . . . She hurried downstairs, grabbed the keys from the hall table, then drove off toward Uddevalla.

Forty-five minutes later, she was sitting in the parking lot, having just realized that she didn't actually have a plan. It had been relatively easy to make a phone call and find out which ward Herman Johansson was in at Uddevalla hospital, but she had no idea whether it would be difficult to get in to see him. Oh, well, it would all work out somehow. She would just have to improvise. To be on the safe side, she went in via the shop in the hospital foyer and bought a large bunch of flowers. She rode up in the elevator and strode confidently into the ward. Nobody seemed to be taking any notice of her. She peered at the room numbers. Thirty-five—that was where he was supposed to be. Now all she had to do was hope that he was alone and that his daughters weren't there, because otherwise there would be hell to pay.

Erica took a deep breath and pushed open the door. She let out a long breath of relief. There were no other visitors. She walked in and gently closed the door behind her. There were two beds, but Herman's roommate appeared to be fast asleep. Herman, on the other hand, was lying on his back staring into space, his arms neatly by his sides on top of the sheet.

"Hello, Herman," Erica said quietly, pulling a chair up to the bed. "I don't know if you remember me. I came to see Britta. You were angry with me."

At first she thought Herman couldn't hear her—or else he didn't want to. Then he slowly turned to look at her. "I know who you are. Elsy's daughter."

"That's right. Elsy's daughter." Erica smiled.

"You were at the house . . . the other day too," he said, his unblinking gaze fixed on her. Erica felt a great tenderness toward him. She remembered him lying beside his dead wife, clutching her tightly. And now he looked so small in the hospital bed, small and frail. This wasn't the same man who had told her off for upsetting Britta.

"Yes, I was there. With Margareta," Erica said. Herman merely nodded. They were silent for a while, then Erica said "I'm trying to find out a bit more about my mother. I came across Britta's name, and when I spoke to Britta, I got the feeling that she knew more than she wanted to tell me—more than she could tell me."

Herman gave a strange smile but didn't reply. Erica took a deep breath and continued. "I also think it's a strange coincidence that two of the people my mom used to hang out with back in those days have died within such a short time. . . ." She paused and waited for his reaction.

A tear rolled down his cheek. He raised his hand and wiped it away. "I killed her," he said, staring into space once more. "I killed her."

Erica heard what he was saying, and, according to Patrik, there wasn't actually any evidence to the contrary. But she knew that Martin was skeptical; she felt the same, and there was an odd tone in Herman's voice that she couldn't quite interpret.

"Do you know what it was that Britta didn't want to tell me? Was it something that happened back then, during the war? Was it something to do with my mother? I think I have the right to know," she persisted. She hoped she wasn't pushing an obviously unstable man too hard, but she so desperately wanted to find out what lay in her mother's past that perhaps her judgment was slightly impaired. When she didn't get a reply, she went on. "When Britta started to get confused, she said something about an unknown soldier. Do you know what she meant? She thought I was Elsy at that point, not Elsy's daughter. And she talked about an unknown soldier. Do you know what she meant?"

At first she couldn't identify the sound Herman was making, then she realized that he was laughing. It was an infinitely sad imitation of laughter, and she couldn't understand what was so funny. But perhaps nothing was.

"Ask Paul Heckel. And Friedrich Hück. They'll be able to answer your questions." He laughed again, louder and louder, until the whole bed was shaking.

His laughter frightened Erica more than his tears, but she still had to ask: "Who are they? Where will I find them? What have they got to do with this?" She wanted to shake Herman, make him answer her questions, make him explain, but at that moment the door opened.

"What's going on here?" A doctor was standing in the doorway with his arms folded, a stern expression on his face.

"Sorry, I got lost. And this gentleman said he wanted a chat. But then. . . ." She got up quickly and rushed out of the room looking apologetic.

Her heart was pounding by the time she got back to her car. She had been given two names. Two names that she had never heard before, that meant nothing to her. What did two Germans have to do with this? Was it something to do with Hans Olavsen? After all, he had been fighting against the Germans before he fled. She didn't understand any of this.

The names were going around and around in her head all the way back to Fjällbacka. Paul Heckel and Friedrich Hück. It was strange. She was sure she hadn't heard them before, and yet at the same time they were vaguely familiar. . . .

"Martin Molin." He answered the phone as soon as it rang, and listened intently for a few minutes, making notes and interrupting with an occasional brief question. Then he picked up his pad and went into Mellberg's office, where he found the chief in a very odd position. Mellberg was sitting in the middle of the floor with his legs stretched out in front of him, straining to touch his toes. Without a great deal of success.

"Sorry—am I disturbing you?" Martin stopped dead in the doorway. Ernst at least was very pleased to see him; he came over, wagging his tail, and started licking Martin's hand. Mellberg didn't reply; he merely scowled and tried to get up, but much to his annoyance he had to give up and hold out a hand to Martin, who hauled him to his feet.

"I was just doing a few stretches," Mellberg muttered, walking stiffly to his chair. Martin covered his mouth to hide a smirk. This was just getting better and better.

"Did you want something in particular, or are you disturbing me for no reason?" Mellberg snapped, reaching for one of the coconut marshmallows he kept in the bottom drawer of his desk. Ernst sniffed the air and made a beeline for the wonderful—and by now familiar—aroma, gazing at Mellberg with liquid, pleading eyes. Mellberg attempted a stern look, but soon gave in and reached for another marshmallow, which he tossed to the mutt. It was gone in a second.

"That dog is getting a bit of a belly," Martin said, looking with concern at Ernst, whose paunch was starting to resemble that of his temporary master.

"He's fine. A bit of extra weight never did anybody any harm," Mellberg said contentedly, patting his stomach.

Martin abandoned the subject of obesity and sat down opposite Mellberg.

"Pedersen just called, and I also had a report from Torbjörn this morning. Their initial conclusions have been confirmed. Britta Johansson was murdered, suffocated with the pillow that was on the bed next to her."

"And how do they know . . . ?" Mellberg began, but Martin interrupted him, consulting his notepad. "Pedersen made things sound more complicated than necessary, as usual, but in simple terms they found a feather from the pillow in her throat. Presumably it got there when she was gasping for breath with the pillow pressed over her face. This led Pedersen to look for further traces of fibers in her throat, and he found cotton fibers that match the pillow. There was also damage to the bones in the throat, which shows that someone also applied direct pressure to that area, probably with the hand. They checked for fingerprints on the skin, but unfortunately they didn't find any."

"Well, that all seems pretty clear. From what I've heard, she was sick. A bit gaga," Mellberg said, tapping his finger against his temple.

"She had Alzheimer's," Martin said tersely.

"Yeah, okay, carry on," Mellberg said, waving away Martin's irritation. "But there doesn't seem to be anything to suggest that the old man didn't do it, does there? Could it have been one of those . . . mercy killings?" he said, pleased with his deductive logic. He decided to reward himself with another marshmallow.

"Well, yes . . . ," Martin said reluctantly, flicking through his notepad. "But there's a very clear fingerprint on the pillowcase, according to Torbjörn. Under normal circumstances it can be difficult to lift prints from fabric, but on this occasion there were two shiny buttons that were used to fasten the pillowcase, and there was a clear thumbprint on one of them. And it doesn't belong to Herman," Martin said firmly.

Mellberg frowned and looked worried for a moment, but then his face brightened. "It's bound to be one of the daughters. Check just to be on the safe side, get confirmation. Then ring the hospital and tell the doctor to give Britta Johansson's husband electric shock therapy or whatever goddamn drugs are necessary to get him back on his feet, because we want to speak to him before the week is out. Understand?"

Martin sighed, but nodded. He didn't like this. Not one bit. But Mellberg was right. There was no evidence pointing anywhere else, apart from a single thumbprint. And if he was really unlucky, Mellberg would be right about that.

On his way out the door, Martin slapped his forehead and turned around. "I forgot something! What an idiot. Pedersen found a significant amount of DNA under Britta's fingernails, both skin and blood. Presumably she scratched the person who suffocated her. And severely, according to Pedersen; she had sharp nails, and had scraped off quite a bit of skin. He thought it was most likely that she had marked her killer on the arms or face." Martin leaned against the doorpost.

"And are there any scratch marks on the husband?" Mellberg said, his elbows propped on the desk.

"I don't know, but it certainly sounds as if we ought to pay Herman a visit right away," Martin said.

"It sure does," Mellberg agreed. "Take Paula with you!" he yelled, but Martin had already gone.

Per had been tiptoeing around at home for the last few days; he couldn't believe this was going to last. In the past, his mother hadn't managed to stay sober for even one day—not since his father left home, anyway. He didn't really remember what things had been like before then, but the few vague memories he had were pleasant ones.

He was still fighting it, but in spite of himself he was beginning to get his hopes up. More and more with each passing hour. Each passing minute, in fact. She was pretty shaky and looked kind of ashamed each time they saw each other in the house, but she was sober. He had checked everywhere, and he hadn't found a single newly purchased bottle. Not one.

And he knew all of her hiding places. He had never understood why she bothered trying to conceal the bottles; she might as well have left them standing on the kitchen counter.

"Shall I make us some dinner?" she said quietly, not quite able to look him in the eye. It was as if they were padding around each other like two frightened animals that had met for the first time, and weren't quite sure how things were going to develop. And perhaps that was exactly what they were. It had been such a long time since he had seen her completely sober; he didn't know who she was without a drink inside her. And she didn't know who he was. How could she, when she had spent all her time enveloped in a fog of alcohol that filtered everything she saw, everything she did? They were strangers to each other, but they were curious, interested, and pretty optimistic strangers.

"Have you heard from Frans?" she said as she began to gather the ingredients for spaghetti Bolognese.

Per didn't really know what to say. All his life he had been told that he was not allowed to have any contact whatsoever with his grandfather, but now Frans was the one who had stepped in and saved the day, at least temporarily.

Carina saw his hesitation and confusion. "It's okay. Kjell can say what he likes, but as far as I'm concerned, I'm happy for you to talk to Frans. Just as long as you . . ." she paused, afraid of saying the wrong thing, destroying the fragile bond they had begun to build up over the past few days. She took a deep breath and went on. "I have nothing against your seeing your grandfather. He . . . well, Frans said things that needed to be said. Things that made me realize . . ." she had started chopping onions, but she put down the knife, and Per could see that she was fighting back tears as she turned to face him. "He made me realize that things have to change around here. And for that I owe him a debt of gratitude. But I want you to promise me that you won't hang out with . . . with those people around him." Her eyes were pleading with him, and her lower lip was trembling. "And I can't promise anything . . . I hope you understand that. It's hard. Every day, every minute is really hard. And I can only promise to try. Okay?" Once again that ashamed, imploring look.

Per felt a little piece of the hard lump in his chest begin to melt. The only thing he had wanted for years, above all during those first years after his father had left them, was to be a child. Instead, he had had to clean up her vomit, make sure she didn't burn the house down when she smoked in bed, do the grocery shopping. He had had to do things that no little boy should ever have to do. All those images flickered through his mind. But none of that mattered now. The only thing he could hear was her voice, her soft, pleading mommy's voice. He took a step forward and put his arms around her. Nestled into her embrace even though he was almost a head taller than she was. And for the first time in ten years, he allowed himself to feel like a little boy.

34
Fjällbacka 1945

"Doesn't it feel great to have a break?" Britta cooed, stroking Hans's arm. He simply laughed and shook off her hand. After getting to know them all over the past six months, he was well aware when he was being exploited to make Frans jealous. The amused expression on Frans's face made it clear that he also knew exactly what Britta was up to. But you had to admire her tenacity; she would probably never stop pining for Frans. Of course Frans himself was partially to blame, occasionally encouraging her crush on him by giving her just a little bit of attention, only to revert to his usual coldness moments later. Hans thought that the game Frans was playing bordered on cruelty, but he didn't want to get involved. What bothered him more was that after a little while he had realized who Frans was actually interested in. He looked at her, sitting just a short distance away from him, and he felt a stab of pain in his chest as she said something to Frans at that very moment and smiled. Elsy had such a beautiful smile. And it wasn't just her smile—it was her eyes, her soul, her slender arms in the short-sleeved dress, the little dimple that appeared at the left-hand corner of her mouth when she smiled. Everything about her, every little detail, both inside and out, was beautiful.

They had been very kind to him, Elsy and her family. He paid a token amount in rent, and Elof had found some work for him on one of the boats. They often invited him to eat with them—virtually every evening, in fact—and there was something about their warmth, their togetherness as a family, that filled every part of him. The emotions that the war had drained away from him were slowly returning. And Elsy. He had tried to fight against the thoughts, the images, and the feelings that came over him when he went to bed at night and she came into his mind. But eventually he had realized that he simply had to give in; he was hopelessly, helplessly in love with her. Jealousy tore at his heart every time he saw Frans gazing at her with the expression he presumably had on his own face. And then there was Britta; she wasn't bright enough to have figured out how things really stood, but she instinctively knew that she wasn't the center of attention when it came to Frans or Hans, and it nagged away at her. She was a shallow, selfish girl, and he didn't really understand why someone like Elsy wanted to spend time with her. But as long as Elsy chose to have her around, he would just have to put up with her.

The person he liked best among his four new friends, apart from Elsy, was Erik. There was something serious, something mature about him that made Hans feel grounded. He liked to sit slightly apart from the others, talking to Erik. They would discuss the war, history, politics, and economics, and Erik had realized to his delight that in Hans he had an equal he had lacked until now. Admittedly he wasn't as well read as Erik when it came to facts and figures, but he had a depth of knowledge about the world and its history, about how things were interconnected. They would sit and talk for hours; Elsy used to tease them, saying they were like two old men sitting on a park bench, but Hans could see that she liked the fact that they enjoyed each other's company.

The only thing they didn't discuss was Erik's brother. Hans had never brought up the subject and, after that first time, neither had Erik.

"I think dinner will be ready soon," Elsy said, getting up and brushing off her skirt. Hans nodded and got to his feet too.

"I'd better come with you," he said, looking at Elsy, who smiled indulgently and set off down the hill. Hans could feel himself blushing. He was eighteen, three years older than Elsy, but she always made him feel like an awkward schoolboy.

He waved good-bye to the other three and slid down the hill after Elsy. She looked both ways before crossing the road and opening the gate leading into the churchyard, which was a shortcut home.

"It's a lovely evening," he said, hearing the sudden nervousness in his voice. He cursed himself; he really must stop behaving like an idiot. Elsy was walking fast along the gravel path, and he quickly caught up with her, his hands pushed deep in his pockets. She hadn't responded to his comment on the weather, which was probably a good thing, given how lame it had sounded.

Suddenly he felt a deep sense of happiness. He was walking along beside Elsy, he was even able to steal a glance at her profile and the curve of her neck from time to time, the breeze was surprisingly warm, and he liked the sound of the gravel crunching beneath their feet. This was the first time in an eternity that he had felt this way. Pure happiness. If he had ever felt this way, in fact. There had been so many obstacles, so many things that had seared his heart with humiliation, hatred, and fear. He had done his best not to think about the past. From the moment he had crept aboard Elof's boat, he had resolved to leave it all behind him. Not to look back.

But now the images came into his mind unbidden. He walked along in silence beside Elsy, trying to push them back into the recesses where he had hidden them, but they forced their way past his barricades, up into his consciousness. Perhaps this was the price he had to pay for that moment of happiness he had just experienced. That brief, bittersweet moment of happiness. If that was the case, perhaps it had been worth it, but it was of no help now as he walked along with Elsy, knowing that the faces, the sights, the smells, the memories, the sounds were demanding his attention. He was starting to panic; he had to do something. His throat was beginning to close up, his breathing was rapid and shallow. He couldn't hold them back any longer, nor could he deal with them. He had to do something.

At that moment Elsy's hand brushed against his. The sensation made him jump. It was soft, electric, and in its simplicity it was all he needed to drive out the things he couldn't think about. He stopped dead on the slope above the churchyard. Elsy was one step ahead of him, and when she turned around, the difference in height meant that her face was exactly level with his.

"What is it?" she said, sounding concerned, and at that moment he didn't know what had gotten into him. He moved half a pace toward her, took her face between his hands, and kissed her gently on the lips. At first she froze, and he felt the panic rising once more. Then she suddenly softened; her mouth relaxed and opened against his. Slowly, slowly her lips parted and, terrified but excited, he cautiously slipped his tongue inside, searching for hers. He realized that she had never been kissed before, but her tongue instinctively met his, and he felt his knees go weak. With his eyes closed, he pulled away from her, looking up only after a few seconds had passed. The first thing he saw was her eyes. And reflected in them, a mirror image of what he was feeling.

As they walked home side by side, slowly and in silence, the images stayed away. It was as if they had never even existed.

35

Christian was completely absorbed in whatever was on his computer screen when Erica walked in. She had gone straight to the library after her visit to Uddevalla, and she still had just as many questions as when she had left Herman at the hospital. She still felt that there was something familiar about the names he had mentioned; she had written them on a piece of paper, which she now handed over to Christian.

"Hi, Christian. Could you help me check if there's anything on these two names, Paul Heckel and Friedrich Hück?" she said, looking hopefully at him.

He studied the piece of paper, and she noticed with some concern that he looked worn out. It was probably just an autumn cold or trouble with the kids, she thought, but she couldn't help feeling a little worried about him.

"Sit down and I'll run a search," he said. Mentally she crossed her fingers as tightly as she could, but hope began to fade when there was no reaction on Christian's face as he studied the results of the search.

"Sorry, I can't find anything," he said eventually, shaking his head mournfully. "Not in our records and databases, at any rate. But you can try an Internet search, of course; the problem is, I don't think they're particularly unusual German names."

"Okay," Erica said, feeling disappointed. "So there's no link between those two names and this area?"

"I'm afraid not."

Erica sighed. "I guess that would have been too easy." Then she brightened up. "Listen, could you just check if there's anything else on someone who was mentioned in the articles you found for me last time? At the time, we were searching for my mother and some of her friends, rather than for this person: he was a Norwegian resistance fighter named Hans Olavsen, and he was living here in Fjällbacka. . . ."

"Toward the end of the war, yes, I know," Christian said laconically.

"Have you heard of him?" Erica said, sounding surprised.

"Not really, but this is the second inquiry I've had about him in two days. He seems to be a popular kind of guy."

"Who else was asking about him?" Erica said, holding her breath.

"Let me just check," Christian said, rolling his chair back toward a small filing cabinet. "He left his card and asked me to call him if I found out any more about Hans Olavsen." He hummed quietly to himself as he riffled through one of the drawers. Finally he found what he was looking for.

"There you go: Kjell Ringholm."

"Thanks, Christian," Erica said with a smile. "I think I'd better have a chat with him."

"Sounds serious," Christian laughed, but the humor failed to reach his eyes.

"Not really; I'm just curious as to why he's so interested in Hans Olavsen . . . ," Erica said, thinking aloud. "Did you find out anything about Hans while Kjell was here?"

"Only the stuff I gave you last time, so unfortunately I can't help."

"Slim pickings today." Erica sighed. "Do you mind if I jot down the number on Ringholm's card?"

"Be my guest," Christian said, pushing the card across to her.

"Thanks," she said, winking at Christian. He winked back, but he still looked tired.

"By the way, how's it going with the book?" she asked. "Are you sure there's nothing I can help you with? *The Mermaid*, wasn't it?"

"It's going well," he said in a slightly odd tone of voice. "And, yes, the title is *The Mermaid*. But if you'll excuse me, I have work to do. . . ." He turned his back on her and started tapping away on the keyboard. Erica walked away feeling baffled; Christian had never behaved like that before. Oh, well, she had other things to think about. A conversation with Kjell Ringholm, for example.

They had agreed to meet out on the peninsula of Veddö. There was little chance that anyone would see them there at this time of year, and if they were spotted, they would just look like two old men out walking.

"Imagine if we'd known what the future held for us," Axel said, kicking a pebble that bounced away across the shore. In the summertime swimmers shared the beach with a herd of cows, and you could just as easily spot a longhaired cow as a child cooling off in the water. But now the place was deserted, and the wind picked up pieces of dried seaweed and whirled them away. They had tacitly agreed not to talk about Erik. Or Britta. Neither of them actually knew why they had arranged to meet; there wasn't any point, after all. It wouldn't change anything. And yet the need was there, like a mosquito bite that just had to be scratched, in spite of the fact that they knew things would be worse after they had given in to temptation, just as with the mosquito bite.

"We're not meant to know," Frans said, gazing out across the water. "If we had a crystal ball showing everything that was going to happen during our lifetime, I don't think we'd ever get out of bed. I guess the idea is that life is doled out in small portions; we're given the sorrows and problems in pieces that are small enough for us to digest."

"Sometimes the pieces are too big," Axel said, kicking at another pebble.

"You're talking about other people, not you and me," Frans said, turning to look at Axel. "Other people might think we're very different, but we're the same, you and I. You know that. We don't give in. Whatever life throws at us."

Axel merely nodded. Then he looked at Frans: "Do you have any regrets?"

Frans thought about the question for a long time, then he said, slowly, "What is there to regret? What's done is done. We all make our own choices. You've made yours, and I've made mine. Do I have any regrets? No—what would be the point?"

Axel shrugged. "I suppose regret is an expression of humanity. Without regret . . . where does that leave us?"

"But surely the question is whether regret changes anything. The same thing applies to what you do: revenge. You've spent your whole life hunting down those who are guilty, and your sole aim has been to exact revenge. Nothing else. And has it changed anything? Six million people still died in the concentration camps. What difference does it make if you hunt down some woman who was a prison guard during the war but has lived as a housewife in the USA ever since? You can drag her into court to face justice for the crimes she committed over sixty years ago, but it doesn't change a thing."

Axel swallowed. He was usually completely convinced of the importance of his work, but Frans had struck a nerve: he had asked the question that Axel had occasionally asked himself in moments of weakness.

"It brings peace to the families of the victims. And it's a signal that there are limits to what we will accept as human beings."

"Bullshit," Frans said, pushing his hands into his pockets. "Do you really think it acts as a deterrent or sends out any kind of signal at all, when the present is so much stronger than the past? Not seeing the consequences of our actions, not learning from the past—that's part of human nature. As for peace . . . if you haven't found peace after sixty years, you're never going to find it. It's the individual's responsibility to cultivate that peace; you can't just wait for some kind of retribution and expect it to turn up."

"Those are cynical words," Axel said, slipping his hands into his coat pockets too. The wind was cold, and he was beginning to shiver.

"I just want you to realize that behind all the noble aims you think you've devoted your life to, there is a highly primitive, basic human emotion: the desire for revenge. I don't believe in revenge. I think we should focus on doing things that can make a difference right here and now."

"And that's what you think you're doing," Axel said, his voice tense.

"You and I are on opposite sides of the barricades, Axel," Frans said drily. "But, yes, that's exactly what I think I'm doing. I change things. I don't seek revenge. I don't have regrets. I look to the future and I follow what I believe in. Which is something completely different from what you believe in, and we are never going to agree on that. We took different roads sixty years ago, and those roads will never meet."

"How did things turn out this way?" Axel said quietly, swallowing hard.

"That's what I'm trying to tell you. It doesn't matter how things turned out this way. It is what it is. And all we can do is try to make changes, to survive. Not to look back, not to wallow in regret or speculation as to how things might have been." Frans stopped and made Axel look at him. "You mustn't look back. What's done is done. The past is the past. There is no such thing as regret."

"That's where you're wrong, Frans," Axel said, bowing his head. "That's where you're very wrong."

It was with considerable reluctance that the doctor responsible for Herman's care had agreed to let them in to speak to him for a few minutes. However, once Martin and Paula had promised that two of his daughters could be present, the doctor had relented.

"Hello, Herman," Martin said, holding out his hand to the man in the bed. Herman shook it, but his grip was extremely weak. "We met at your house, but you might not remember. This is my colleague Paula Morales. We'd like to ask you one or two questions, if that's okay?" He spoke softly, and he and Paula sat down by the side of the bed. Martin had no idea that he was sitting on the chair that had been occupied by Erica a short while earlier.

"It's fine," said Herman, who now seemed slightly more aware of his surroundings. His daughters had sat down at the opposite side of the bed, and Margareta was holding her father's hand.

"We're very sorry for your loss," Martin said. "I understand you and Britta had been married for a long time?"

"Fifty-five years," Herman replied, and for the first time since they arrived there was a spark of life in his eyes. "We were married for fifty-five years, me and my Britta."

"Could you tell us what happened? When she died?" Paula said, trying to match Martin's gentle tone of voice.

Margareta and Anna-Greta looked at them anxiously and were about to protest when Herman waved away their concern.

Martin had already noted that there were no scratch marks on Herman's face. He tried to peer under the sleeves of the hospital gown to see if there were any telltale marks, but without success. He decided to wait until they had finished the interview before checking properly.

"I'd gone over to Margareta's for coffee," Herman said. "They're so good to me, my girls. Especially since Britta's been ill." Herman smiled at his daughters. "We had things to discuss. I . . . I'd decided that Britta would be better off living in a place where someone could take better care of her. . . ." His voice was anguished.

Margareta patted his hand. "It was the only way, Dad. There was no other solution, you know that."

Herman didn't seem to hear her. "Then I went home. I was a bit worried, because I'd been gone for such a long time—almost two hours. If I have to go out, I usually make sure I'm not away for longer than an hour, while she has her afternoon nap. I'm so afraid . . . I was so afraid that she would wake up and set fire to the house and herself." He was shaking, but he took a deep breath and continued. "I called out as soon as I got in the door, but there was no reply. I assumed she must still be asleep, thank goodness, so I went upstairs. And she was lying there. . . . I thought it was a bit strange because there was a pillow over her face—why would she be lying like that? So I went over and lifted it off. I could see right away that she'd gone. Her eyes . . . her eyes were just staring at the ceiling, and she was absolutely still." The tears began to trickle down his cheeks, and Margareta gently wiped them away.

"Is this really necessary?" she pleaded, looking at Martin and Paula. "My father is still in shock, and—"

"It's fine, Margareta," Herman said. "It's fine."

"Okay, but just a few minutes more, Dad. Then I'll throw them out myself if I have to; you need to rest."

"She's always been the feisty one," Herman said with a wan smile. "A real battle-ax."

"Hush now, Dad—there's no need to start insulting me," Margareta said, looking pleased that he was up to a bit of banter.

"So what you're saying is that she was already dead when you walked into the room?" Paula said, sounding surprised. "But why did you say that you were the one who killed her?"

"Because I did kill her," Herman said, his face closing down. "But I never said I murdered her. Although I might just as well have." He looked down at his hands, unable to meet the eyes of either the police officers or his daughters.

"But, Dad, we don't understand." Anna-Greta was in despair, but Herman refused to answer.

"Do you know who murdered her?" Martin said, instinctively realizing that right now Herman had no intention of telling them why he kept insisting that he had killed his wife.

"I can't talk anymore," Herman said, staring down at the sheet. "No more."

"You heard what my father said." Margareta got to her feet. "He's told you what he wanted to tell you. But the most important thing is that you heard him say that he didn't murder my mother. As for the rest . . . that's just the grief talking."

Martin and Paula stood up. "Thank you for sparing us a few minutes. But I do have one more request," Martin said, turning to Herman. "Just to confirm what you say, could we possibly take a look at your arms? Britta scratched the person who suffocated her."

"Is that really necessary? He's already told you—" Margareta had started to raise her voice, but Herman quietly pushed up his sleeves and held out his arms. Martin looked at them closely; no scratch marks.

"There, you see!" Margareta looked as if she would like to throw Martin and Paula out herself, as she had threatened.

"We're done now. Thank you for your time, Herman. And once again, our condolences," Martin said, with a wave of his hand to indicate that he would like Margareta and Anna-Greta to accompany him.

Out in the corridor he explained the situation with the fingerprint, and they were happy to provide theirs for elimination purposes. Birgitta arrived just as they were finishing, and was able to provide her prints too. All three sets would be sent to the National Forensics Lab in Linköping.

Paula and Martin sat in the car for a few moments before setting off. "Who do you think he's protecting?" Paula asked, inserting the key in the ignition without turning it.

"I don't know. But I got exactly the same impression as you. He knows who killed Britta, but he's shielding that person. And somehow he believes he was responsible for her death."

"If only he could tell us," Paula said, starting up the engine.

"Yes, for the life of me I can't. . . ." Martin shook his head, drumming his fingers crossly on the dashboard.

"But you believe him?" Paula already knew what the answer would be.

"Yes, I do. And the fact that he has no scratch marks proves I'm right. But for the life of me, I can't understand why he's protecting the person who murdered his wife. And why he thinks he's responsible."

"We may never know," Paula said as she drove out of the parking lot. "We've got the daughters' prints now, so we can send those off and eliminate them. Meanwhile, we can start trying to find out who actually left that print on the pillowcase."

"I guess that's all we can do at the moment," Martin said with a heavy sigh as he gazed out the side window.

Neither of them noticed when they passed Erica's car just north of Torp.

36
Fjällbacka 1945

It was no accident that Frans saw what happened. He had watched Elsy all the way; he wanted to see her until she vanished out of sight beyond the brow of the hill. Therefore, he couldn't help seeing the kiss. It was as if someone had plunged a dagger straight into his heart. He felt a rush of blood, while at the same time an icy chill spread through his limbs. It hurt so much, he thought he might drop dead on the spot.

"Would you look at that. . . ." Erik had also spotted Hans and Elsy. "Well, I'll be. . . ." He laughed and shook his head. The sound of Erik's laughter made a white light explode inside Frans's head. He needed an outlet to get rid of all the pain, so he hurled himself at Erik and grabbed him by the throat.

"Shut up shut up shut UP you stupid fucking. . . ." He tightened his grip on Erik's throat, watching as the boy gasped for air. It felt good to see the fear in Erik's eyes; it somehow diminished the ever-present hard knot in Frans's stomach. The kiss had made it grow ten times as big in one fell swoop.

"What are you doing?" Britta screamed as she stared at the two boys, Erik on his back and Frans on top of him. Without thinking, she rushed forward and started pulling at Frans's shirt, but he lashed out with his arm and sent her flying.

"Stop it, Frans, stop!" she yelled, shuffling backward away from him with tears pouring down her cheeks. Something in her tone of voice brought him to his senses. He looked down at Erik, who had gone a very strange color, and immediately let go of him.

"Sorry," he mumbled, running a hand over his eyes. "Sorry . . . I. . . ."

Erik sat up and stared at him, rubbing his throat. "What the hell was all that about? What got into you? You nearly strangled me, for fuck's sake! Have you gone crazy?" Erik's glasses had been knocked sideways; he took them off and put them back on properly.

Frans was staring blankly into space, saying nothing.

"He's in love with Elsy—didn't you know?" Britta said bitterly, wiping away the tears with the back of her hand. "And I expect he thought he had a chance with her. But you're stupid if you believe that, Frans! She's never so much as looked at you. And now she's thrown herself at that Norwegian. Whereas I. . . ." She burst into tears and started scrambling down the hill. Frans watched her go, his eyes empty. Erik was still furious.

"For God's sake, Frans. I mean, you're . . . is it true? Are you in love with Elsy? If that's the case, then I can understand why you got mad. But you can't just. . . ." Erik broke off, shaking his head.

Frans didn't answer. He couldn't. His head was completely filled with the image of Hans leaning over to kiss Elsy. And Elsy, returning his kiss.

37

These days Erica always paid more attention when she saw a police car, and she thought she spotted Martin in the one she passed just outside Torp as she drove toward Uddevalla for the second time that day. She wondered where they had been.

Although there was no real urgency to tackle this now, she knew she wouldn't get anything written until she had gotten to the bottom of the new information she had been given. And she was very curious as to why Kjell Ringholm, a newspaper journalist, was also interested in the Norwegian resistance fighter.

As she sat waiting in the reception area at *Bohusläningen* a little while later, she considered various possible reasons for his interest, but decided to avoid speculation until she had the chance to speak to him. After a few minutes, she was shown to his office, and he looked at her with a quizzical expression as they shook hands.

"Erica Falck? You're a writer, aren't you?" he said, gesturing toward a chair. She sat down and took off her jacket.

"That's right."

"Unfortunately, I haven't read any of your books, but I've heard they're very good," he said politely. "Are you here to do some research for a new book? I'm not a crime reporter, so I don't really know how I can help. You write about true-life murder cases, if I've understood correctly."

"My visit has nothing to do with my books," Erica said. "I've actually started doing some research into my mother's past, for various reasons. She was a good friend of your father's, by the way."

Kjell frowned. "When was that?" he asked, leaning forward.

"They spent a lot of time together when they were children and teenagers, from what I understand. I've focused mainly on the last years of the war in my research; as you know, they were about fifteen then."

Kjell nodded, waiting for her to go on.

"They were part of a group of four teenagers who hung out together back then, and it seems they were all pretty close. Apart from your father and my mother, there was Britta Johansson and Erik Frankel. And as I'm sure you know, those two have been murdered within the space of just two months. Which is a bit too much of a coincidence, don't you think?"

Still no response from Kjell, but Erica noticed that his body had tensed and there was a glint in his eye.

"And then. . . ." She paused. "Another person became part of the group. In 1944 a Norwegian resistance fighter came to Fjällbacka. He was just a boy, really; he had stowed away on board my grandfather's boat, and was given a room in my grandparents' house. His name was Hans Olavsen. But you already know that, don't you? I've discovered that you've also started to show an interest in him, and I'm just wondering why."

"I'm a journalist; I can't discuss that kind of thing," Kjell said defensively.

"No, you can't reveal your sources," Erica said calmly. "But I can't see any reason why we shouldn't be able to help each other on this. I'm very good at tracking things down and, as a journalist, that's what you do all the time. We're both interested in Hans Olavsen. I can live with the fact that you don't want to tell me why, but can't we at least exchange the information we already have, as well as anything we might find out in the future?" She stopped and waited, feeling the tension.

Kjell considered what she had said. He drummed his fingers on the desk as he weighed the possible pros and cons of the arrangement Erica had suggested.

"Okay," he said eventually, taking a folder out of his top drawer. "I can't see any real reason why we can't help each other out. And my source is dead, so I might as well tell you everything. I came into contact with Erik Frankel on a . . . private matter." He cleared his throat and pushed the folder over to her. "He said there was something he wanted to tell me, something that I might find useful and that ought to come out."

"Is that exactly how he put it?" Erica picked up the folder. "That there was something that ought to come out?"

"Yes, as far as I remember. Then he came here a few days later. He'd brought the articles in that folder, and he just gave them to me without saying any more about his reasons. I asked him lots of questions, of course, but he just kept on saying that if I was as good at digging up information as he'd heard, then the material in the folder should be enough."

Erica leafed through the papers, which consisted of the same articles she had already been given by Christian, the articles from the library archive that mentioned Hans Olavsen and his time in Fjällbacka. "Nothing else?" She sighed.

"That's exactly how I felt. If he knew something, why couldn't he just come right out with it? But for some reason it was important to him that I should find out the rest for myself.

So that's what I've been trying to do, and I'd be lying if I didn't admit that my interest increased by several thousand percent when Erik Frankel was found murdered. And I've been wondering if there might be any connection with this. . . ." He pointed to the folder in front of Erica. "And of course I'd heard about the murder of an elderly woman last week, but I had no idea there was a link. . . . That certainly raises a number of questions."

"Have you found out anything about the Norwegian?" Erica asked eagerly. "I haven't gotten very far yet; apparently he and my mother were in love, but he seems to have left both her and Fjällbacka very suddenly. I was thinking of trying to track him down as my next step, find out where he went, whether he went back to Norway or. . . . But maybe you're ahead of me there?"

There was no simple yes-or-no answer to that question. Kjell told her about his conversation with Eskil Halvorsen, who had said that he was unable to identify Hans Olavsen off the top of his head, but had promised to undertake further inquiries.

"Of course, he might have stayed on in Sweden," Erica mused. "If that's the case, it ought to be possible to track him down through the Swedish authorities; I can check on that. But if he's disappeared abroad somewhere, then we have a problem."

She passed the folder back to Kjell. "That's worth looking into," he said. "After all, there's no reason to assume he went back to Norway; lots of his countrymen stayed on in Sweden after the war."

"Did you send Eskil Halvorsen a picture of him?"

"No, I didn't, now that you mention it," said Kjell, leafing through the folder. "But you're right—that would be a good idea. You never know; the least little thing can help. I'll get in touch as soon as you've gone and see if I can fax him one of these pictures. Maybe this one? It's the clearest—what do you think?" He held up the article with the group picture that Erica had studied so closely a couple of days ago.

"That should do nicely. And you've got the whole group there. That's my mother." She pointed to Elsy.

"So you're saying they spent a lot of time together back then?" Kjell said thoughtfully. He cursed himself for not making the connection between the Britta in the photograph and the Britta who had been murdered, but he consoled himself with the thought that most people would have done the same thing. It was difficult to spot any similarities between the fifteen-year-old girl and the seventy-five-year-old woman.

"Yes, as I understand it, they were a very close-knit group, even though their friendship probably wasn't completely accepted in those days. There was a very clear class divide in Fjällbacka; Britta and my mother would have belonged to the poorer side, while Erik Frankel and your father were part of the 'upper crust.'" Erica drew quotation marks in the air.

"Oh, yes, very upper crust," Kjell muttered, and Erica sensed that a great deal lay beneath the surface of his words.

"Actually, I never thought of speaking to Axel Frankel," Erica said excitedly. "He might know something about Hans Olavsen. Even if he was slightly older, he seems to have been there in the background, and maybe he—" Her thoughts and expectations went spiraling away, but Kjell held up a warning hand.

"I wouldn't get your hopes up too much. I had the same idea, but fortunately I did a little research on Axel first. I'm sure you know he was taken prisoner by the Germans during a trip to Norway?"

"Yes, but I don't know much about it," Erica said, looking at Kjell with interest. "What did you find out?"

"As I said, Axel was captured by the Germans when he was supposed to be handing over some documents to the resistance movement. He was taken to Grini prison outside Oslo, where he remained until the beginning of 1945. The Germans then transported him and a large number of other prisoners from Grini to Germany by boat and train, and at first Axel Frankel ended up in a concentration camp called Sachsenhausen, where many Scandinavian prisoners were taken. Then, toward the end of the war, he was moved to Neuengamme."

Erica gasped. "I had no idea. So Axel Frankel was in concentration camps in Germany? I didn't even know that had happened to Norwegians or Swedes."

Kjell nodded. "Yes, it was principally Norwegian prisoners who ended up there, along with odd individuals from other countries who had been captured by the Germans after being involved in the resistance movement. They were known as NN prisoners, *Nacht und Nebel*—night and fog. The name has its origins in a decree issued by Hitler in 1941, which stated that civilians in occupied countries would not be tried in their homelands but would be sent to Germany, where they would disappear 'into the night and the fog.' Some were executed; the rest were condemned to work themselves to death in the camps. Anyhow, the fact is that Axel Frankel wasn't in Fjällbacka when Hans Olavsen was there."

"But we don't know exactly when Olavsen left Fjällbacka," Erica said with a frown. "At least I haven't found that information anywhere. I have no idea when he left my mother."

"But I do," Kjell said triumphantly, rummaging among the papers on his desk. "Roughly, at least," he added. "Aha!" He pulled out a sheet of paper, placed it in front of Erica, and pointed to a passage in the middle of the page. Erica leaned forward and read aloud, "*This year the Fjällbacka Society has arranged an extremely successful—*"

"No, no, next column," Kjell said, pointing again.

"Oh, right." Erica tried again. "*It has come as a great surprise to discover that the Norwegian resistance fighter who found refuge here in Fjällbacka has left us so abruptly. Many residents regret that they did not have the opportunity to say good-bye, and to thank him for his efforts during the war, which has ended at long last. . . ."* Erica glanced at the date at the top of the page, then looked up at Kjell. "June 19, 1945."

"Yes. Which means he disappeared immediately after the end of the war, if I've interpreted it correctly," Kjell said, placing the article on top of one of the piles of paper.

"But why?" Erica tilted her head to one side as she pondered. "I still think it might be worth speaking to Axel, though. His brother might have said something to him. I can do that. Is there any chance you could talk to your father?"

Kjell remained silent for a long time, but eventually he said "Of course I can. I'll let you know if I hear anything from Halvorsen—and you'll get in touch with me right away if you come up with anything. Deal?" He wagged a warning finger at her. He wasn't used to working with anyone else, but in this case he could see the advantages of having Erica's help with the groundwork.

"I'll check with the Swedish authorities too," Erica said, getting to her feet. "And I promise to let you know as soon as I hear anything." She started to put on her jacket but stopped in midmovement.

"Actually, Kjell, there was one more thing. I don't know if it means anything, but. . . ."

"Go on—anything might be useful at this stage," he said encouragingly, looking up at her.

"Well, I was talking to Britta's husband, Herman. He seems to know something about all this. . . . I can't be certain, but that's the feeling I get. I asked him about Hans Olavsen, and his reaction was very strange, but then he said I should ask Paul Heckel and Friedrich Hück. I've tried to look them up, but I can't find anything. And yet. . . ."

"What?" Kjell said.

"Oh, I don't know. I'm sure I've never come across either of them, and yet there's something familiar . . . no, it's no good, I can't put my finger on it."

Kjell tapped his pen on the desk. "Paul Heckel and Friedrich Hück?" he repeated, and when Erica nodded, he jotted down the names.

"Okay, I'll see what I can do. But they don't ring any bells at the moment."

"So we've both got plenty to do," Erica said with a smile as she paused in the doorway. It felt good to be working with someone else on this.

"Indeed we have," Kjell said, sounding slightly distracted.

"I'll be in touch," Erica said.

"Me too," Kjell replied, picking up the phone without looking at her as she left. He was keen to get to the bottom of this. His journalistic nose could definitely smell a rat.

"Shall we sit down and go through everything one more time?" It was Monday afternoon, and the station was quiet.

"Sure," Gösta said, reluctantly getting to his feet. "Paula too?"

"Of course," Martin said and went to fetch her. Mellberg had taken Ernst for a walk, and Annika looked busy in reception, so the three of them settled down in the kitchen with all the existing case material in front of them.

"Erik Frankel," Martin said, his pen poised over a clean page in his notepad.

"He was murdered in his own home with an object that was already there," Paula said as Martin made notes.

"Which could suggest that it wasn't premeditated," Gösta said, and Martin nodded.

"There are no prints on the bust that was used as the murder weapon, but it does not appear to have been wiped, so the killer must have been wearing gloves, which could in fact contradict the idea that it wasn't premeditated," Paula interjected. She looked at Martin's writing on the pad.

"Will you actually be able to read that later?" she asked skeptically, since the words looked like hieroglyphics. Or shorthand.

"As long as I type it up right away," Martin smiled as he continued to make notes. "Otherwise—no chance."

"Erik Frankel died from a single heavy blow to the temple," Gösta said, laying out the pictures from the crime scene. "And the killer left the murder weapon behind."

"Which also makes it look as if this wasn't a particularly cold-blooded or calculated murder," Paula said, getting up to pour them all a cup of coffee.

"The only potential threat we've been able to identify comes from Erik's expertise in Nazism, which led to conflict with the neo-Nazi organization known as Sweden's Friends." Martin reached for the five letters in their plastic sleeves and spread them out on the table. "Erik also had a personal connection with the organization through his childhood friend Frans Ringholm."

"Do we have anything that could link Frans to the murder? Anything at all?" Paula was staring at the letters as if she might be able to make them talk.

"Three of his Nazi pals claim that he was in Denmark with them during the relevant period. It's not exactly a watertight alibi, if such a thing exists, but we haven't much physical evidence to go on. The footprints we found belong to the boys who discovered the body, and there were no other footprints or fingerprints apart from what we would expect to find there."

"Are you going to pour the coffee, or are you just going to stand there holding the pot?" Gösta said to Paula.

"Say please and I'll pour you a cup," Paula teased, and Gösta reluctantly muttered "Please."

"Then there's the date," Martin said, nodding his thanks to Paula as she passed him a cup of coffee. "We can be fairly certain that Erik Frankel died sometime between June 15 and 17. Two days to play with. Then he was left sitting there, because his brother was away and nobody was expecting to hear from Erik. The only person who might have tried to contact him was Viola, and he had finished with her on the fifteenth, or at least that was how she interpreted it. Gösta, you've spoken to all the neighbors; did anybody see anything? Any unfamiliar cars? Anyone hanging around who looked suspicious?"

"There aren't many neighbors to talk to out there," Gösta mumbled.

"Shall I take that as a no?"

"Yes, I spoke to all the neighbors, and no, none of them saw anything."

"Okay, we'll leave that for now." Martin sighed and took a sip of his coffee.

"What about Britta Johansson then? It's certainly a strange coincidence that she seems to have had some kind of connection with Erik Frankel. And with Frans Ringholm, for that matter. Admittedly, it was a long time ago, but the phone records show that there was some contact between them in June, and both Frans and Erik went to see Britta around that time." Martin paused and gave his two colleagues a challenging look. "Why choose that particular moment to make contact again after sixty years? Do we believe Britta's husband when he says it was because her illness was getting worse and that she wanted to remember the good old days?"

"Personally I think that's bullshit," Paula said, reaching for an unopened package of Ballerina cookies. She tore off the plastic strip at one end and took three before passing the package around. "I don't believe a word of it. I think if we could find out the real reason why they met, the whole case would open up. But Frans won't say a word, and Axel is sticking to the same story as Herman."

"And let's not forget the regular payments," Gösta said as he removed the top layer of a cookie with surgical precision. He licked off every scrap of the chocolate cream filling before he went on. "In the Frankel case, I mean."

Martin looked at his colleague in surprise. He hadn't realized that Gösta was up to speed on that part of the investigation, since he usually adopted the "I only pay attention to the information I'm given" strategy.

"Yes, Hedström helped us out with that on Saturday," Martin said, finding the notes he had made when Patrik called to report on his visit to Wilhelm Fridén's family.

"And what did he find out?" Gösta took another cookie and carried out the same maneuver, removing the top layer, licking off the chocolate filling, then discarding the actual pieces of cookie.

"You can't just sit there licking off the chocolate and leaving the rest, Gösta!" Paula said crossly.

"Who are you—the Ballerina cookie cop?" Gösta said, deliberately taking another. Paula merely snorted in response, but picked up the package and put it on the counter out of Gösta's reach.

"Unfortunately, Patrik didn't get much information," Martin said. "Wilhelm Fridén died just a couple of weeks ago, and neither his widow nor his son knew anything about the payments. Of course, we can't be sure they were telling the truth, but Patrik said it sounded likely. The son has promised to ask their lawyer to send over a copy of all his father's papers, so, if we're lucky, there might be something there."

"What about the brother? Did he know anything about it?" Gösta was eyeing the cookies on the counter, and seemed to be considering whether to actually get up and retrieve them.

"We called Axel and asked him," Paula said, giving Gösta a warning look. "But he had no idea what the reason might be."

"And we believe him?" Gösta measured the distance from the chair to the counter. A quick sortie just might work.

"I don't know, to be honest. He's hard to read. What did you think, Paula?" Martin turned to her and, as she pondered the question, Gösta saw his chance. He jumped up and hurled himself at the package, but Paula's left hand shot out with lightning speed and grabbed it.

"Too slow, Gösta, way too slow!" She gave him a teasing wink, and he couldn't help smiling back. He had started to enjoy their banter.

Paula turned to Martin, the package of cookies safely in her grasp.

"I agree. He's hard to read. So . . . I don't know." She shook her head.

"Let's get back to Britta," Martin said. He wrote BRITTA in capital letters on his notepad and drew a line underneath it.

"I think our best lead is the fact that Pedersen found what is probably the killer's DNA under her fingernails, and that she probably scratched the person who suffocated her on the face or arms quite severely. We went to the hospital and spoke briefly to Herman this morning, and he has no scratches. He also said she was already dead when he got home—she was lying on the bed with the pillow over her face."

"But he still insists that he's responsible for her death," Paula added.

"So, what does he mean?" Gösta frowned. "Is he protecting someone?"

"That's what we're thinking too." Paula's expression softened, and she passed the cookies over to Gösta. "There you go—knock yourself out."

"Then there are the fingerprints," said Martin, amused by Gösta and Paula's amiable teasing. If he didn't know better, he'd think the old man was starting to soften.

"A single thumbprint on one of the buttons on the pillowcase. Not much to shout about," Gösta said gloomily.

"Not on its own, admittedly, but if the print belongs to the same person who left his or her DNA under Britta's fingernails, then I think it's quite promising." Martin underlined "DNA" on his pad.

"When will the DNA profile be ready?" Paula asked.

"Thursday, according to the lab."

"Okay, so we can do a round of DNA sampling after that." Paula stretched out her legs. Sometimes she wondered if Johanna's pregnancy symptoms were catching. So far, she had experienced shooting pains in her legs, odd little cramps, and a voracious appetite.

"Do we have any candidates for sampling?" Gösta was now on his fifth cookie.

"I was thinking of Axel and Frans, to begin with."

"In which case, do we really need to wait until Thursday? I mean, it will take a while to get the results, and scratch marks heal fairly quickly, so it might be a good idea if we get it done as soon as possible."

"Good thinking, Gösta," Martin said, surprised. "We'll do it tomorrow. Anything else? Anything we've missed or forgotten?"

"Missed? What do you mean, 'missed'?" came a voice from the doorway. Mellberg walked in with Ernst trailing behind him, panting slightly. The dog immediately caught the smell of Gösta's pile of denuded cookies; he rushed over and sat down at Gösta's feet, a pleading expression on his face. It worked, and the pile disappeared in a trice.

"We're just going through a few things, trying to figure out whether we *might* have missed anything," Martin said, pointing to the documents on the table. "We've just decided to collect DNA samples from Axel Frankel and Frans Ringholm tomorrow."

"Yes, yes, fine," Mellberg said impatiently, afraid of getting dragged into the practical work that would have to be done. "Carry on with what you're doing. It looks good." He called Ernst, who followed him into his office with his tail wagging, then settled down in his usual place, lying on Mellberg's feet under the desk.

"The idea of finding someone to adopt the dog seems to have been put on ice," Paula said, sounding amused.

"I think Ernst has already been adopted, although it's difficult to say who's taking care of whom. There's also a rumor going around that Mellberg has become a salsa king in his old age." Gösta snickered.

Martin lowered his voice and whispered "Yes, I'd heard that too. . . . And this morning when I walked into his office, he was sitting on the floor doing *stretches* . . . !"

"You're kidding me!" Gösta said, his eyes wide. "And how did that go?"

"Not too well," Martin laughed. "He was trying to touch his toes, but his belly was in the way. To name just one reason."

"Listen, guys, it's actually my mom who teaches the salsa class Mellberg goes to," Paula said sternly. Gösta and Martin stared at her, lost for words.

"And Mom invited Mellberg home for lunch the other day, and . . . and he was really nice," she concluded.

By this time, both Martin and Gösta were gaping at her, openmouthed. "Mellberg is taking salsa classes with your mother? And he's been to your place for lunch? You'll be calling him 'Daddy' before long," Martin cackled, and Gösta joined in.

"Cut it out, okay?" Paula said crossly, getting to her feet. "Are we done here?" She sailed out of the room. Martin and

Gösta exchanged a shamefaced look, then burst out laughing again. This was too good to be true.

Open warfare had broken out over the weekend. Dan and Belinda had been yelling at each other virtually nonstop, and Anna thought her head was going to explode with all the noise. She had shouted at them several times, asking them to think of Adrian and Emma, and fortunately that seemed to have the desired effect on both of them. Even if Belinda would never admit it, Anna could see that she thought the world of Anna's children, which meant that Anna was prepared to excuse some of her teenage tantrums. She also thought that sometimes Dan didn't really understand how his seventeen-year-old daughter felt, and why she reacted as she did. It was as if they were each locked into an entrenched position, and neither of them knew how to get out of it. Anna sighed as she moved around the living room picking up the children's toys, which they had somehow managed to scatter over every inch of the floor.

She had also spent the last few days trying to absorb the realization that she and Dan were having a child together. Her mind was whirling, and she had put a lot of energy into suppressing the fear. She had started to feel nauseous too, just as she had during her earlier pregnancies. She wasn't throwing up quite so often, but she had a queasy, bilious feeling in her stomach all the time, like permanent seasickness. Dan had anxiously pointed out that she seemed to have lost her appetite and ran around after her like a mother hen, trying to tempt her with different kinds of food.

She sat down on the sofa and lowered her head toward her knees, trying to focus on her breathing in order to control the nausea. With Adrian this had gone on until the sixth month, and it had felt like an eternity. . . . From upstairs she could hear angry voices, rising and falling to the accompaniment of

Belinda's loud music. She couldn't stand it. She really couldn't stand it. She started to retch, and bile surged up into her throat. She quickly got up and rushed into the bathroom, knelt down in front of the toilet, and tried to bring up whatever it was that kept rising and falling in her gullet. But nothing came, just dry heaves that didn't even provide a temporary respite.

She stood up wearily, wiped her mouth with a towel, and looked at her face in the bathroom mirror. She was as pale as the white towel she was holding in her hand, and her eyes were big and frightened. This was more or less what she had looked like when she was with Lucas, and yet everything was so different now. So much better. She stroked her still-flat stomach with one hand. So much hope, so much fear gathered in one tiny spot in her belly, in her womb. So small, so dependent. She had certainly thought about having children with Dan, but not now, not so soon. At some point, in a distant, unspecified future. When things had calmed down, stabilized. However, it had never occurred to her to do something about the pregnancy now that it was a fact. The bond had already formed, the invisible, fragile, yet unbreakable bond between Anna and the fetus that wasn't yet visible to the naked eye. She took a deep breath and walked out of the bathroom; the loud voices had moved into the hallway.

"I'm only going over to Linda's; how fucking difficult is it to understand that? I've got to have friends! Or are you saying I'm not allowed to do that either? Fuck you!"

Anna heard Dan take a deep breath before delivering a vicious response, but at that point she ran out of patience. She marched over and let them have it with both barrels: "Will you shut UP, BOTH of you! You're behaving like kids, and it stops RIGHT NOW!" She held up her finger and went on before either of them could interrupt. "Dan, you are to STOP yelling at Belinda! For God's sake, you can't lock her up and throw away the key! She's seventeen years old, and she needs to see her friends!"

Belinda broke into a smug smile, but Anna hadn't finished by a long shot.

"And YOU can stop behaving like a child and start acting like an adult if you want to be treated like one! I don't want to hear any more crap about the fact that the kids and I are living here, because that's a done deal whether you like it or not, and we're ready to get to know you if you give us the chance!"

Anna took a deep breath, then went on in a tone of voice that made Dan and Belinda stand to attention in front of her like toy soldiers in sheer terror. "What's more, we have no intention of disappearing anytime soon, if that's your plan, because your father and I are having a baby, so my children and you and your sisters will be linked by a half sibling. I really, really want us all to get along, but I can't do it on my own; the two of you have to help. There will be a baby in the spring, whether you accept me or not, and there is no way I'm putting up with this crap until then!" Anna burst into tears, while Dan and Belinda stood there as if they had been turned to stone. Then Belinda let out a sob, stared at Dan and Anna, and ran out the front door, which slammed shut behind her.

"Nice one, Anna. Was that really necessary?" Dan said wearily. The fight had brought Emma and Adrian into the hallway, and they were looking utterly bewildered.

"Oh, go to hell," Anna said, grabbing a jacket. The front door slammed shut for the second time.

"Hi, where've you been?" Patrik met Erica in the doorway and kissed her on the lips. Maja also wanted a kiss from Mommy, and came running along a little unsteadily, arms outstretched.

"Well, I've certainly had two interesting conversations." Erica took off her jacket and followed Patrik into the living room.

"What about?" he asked curiously. He sat down on the floor and continued what he and Maja had been doing when they heard Erica come in: constructing the world's tallest tower from building blocks.

"I thought this was supposed to help *Maja*'s development!" Erica couldn't help laughing as she sat down beside them. She watched with amusement as her husband attempted to place a red block at the top of a tower that was now taller than Maja.

"Ssh . . . ," Patrik said, his tongue sticking out the corner of his mouth as he tried to steady his hand in order to carry out the tricky maneuver; the tower was looking distinctly wobbly by this stage.

"Maja, could you give Mommy that yellow block there?" Erica whispered theatrically to her daughter, pointing at a block right at the bottom. Maja's face lit up at the chance to do something for Mommy; she bent forward and yanked out the block, which brought Patrik's carefully constructed edifice tumbling down.

Patrik sat there with the red block poised in the air. "Thanks for that," he said, glaring at Erica. "Do you have any idea of the skill required to build a tower as tall as that? The precision? The steady hand?"

"Is someone starting to understand what I meant by 'lack of stimulation' for a whole year?" Erica laughed, leaning forward to kiss her husband.

"Maybe," he said, returning her kiss with just a hint of tongue. Erica responded to the invitation, and what had begun as a kiss turned into something more, which was interrupted when Maja threw a building block at her father's head with impressive accuracy.

"Ow!" He rubbed his head and wagged a finger at Maja. "What do you think you're doing? Throwing blocks at Daddy when he gets to make out with your mom for once!"

"Patrik!" Erica thumped him on the shoulder. "I don't think our daughter needs to hear about making out when she's only one year old. . . ."

"If she wants little brothers and sisters, I guess she's going to have to put up with the sight of her mom and dad making out," he said, and Erica could see that familiar look in his eye.

She got up. "I think little brothers and sisters can wait a while. But we can put in some practice tonight. . . ." She winked and went into the kitchen. They had finally managed to recapture that aspect of their lives together. It was amazing to think what a devastating effect the arrival of a baby could have on a couple's sex life, but after a pretty thin year on that front, things were starting to improve. However, after spending a year at home with Maja, she hadn't even given a thought to the question of a brother or sister for her yet. She felt as if she needed to get used to being an adult again before she was absorbed into the world of babies once more.

"So, tell me about these interesting conversations you had today," Patrik said, following her into the kitchen.

Erica told him about her two visits to Uddevalla and what she had gotten out of them.

"So you don't recognize the names?" Patrik asked with a frown after she had recounted what Herman had said.

"That's what's so odd. I can't remember ever having heard them, and yet there's something . . . I don't know. Paul Heckel and Friedrich Hück. They sound kind of familiar, somehow."

"And you and Kjell Ringholm are pooling your resources to try and track down this . . . Hans Olavsen?" Patrik looked skeptical, and Erica could see what he was thinking.

"I know it's a long shot. I have no idea what role he might have played, but something tells me it was significant. And even if it has nothing to do with the murders, it seems as if he meant something to my mother, which is where all this started as far as I'm concerned. I just want to find out more about her."

"Okay, but just be a little bit careful." Patrik put a pan of water on the stove. "Tea?"

"Yes, please." Erica sat down at the kitchen table. "What do you mean, be careful?"

"It's just that, from what I've heard, Kjell is a very skilled journalist; make sure he's not just using you."

"I don't see how he could do that. I mean, he could take the information I come up with and then give nothing back, but surely that's the worst that can happen? I'll just have to take that risk, but I don't think he'll do that. We've agreed that I'm going to speak to Axel Frankel about Olavsen, and I'll check to see if he's registered anywhere in Sweden, while Kjell is going to have a word with his father. Not that he was exactly thrilled with that particular task. . . ."

"No, those two don't seem to have a very good relationship," Patrik said, pouring boiling water into two mugs, each of which contained a tea bag. "I've read some of Kjell's articles, and he doesn't hold back from saying what he thinks about his father."

"It should be a fascinating conversation, in that case," Erica said laconically as Patrik passed her a mug. She looked at him as she sipped the hot tea. From the living room, she could hear Maja babbling away to some unknown audience—probably the doll, who had been her constant companion over the past few days.

"How does it feel, not being part of what's going on at the station at a time like this?" she asked.

"I'd be lying if I said it was easy. But I realize what a wonderful opportunity this is to be at home with Maja, and the job will still be there when I go back. Not that I'm hoping for more homicide cases, but . . . you know what I mean."

"And how's Karin getting on?" Erica said, trying to keep her tone as neutral as possible.

Patrik took a few seconds to answer. "I don't know. She seems so . . . unhappy. I don't think things have turned out the way she'd expected, and now she's stuck in a situation that . . . no, I don't know. I feel a bit sorry for her."

"Does she regret losing you?" Erica waited anxiously for the response. They had never really talked about Patrik's marriage to Karin, and on the few occasions when she had ventured to ask, his answers had been terse and monosyllabic.

"I don't think so. Or maybe . . . I've no idea. I think she regrets what she did, and the fact that I found them the way I did." He let out a bitter laugh as an image he hadn't seen for a long time came into his mind; he'd thought he'd put all that behind him. "But then again . . . she did what she did largely because things between us weren't good."

"Do you think she remembers that now?" Erica said. "Sometimes we have a tendency to put a positive spin on things in retrospect."

"That's true, but I think she remembers. She must," Patrik said, but he sounded thoughtful. "Anyway, what's on the agenda for tomorrow?" he said abruptly, changing the subject.

Erica realized what he was doing, but decided to let it go. "I thought I might go and see Axel, as I said. And I'll start asking the tax authorities a few questions and looking into electoral rolls regarding Hans."

"Hey, aren't you supposed to be writing a book?" Patrik laughed, but he sounded slightly concerned.

"There's plenty of time for that; I've already done most of the research. And I can't really focus on the book until I've gotten this out of my system, so just let me continue. . . ."

"Okay, okay," Patrik said, holding up his hands. "You're a big girl, you can make your own decisions about how you spend your time. Maja and I will take care of our business and you take care of yours." He got up and kissed the top of Erica's head as he walked past.

"Time to construct a new masterpiece. I'm considering a scale model of the Taj Mahal," he said.

Erica shook her head, laughing. Sometimes she wondered if the man she had married was completely sane. Probably not, she decided.

Anna spotted her from a distance. A small, lonely figure right at the end of one of the pontoon jetties. She hadn't intended to go looking for her, but when she saw Belinda as she walked down Galärbacken, she knew she had to go to her.

Belinda didn't hear her coming. She was sitting smoking, with a package of cigarettes and a box of matches by her side.

"Hi," Anna said.

Belinda gave a start. She looked at the cigarette in her hand and for a second she seemed to be wondering whether to hide it, but then she defiantly brought it to her lips and took a deep drag.

"Can I have one?" Anna said, sitting down next to Belinda.

"You smoke?" Belinda sounded surprised, but passed her the package.

"I used to. For five years. But my . . . ex-husband . . . he didn't like it." That was something of an understatement. On one occasion at the beginning when Lucas had caught her smoking on the sly, he had stubbed the cigarette out in the crook of her arm. A faint scar was still visible.

"You won't tell Dad about this, will you?" Belinda said sullenly, waving the cigarette around. However, she did manage a faint "Please."

"If you don't tell on me, I won't tell on you," Anna said, closing her eyes as she took the first drag.

"Should you really be doing that? I mean, what about the baby?" Belinda said, suddenly sounding like an indignant old lady.

Anna laughed. "This will be my first and last cigarette during this pregnancy, I promise you."

They sat in silence for a while, blowing smoke rings. The warmth of summer had completely disappeared now, and had been replaced by the chill of September. But there wasn't a breath of wind, and the water lay still and shining before them. The harbor looked deserted; just a few boats were at their moorings, in contrast to the summer months when there were row upon row.

"It's not easy, is it?" Anna said, gazing out across the water.

"What?" Belinda said in a surly tone, still unsure what attitude to adopt.

"Being a kid, although you're almost grown up now."

"And what would you know about it?" Belinda said, kicking a pebble into the water.

"Oh, sure, I was born this age," Anna laughed, nudging Belinda in the side. She was rewarded with a tiny, tiny smile that disappeared almost immediately. Anna let her be. She could set the pace. They sat in silence for several minutes, then, from the corner of her eye, Anna saw Belinda steal a glance at her.

"Do you feel very sick?"

Anna nodded. "Like a seasick polecat."

"Why would a polecat be seasick?" Belinda snorted.

"Why not? Do you have any evidence to suggest that a polecat can't get seasick? If so, I would very much like to see it. Because that's exactly how I feel. Like a seasick polecat."

"You're kidding me," Belinda said, but she couldn't help laughing.

"Okay, but, joking aside, I feel pretty rough."

"Mom felt real bad when she was carrying Lisen. I was old enough to realize that. She was—sorry, maybe I shouldn't be talking about Mom and Dad. . . ." She fell silent, clearly embarrassed; she reached for another cigarette and lit it between cupped hands.

"Listen, you're very welcome to talk about your mom. Whenever you like. I have no problem with the fact that Dan had a life before he met me and, after all, he had the three of you in that life. With your mom. So believe me, you don't have to feel as if you're betraying your dad because you love your mom. And I promise not to mind if you talk about Pernilla. Not at all." Anna placed her hand on the hand with which Belinda was supporting herself on the jetty. At first, Belinda seemed about to pull away reflexively, but then she let her hand remain where it was. After a few seconds, Anna reached for another cigarette. She would have two cancer sticks during this pregnancy. But that was it. No more.

"I'm really good at helping out with babies," Belinda said, meeting Anna's gaze. "I helped Mom out a lot with Lisen when she was little."

"Yes, Dan told me. He said he and your mom used to have to practically force you to go and play with your friends instead of taking care of the baby. He also said you were really good at it. So I hope I can count on some assistance in the spring. You can deal with all the shitty diapers." She nudged Belinda again, and this time Belinda nudged her right back.

With a smile twinkling in her eyes, Belinda said "Sorry, I'm only dealing with wet diapers. Deal?" She held out her hand and Anna shook it.

"Deal. The wet diapers are yours." Then she added "Your dad can have the shitty ones."

Their laughter echoed out across the deserted harbor.

Anna would always remember that particular moment as one of the best in her life. The moment the ice broke.

Axel was busy packing when Erica arrived. He met her in the doorway with a shirt on a hanger in each hand. A folding travel bag was hanging from a door in the hallway.

"Are you going somewhere?" Erica asked.

Axel nodded as he carefully inserted the shirts so that they wouldn't crease.

"Yes, I have to start work again soon. I'm going back to Paris on Friday."

"Can you go without knowing who. . . ." She left the words hovering in the air and didn't complete the sentence.

"I have no choice," Axel said grimly. "Obviously I'll catch the first flight home if the police require my assistance in any way, but I really do have to get back to work. Sitting here brooding isn't very constructive." He rubbed his eyes with a weary gesture, and Erica noticed how haggard he was beginning to look. He seemed to have aged several years since she last had seen him.

"I think getting away for a little while might do you good," she said softly. She hesitated. "I have one or two questions, a couple of things I'd really like to talk to you about. Could you spare a few minutes? Do you feel up to it?"

Axel nodded, looking tired and resigned, and led the way into the house. Erica stopped by the sofa on the veranda where they had sat last time, but he continued into the next room.

"This is lovely!" she said breathlessly, gazing around. It was like stepping into a bygone age. Everything in the room dated from the 1940s, and although it was clean and tidy, there was still a smell of the past about it.

"Neither our parents nor Erik and I were very fond of newfangled things. Mother and Father never made any great changes to the house, nor did we. I also think it was an age that produced beautiful objects, and I see no reason to exchange the furniture for modern—and in my opinion, ugly—replacements." He ran a hand over an elegant chest of drawers.

They sat down on a brown sofa. It wasn't particularly comfortable, and it made them sit up nice and straight.

"You wanted to ask me some questions," Axel said pleasantly but with a hint of impatience.

"Yes, of course," Erica said, suddenly feeling embarrassed. This was the second time she had come here disturbing Axel Frankel with her questions, when he had so many other things on his mind. But just as before, she decided that since she was here, she might as well do what she had come for.

"I've been doing some research into my mother's life, and that has led me to her friends: your brother, Frans Ringholm, and Britta Johansson."

Axel nodded, twiddling his thumbs as he waited for her to go on.

"There was another person who became part of their group."

Axel still didn't speak.

"Toward the end of the war, a Norwegian resistance fighter arrived onboard my grandfather's boat . . . the same boat you often traveled on, I believe."

He stared at her without blinking, but she saw his body tense when she mentioned his trips to Norway.

"He was a good man, your grandfather," Axel said quietly after a while. His hands grew still. "One of the best men I've ever met."

Erica had never known her maternal grandfather, and it warmed her heart to hear him spoken of so positively.

"As I understand it, you were in prison at the time Hans Olavsen came to Fjällbacka on my grandfather's boat. He arrived in 1944, and according to what we have managed to find out so far, he stayed until just after the end of the war."

"You said 'we,'" Axel broke in. "Who's 'we'?" He sounded tense.

Erica hesitated, then she simply said: "I just mean I've had some help from Christian at the library, that's all." She didn't want to mention Kjell, and Axel seemed to accept her explanation.

"Yes, I was in prison then," Axel said, his body stiffening once more. It was as if every muscle suddenly remembered what it had suffered, and reacted by contracting.

"Did you ever meet him?"

Axel shook his head. "No, he'd already gone when I came home."

"When was that?"

"June 1945. On the white buses."

"The white buses?" Erica said, but suddenly she recalled a little of what she had learned in her history classes; a man named Folke Bernadotte had been involved in some way.

"It was a scheme initiated by Folke Bernadotte," Axel said, confirming her vague memories. "He arranged for Scandinavian prisoners held in German concentration camps to be brought home. The buses were white, with a red cross painted on the roof and sides so that they wouldn't be mistaken for military targets."

"Why was that a risk if they were collecting prisoners after the war ended?" Erica was confused.

Axel smiled gently at her lack of knowledge and started twiddling his thumbs again. "The first buses picked up prisoners in March and April 1945, following negotiations with the Germans. They brought home fifteen thousand prisoners that time around. Then after the end of the war they collected another ten thousand in May and June. I was in the very last batch. June 1945." The facts sounded dry as he reeled them off, but beneath the detached tone of voice Erica could hear an echo of the horror he had experienced.

"But as I said, Hans Olavsen left here in June 1945. He must have gone just before you got back," she said.

"I think it was only a matter of days." Axel nodded. "But you'll have to forgive me if my memory is a little unclear on that point. I was . . . in pretty bad shape when I got back."

"I understand," Erica said, looking down at the floor. It was a strange feeling to be sitting here with someone who had seen the German concentration camps from the inside.

"Did your brother say anything about him? Anything you can remember? Anything at all? I have no real proof, but I get the feeling that Erik and his friends spent a lot of time with Hans Olavsen during the year he spent in Fjällbacka."

Axel stared out the window, looking as if he was trying to think back. He tipped his head to one side and frowned slightly.

"I seem to recall that there was something between the Norwegian and your mother, if you don't mind my saying so."

"Of course not." Erica waved a hand dismissively. "It's a lifetime ago, and I've already heard the same thing."

"There you go; my memory isn't quite as bad as I sometimes fear." He gave a little smile and turned to look at her. "Yes, I'm pretty sure Erik told me there was some kind of romance between Elsy and Hans."

"How did she react when he left? Do you remember anything about what she was like around that time?"

"Not much, I'm afraid. Of course she wasn't really herself anyway, after what had happened to your grandfather. And she left Fjällbacka soon after that to start studying . . . home economics, I think it was. And then we kind of lost touch. When she came back here a couple of years later, I had already started working abroad, and I wasn't home very often. She and Erik didn't have any contact either, as far as I can remember. But that's nothing unusual; you can be good friends with someone during your childhood and teens, but when adult life comes along with all its concerns, you drift apart." He gazed out the window once more.

"I know what you mean," Erica said, feeling disappointed. Axel didn't seem to know anything about Hans either. "And nobody ever mentioned where Hans Olavsen went? He didn't say anything to Erik?"

Axel shook his head regretfully. "I'm very sorry. I wish I could help you, but I wasn't really myself when I came home, and then I had other things to think about. But surely you should be able to trace him through the authorities?" he said optimistically as he got to his feet. Erica took the hint and stood up as well.

"That's the next step, I guess. If I'm lucky, that should provide the answers. Perhaps he didn't go very far after all."

"I wish you luck, I really do," Axel said, taking her hand. "I understand perfectly how important it is to deal with the past so that we can live in the present. Trust me, I do know." He patted her hand, and Erica smiled gratefully at his attempt to console her.

"By the way, did you find out any more about that medal?" he asked as she was about to open the front door.

"I'm afraid not," she said, feeling more disheartened with every passing minute. "I went to see an expert on Nazi medals in Gothenburg, but unfortunately it's too common to be traced."

"I'm so sorry I couldn't be of more help."

"Don't worry, it was a long shot," she said, waving good-bye.

The last thing she saw was Axel standing in the doorway, watching her go. She felt terribly sorry for him, but something he had said had given her an idea. Erica headed purposefully toward Fjällbacka.

Kjell hesitated before knocking. Standing here outside his father's door, he suddenly felt like a frightened little boy again. His memory took him back to all those times he had stood outside the imposing prison doors, clutching his mother's hand with an equal measure of fear and anticipation in his belly at the thought of seeing his father. Because there had been anticipation at first. He had longed to see Frans. Missed him. He had remembered only the good times, those brief periods when his father had been outside the prison walls, how Frans had swung him high in the air, taken him for walks in the forest holding his hand, told him about all the different mushrooms, the bushes, and the trees. Kjell had believed that his father knew everything in the whole wide world. But in his bedroom at night he had had to bury his head in his pillow to shut out the noise of the quarrels—the horrible, vicious quarrels that seemed to have no beginning and therefore no end. His mother and father simply resumed where they had left off the last time Frans went to prison, and they just continued along the same route, the same arguments and blows, over and over again until the next time the police came knocking and took his father away.

And so the anticipation dwindled with every passing year, until in the end only the fear was left as he stood in the visitors' room, confronted with the expectant look on his father's face. And then the fear had turned to hatred. In a way it would have been easier if he hadn't had those forest walks to remember, because what sparked the hatred, fed its fire, was the question he had constantly asked himself when he was a little boy: How could his father reject all this, over and over again? Reject Kjell in favor of a world that was gray and cold, a world that took away something in his father's eyes every time he went back there.

Kjell hammered on the door, annoyed at having allowed himself to be overwhelmed by memories.

"I know you're in there—open up!" he yelled, listening hard. Then he heard the sound of the safety chain being lifted off and the latch turning.

"I presume you need all this security to protect you from your pals," Kjell said nastily, pushing past Frans into the hallway.

"What do you want this time?" Frans said.

Kjell was struck by the realization that his father suddenly looked old. Frail. Then he dismissed the thought; the old man was tougher than most. He'd probably outlive them all.

"I want some information from you." Kjell walked in and sat down on the sofa without waiting for an invitation.

Frans sat down in the armchair opposite his son; he didn't say a word.

"What do you know about a man by the name of Hans Olavsen?"

Frans gave a start, but quickly regained control of himself. He leaned back in his chair and casually placed his hand on the armrest. "Why?" he said, looking his son in the eyes.

"That's none of your business."

"And why should I help you if that's your attitude?"

Kjell leaned forward so that his face was only inches from his father's. He stared at him for a long time, then said coldly "Because you owe me. You need to take every single opportunity to help me if you want to reduce the chances of my dancing on your grave."

For a moment, there was a glint of something in Frans's eyes. Something lost. It might have been the memory of walks in the forest and a little boy being lifted high in the air in strong arms. Then it was gone. He gazed at his son and said, calmly, "Hans Olavsen was a Norwegian resistance fighter who was seventeen years old when he arrived in Fjällbacka. I think it was in 1944. He left a year later. That's all I know."

"Crap," Kjell said, leaning back on the sofa. "I know you spent a lot of time together, you and Elsy Moström, Britta Johansson, and Erik Frankel. And now two of them are dead, murdered, within the space of two months. Don't you think that's a little strange?"

Frans ignored the question and said "What's that got to do with the Norwegian?"

"I don't know. But I intend to find out," Kjell hissed between clenched teeth, trying to keep his anger in check. "What else do you know about him? Tell me about the time you spent together, tell me what happened when he left. Every detail you can recall."

Frans sighed and looked as if he were trying to go back in time. "So you want details. . . . Let's see what I can remember. He lodged with Elsy's parents; he came over on her father's boat."

"I already know that. More."

"He worked on the cargo ships sailing down the coast, but whenever he had any free time, he'd spend it with us. We were several years younger than he was, but he didn't seem to mind; we all got on very well. Some of us better than others," he said; sixty years hadn't wiped away the bitterness he had felt back then.

"Hans and Elsy," Kjell said drily.

"How did you know that?" Frans said, surprised that he still felt a stab of pain when he thought about the two of them together. The heart definitely had a longer memory than the head.

"I just know. Keep going."

"Well, he and Elsy got together and, as I'm sure you also know, I wasn't exactly pleased about it."

"No, I didn't know that."

"Well, that's how it was. I had a thing for Elsy, but she chose him. And the irony of it was that Britta was besotted with me, but I wasn't interested in her. I would have been happy to go to bed with her, but something always told me that that would bring more trouble than pleasure, so I didn't."

"Very chivalrous of you," Kjell said sarcastically. Frans merely raised an eyebrow.

"So what happened? If Hans and Elsy were more than friends, why did he take off?"

"I suppose it was the oldest story in the world. He promised her the moon, and when the war ended he said he was just going to go back to Norway to see his family, then he would return. But. . . ." Frans shrugged and gave a tight little smile.

"You think he was lying to her?"

"I don't know, Kjell. To be perfectly honest, I don't know. It was sixty years ago, and we were young. Perhaps he meant what he said to Elsy, but then he had too many commitments at home and couldn't get back. Or perhaps he intended to run away all along, as soon as he got the chance." Another shrug. "All I know is that he said good-bye to us and told us he'd be back as soon as he'd sorted things out with his family. And then he left. To tell the truth, I've hardly thought of him since then. I know that Elsy was very upset for a while, but her mother got her into some kind of training college, and I have no idea what happened after that. I'd already left Fjällbacka by then, and . . . well, you know the rest."

"Indeed I do," Kjell said grimly, seeing the enormous gray prison doors in his mind's eye once more.

"I just don't see how this can be of any interest to you," Frans said. "He turned up, and after a while he disappeared. And I don't think any of us has been in touch with him since then. So why the questions?" Frans stared at Kjell.

"I can't tell you that," his son answered angrily. "But if there's something to find out, I'm going to get to the bottom of it, I promise you." His gaze was challenging.

"I believe you, Kjell, I believe you," Frans said wearily.

Kjell looked at his father's hand, resting on the arm of the chair. It was an old man's hand, wrinkled and sinewy, shrunken and marked with liver spots. So different from the hand that had held his on those forest walks. That hand had been so strong, so smooth, so warm as it enveloped his own small hand. It had made him feel safe and secure.

"It looks as if it's going to be a good year for mushrooms," he heard himself say, and Frans looked at him in astonishment. Then his face softened and he answered, quietly, "I think you're right, Kjell. I think you're right."

Axel was packing with military discipline. All the years of traveling had taught him that; nothing must be left to chance. A pair of pants folded carelessly would result in a laborious bout of ironing using the inadequate ironing board in some hotel room. Not checking that the cap of the toothpaste tube had been screwed on tightly would lead to a minor catastrophe and the need for some urgent washing. So everything was placed in the large suitcase with meticulous precision.

He sat down on the bed. This had been his bedroom when he was growing up, but he had actually changed a few things over the years when it came to the decor. Model planes and comic books didn't seem quite right for a grown man's bedroom. He wondered whether he would ever come back here. It had been difficult, staying in the house these last few weeks, yet at the same time he had felt that he had to do it.

He got up and went into Erik's bedroom, a few doors down along the landing. Axel smiled as he walked in and sat down on his brother's bed. The room was full of books. Of course. The shelves were overstuffed, and there were piles of books on the floor, many of them marked with small Post-it notes. Erik had never tired of his books, his facts, his dates, and the steadfast reality they offered him. In that way, things had been easier for Erik. Reality was there on paper, in black and white. No gray areas, none of the political twists and turns or moral dilemmas that were standard fare in Axel's world. Just concrete facts. Battle of Hastings, 1066. Death of Napoleon, 1821. German surrender, May 8, 1945. Axel reached for a book that was still lying on Erik's bed, a thick tome on how Germany had been rebuilt after the war. He put it down again. He knew all about that. His life had been centered on the war and its aftermath for sixty years. But perhaps it had been about himself more than anything. Erik had realized that, had pointed out the shortcomings in Axel's life, and in his own. He had recounted them as dry facts, apparently without emotion. But Axel knew his brother very well, and was aware that behind all those facts there was more emotion than most people he had met were capable of feeling.

He wiped away a tear that had begun to trickle down his cheek. Here, in Erik's room, suddenly things weren't as crystal-clear as he would have liked them to be. Axel's entire life was built on the premise that there must be no ambiguities. He had constructed a life based on right and wrong, set himself up as the person who could point the finger and say in which of these camps people belonged. And yet it was Erik, in his quiet little world of books, who had been the one who knew all about right and wrong. Somewhere deep inside, Axel had always known that. Known that the struggle to escape from the gray area between good and evil would take more of a toll on his brother than on him.

But Erik had fought. For sixty years he had watched Axel come and go, heard him talk about his efforts in the service of good. He had permitted Axel to build up an image of himself as the man who put everything right. Erik had watched and listened in silence. Looked at his brother with that gentle expression from behind his glasses, allowed him to live in a state of delusion. But somewhere deep down Axel had always known that it was himself he was fooling, not Erik.

And now he would keep on living the lie. Back to work. Back to the diligent hunt that must go on. He couldn't slow down because soon it would be too late, soon there would no longer be anyone left alive who could remember, and no one left to punish. Soon there would be nothing but the history books to bear witness to what had taken place.

Axel got up and looked around the room one more time before he went back to his own bedroom. He still had a lot of packing to do.

It was a long time since Erica had visited her maternal grand-parents' grave. The conversation with Axel had reminded her, and she had decided to go home via the churchyard. She opened the gate and heard the gravel crunch beneath her feet as she set off along the path.

She passed her parents' grave first; it was straight ahead and on the left-hand side. She crouched down and pulled up a few weeds around the headstone to make it look tidy, and reminded herself that she must come again soon with fresh flowers. She stared at her mother's name on the stone. Elsy Falck. There were so many questions she would have liked to ask her. If only Elsy hadn't died in that car accident four years ago, Erica would have been able to speak to her directly rather than feeling her way along, trying to find out more about why Elsy had been the way she was.

As a child, Erica had blamed herself. And as an adult too. She had thought that there was something wrong with her, that she wasn't good enough. Why else would her mother not want to touch her? Why else did her mother talk at her rather than with her? Why else did her mother never tell her that she loved her, or that she was fond of her at least? For a long time Erica had carried a sense of being inadequate, lacking in some way. Admittedly, her father had done all he could to make up for her mother's coldness. Tore had invested a great deal of time and love in Erica and Anna. He always listened, was always ready to make a wound better with a kiss when they fell and scraped their knees, and they always felt safe in the shelter of his arms. But it hadn't been enough, not when it seemed as if their mother could hardly bear the sight of them sometimes, let alone give them a hug.

That was why Erica was so astonished by the picture of her mother as a young girl that was gradually emerging. How could the quiet but warm and gentle girl everyone described have metamorphosed into someone who was so cold, so distant, that she even treated her own children like strangers?

Erica reached out and touched her mother's name, engraved on the stone.

"What happened to you, Mom?" she whispered, feeling her throat tighten. When she stood up a little while later, she was even more determined to follow her mother's story as far as she could. There was something there, something that was still mocking her, and it needed to be brought out into the light. Whatever it cost her, she was going to find it.

After a final glance at her parents' headstone, Erica moved on to her grandparents' grave just a few yards away. Elof and Hilma Moström. She had never met them. The tragedy that took her grandfather's life had struck long before Erica was born, and her grandmother had passed away ten years later. Elsy had never talked about them, but Erica was happy that everything she had heard about them so far during her research had indicated that they were warmhearted and well liked. She crouched down again and stared at the headstone, almost as if she thought she might be able to make it speak to her. But the stone remained silent. She wasn't going to find out anything here. If she wanted to get to the truth, she would have to look elsewhere.

She headed toward the slope leading up to the community center and a shortcut home. At the foot of the slope she automatically glanced to the right at the large, gray, moss-covered gravestone that stood by itself at the foot of the granite cliff that ran along one side of the churchyard. She took one step up the slope, then stopped dead. She moved back until she was standing right in front of the big gray stone, her heart pounding in her chest. Disconnected facts, disconnected comments started spinning around in her mind. She squinted, peering at the stone to make sure she was right, then took a step forward so that she was standing as close to the stone as possible. She even followed the words with her finger to check that her brain wasn't playing tricks on her.

Then everything fell into place with an audible clunk inside her head. Of course. Now she knew what had happened, or at least part of it. She took out her cell and called Patrik, her fingers trembling. It was time for him to intervene.

His daughters had just been to visit him again. They came every day, his wonderful, wonderful girls. It did his heart good to see them sitting side by side next to his bed, so alike and yet so different. And he could see Britta in all of them. Anna-Greta had her nose, Birgitta her eyes, and Margareta, the youngest, had those little dimples in her cheeks that Britta had when she smiled.

Herman closed his eyes to stop himself from crying. He just didn't have the strength to cry anymore. He had no tears left. But he had to open his eyes again; every time he closed them, he saw Britta as she had looked when he lifted the pillow from her face. He had known without picking up the pillow, but he had done it anyway. He had wanted the confirmation, wanted to see what he had done through one unconsidered action. Because he had definitely understood. The second he had walked in through the bedroom door to see her lying there motionless with the pillow over her face, he had understood.

When he picked up the pillow and saw her empty gaze, he had died. At that very moment, he too had died. All he could do was lie down beside her, as close as he could get, with his arms around her body. If it had been up to him, he would still be lying there now. He had wanted to hold her tight as her body grew cold, the memories drifting through his mind.

Herman stared up at the ceiling as he remembered. Summer days when they took the rowboat over to the beach on the island of Valö, with the girls on board and Britta in the prow with her face turned up to the sun, her long legs stretched out in front of her, and her long blond hair hanging down her back. He would watch as she opened her eyes and turned to face him, smiling happily. He would wave to her from his place at the tiller, feeling as rich as a king.

Then a shadow passed over his face as he remembered the first time she had talked to him about the unmentionable matter. It was a dark winter afternoon, and the girls were in school. She had told him to sit down, said she needed to talk to him about something. His heart had almost stopped, and he was ashamed to admit that his first thought had been that she was leaving him, that she had met someone else. For that reason, what she actually said had almost come as a relief. He had listened. She had talked. For a long time. And by the time they had to go and pick up the girls, they had agreed that they would never talk about it again. What was done was done. He hadn't looked at her any differently afterward, hadn't felt differently toward her or changed the way he spoke to her. How could he have? How could that have pushed aside the images of the quiet, happy life they had shared together, the wonderful nights? What she had told him could never outweigh all that, not by a long shot, and so they had agreed never to touch upon it again.

But her illness had changed all that, changed everything. It had swept through their lives like a typhoon, ripping every thing up by the roots. And he had allowed himself to be swept along with it. He had made a mistake. One fateful mistake.

One phone call he shouldn't have made. But he had been naïve, thought it was time to bring all that was musty and rotten out into the air. He had thought that if he just showed Britta how she was suffering because of the knowledge that had been hidden deep inside her brain—the brain that was now deteriorating little by little—it would be obvious to her that the time had come. She would realize that it was wrong to keep on fighting; the past must come out so that they could both find peace of mind. So that Britta could find peace of mind. Good God, he had been so naïve. He might just as well have placed the pillow over her face himself and held it there. He knew that, and the pain of that knowledge was unbearable. Herman closed his eyes once more to try to escape the pain, and this time he didn't see Britta's empty gaze. Instead he saw her in the hospital bed, pale and exhausted but happy. With Anna-Greta in her arms. She raised her hand and waved to him, beckoning him closer.

With one last sigh he let go of everything that was causing him pain, smiling as he walked toward them.

Patrik was staring blankly into space. Could Erica be right? It sounded completely insane yet . . . logical. He sighed, well aware of the difficult task before him.

"Come on, sweetie, we're going for a little outing," he said, carrying Maja into the hallway. "And we're picking up Mommy on the way."

A short while later he pulled up in front of the gate leading to the churchyard; Erica was waiting, practically jumping up and down on the spot with excitement. Patrik had begun to feel the same, and had to remind himself not to drive too fast as they headed toward Tanumshede. He could be a slightly careless driver at times, but when Maja was in the car he always drove with extreme caution.

"I'll do the talking, okay?" Patrik said as they parked in front of the station. "You can come in because I don't have the strength to try and talk you out of it and because I know I wouldn't succeed. But he's my boss, and I'm the one who's done this before—understood?"

Erica nodded reluctantly as she lifted Maja out of the car.

"Perhaps we should drive over to Mom's and see if she can look after Maja for a while? I mean, you don't like her spending time at the station . . . ," Patrik teased, and was rewarded with a glare from Erica.

"You know I want this done as soon as possible. And she doesn't seem to have come to any harm from her previous time with the police," she said with a wink.

"Well, look who's here!" Annika said in surprise, her face lighting up as Maja beamed at her.

"We need to speak to Bertil," Patrik said. "Is he in?"

"Yes, he's in his office," Annika said with an inquiring glance. She let them in, and Patrik marched quickly down to Mellberg's office, with Erica following behind, Maja in her arms.

"Hedström! What the hell are you doing here? I see you've brought the family with you," Mellberg said morosely, not bothering to get up to say hello.

"There's something we need to discuss with you," Patrik said, sitting down without waiting to be invited. Maja and Ernst had just caught sight of one another, to their mutual delight.

"Is he used to children?" Erica said, unwilling to put down her daughter, who was struggling to escape.

"How the hell should I know?" Mellberg said, before softening slightly. "He's the gentlest dog in the world. Wouldn't hurt a fly." His voice betrayed a certain amount of pride, and Patrik raised an eyebrow in amusement. Mellberg had definitely fallen for that dog.

Erica put Maja down next to Ernst, still feeling a little wary; he immediately started licking her face enthusiastically, and Maja reacted with a mix of joy and fear.

"So, what do you want?" Mellberg was staring at Patrik with a hint of curiosity.

"I want you to apply for permission to open up a grave."

Mellberg made a choking sound as if he had something stuck in his throat, his face turning redder and redder as he tried to get some air.

"Open up a grave? Have you gone crazy?" he managed after a bout of coughing. "Being on paternity leave must have affected your brain! Do you know how rare it is to open up a grave? And we've done it twice in the past few years. If I tell them we want to do it again, I'll end up in the funny farm! Who do you want to dig up this time, by the way?"

"A Norwegian resistance fighter who disappeared in 1945," Erica said calmly from a crouching position next to Patrik as she scratched Ernst behind the ear.

"I'm sorry?" Mellberg stared at her blankly, as if he thought he might have misheard.

Patiently Erica told him everything she had found out about the four friends and the Norwegian who'd arrived in Fjällbacka a year before the war ended. She told him about how there was no trace of Hans Olavsen after June 1945, and that they hadn't yet managed to track him down.

"Couldn't he have stayed in Sweden? Or gone back to Norway? Have you checked with the authorities in both countries?" Mellberg looked immensely skeptical.

Erica straightened up, then sat down in the other visitor's chair. She stared at Mellberg as if she was trying to get him to take her seriously through sheer willpower. Then she told him what Herman had said to her: that Paul Heckel and Friedrich Hück would be able to answer her questions.

"I thought the names were vaguely familiar, but I couldn't remember where I'd come across them before. Until today. I went to the churchyard to visit the graves of my parents and grandparents, and that was when I saw it."

"Saw what?" Mellberg asked, completely lost.

She waved her hand dismissively. "I'll get there, if you'll just let me continue."

"Of course, of course," Mellberg said; he was starting to get interested in spite of himself.

"There's a grave in Fjällbacka churchyard that's a little bit different. It's from the First World War, and ten German soldiers are buried there. Seven were identified and are named, and three are unknown."

"You forgot to mention what was scribbled on the pad," Patrik said, having resigned himself to the fact that his wife was doing the talking. A good man knows when to give in.

"Oh, yes, that's another piece of the puzzle." Erica told Mellberg about the words she had seen on the notepad when she was studying the photograph from the scene of Erik Frankel's murder: *Ignoto militi.*

"How come you were looking at pictures from a crime scene?" Mellberg said crossly, glaring at Patrik.

"We can discuss that later," Patrik said. "Just listen to what she has to say, please."

Mellberg grunted but let it go, and Erica went on.

"He'd written those words over and over again, so I looked them up. It's an inscription from the Arc de Triomphe in Paris, on the grave of the Unknown Soldier, to be exact. And that's exactly what the quotation means: *To the Unknown Soldier.*"

Mellberg seemed none the wiser, so Erica kept on talking and waving her hands around.

"It was all in the back of my mind. We have a Norwegian resistance fighter who disappeared in 1945, and nobody knows where he went. We have Erik's words on the pad: the unknown soldier. Britta Johansson said something about 'old bones,' then we have the names Herman gave me. A little while ago I was walking past that grave in Fjällbacka churchyard, and I realized why those two names were so familiar: they're engraved on the headstone." Erica paused to catch her breath. Mellberg stared at her.

"So Paul Heckel and Friedrich Hück are the names of two Germans who are lying in a First World War grave in Fjällbacka churchyard?"

"Yes," Erica said, wondering how to proceed. But Mellberg got there first.

"So what you're saying is that . . . ?"

She took a deep breath and glanced at Patrik before going on. "What I'm saying is that there is probably an extra body in that grave. I believe that Hans Olavsen, the Norwegian resistance fighter, is buried there. And I don't know how, but I also believe this is the key to the murders of Erik and Britta."

The room fell silent. No one said a word, and the only sounds in Mellberg's office came from Maja and Ernst, happily playing together. Eventually Patrik said quietly, "I know this might sound crazy, but I've talked it through with Erica, and I think there's a great deal in what she says. I can't offer any concrete proof, but there's enough circumstantial evidence. There's also a good chance that Erica is right, and that this is somehow linked to the two murders. I don't know how or why, but the first step is to find out if there really is another body in the grave, and if so, how he died and ended up there."

Mellberg didn't reply. He clasped his hands and sat in silence, thinking. Eventually he sighed deeply.

"I've probably lost my mind, but I think you might be right. I can't guarantee that I'll succeed; we do have something of a track record, as I said, and the prosecutor will probably hit the roof, but I can try. That's the best I can do."

"That's all we ask," Erica said eagerly, looking as if she was about to throw her arms around Mellberg.

"Okay, calm down. I don't think I'll get anywhere, but I will try. And now I need some peace and quiet to get on with it."

"We'll get out of your way," Patrik said, getting to his feet. "Give me a call as soon as you know anything, won't you?"

Mellberg merely waved them away as he picked up the phone to begin what would probably be the most difficult test of his powers of persuasion in his entire career.

38
Fjällbacka 1945

Hans had been lodging with them for six months, and he and Elsy had known that they loved each other for three months when disaster struck. Elsy was standing on the veranda watering her mother's plants when she saw them coming up the steps. She had known the moment she saw their grim faces. Behind her she could hear her mother clattering about with the dishes in the kitchen, and a part of her wanted to rush in there and take her away, get her out of the house before she had to hear the words Elsy knew she wouldn't be able to bear. But she realized it was futile. Instead, she moved stiffly over to the front door and opened it to let in three men from one of the other fishing boats in Fjällbacka.

"Is Hilma at home?" the oldest man asked. Elsy knew he was the skipper; she nodded and showed them in. They walked into the kitchen in front of Elsy; when Hilma turned around and saw them, she dropped the plate she was holding and it smashed to pieces on the floor.

"No, no, please God, no!" she screamed.

Elsy just managed to catch her mother before she collapsed. She got her onto a chair and held her tightly, while at the same time she felt as if her heart were being ripped from her chest. The three fishermen stood by the table looking embarrassed, twisting their caps in their hands, but eventually the skipper spoke.

"It was a mine, Hilma. We saw everything from our boat, and we got there as fast as we could. But . . . there was nothing we could do."

"Oh God, oh God," Hilma repeated, gasping for breath. "And the rest of the crew. . . ."

Elsy was amazed that her mother could think of others at a moment like this, but then she pictured her father's crew, the men they knew so well. Their families would be getting the same news before long.

"Nobody could have survived," the skipper said, swallowing hard. "There was only the wreckage of the boat left; we stayed and searched for a long time, but we didn't find anyone except Oscarsson, the boy. But he was already dead when we got him into our boat."

Tears were pouring down Hilma's face and she was biting her knuckles to stop the scream from coming out. Elsy swallowed her tears and tried to be strong. How was her mother going to get through this? And how would she? Father was such a good, kind person, always quick to offer a friendly word and a helping hand. How would they get by without him?

They were interrupted by a cautious knock on the door, and one of the men went to open it. Hans came into the kitchen, his face ashen.

"I saw that you had company. I thought . . . I wondered. . . ." He looked down at the floor. Elsy realized that he was afraid of intruding, but she was grateful for his presence.

"Father's boat hit a mine," she said, her voice thick with tears. "There were no survivors."

Hans swayed unsteadily, then he walked over to the cupboard where Elof kept his strong drink, and resolutely poured six shots, which he placed on the table.

"I think we could all use a stiff drink right now," he said in his lilting Norwegian accent, which was becoming more and more Swedish the longer he stayed with them.

Everyone gratefully reached for a drink except Hilma. Elsy carefully picked up a glass and put it in front of her mother. "Please try, Mom." Hilma obeyed her daughter; she brought the glass to her lips with a shaking hand and swallowed the contents with a grimace. Elsy gave Hans a look full of gratitude. It was good to know that she wasn't alone at a time like this.

There was another knock on the door, and Hans went to open it. The women had begun to arrive, those who knew what it was like to live with the threat of losing their husbands to the sea. They understood what Hilma was going through, and realized that she would need them around her. They brought food and capable hands and consoling words about the will of God. And it helped. Not a great deal, but they were all aware that they might need the same solace one day, and they did their best to ease the pain of their sister in her sorrow.

Her heart bursting with grief, Elsy took a step back and watched as the women flocked around Hilma, while the men who had brought the sad news bowed their heads and took their leave, on their way to tell other families.

By the time night fell, Hilma had finally fallen into an exhausted sleep. Elsy was lying in her bed gazing up at the ceiling, empty, incapable of taking in what had happened.

She could see her father's face before her. He had always been there for her, listened to her, talked to her. She had been the apple of his eye, and she had always known it. She had been more precious to him than anything, and she knew that he had probably realized there was something going on between her and the Norwegian boy he had grown so fond of. But he had let them carry on, keeping a watchful eye on them while giving his tacit approval, perhaps hoping that Hans would be his son-in-law someday. Elsy didn't think he would have objected. And she and Hans had respected both her father and mother, kept their affection to stolen kisses and chaste hugs; they had done nothing that would make it difficult to look her mother and father in the eye.

But as she lay there staring into the darkness, that no longer mattered. The pain in her breast was so great that she couldn't endure it alone, and she quietly slipped out of bed. There was still something within her that was unsure, but the grief tore at her heart, driving her to seek the only relief she knew she could find.

Cautiously she crept down the stairs, peeping in at her mother as she passed the door of her parents' bedroom; it was painful to see how small she looked, lying there alone. At least she was fast asleep, which brought her a temporary respite from reality.

The front door creaked slightly as she turned the latch and opened it. The night air was so chilly that it took her breath away as she stepped out onto the porch wearing only her nightdress, and the cold stone steps hurt the soles of her feet. She quickly padded down to the basement and found herself hesitating outside his door. But only for a moment. She had to ease this pain.

He opened at her first gentle tap, stepping aside to let her in without a word. She walked in and stood there in her nightdress, her eyes locked on his, without speaking. There was an unspoken question in his gaze, and she responded by taking his hand.

For a few blessed moments that night, she was able to forget the pain in her heart.

39

Kjell felt strangely agitated after the encounter with his father. For years he had managed to maintain the status quo, to keep the hatred alive. It had been so easy to see only the negatives, to focus solely on all the mistakes Frans had made during Kjell's childhood. However, perhaps everything wasn't just black or white. He shook himself, trying to dismiss the idea. It was so much easier not to see any gray areas, just wrong or right. But Frans had looked so old and frail today. For the first time, Kjell realized that his father wasn't going to live forever; he wouldn't always be there as a symbol of Kjell's hatred. One day his father would be gone, and then he would be forced to look at himself in the mirror. Deep inside, he knew that the hatred burned as strongly as it did because he still had the opportunity to reach out, to take the first step toward reconciliation. He didn't want to do that, he had absolutely no desire to do it, but the possibility was there, and it had always given him a sense of power.

But the day his father died, it would all be too late. All he would have left would be a life of hatred. Nothing else.

His hand was shaking slightly as he picked up the phone to make some calls. Erica had said that she would check with the authorities, but he wasn't used to relying on someone else; it was probably best if he checked for himself. However, one hour later, after five calls within Sweden and to Norway, he had to admit that his inquiries had produced nothing concrete. It was undeniably difficult when they had only a name and an approximate age, but there was always a way. He had not yet exhausted all the possibilities, and the information he had acquired was sufficiently reliable for him to be fairly sure that the Norwegian had not remained in Sweden. That left the most likely scenario, which was that he had returned to his homeland once the war was over and he was no longer in any danger.

Kjell reached for the folder of articles and suddenly realized that he had forgotten to fax a picture of Hans Olavsen to Eskil Halvorsen. He picked up the phone again to call him and get a fax number.

"I'm afraid I haven't found anything yet," Halvorsen said as soon as Kjell spoke, and Kjell quickly explained that that wasn't why he had called again so soon.

"A picture might be useful. You can fax it to my office at the university," Halvorsen said, reeling off a number that Kjell jotted down. He sent off a copy of the article with the clearest picture of Hans Olavsen, then sat down at his desk once more. He hoped Erica would be able to come up with something; he felt as if he had hit a dead end.

At that moment the telephone rang.

"Gramps is here," Per called out, and Carina emerged from the living room.

"Can I come in for a little while?" Frans said.

Carina was concerned to see that he didn't look like himself at all. Not that she had ever been particularly fond of Kjell's father, but what he had done for her and Per had at least secured him a place on the list of people to whom she was grateful.

"Sure, come on in," she said, leading the way into the kitchen. She could see that he was scrutinizing her closely, and in answer to his unspoken question, she said "Not a drop since you were last here. Per can vouch for me."

Per nodded and sat down opposite Frans at the kitchen table. The expression on his face when he looked at his grandfather was very close to adoration.

"Your hair is starting to grow," Frans said, sounding amused as he patted the stubble on his grandson's head.

"I guess so," Per said in embarrassment, but he looked pleased as he ran a hand over his head.

"That's good," Frans said. "Really good."

Carina threw him a warning glance as she measured out the coffee. He gave her an almost imperceptible nod to reassure her that he wouldn't discuss his political views with Per.

When the coffee was ready and Carina had joined them at the table, she looked questioningly at Frans. He stared down into his cup. Once again she noticed how tired he seemed; in spite of the fact that he used his energy in the wrong way, in her opinion, she had always thought of him as the epitome of strength.

"I've opened an account in Per's name," Frans said eventually, still without looking at either of them. "He'll have access to it when he turns twenty-five, and I've already put some money in there."

"Where did you get—" Carina began, but Frans held up his hand and went on.

"For reasons I can't go into, the account is not in a Swedish bank; it's in Luxembourg."

Carina raised an eyebrow, but she wasn't entirely surprised. Kjell had always maintained that his father had money tucked away somewhere, from one of the criminal activities that had led to his frequent spells in jail.

"But why now?" she said, looking at him.

At first Frans seemed reluctant to answer the question, but finally he said "If anything happens to me, I want this taken care of."

Carina didn't speak. She didn't want to know any more.

"Cool," Per said, gazing admiringly at his grandfather. "How much cash do I get?"

"Per!" Carina said, glaring at her son, who merely shrugged.

"A lot," Frans said drily, but without going into detail. "However, although the account is in your name, I have set one condition. You can't access it until you're twenty-five, as I said, but"—he held up a warning finger—"I've also specified that you are not allowed access until your mother agrees that you are mature enough to handle the money and gives her permission. And that applies even after you turn twenty-five. If she decides you're not smart enough to do something sensible with the money, you won't see a cent of it. Is that clear?"

Per mumbled something, but accepted what Frans had said without protest.

Carina didn't know how to react. There was something about the way Frans was behaving, something about his voice, that worried her, yet at the same time she felt an enormous sense of gratitude toward him on Per's behalf. She didn't care where the money had come from. It was a long time since anybody had missed it, and if it could help Per in the future, she wasn't about to complain.

"What about Kjell?" she said.

Frans raised his head and looked at her. "I don't want Kjell to know anything about this until the day Per gets the money.

I want your word that you won't say anything to him—you too, Per!" He turned to his grandson with a stern expression. "That's the only demand I'm making: your father is not to know about this until he is faced with a fait accompli."

"No problem. I won't say a word," Per said. In fact, he seemed delighted at the idea of keeping something from his father.

Frans added, in a slightly calmer tone of voice, "I know you'll probably end up being punished in some way for your stupid antics recently, but listen to me, Per." He forced the boy to meet his eye.

"You take your punishment. They'll probably send you to a juvenile detention center. You stay away from trouble, stay away from any kind of crap that's going on, you serve your time without causing any problems, then you make sure you don't do anything stupid in the future. Do you hear me?" He spoke slowly and clearly, and every time Per tried to look away, Frans held his gaze.

"You don't want my life, trust me. My life has been crap from start to finish. The only thing that has ever mattered to me is you and your father, even though he would never believe me. But it's true. So promise me you'll stay away from the bad stuff. Promise me!"

"Yeah, yeah," Per said, squirming uncomfortably, but it was obvious that he was listening and taking notice.

Frans just hoped it would be enough. He knew from experience how difficult it was to change direction once you had embarked on a certain course, but with any luck he had gotten through sufficiently in order to give his grandson a little push onto a different route. At any rate, there was nothing more he could do now.

He got to his feet. "That's all I wanted to say. Everything you need in order to access the money is written down here." He placed a sheet of paper in front of Carina on the kitchen table.

"Won't you stay a while?" she said, still worried about him. Frans shook his head. "Things to do." He moved toward the door, but turned back. He hesitated for a moment, then said, quietly, "Take care of yourselves." He raised his hand and gave them a little wave, then walked away and let himself out of the apartment.

Carina and Per remained sitting at the kitchen table; neither of them spoke. They had both recognized a farewell.

"This is starting to become something of a tradition," Torbjörn Ruud said drily as he stood beside Patrik, watching the macabre task unfolding in front of them. Anna had offered to babysit, so Erica was there too, following the excavation with ill-concealed excitement.

"Yes, it can't have been easy for Mellberg to get permission," Patrik said, giving his boss credit for once.

"From what I've heard, it was ten minutes before the guy in the prosecutor's office stopped yelling at him," Torbjörn said without taking his eyes off the grave, where layer after layer of soil was being removed.

"Are we going to have to dig up the whole lot?" Patrik asked with a shudder.

Torbjörn shook his head. "If you're right, the person you're looking for should be at the top. I find it difficult to believe that someone would have gone to the trouble of burying him right at the bottom, underneath the others," he said with a hint of sarcasm. "He's probably not in a coffin either, and his clothes might give us an indication as to whether or not we're right."

"How quickly will we be able to get a preliminary report on the cause of death?" Erica said. "If we find him," she added, although she was pretty sure the exhumation would prove her right.

"They've promised we can have it by the day after tomorrow," Patrik said. "I spoke to Pedersen this morning, and they're giving this top priority. He can start work on it tomorrow, and get back to us by Friday. He was very eager to stress that it will only be a preliminary report, but he hopes it will at least give us the cause of death."

He was interrupted by a shout from the excavation, and they moved closer, curious to see what was going on.

"We've found something," one of the technicians called out, and Torbjörn went over to join him. They had a brief discussion, their heads close together, then Torbjörn came back to Patrik and Erica, who hadn't dared go too close.

"It looks as if someone who wasn't in a coffin has been buried pretty close to the surface. We're going to take things a little more slowly from now on to make sure we don't destroy any evidence, so it's going to take a while to get the guy out." He hesitated. "But it certainly looks as if you were right."

Erica nodded and took a deep breath, feeling very relieved. A short distance away, she saw Kjell approaching, but he was stopped by Martin and Gösta, who were there to keep unauthorized visitors away. She hurried over.

"It's okay, I called him and told him what was going on."

"No press and no unauthorized persons—those were Mellberg's express orders," Gösta muttered, placing a hand on Kjell's chest to stop him.

"Let him through." Patrik had joined them. "I'll take the responsibility." He glanced sharply at Erica, making it very clear that she was now accountable for any possible consequences. She gave a brief nod and led Kjell toward the grave.

"Have they found something?" he said, his eyes sparkling with excitement.

"Looks like it. I think we've found Hans Olavsen," she said, watching in fascination as the technicians carefully continued to expose a shapeless bundle in a hole barely eighteen inches deep.

"So he never left Fjällbacka," Kjell said breathlessly. He couldn't take his eyes off what was going on.

"Looks that way. So the question is, how did he end up here?"

"Erik and Britta knew he was here, anyway."

"Yes, and they've both been murdered." Erica shook her head as if she might be able to make all the details fall into place that way.

"But that means he's been here for sixty years. Why now? What is it that suddenly made him so important?" Kjell said thoughtfully.

"Did you get anything out of your father?" Erica said, turning to look at him.

He shook his head. "Not a thing. And I have no idea whether that's because he doesn't know anything, or because he just doesn't want to tell me."

"Do you think he could have . . . ?" She couldn't quite bring herself to complete the sentence, but Kjell understood what she meant.

"I think my father is capable of anything, that's all I know for sure."

"What are you two talking about?" Patrik said as he came to join them, pushing his hands deep into his pockets.

"We're discussing whether my father might have committed murder," Kjell said calmly.

Patrik was taken aback by his honesty. "Did you come to any conclusions?" he said after a moment. "We've had our suspicions, but evidently your father has an alibi for the time of Erik's murder."

"I didn't know that," Kjell replied. "But I hope you've double-checked and triple-checked the information in that case, because I find it hard to believe that an old jailbird like my father would have trouble coming up with an alibi."

Patrik realized that he was right, and made a mental note to ask Martin how thoroughly they had checked Frans Ringholm's alibi.

Torbjörn came over, with a nod of recognition to Kjell. "So . . . the fourth estate has permission to be here?"

"I have a personal interest in all this," Kjell said. Torbjörn shrugged; if the police had decided to allow a journalist to be present, he wasn't about to get involved. That was their problem.

"We'll be done here in about an hour," he said. "Pedersen is ready to start work right away."

"Yes, I spoke to him earlier," Patrik said.

"Okay. In that case, let's get whoever it is out of there and see what secrets this guy is hiding." He turned away and went back to the grave.

"Yes, let's find out what his secrets are," Erica said quietly, staring at the hole. Patrik put his arm around her shoulders.

40
Fjällbacka 1945

The months following her father's death were confusing and painful. Elsy's mother continued to carry out her daily chores and to do what was required of her, but there was something missing. Elof had taken a part of Hilma with him, and Elsy no longer recognized her mother. In a way, she had lost not only her father but her mother too. The only security she had left was the nights she shared with Hans. Every night after her mother had fallen asleep, Elsy crept downstairs and slipped into his arms. She knew it was wrong, she knew there were conse-quences that she couldn't ignore, but she couldn't help herself. When she was lying there beneath the covers with him, his arm around her as he gently stroked her hair, the world was whole again. When they kissed and the now familiar yet still surprising heat spread through her whole body, she couldn't understand how this could be wrong. How could love be wrong in a world that could suddenly and brutally be blown to pieces by a mine?

Hans had also been a boon to the family in practical terms. Money was a huge worry, now that Father was gone, and they only managed to get by because Hans had taken extra shifts on the boat and gave them every krona he earned. Sometimes Elsy wondered whether her mother actually knew that she crept downstairs to him at night but pretended it wasn't happening because she couldn't afford to do anything else.

Elsy caressed her stomach as she lay in bed beside Hans, listening to his steady breathing. It had been over a week since she had realized that she was expecting a child. No doubt it had been inevitable, but she had ignored the risks and, in spite of the circumstances, she was filled with a sense of serenity. She was carrying Hans's child, and that changed everything in terms of shame and consequences as far as she was concerned. There was no one in the world she trusted more than him. She hadn't said anything yet, but deep inside she knew that everything would be fine. He would be overjoyed. They would help each other, and somehow they would make it.

She closed her eyes, her hand resting on her stomach. Somewhere inside there was something tiny, something that had been created through love, the love between her and Hans. How could that be wrong? How could their child ever be wrong?

Elsy fell asleep with her hand on her stomach and a faint smile on her lips.

41

There was an air of tense expectation at the station following the previous day's exhumation. Naturally, Mellberg was claiming all the credit for the discovery, but nobody was taking much notice of him.

Martin couldn't hide the fact that he found the whole thing incredibly exciting, and even Gösta had had a spark in his eyes when they were standing guard in the churchyard. Like the others, Martin had begun to speculate on how everything might hang together. Even if they didn't know very much at this stage and couldn't yet see the connections, they all felt strongly that the previous day's discovery had been a breakthrough and that the solution was close.

A knock on the door interrupted Martin's thoughts.

"Am I disturbing you?" Paula looked inquiringly at him, and he shook his head.

"Not at all. Come on in."

She came in and sat down. "So, what are you thinking?"

"I don't know yet, but I'm looking forward to hearing what Pedersen has to say."

"Do you think we have another murder?"

"Why hide the body otherwise?" Martin said, and she nodded in agreement. She had already reached the same conclusion.

"But the question is why it's suddenly become important now, after sixty years. I think we have to assume that the murders of Britta and Erik are linked to the 'possible'"—she formed air quotes with her fingers—"murder of this boy. But why now? What's triggered this chain of events?"

"I don't know," Martin said with a sigh. "But I hope the autopsy will give us something to go on."

"And if it doesn't?" Paula said, putting into words the thought that had also crossed Martin's mind.

"We'll cross that bridge when we come to it," he said quietly.

"By the way," Paula said, changing the subject, "in the middle of all this upheaval, we've forgotten to collect the DNA samples. Weren't the DNA results supposed to be in today? They won't be much use if we haven't got anything to compare them with."

"You're right," Martin said, quickly getting to his feet. "We'll do it right away."

"Who shall we go and see first, Axel or Frans? I presume we're mainly concentrating on those two?"

"Frans," Martin said, pulling on his jacket.

Grebbestad was just as deserted as Fjällbacka now that the season was over, and they saw only a few residents as they drove through the small town. Martin parked outside the restaurant, and they crossed the street to Frans's apartment. There was no answer when they rang the bell.

"Damn, he's not home. We'll have to come back later or give him a call first," Martin said, turning to go back to the car.

"Hang on," Paula said, holding up her hand to stop him. "The door's open."

"But we can't . . . ," Martin objected. Too late; his colleague had already pushed it open and gone in.

"Hello?" she called out, and he followed reluctantly. There wasn't a sound inside the apartment. They moved cautiously through the hallway and glanced into the kitchen and living room. No Frans. Everything was quiet.

"Let's just check the bedroom," Paula said eagerly. Martin hesitated. "Come on, we might as well," she insisted. He sighed and followed her.

The bedroom was also empty; the bed was neatly made, and there was no sign of Frans.

"Hello?" Paula called again when they went back into the hallway. No answer. Slowly they approached the only door they hadn't opened.

They saw him as soon as the door swung inward. The room was a small study, and Frans was slumped over the desk with the gun still in his mouth and a gaping hole in the back of his head. Martin felt the blood drain from his face; he swayed briefly and swallowed hard before he managed to pull himself together. Paula, on the other hand, looked completely unmoved. She pointed at Frans, forcing Martin to look even though he really didn't want to, and said, calmly, "Look at his arms."

With waves of nausea rising and falling and a sour taste in his mouth, Martin made himself focus on Frans's forearms. He gave a start; there was no doubt about it. They were covered in deep scratches.

The mood at Tanumshede police station on that Friday was a strange combination of elation and anticipation. The discovery that Frans was in all probability the person who had murdered Britta just had to be confirmed through DNA and fingerprints, and no one doubted that they would find a link to the murder of Erik Frankel. During the day they would also receive a preliminary report on the body found in the soldiers' grave in Fjällbacka, and they were all very curious about the contents of that report.

Martin took the call from the medical examiner, and with the faxed autopsy report at the ready he went around knocking on doors, summoning everyone to a meeting in the kitchen.

When they had all sat down, he stood leaning against the counter so that everyone would be able to hear him properly.

"As I said, I've just had the preliminary report from Pedersen," Martin began, turning a deaf ear as Mellberg mumbled crossly that the call should have come to him.

"Since we don't have any DNA or dental records for comparison purposes, we can't be absolutely certain that the man in the grave is Hans Olavsen. But the age fits, and the time of his disappearance may also match, although it's impossible to be precise after such a long time."

"So, how did he die?" Paula asked, tapping her foot in her eagerness to continue.

Martin paused for effect, enjoying his moment in the limelight. Then he said "According to Pedersen, the victim sustained multiple serious injuries: stab wounds from a sharp object and crush injuries from kicks or blows or both. Someone was really, really furious with Hans Olavsen and took out their rage on him. You can read more details in the report Pedersen faxed us." He placed the copies on the table in front of them.

"So the cause of death was . . . ?" Paula was still tapping her foot.

"It's hard to determine whether one particular blow led to his death; several of the injuries could have been fatal, according to Pedersen."

"I wouldn't mind betting that Ringholm was responsible for this, and that's why he murdered Erik and Britta," Gösta muttered, saying out loud what everyone in the room was thinking. "He always did have a temper," Gösta added, nodding grimly.

"That's one hypothesis," Martin agreed. "But we mustn't jump to conclusions. Frans's forearms certainly bear the scratch marks that Pedersen told us to look out for, but we still haven't gotten the results of the samples we took from him yesterday, which means we haven't yet been able to establish that Frans's DNA matches the fragments of skin found under Britta's nails, or that it was his thumbprint on the button on the pillowcase. So let's not make too many assumptions. Until everything is confirmed, we carry on as usual." Martin was surprised to hear how calm and professional he sounded. This was exactly how Patrik sounded when he spoke to the team. He couldn't help glancing at Mellberg to see if he was put out because Martin had stepped into what should have been Mellberg's role in his capacity as station chief. As usual, though, he appeared perfectly happy to avoid anything that looked like real work. He would soon come to life and take all the credit, once the case was solved.

"So, what do we do now?" Paula said, looking at Martin. She gave him a quick wink to show that she thought he was doing really well. Martin felt himself grow taller with the praise, even though it was unspoken. He had been the station rookie for such a long time that he hardly dared step forward, but Patrik's paternity leave had given him the opportunity to show what he was made of.

"As far as Frans is concerned, I think we wait for the DNA results from the lab. Meanwhile, let's start again from the beginning and go through the investigation into Erik Frankel's death to see if we can find a link to Frans, apart from the things we already know about. Paula, perhaps you could take that?" Paula nodded, and Martin turned to Gösta.

"Gösta, could you see if you can find out any more about Hans Olavsen? What's his background, is there anyone who has any further details about his time in Fjällbacka, that kind of thing. Have a word with Patrik's Erica; apparently she's found out quite a bit, and Kjell Ringholm seems to be on the same track. Make sure they pass on any information they have. I don't think Erica will be a problem, but you might have to push Kjell a bit harder."

Gösta also nodded, but with considerably less enthusiasm than Paula. Digging into events that took place sixty years ago would be neither easy nor enjoyable. He sighed. "I suppose so," he said, looking as if he'd just been told that he was facing seven years of bad luck.

"Annika, could you let us know as soon as you hear from the National Forensics Lab?"

"Of course," Annika said, putting down her pad; she had been taking notes while Martin was speaking.

"Okay, so we've all got plenty to do." Martin was flushed with satisfaction at having led his first briefing.

They all got up and trooped out of the room, their thoughts filled with the mysterious fate of Hans Olavsen.

Patrik put down the phone after speaking to Martin. He went upstairs to Erica's study and tapped gently on the door.

"Come in!"

"Sorry to disturb you, but I thought you'd want to hear this." He sat down in the armchair in the corner and went through what Martin had told him about Hans Olavsen's terrible injuries—or at least the person they assumed was Hans Olavsen.

"I presumed he'd been murdered. . . . But like this . . . ," Erica said, noticeably affected.

"Someone certainly had a problem with him," Patrik said. Then he saw that he had interrupted Erica while she was going through her mother's diaries once again.

"Have you found anything else in there?" he asked, pointing at the books.

"No, unfortunately," she said, running a hand through her blond hair in frustration. "They end just as Hans Olavsen arrives in Fjällbacka, which is exactly when it starts to get interesting."

"And you've no idea why she stopped keeping a diary at that particular point?"

"No, that's the thing. I'm not convinced that she did stop. Writing for a little while every day seems to have been a deeply ingrained habit with her, so why would she suddenly stop? I think there must be some more books somewhere, but God knows where . . . ," she said pensively, winding a strand of hair around her finger in a gesture that Patrik had come to know well by this stage.

"You've gone through everything in the attic, so they can't be there," he said, thinking aloud. "Could they be in the cellar?"

Erica considered the possibility, then shook her head. "No, I went through more or less everything down there when I cleared things out before you moved in. I find it difficult to believe they're here, but I don't have any other theories."

"At least you'll have some help now as far as Hans Olavsen is concerned. You've got Kjell, and I have great faith in his ability to dig things out. Martin also said they were continuing to work on that line of inquiry, and he's asked Gösta to speak to you to find out what you've come up with so far."

"I don't have any problem with sharing what I know," Erica said. "I just hope Kjell feels the same."

"I don't suppose you can count on that," Patrik said drily. "After all, he is a journalist, and there's a story in it."

"I'm still wondering . . . ," Erica said slowly, rocking her chair back and forth. "I'm still wondering why Erik gave those articles to Kjell. What did he know about the murder of Hans Olavsen that he wanted Kjell to find out? And why didn't he just tell him? Why such a cryptic approach?"

Patrik shrugged. "I don't suppose we'll ever know. But according to Martin, the feeling at the station is that everything is connected with Frans Ringholm's death. They believe it was Frans who murdered Hans Olavsen, and that Erik and Britta were murdered to conceal that fact."

"Okay, I suppose there's a lot of evidence pointing in that direction," Erica said. "But there's still so much. . . ." She let the sentence die away. "There's still so much that I just don't get. For example, why now? After sixty years? If he's lain undisturbed in his grave for sixty years, why did this start to come to the surface now?" She chewed the inside of her cheek as she pondered.

"No idea," Patrik said. "It could be just about anything. But as I said, we'll probably have to accept that some of this happened so long ago that we'll never be able to see the whole picture."

"You're probably right," Erica said, sounding disappointed. She reached for the bag on her desk. "Chocolate caramel?"

"Yes, please," Patrik said, taking one. They chewed away in silence, contemplating the mystery of Hans Olavsen's violent death.

"Do you really think it was Frans? That he murdered Erik and Hans as well?" Erica said after a while, staring intently at Patrik.

He considered her question for a long time, then said slowly, "Yes, I do. Or at least there's not much to suggest that it wasn't him. Martin thought they would get the results on the DNA samples on Monday, which should prove that he killed Britta I expect once that's confirmed, they should be able to find evidence linking him to Erik's death. Hans was murdered such a long time ago that I doubt if we'll ever find out the whole truth. The only thing is. . . ." He made a face.

"What? Is something bothering you?" Erica said.

"It's just that Frans actually has an alibi for the time of Erik's murder. But then again, his pals could be lying. Martin and the team will have to check it out. That's my only objection."

"And there were no question marks around Frans's death? No doubt that it was suicide, I mean?"

"It seems not." Patrik shook his head. "It was his own revolver, it was still in his hand, and the barrel was in his mouth."

Erica grimaced at the image that came into her mind. Patrik went on: "So as long as we get confirmation that his fingerprints are on the gun, and that there's powder residue on the hand that was holding it, with the best will in the world you can't say that the evidence points to anything other than suicide."

"But you didn't find a note?"

"Not according to Martin. But people who kill themselves don't always leave a note." He got up and threw the caramel wrapper in the wastepaper basket. "Okay, I'll leave you in peace, honey. Try and do some work on your book, otherwise your publisher will be out for blood!" He went over and kissed her on the lips.

"I know, I know," Erica sighed. "I have actually done quite a bit today. What are you and Maja going to do?"

"Karin called," Patrik said airily. "I think we're going to go for a walk as soon as Maja wakes up."

"You seem to be going for quite a lot of walks with Karin," Erica said, shocked at how poisonous she sounded. Patrik looked at her in surprise.

"Are you jealous? Of Karin?" He laughed and kissed her again. "There's no reason whatsoever for you to feel that way."

His expression suddenly grew serious. "But if you've got a problem with me and Karin meeting up with the kids, you only have to say."

Erica shook her head. "No, of course not. I'm just being stupid. There aren't many people you can hang out with while you're on paternity leave, so you should grab the chance of some adult company."

"Sure?" Patrik studied her intently.

"Positive," Erica said, waving him away. "Now get out of here—*someone* in this family has to work!"

He laughed; just as he was closing the door, he saw her reach for another of the blue diaries.

42
Fjällbacka 1945

It was impossible to take in. The war that had seemed as if it would never end was finally over. Elsy was sitting on Hans's bed reading the paper as she tried to get her brain to understand the significance of the word printed in huge black letters: PEACE!

She felt the tears spring to her eyes and had to blow her nose on the apron she was still wearing after helping her mother with the dishes.

"I can't believe it, Hans," she said, and felt his arm around her shoulders give a reassuring squeeze in response. He too was staring at the paper, apparently incapable of grasping what they were reading. Elsy glanced up at the door, afraid that someone would catch them; they had forgotten to be careful, and were alone together during the daytime. But Hilma had gone over to see the neighbors, and she didn't think anyone else was likely to disturb them. In any case, it would soon be time to tell everyone about her and Hans. Her skirts had begun to feel a little tight around her waist, and this morning she had only just managed to get the top button fastened. But she was sure everything would be fine. Hans had reacted exactly as she had thought when she told him a few weeks ago how things were. His face had lit up, and he had kissed her as he tenderly placed a hand on her stomach, before assuring her that they would manage just fine. He had a job, after all, and was able to support her. Elsy's mother liked him, and even though Elsy was young, they could apply for permission to get married. It would all work out somehow.

Every word he spoke had eased a little of the anxiety that had been gnawing away at her, in spite of the fact that she knew him so well and trusted him completely. And he had been so calm, guaranteeing her that their child would be the most loved in the whole world, and that they would cope with all the practical matters. The waters might be a little choppy for a while, but as long as they held on tight to each other, everything would settle down, and both the family and God would give their blessing.

Elsy rested her head on his shoulder. At this precise moment, life was so good. The news that peace had finally come spread through her breast like a warm glow, melting the emotions that had turned to ice when her father died. She just wished he could have been here to experience this moment. If only he and the boat had made it through just a few months more. . . . She pushed aside the thought. God's will be done; it wasn't up to man to decide what happened, and she believed that there was a plan behind everything, however dreadful things might seem. She trusted in God and she trusted Hans, and that was a gift that meant she could look forward to the future with confidence.

Her mother was a different matter. Elsy had grown more and more concerned about Hilma over the past few weeks.

Without Elof she had shriveled, shrunk, and there was no longer any joy left in her eyes. When the news about peace had come today, for the first time since her father had died Elsy had seen the hint of a smile. Perhaps the child she was expecting would give her mother back some of her joy in life, once she got over the initial shock? Admittedly, Elsy was afraid that her mother would be ashamed of her, but she and Hans had agreed that they would tell her as soon as possible, so that they would have the chance to put everything in order in plenty of time before the child arrived.

Elsy closed her eyes and smiled as she sat there with her head resting on Hans's shoulder, breathing in his familiar smell.

"I'd really like to go home and see my family now that the war is over," Hans said, stroking her hair. "But I'll only be gone for a few days, so there's no need to worry. I won't run away from you." He kissed the top of her head.

"You'd better not," Elsy said with a grin. "Because otherwise I'd hunt you down to the ends of the earth."

"I'm sure you would," he laughed. Then he grew serious. "I've just got one or two things to sort out now that I can go back to Norway."

"That sounds serious," she said, raising her head and looking up at him. "Are you afraid that something might have happened to your family?"

He didn't say anything for a while. "I just don't know. It's such a long time since we spoke. But I won't go right away; I'll give it a week or so, and I'll be back before you know it."

"Sounds good," Elsy said, settling down once more. "Because I never want to be without you."

"And you won't be," he said, kissing her hair again. "Never." Hans closed his eyes as he hugged her tightly. The open newspaper lay beside them, with the word "PEACE" filling the entire front page.

43

It was strange. It was only the previous week that he had realized for the first time that his father was not immortal, and then on Thursday the police had turned up to give him the news. The strength of his feelings had surprised him. His heart had missed a beat, and when he reached out he could feel himself holding his father's hand, a small hand enveloped in a big one, and then those two hands slowly drifted away from one another. At that moment he realized that something even more powerful than hatred had been there all along: hope. It was the only thing that had managed to survive, the only thing that had been able to exist alongside the all-consuming hatred he had felt toward his father without being suffocated. Love had died long ago, but hope had hidden itself away in a tiny corner of his heart; even Kjell himself hadn't known it was there.

As he stood in the hallway after the police had left, he had felt the hope break free, disclose itself, and with it came a pain that made everything go black before his eyes. Because somewhere that little boy inside him had longed for his daddy. Hoped that there might be some way around the walls they had built up. Now it was too late. The walls would remain standing until they crumbled, with no chance of reconciliation.

All weekend his brain had tried to grasp the fact that his father was dead. And by his own hand. Even though it had always been in the back of Kjell's mind that his father's life could end like this—his life had been so destructive in so many ways—it was still hard to take in.

On Sunday, he had gone to visit Carina and Per. He had called Carina on Thursday and told her what had happened, but couldn't bring himself to go there until his own thoughts and the images in his mind had settled down. He had been very surprised when he arrived at their apartment. There was something fundamentally different about the atmosphere, and at first he hadn't been able to put his finger on what it was. Then he had exclaimed: "You're sober!" He didn't just mean temporarily, for the time being; that had happened before, albeit not very often over the years. But now something had changed. There was a calmness, a resolve in her eyes that had replaced the hurt expression she had worn ever since he had left her, making him feel so guilty. And Per was different too. They had talked about what would happen after the hearing for the assault on Mattias, and Per had astonished him with his composure and his thoughts on how he intended to deal with the situation. When Per went to his room, Kjell had asked Carina what had happened. He listened with growing amazement as she told him about his father's visit, and the fact that he had somehow managed to achieve what Kjell had failed to accomplish in ten years.

That knowledge had made everything so much worse. It had validated the hope that now chafed in vain at his heart. Because Frans was gone. What hope was there now?

Kjell went and stood by the window of his office and gazed out. For a brief, naked moment of self-examination he looked at himself and his life for the first time with the same harsh judgment he had applied to his father. And what he saw frightened him. Admittedly, his betrayal of those he loved hadn't been as obvious or as unforgivable in the eyes of society. But did that mean it was any less of a betrayal? Hardly. He had abandoned Carina and Per, thrown them away. Nor had Beata escaped his betrayal. He had let her down even before their relationship began. He had never loved her, he had loved only what she represented at the time, in a weak moment when he needed what she stood for. He had never loved Beata herself. To be honest, he didn't even like her. He had never felt the way he had about Carina that first time he saw her sitting on the sofa, in a yellow dress and a yellow hair band. And he had let down Magda and Loke, because the shame at having left behind one child had built barriers inside him, so that he was no longer able to feel that deep, raw, all-encompassing love he had felt for Per the very first time he saw him in Carina's arms. He had withheld that love from the children he had with Beata, and he didn't think he was capable of finding it again. That was the betrayal he had to live with—the betrayal his family had to live with.

His hand was shaking slightly as he brought his coffee cup to his lips. He frowned as he realized the coffee had gone cold while he was lost in thought, but he had already taken a mouthful and had to force himself to swallow it.

He heard a voice from the doorway: "Your mail."

Kjell turned around and nodded distractedly. "Thanks." He reached out and took the pile of envelopes addressed to him personally, and flicked through them. Junk mail, a couple of invoices . . . and a letter. Addressed in familiar handwriting. His entire body began to shake, and he had to sit down. He placed the letter on the desk in front of him, and spent a long time simply staring at it. At his name and work address. At the ornate, old-fashioned writing. The minutes ticked by as he tried to send signals from his brain to his hand, instructing it to pick up the letter and open it. But it was as if the signals became confused along the way and instead produced a total inability to move.

Eventually the message got through and he opened the letter very, very slowly. It consisted of three handwritten pages, and he had to read a few sentences before he got used to the style. But he managed it. Kjell read the letter, and when he had finished he put it down on the desk. For the last time he felt the warmth of his father's hand in his, then he picked up his jacket and car keys, and tucked the letter safely in his pocket.

There was only one thing he could do now.

44

Germany 1945

They had been gathered together in Neuengamme concentration camp. There was a rumor that the white buses first had to remove a number of other prisoners, including Poles, in order to make room for the Scandinavians. Rumor also had it that this had cost lives. The prisoners of other nationalities had been in considerably worse shape than the Scandinavians, who had received food parcels by various means and had therefore coped considerably better during their time in the concentration camps. Many were said to have died during transportation, while others had suffered very badly; but even if the rumor was true, no one cared about that now, not when freedom was suddenly within reach. Bernadotte had negotiated with the Germans and had been given permission to send buses to bring home Scandinavian prisoners, and now they were here.

Axel's legs were unsteady as he climbed aboard the bus. For him this was the second transfer within just a few months. They had suddenly been moved from Sachsenhausen to Neuengamme, and he often woke at night reliving that terrifying journey. They had been locked inside freight cars, powerless and apathetic as the bombs fell around them on their journey through Germany. Some of the bombs landed so close that they could hear debris raining down on the roof, but at least none of them had hit the train. For some reason, he had survived this ordeal too, and now, when the will to live had almost been extinguished, the news had come that liberation was here at last. The buses would take them to Sweden, take them home.

He was able to get to one of the buses under his own steam; others were in such a poor state that they had to be carried onboard. There wasn't much room, and a great deal of misery was contained in that small space. He found a spot on the floor and carefully settled down, drawing up his knees and wearily resting his head upon them. He couldn't believe it. He was going home. To Mother and Father. And Erik. To Fjällbacka. In his mind he could see everything so clearly, all the things he hadn't allowed himself to think about for so long. But finally, now that he knew they were in reach, he dared to allow his thoughts and memories to run free. At the same time, he knew that nothing could ever be the same. He would never be the same. He had seen things, experienced things, that had changed him forever.

He hated that change, hated what he had had to do, what he had been forced to witness. And getting on the bus didn't mean it was over. The journey was long and full of pain, bodily fluids, sickness, and horror. Along the way they saw burning buildings and a country in ruins. Two of their number died en route; he had leaned against one of them in brief moments of sleep as the bus traveled through the night. When he woke up in the morning and shifted his weight, the man beside him had collapsed. Axel had simply pushed him away and called to one of the supervisors, then he had sunk back into his place. It was just another dead body. He had seen so many.

He realized he kept on touching his ear. Sometimes he could hear a rushing noise, but mostly it was filled with nothing but an empty, soughing silence. He had relived it so many times. Even though he had experienced far worse in the subsequent weeks and months, somehow the sight of the young soldier's rifle butt coming toward him had represented the ultimate betrayal. They had met as human beings, hadn't they? In spite of the fact that they were on different sides, they had found a friendly tone that had given him a sense of respect and security. But in the moment when he saw the boy raise his rifle, in the moment when he felt the pain as something burst when the rifle hit his ear, he had lost all his illusions about the innate goodness of mankind.

Sitting there on the bus on the way home, surrounded by sick, injured, and traumatized individuals, he made a solemn vow that he would never rest until he had brought those responsible to justice. They had crossed the line as far as their own humanity was concerned, and it was his duty to make sure that none of them escaped.

Axel touched his ear again as he pictured his home. Soon, soon he would be there.

45

Paula was chewing a pen as she meticulously went through one document after another. Everything relating to the murder of Erik Frankel was in front of her, and she was checking it one more time. There had to be something somewhere. One little detail they had missed, one little piece of information that would prove what they already suspected: that Frans Ringholm had also murdered Erik. She knew it was dangerous to go through case material wearing those particular glasses—trying to find evidence that would point in a certain direction—but she was attempting to keep an open mind as far as possible, searching for anything at all that would raise a question in her mind. So far, she had found nothing, but she still had a considerable amount of material to go through.

However, sometimes it was hard to concentrate. Johanna didn't have long to go until her due date, and theoretically it could all kick off at any time. Paula felt a strange mixture of fear

and joy at the thought of what was to come. A child. Someone
to be responsible for. If she had spoken to Martin, she would no
doubt have recognized every single thought about the future,
but she had kept her worries to herself. In her case, the anxiety
was so much greater than that experienced by other parents-
to-be. Had she and Johanna done the right thing in realizing
their dream of having a child together? Would it turn out to
be a selfish act, something for which their child would one day
pay the price? Perhaps they should have stayed in Stockholm
and allowed the child to grow up there instead? That might
have been easier than in this small community, where their
family would stick out like a sore thumb and attract attention.
But something told her that it had still been the right thing to
do. People had been so kind and friendly, and so far no one
had looked askance at them, as far as she could tell. Although
perhaps it would be different when the baby was born. . . .

Paula sighed and reached for the next document in the pile.
The forensic analysis of the murder weapon: the stone bust
that normally stood in the window, but which they had found
under the desk, covered in blood. There wasn't much to go on:
no fingerprints, no traces of foreign substances, nothing. Just
Erik's blood, hair, and brain matter. She threw down the piece
of paper and picked up the pictures from the scene of the crime;
she'd lost count of how many times she'd studied them. She
was amazed that Patrik's wife had noticed something scribbled
on the notepad on the desk: *Ignoto militi* . . . To the Unknown
Soldier. Paula hadn't spotted it when she was scrutinizing the
photographs, and even if she had, she had to admit that she
probably wouldn't have thought of checking what the words
meant. Not only had Erica noticed the words, she had also
managed to link them to the tangle of clues and circumstantial
evidence that had led them to the discovery of Hans Olavsen's
body in the grave in the churchyard.

However, one of the most important aspects of the case was the issue of time. It was impossible to say exactly when Erik Frankel had been murdered; they had managed to establish only that it must have happened sometime between June 15 and 17. Perhaps it was worth another look, Paula thought, taking out her notepad. She began to write down all the date-related information they had, and drew a timeline to show elements such as Erica's visit, Erik's drunken encounter with Viola, Axel's trip to Paris, and the cleaner's attempts to gain access to the house. She searched among the case notes for something that would show where Frans was during the relevant period, but found only statements from members of Sweden's Friends maintaining that Frans had been in Denmark at that time. Damn it. They should have pressed him for more details while they had the chance, but no doubt he had made sure that he had the necessary documentation to back up his alibi. He knew what he was doing. Then again, what was it Martin had said during one of their briefings? That there was no such thing as a watertight alibi. . . .

Suddenly Paula sat up straight. Something had occurred to her, and her conviction was growing stronger by the second. There was one thing they hadn't checked.

"Hi, it's Karin. Listen, could you possibly come over and help me with something? Leif left this morning, and one of the pipes in the cellar has started leaking."

"Well, I'm no plumber," Patrik said slowly, "but I can pop over and see how bad it looks, then I can help you find someone if necessary."

"Thank you so much," she said, sounding relieved. "Bring Maja with you if you like; she and Ludde can play together."

"Erica's working, so I'll *have* to bring her," he said, promising to get there as soon as possible.

He had to admit that it felt a little strange pulling into the drive at Karin and Leif's house fifteen minutes later, seeing the house where his ex-wife lived with the man whose white ass he still saw bobbing up and down in his mind's eye from time to time. He had caught them in bed together—something that wasn't easy to forget.

She opened the door with Ludde in her arms before he'd even rung the bell. "Come on in," she said, stepping to one side.

"Emergency services at your disposal," he joked, putting Maja down. Ludde immediately grabbed her hand and dragged her off to what appeared to be his room, just down the hallway.

"It's down here." Karin opened a door to a flight of stairs leading into the cellar and led the way.

"Will the kids be okay?" Patrik said anxiously, looking toward Ludde's room.

"They'll be fine for a few minutes," Karin said, gesturing to Patrik to follow her.

At the foot of the stairs she pointed to a pipe on the ceiling, looking worried. Patrik went over to have a look, then said reassuringly, "It's a bit of an exaggeration to say it's leaking. I think it's just condensation." He pointed to a few small drops of water on top of the pipe.

"Oh, what a relief. I got so worried when it looked wet," Karin said, letting out a long breath. "It was really kind of you to come over. Can I make you a cup of coffee to say thanks? Or do you have to rush back?" She looked at him inquiringly as she set off up the stairs.

"No, we're in no hurry. Coffee would be good."

A little while later, they were sitting at the kitchen table sharing a plate of cookies.

"I don't suppose you were expecting something homemade," Karin said with a smile.

He reached for a cookie and shook his head, laughing. "No, baking was never your specialty. Nor was cooking in general, to be honest."

"Hey," Karin said, looking insulted. "I wasn't that bad, was I? You used to like my meat loaf, anyway."

Patrik made a face and wiggled his hand to indicate that he wasn't too sure about that. "I used to make the right noises because you were so proud of it, but actually I wondered if I ought to sell the recipe to the local defense volunteers so they could use it instead of cannonballs."

"Hey," Karin said again. "Enough already!" Then she laughed. "You're probably right. Cooking isn't my strong point, which Leif is very fond of making clear. In fact, he doesn't seem to think that I have any strong points." Her voice broke and tears welled up in her eyes. Spontaneously Patrik covered her hand with his.

"Are things between you that bad?"

She nodded and dabbed away the tears with her napkin. "We've decided to separate. We had a hell of a fight last weekend, and realized we can't keep on like this. So he's gone for good this time; he's not coming back."

"I'm sorry," Patrik said, his hand still resting on hers.

"Do you know what hurts the most?" she said. "The fact that I don't even miss him. I realize now that the whole thing was just a huge mistake." Her voice gave way again, and Patrik began to feel uneasy about where this conversation was going.

"I mean, things were so good between you and me, weren't they? If only I hadn't been so stupid. . . ." She sobbed into the napkin and gripped Patrik's hand tightly. He couldn't pull it away, although he knew he should.

"I realize you've moved on. I know you've got Erica. But we had something special, didn't we? Didn't we? Is there any chance that we could . . . that you and I could. . . ." Incapable of finishing the sentence, she clutched his hand even more tightly, pleading with him.

Patrik swallowed, then said, calmly, "I love Erica. That's the first thing you have to understand. And second, the image you have of our marriage is nothing more than a fantasy; you're looking back through rose-tinted glasses now that you and Leif are having problems. We were okay, but it was nothing special. That's why things turned out the way they did; it was only a matter of time." Patrik looked her in the eye. "And you know that, if you think back. We stayed married largely out of convenience, not because we were in love. So in a way you did us a favor, although obviously I wouldn't have wanted things to end as they did. But right now you're fooling yourself. Okay?"

Karin burst into tears once again, largely because she was feeling so humiliated. Patrik understood, and moved to sit beside her. He put his arms around her and leaned her head against his shoulder as he stroked her hair. "Ssh," he said. "It's okay. . . . Everything will be fine."

"How . . . can . . . you . . . be . . . so . . . when . . . I've . . . just . . . made . . . such . . . a . . . fool . . . of . . . myself . . . ?" Karin sobbed, trying to turn her head away in embarrassment. But Patrik simply kept stroking her hair.

"You have nothing to be ashamed of," he said. "You're upset and you're not thinking straight right now. But you know I'm right." He used his napkin to wipe away the tears from her blotchy cheeks.

"Do you want me to leave, or shall we finish our coffee?" he said, gazing steadily at her. She hesitated for a moment, then the tension in her body suddenly evaporated.

"If we can forget that I practically threw myself at you just now," she said calmly, "I'd really like you to stay a while longer."

"Excellent," Patrik said, moving back to his own chair. "I've got a memory like a goldfish, so in ten seconds I won't remember anything except these delicious cookies," he said, reaching for another.

"What's Erica working on at the moment?" Karin asked in a desperate attempt to change the subject.

"She's supposed to be working on her new book, but she's gotten a bit tied up in researching her mother's background," Patrik said, grateful for the chance to talk about something else.

"How come?" Karin asked, genuinely curious; she too reached for another cookie.

Patrik told her about what they had found in the chest, and how Erica had discovered links to the murders everyone was talking about.

"What's frustrating her most is that her mother kept a diary, but Erica can't find anything after 1944. Either she suddenly stopped at that point, or there's a pile of blue notebooks tucked away somewhere else, not in our house," Patrik explained.

Karin gave a start. "Sorry, what did you say the diaries look like?"

Patrik frowned and stared at her quizzically. "They're thin blue notebooks, similar in size to the exercise books you have in school. Why do you ask?"

"Because in that case, I think I know where they are," Karin said slowly.

"You have a visitor," Annika said, sticking her head around the door of Martin's office.

"Who is it?" he said curiously, but got his answer immediately as Kjell Ringholm walked in.

"I'm not here in my capacity as a journalist," he said right away, holding up his hands defensively as Martin began to voice an objection to his visit. "I'm here as Frans Ringholm's son," he said, sitting down heavily on the visitor's chair.

"My condolences . . . ," Martin said, unsure how to continue. After all, everyone had known what their relationship had been like.

Kjell waved away his embarrassment and reached into his pocket. "I received this today." His tone was neutral, but his hand shook as he threw the letter down onto the desk. Martin picked it up and opened it after a nod from Kjell confirmed that this was the intention. He read the three handwritten pages in silence, raising an eyebrow several times.

"He's admitting responsibility not only for the murder of Britta Johansson, but also Hans Olavsen and Erik Frankel," Martin said, staring at Kjell.

"That's what it says," Kjell replied, looking away. "But I presume you were already thinking along those lines, so it can't come as much of a surprise."

"I'd be lying if I said anything else," Martin nodded. "But we've only got firm evidence for Britta's murder."

"In that case, this ought to help," Kjell said, pointing to the letter.

"And you're sure that. . . ."

"That this is my father's handwriting, yes," Kjell supplied. "I'm absolutely certain that my father wrote this letter. And I suppose I'm not surprised," he added bitterly. "But I never would have thought . . " he shook his head.

Martin read through the letter again. "In actual fact, he only confesses to murdering Britta; after that he expresses himself rather more vaguely: *I am to blame for Erik's death, and also for that of the man you have found in a grave that should not have been his.*"

Kjell shrugged. "I can't see the difference. He's just being pompous. No, I have no doubt that it was my father who . . ." he didn't continue but took a deep breath as if to keep his emotions in check.

Martin read on, sounding thoughtful: "*I thought I could fix everything the way I usually fix things, I thought that one decisive act would solve everything, hide everything. But as soon as I lifted the*

pillow from her face, I knew that it had solved nothing. And I real-
ized that only one option remained, that I had reached the end of the
road. The past had caught up with me at last." Martin looked up at
Kjell. "Do you know what he means? What was it that had to
be hidden? What is he talking about when he refers to the past
catching up with him?"

Kjell shook his head. "I have no idea."

"I'd like to hang on to this for a while," Martin said, waving
the handwritten letter.

"Sure," Kjell said wearily. "You keep it. I was going to burn it."

"By the way, I've asked one of my colleagues to have a word
with you when it's convenient, but perhaps we could deal with
the matter now instead?" Martin slipped the letter into a plastic
sleeve and set it to one side.

"What's it about?"

"Hans Olavsen. I understand you've been doing some
research on him?"

"Surely that's no longer relevant? I mean, my father confesses
to his murder in the letter."

"That's one possible interpretation, yes. But there are still a
number of question marks surrounding Olavsen and his death,
and we'd like to clear them up. So if there's anything at all you
can tell us, then. . . ." Martin spread his hands wide and leaned
back in his chair.

"Have you spoken to Erica Falck?"

"No, but we will. However, as you're already here. . . ."

"There's not much I can tell you." Kjell relayed the details of
his conversation with Eskil Halvorsen, and said that he hadn't
yet heard anything from him about Hans Olavsen, nor was there
any guarantee that such information would be forthcoming.

"Would you mind giving him a call now, just to check if
he's found anything?" Martin said curiously, pointing to the
telephone on his desk.

Kjell shrugged and took a well-thumbed address book out of his pocket. He leafed through it until he reached a page marked with a yellow Post-it note bearing Eskil Halvorsen's name.

"I don't really think he'll have come up with anything, but I'm happy to give him a call if you want." Kjell sighed, then pulled the telephone closer and punched in the number. After quite some time, the Norwegian answered.

"Good afternoon. Kjell Ringholm. I'm sorry to bother you again, but I just thought I'd ask whether. . . . Oh, good, you got the photograph I sent on Thursday. Have you. . . ."

He nodded as he listened to what the man on the other end of the line was saying, and as Kjell's expression grew more animated, Martin sat up straight, studying him intently.

"So it was the photograph that . . . ? But the name was wrong? The name was actually. . . ." Kjell snapped his fingers, signaling to Martin that he needed a pen and paper.

Martin grabbed the pen holder and managed to knock it over so that all the pens fell out, but Kjell managed to catch one; he snatched a report out of Martin's in-box and started scribbling frantically on the back of it.

"So he wasn't. . . .

"Yes, I realize this is extremely interesting. We feel the same, believe me. . . ."

Martin was staring at Kjell, about to explode with tension.

"Okay, thank you so much. This puts things in a completely different light. Absolutely. Thank you. Thank you." Finally Kjell put the phone down and grinned at Martin.

"I know who he is! I know who he damned well is!"

"Erica!"

The front door slammed, and Erica wondered why Patrik was shouting.

"What's the matter? Is the house on fire?" She went out onto the landing and looked down at him.

"Come down, there's something I have to tell you." He waved eagerly, and she did as he asked.

"Sit down," he said, going into the living room.

"Okay, now I'm really, really curious," she said once they were settled on the sofa. She looked at him encouragingly. "Talk."

Patrik took a deep breath. "You know you kept saying there must be more diaries somewhere?"

"Yeees," Erica said, a flutter of excitement in her stomach.

"Well, I went over to Karin's a while ago."

"Did you?" Erica said in surprise. Patrik waved dismissively.

"Never mind that, just listen. I happened to mention the diaries to Karin, and she thought she knew where there might be some more!"

"Are you kidding me?" Erica said, staring at him in astonishment. "How could she know that?"

Patrik explained, and Erica's face cleared. "Of course. But why didn't she say anything?"

"No idea; you'd better go and ask her," Patrik said. He'd hardly finished the sentence before Erica was on her feet and heading for the door.

"We'll come with you," Patrik said, scooping up Maja from the floor.

"Hurry up then," Erica said; she was already halfway out the door, car keys at the ready.

A little while later, Kristina opened her door looking somewhat taken aback. "Hi, this is a surprise! What are you doing here?"

"We just thought we'd come by," Erica said, exchanging a glance with Patrik.

"Lovely. Come on in and I'll make some coffee," Kristina said, still looking puzzled.

Erica waited impatiently for the right moment. She let Kristina make the coffee and sit down at the table, then with ill-concealed excitement she said, "You remember I told you I found Mom's diaries in the attic? And that I've spent a lot of time reading them lately, trying to find out more about who Elsy Moström really was?"

"Oh, yes, you did mention something about it," Kristina said, refusing to look her in the eye.

"The last time I was here, I think I also said I found it strange that she'd stopped keeping a diary in 1944, and that there weren't any more."

"Yes," Kristina said, studying the tablecloth intently.

"And today when Patrik was having coffee at Karin's, he mentioned the diaries and described them to her. She had a clear recollection of having seen some similar books here, in your apartment." Erica paused and gazed at her mother-in-law. "According to Karin, you asked her to get a cloth from the linen closet, and she remembers seeing some blue notebooks right at the back, with 'Diary' written on the covers. She assumed they were your old diaries and didn't say anything about them, but when Patrik was talking about my mom's diaries today . . . well, she made the connection. And my question is," Erica said quietly, "why didn't you tell me about them?"

Kristina sat in silence for a long time, staring down at the table. Patrik tried not to look at either of them, and concentrated on sharing a cake with Maja. Eventually Kristina got to her feet and went into the living room. Erica watched her go, hardly daring to breathe. She heard a closet door open and close, and a moment later Kristina came back into the kitchen with three blue notebooks in her hand. They were exactly the same as the ones Erica had at home.

"I promised to look after these for Elsy. She didn't want you or Anna to see them. But I guess . . ." Kristina hesitated, then handed them over. "I guess there's a time when things have to come out, and it feels as if that time is now. I think Elsy would have given her consent."

Erica took the diaries and ran her hand over the cover of the one on top.

"Thank you," she said, looking at Kristina. "Do you know what's in here?"

Kristina hesitated once more, and seemed unsure of how to answer.

"I haven't read them. But I do have some idea what Elsy wrote about."

"I'm going to read them in the living room," Erica said, her whole body trembling as she went into the other room and settled down on the sofa. Slowly she opened the first page and began to read. Her eyes moved along the lines, taking in the now-familiar handwriting as she learned about her mother's story, and thus her own. With growing astonishment and consternation she read about the love story between her mother and Hans Olavsen, and Elsy's discovery that she was pregnant. By the time she got to the third notebook, she had reached Hans's departure for Norway. And his promises. Erica's fingers were shaking more and more, and she could actually feel her mother's rising panic as she wrote about the days and weeks that passed without a word from Hans. When Erica came to the final pages, she started to cry and couldn't stop. Through her tears she read her mother's beautiful handwriting:

Today I traveled to Borlänge on the train. Mother didn't come to see me off. It is getting difficult to hide my condition, and I don't want Mother to have to deal with the shame. It's hard enough for me, but I have prayed to God, asking Him to give me the strength to get through this. The strength to give away the child I have never met, but already love so very, very much. . . .

46
Borlänge 1945

He never came back. He had kissed her good-bye, said that he would be back soon, and left. And she had waited, at first with utter certainty, then with a small pang of anxiety, which turned into sheer panic as time went by. Because he never came back. He had broken his promise to her. Let down both her and the child. She had been so sure of him. She had never even doubted his promise to her; instead she had taken it for granted that he loved her as much as she loved him. So stupid, so naïve. How many girls had been fooled in the same way throughout history?

When it was no longer possible to hide her condition, she had gone to her mother. With her head bowed, incapable of looking Hilma in the eye, she had told her everything: that she had let herself be taken in, that she had believed his promises, and that she was now carrying his child. At first her mother hadn't said a word. An icy, dead silence had settled over the kitchen where they sat, and only then had fear gripped Elsy's heart. A tiny, tiny part of her had hoped that her mother would take her in her arms, rock her gently, and say "Darling girl, everything will be fine. We'll manage somehow." That was what the mother she had had before her father died would have done. She would have had the strength to love Elsy in spite of the shame, but Mother was no longer the same person. Part of her had died along with Father, and the part that was left wasn't strong enough.

So instead she hadn't said a word, but had packed a suitcase for Elsy containing the essentials. Then she had put her pregnant fifteen-year-old daughter on a train to Borlänge, where her sister had a farm, with a handwritten letter in her pocket. She hadn't even been able to bring herself to go and see her daughter off at the station; instead she had said a brief good-bye on the porch before turning her back on Elsy and going into the kitchen. People would be told that Elsy had gone away to study domestic science.

Five months had passed since that day. It hadn't been easy. In spite of the fact that her belly was getting bigger and bigger by the week, she had had to work as hard as everyone else on the farm. From morning till night she had toiled at the tasks that were allocated to her, while her back ached more and more from the burden that was now kicking inside her. Part of her wanted to hate the child, but she couldn't. It was a part of her and a part of Hans, and she couldn't even bring herself to hate him, not completely. So how could she hate the child that united them both? But everything was arranged. The child would be taken away from her as soon as it was born and given up for adoption. There was no other way, according to Hilma's sister Edith. Anton, her husband, had organized all the practical details while constantly muttering about the shame of his wife having a niece who opened her legs for the first man who came along. Elsy was incapable of protesting. She took the harsh words without raising any objections, unable to give him any other explanation, because it was hard to argue with the fact that Hans had deserted her. In spite of his promises.

The contractions started early one morning. At first she thought it was the usual backache that had waked her, but then the nagging pain had increased, coming and going, growing stronger and stronger. She lay in bed writhing in agony for two hours before she gradually realized what was happening and laboriously rolled out of bed. With her hands pressed against the small of her back, she had padded into Edith and Anton's bedroom and cautiously waked her aunt. Then there had been a flurry of activity. She had been told to go back to bed, and Edith's oldest daughter had been sent to fetch the midwife. Boiling water and clean towels were laid out, and as she lay there in bed, Elsy grew more and more terrified.

After ten hours, the pain was unbearable. The midwife had arrived several hours earlier and had briskly examined her. She had been rough and unfriendly, making it very clear what she thought of unmarried girls who got pregnant. Elsy felt as if she were in the middle of enemy territory. No one had a kind word or a smile for her as she lay there, convinced she was going to die. That was how much it hurt. Every time a wave of pain washed over her, she grabbed hold of the bed frame and clenched her teeth to stop herself from screaming. It felt as if someone were trying to split her in two. At the beginning she had been able to rest for a little while between contractions, a few minutes when she could catch her breath and try to gather her strength once more. But now they were so close together that there was no chance to rest. The same thought kept running through her mind: I'm going to die.

She realized through the fog of pain that she must have spoken the words out loud as the midwife glared at her and

473

said "Stop making such a fuss. You've only yourself to blame, and the best thing you can do is put up with the pain without complaining. Think about that, my girl."

Elsy was too weak to protest. She gripped the bed frame so tightly that her knuckles whitened as a different level of pain surged through her abdomen and down her legs. She had never imagined that such pain could exist. It was everywhere, penetrating every fiber, every cell in her body. And she was starting to tire. She had battled with the agony for so long that part of her just felt like giving in, sinking back on the bed and letting the pain take her, letting it do whatever it wanted with her. But she knew that wasn't an option. This child belonged to her and Hans, and she was going to give birth to it if it was the last thing she ever did.

A new kind of pain began to merge with the contractions that were so familiar by now. She felt pressure, and the midwife nodded in satisfaction to Elsy's aunt, who was standing beside her.

"Not long now," she said, pressing on Elsy's stomach. "You need to bear down when I say so, and the baby will soon be here."

Elsy didn't reply, but paid attention to what she had said and waited for what was to come. The urge to push was growing stronger, and she took a deep breath.

"Right, now push as hard as you can." The midwife made it sound like the command it was; Elsy lowered her chin to her chest and strained as hard as she could. It didn't feel as if anything was happening, but the midwife gave her a brief nod to indicate that she had done the right thing.

"Now wait for the next contraction," she said brusquely, and Elsy did as she was told. She felt the pressure building again, and when it was at its height, the order came to push once more. This time she felt something loosen; it was hard to describe, but it was as if something had given way.

"The head is out. Just one more contraction, and then. . . ."

Elsy closed her eyes for a moment and pictured Hans. She didn't have the strength to grieve for him now, so she opened her eyes again.

"Now!" the midwife barked from her position between Elsy's legs, and with her last scrap of energy Elsy pressed her chin to her chest and pushed, her knees drawn up.

Something wet and slippery slid out of her, and she fell back onto the sweat-drenched sheets. Her initial feeling was one of relief that all the hours of torment were over. She had never known tiredness like it; every part of her body was utterly exhausted, and she couldn't move even a fraction of an inch. Until she heard the cry. A shrill, angry cry that made her prop herself up on her elbows so that she could see where it was coming from.

She let out a sob when she saw him. He was . . . perfect. Slimy and bloody, and angry at emerging into the cold, but perfect. Elsy flopped back against the pillows as she was struck by the realization that this was the first and last time she would see him. The midwife cut the umbilical cord and gently washed him with a piece of cloth. Then she put him in a little embroidered dress provided by Edith. Everyone was ignoring Elsy, but she couldn't take her eyes off all the activity surrounding the boy. Her heart felt as if it would burst with love, and her eyes were hungry as they devoured every detail of him. It wasn't until Edith picked him up and was about to leave the room that Elsy managed to speak: "I want to hold him!"

"That's not advisable under the circumstances," the midwife said crossly, gesturing to Edith to go on. But Elsy's aunt hesitated.

"Please, let me hold him. Just for a minute, then you can take him." Elsy's voice was pleading, and Edith couldn't refuse her. She walked over to the bed and placed the boy in his mother's arms; Elsy held him carefully as she gazed into his eyes.

"Hello, sweetheart," she said, rocking him gently.

"You're getting blood on his dress," the midwife said, looking annoyed.

"I can find another," Edith said, giving her a glance that shut her up.

Elsy couldn't get enough of him. He felt warm and heavy in her arms, and she stared in fascination at the little fingers, the tiny, perfect nails.

"He's a beautiful boy," Edith said, moving to stand beside her.

"He's like his father," Elsy said, smiling as he took a firm grip on her index finger.

"Time for you to let him go. He needs feeding," said the midwife, taking the boy out of Elsy's arms. Her first instinct was to resist, to seize him and never let him go, but then the moment passed, and the midwife roughly pulled off the bloodstained dress and put on a clean one. Then she gave him to Edith, who carried him out of the room after one last look at Elsy.

At that moment Elsy felt something break inside her. Somewhere deep in her heart, something was torn apart as she looked at her son for the last time. She knew she could never survive pain like this again. And as she lay there in her sweat-soaked, bloodstained bed, with an empty belly and empty arms, she decided she would never expose herself to such anguish in the future. Never, ever. With tears pouring down her cheeks she made herself that promise as the midwife roughly dealt with the afterbirth.

47

"Martin!"

"Paula!"

The exclamations came at exactly the same moment, and it was apparent that each had been on the way to see the other on urgent business. They stood in the corridor, staring at one another with glowing cheeks. Martin came to his senses first.

"Come into my office," he said. "Kjell Ringholm has just left, and I've got something to tell you."

"I've got something to tell you as well," Paula said, following Martin into his office.

He closed the door behind her and they both sat down; Paula was so eager to share what she had found out that she had trouble sitting still.

"First of all, Frans Ringholm has confessed to the murder of Britta Johansson, and he also implies that he killed Erik

Frankel and . . . ," Martin hesitated, "the man we found in the grave."

"You mean he confessed to his son before he died?" Paula was taken aback. Martin pushed the plastic sleeve containing the letter across the desk.

"After he died, in a way. Kjell received this in the mail today. Read it, then give me your initial reaction."

Paula took out the letter and read with concentration. When she had finished, she put it back in the sleeve and said, with a pensive frown, "Well, he definitely states that he murdered Britta. But Erik and Hans Olavsen . . . he writes that he's to blame for their deaths, but it's a slightly odd way of expressing himself under the circumstances, particularly as he is so clear about the fact that he killed Britta. So I don't know . . . I'm not sure he means that he literally murdered the other two. And besides—" She leaned forward, ready to tell him what she had found out, but Martin stopped her.

"Hang on, there's more." He held up a hand and she closed her mouth, feeling slightly put out.

"Kjell has been looking into this . . . Hans Olavsen. He's been trying to find out where he went, and to track down any information about him."

"And?" Paula said impatiently.

"He's been in touch with a Norwegian professor who's an authority on the German occupation of Norway. Because he has so much material on the Norwegian resistance movement, Kjell thought he might be able to help track down Hans Olavsen."

"So . . . ," Paula said, starting to look annoyed; was Martin ever going to get to the point?

"He didn't find anything at first . . ."

Paula sighed loudly.

". . . until Kjell faxed over an article with a photograph of Hans Olavsen, the 'Norwegian resistance fighter.'" Martin drew quotation marks in the air.

"And?" Paula's interest had definitely been aroused now, and for a moment she forgot about her own news.

"The guy wasn't a resistance fighter at all. He was the son of an SS officer by the name of Reinhardt Wolf. Olavsen was his mother's maiden name, which he decided to use when he fled to Sweden. His Norwegian mother married a German, and when the Germans occupied Norway, Wolf was appointed to an important position with the SS there, due to the fact that he had learned Norwegian from his wife. Hans actually worked under him. At the end of the war, the father was captured and sent to prison in Germany. The mother's fate is unknown, but Hans disappeared from Norway in 1944 and was never seen again. And we know why. He fled to Sweden, passed himself off as a resistance fighter, and somehow ended up in a grave in Fjällbacka churchyard."

"Unbelievable. But where does that get us, as far as the case is concerned?" Paula asked.

"I don't know yet, but I just have a feeling it's important," Martin said thoughtfully. Then he smiled. "Okay, so I've told you my big news. What's on your mind?"

Paula took a deep breath and quickly went through what she had discovered. Martin looked appreciatively at his colleague.

"Well, that definitely puts things in a different light," he said, getting to his feet. "We need to search the house right away. Bring the car around; I'll call the prosecutor and get a warrant."

Paula didn't need to be told twice. She bounced up from her chair, the blood singing in her ears. They were close now, she could feel it. They were close.

Erica hadn't said a word since they got in the car. She had simply stared out the window with the diaries on her knee, her mother's words and pain spinning around and around in her head. Patrik had left her alone, realizing that she would talk to him when she was ready. He hadn't actually read the diaries, so he didn't know as much detail as Erica did, but while Erica was reading them Kristina had told him about the child Elsy had given up.

At first he had been angry with his mother. How could she have kept such a thing from Erica? And from Anna too. But gradually he had begun to see it from her point of view. She had promised Elsy that she wouldn't tell anyone; she had made a promise to a friend and kept it. She said she had sometimes thought about telling Erica and Anna that they had a brother, but at the same time she had been afraid of the consequences if she spoke out, and had always come to the conclusion that it was best to leave things as they were. Part of Patrik still wanted to protest, but he absolutely believed Kristina when she assured him that she had tried to do what she thought was best.

But now the secret was out, and he could see that Kristina was relieved. The only question now was how his wife would react to what she had discovered. Then again, he already knew the answer. He knew Erica well enough to realize that she would leave no stone unturned to find her brother. He turned and glanced at her profile as she sat staring blankly out of the window. He was suddenly struck by how very much he loved her. It was so easy to forget that fact as everyday life took over, with work and jobs to do at home and just . . . days passing by. But at certain moments like this, it hit him with almost terrifying force: how much the two of them belonged together, and how much he loved waking up beside her every morning.

When they got home, Erica went straight up to her study, still without having said a word, and still with that same distant look on her face. Patrik occupied himself downstairs and settled Maja for her afternoon nap before he ventured to disturb her.

"Can I come in?" he said, tapping gently on the door. Erica turned around and nodded; she was still pale, but her expression was a little more alert.

"How are you feeling?" he asked, sitting down in the arm-chair in the corner.

"To be honest, I don't really know," she said, taking a deep breath. "Stunned."

"Are you angry with Mom because she didn't say anything?"

Erica thought for a moment, then shook her head. "No, I'm not. My mom made her promise, and I can understand that Kristina was afraid of doing more harm than good if she told me."

"Are you going to tell Anna?"

"Of course. She has a right to know. But I just need to deal with it first."

"I suspect you've already started searching," Patrik said, smiling as he nodded toward the computer, where her web browser was open.

"Absolutely," Erica said with a faint smile. "I've been checking to find out how to trace adopted children, and I don't think it will be a problem."

"Is it scary?" Patrik asked. "I mean, you have no idea what he's like, or what kind of life he's had."

"Super scary," Erica nodded. "But not knowing would be even worse. I mean, I've got a brother out there somewhere. And I've always wanted a big brother. . . ." She smiled wryly.

"Your mother must have thought about him over the years. Does this change the picture you have of her?"

"Definitely. I can't say I think she was right to shut out Anna and me as she did, but . . ." she searched for the right words. "But I can understand that she was afraid to let anyone in again. Just think about it: first of all she was abandoned by her child's father, or that's what she thought. Then she was forced to give up her baby for adoption. She was only fifteen years old! I can't even imagine how painful it must have been. And on top of all that, she'd just lost her father—and in some ways her mother too, or so it seems. No, I can't blame her. However much I'd like to, I just can't."

"If only she'd known that Hans hadn't deserted her." Patrik shook his head.

"Yes, that's almost the cruelest blow of all. He never even left Fjällbacka. He didn't leave Elsy; instead he was beaten to death." Erica's voice broke. "Why? Why was he killed?"

"Would you like me to give Martin a call to see if they've found out anything more?" Patrik said. It wasn't only on Erica's behalf that he wanted to call the station; he himself had become fascinated by the Norwegian's fate, even more so now that they knew he was the father of Erica's half-brother.

"Could you?" Erica said eagerly.

"Sure, I'll do it right now."

Fifteen minutes later, he was back in Erica's study, and she could see right away that he had news.

"A possible motive for the murder of Hans Olavsen has emerged," he said.

Erica could hardly sit still. "Yes?"

Patrik hesitated for a second before passing on what Martin had told him.

"Hans Olavsen wasn't a resistance fighter. He was the son of a high-ranking SS officer, and he worked for the Germans during the occupation of Norway."

The room fell completely silent. Erica stared at him; for once she was lost for words. Patrik went on. "Kjell Ringholm has been at the station today with a suicide letter from Frans that he received in the mail. Frans has confessed to Britta Johansson's murder, and he writes that he's to blame for the deaths of Erik and Hans. I asked Martin whether he interpreted that as an admission that Frans had murdered Erik and Hans, but he wasn't prepared to say."

"What does Frans mean when he says that he's to blame for their deaths?" Erica said once she had regained the power of speech. "So Hans wasn't a resistance fighter . . . did my mother know? How . . . ?" She shook her head.

"What do you think, having read the diaries? Did she know?" Patrik asked, sitting down in the armchair.

Erica thought it over, then shook her head. "No," she said firmly. "I don't think Mom knew. No, definitely not."

"The question is whether Frans found out somehow," Patrik said, thinking aloud. "But why doesn't he come right out and say that he killed them, if that's what he meant? Why say he's 'to blame'?"

"Did Martin say how they were going to proceed?"

"No, he just said that Paula had found a possible lead; they were going to go and check it out, and he'd be in touch when he knew more. He sounded pretty excited," Patrik added, feeling a pang of regret. He wasn't used to being out of the loop, and he was finding it hard to deal with.

"I know what you're thinking," Erica said, sounding amused.

"I'd be lying if I said I wouldn't like to be at the station right now," he replied. "But I wouldn't change a thing, you know that."

"I do," Erica said. "And I understand. It's only to be expected."

As if to underline what they had just been talking about, a loud yell came from Maja's room. Patrik got to his feet.

"There you go, time to clock in."

"Off you go down the mine," Erica laughed. "But bring the little slave driver in here first so that I can give her a kiss."

"Will do," Patrik said. As he was on his way out the door, he heard Erica gasp.

"I know who my brother is," she said. She was laughing as the tears began to flow. "Patrik, I know who my brother is."

They were already on their way when Martin heard that a search warrant had been issued. They'd taken a risk and set off anyway. Neither of them said anything during the drive. They were both deep in thought, trying to put together the pieces, make out the pattern that was beginning to emerge.

No one answered when they knocked on the door.

"Seems as if no one's home," Paula said.

"So how do we get in then?" Martin wondered, contemplating the sturdy door that looked as if it would be difficult to force.

Paula smiled and reached up, running her hand over one of the beams above the door.

"With the key," she said, holding up what she had found.

"What would I do without you?" Martin said, and he meant every word.

"You'd probably break your shoulder trying to smash through this," she said, unlocking the door.

They went inside. There was an eerie silence, and the place felt warm and stuffy as they took off their jackets in the hallway.

"Shall we split up?" Paula suggested.

"I'll take downstairs, you take upstairs."

"What are we looking for?" Paula suddenly seemed unsure of herself. She was convinced that they were on the right track; but now they were standing here, she was no longer quite so certain that they would find the necessary proof.

"I don't really know." Martin appeared to have been struck with the same uncertainty. "But let's check everywhere as carefully as we can, and we'll see what we find."

"Okay." Paula nodded and headed upstairs.

An hour later she came back down. "Nothing so far; do you want me to keep on up there or shall we swap for a while? Have you found anything interesting?"

"Not yet." Martin shook his head. "Swapping is probably a good idea. But . . ." he pointed to a door in the hallway. "We could check out the cellar first. Neither of us has been down there."

"Okay," Paula said, opening the door. The staircase was pitch-dark, but she located a switch in the hallway, just by the door, and flicked on the light. She led the way and stopped for a few seconds at the bottom of the steps as she allowed her eyes to grow accustomed to the dim lighting.

"What a creepy place," Martin said. He glanced around the walls, and what he saw made his jaw drop.

"Ssh . . . ," Paula said, putting a finger to her lips. She frowned. "Did you hear something?"

"No. . . ." Martin listened. "No, I didn't hear a thing."

"I thought it sounded like a car door closing. Are you sure you didn't hear anything?"

"Yes. It was probably just your imagination. . . ." He fell silent as they suddenly heard the distinct sound of footsteps on the floor above.

"My imagination, was it? We'd better get up there," Paula said, placing her foot on the bottom step. At that moment the cellar door slammed shut, and they heard a key turn.

"What the hell. . . ." Paula set off up the stairs two at a time, just as the light went out, leaving them standing in total darkness.

"Fucking hell!" Paula swore, banging on the door. "Let us out! This is the police! Do you hear me! Open this door and let us out!"

But when she paused for breath, they heard the sound of a car door slamming and an engine starting up.

"Shit!" Paula said, feeling her way back down the stairs.

"We'll have to call for help," Martin said as he reached for his phone, only to realize that he had left it in his jacket pocket.

"You'll have to use your phone; mine's upstairs in my jacket," he said. Silence was the only response from Paula, and he began to feel anxious.

"Don't tell me yours is. . . ."

"Yes," Paula said feebly. "My phone's in my jacket pocket too. . . ."

"Goddamn it!" Martin groped his way up the stairs, hell-bent on breaking out.

"Jesus!" he yelled when the only result was a sore shoulder. Sheepishly he went back down to Paula.

"It won't budge."

"So what do we do now?" Paula said gloomily. Then she gasped. "Johanna!"

"Who's Johanna?" Martin said, feeling confused.

Paula didn't say anything for a few seconds, then she explained: "Johanna is my partner. We're expecting a baby in two weeks. But you never know . . . and I've promised I'll always be accessible by phone."

"I'm sure there's nothing to worry about," Martin said as he tried to digest the deeply personal information he had just been given by his colleague. "The first one is usually late, isn't it?"

"Let's hope so. Otherwise she'll have my head on a plate. Luckily she can always get hold of Mom. If worse comes to worst, then. . . ."

"Don't even think about it," Martin said reassuringly. "I don't think we'll be here for long, and if she's still got two weeks to go, I'm sure it'll be fine."

"But nobody knows where we are," Paula said, sitting down on the bottom step. "And while we're sitting here, the killer is getting away."

"Look on the bright side—at least there's no doubt that we were right," Martin said in an attempt to lighten the atmosphere. Paula didn't even dignify the comment with an answer.

Upstairs, Paula's cell began to ring frantically.

Mellberg hesitated outside the door. Friday's class had been great, but he hadn't seen Rita since then, in spite of frequent walks along her usual route. And he really missed her. He was surprised at the strength of his emotions, but he could no longer deny the fact that he really, really wanted to see her. It seemed as if Ernst felt the same, because he had eagerly pulled on the leash as they headed toward the apartment block where Rita lived, and Mellberg hadn't exactly resisted. But now he wasn't sure. For one thing he didn't even know if she was home, and for another he felt uncharacteristically shy, afraid of appearing too forward. After a moment he shook off the unfamiliar feeling and pressed the intercom. No one answered, and he was just turning away when there was a crackle and the sound of a stressed voice panting something.

"Hello?" he said. "It's Bertil Mellberg."

At first there was no reply, then came a barely audible "Come up," followed by a groan. He frowned. Strange. With Ernst at his heels, he hurried up the two flights of stairs to Rita's apartment. The door was ajar, and he walked in, wondering what was going on.

"Hello?" he called out tentatively. After a moment he heard a groan coming from somewhere close by, and when he turned in the direction of the sound he saw a figure lying on the floor.

"Contractions . . . started . . . ," Johanna gasped; she had curled up into a ball, panting to ride out the pain.

"Oh, my God," Mellberg said as sweat broke out on his forehead. "Where's Rita? I'll call her! And Paula, we must get hold of Paula, and an ambulance . . . ," he stammered, looking around for the nearest phone.

"Tried . . . can't get . . . hold of . . . ," Johanna whimpered, but was unable to continue until the pain diminished. Laboriously she hauled herself to her feet with the help of the closet door handle; she stared wildly at Bertil, clutching her belly.

"Do you think I haven't tried calling them? But there's no answer! How hard can it be to . . . fucking hell—" The stream of curses was interrupted by a fresh contraction, and she fell to her knees, breathing hard.

"Drive me . . . hospital," she said, pointing to a set of car keys lying on the table in the hall. Mellberg stared at them as if they might turn into a venomous snake at any moment, then saw his hand reaching for the keys as if in slow motion. Without really knowing how he did it, he more or less carried and dragged Johanna out to the car and bundled her into the back seat, leaving Ernst in the apartment. Then Mellberg put his foot down and drove to NÄL, Norra Älvsborg County Hospital. As the noises from the back seat grew more intense, he could feel the panic rising, and the journey to the hospital between Vänersborg and Trollhättan seemed endless. However, at long last he screeched to a halt outside the maternity unit and dragged Johanna, her eyes wide with fear, to the reception desk.

"She's having a baby," Mellberg said to the nurse behind the glass. She looked at Johanna with an expression that suggested she found that particular piece of information slightly superfluous.

"This way," she said, showing them to a room close by.

"I'll leave you to it . . . ," Mellberg said nervously as Johanna was told to remove her pants. But Johanna seized his arm just as he was about to make his escape, and hissed quietly during yet another contraction: "You're . . . not . . . going . . . anywhere. . . . I'm not . . . doing this . . . alone. . . ."

"But . . . ," Mellberg began to protest before realizing that he couldn't bring himself to leave her on her own. With a sigh he sat down and tried to concentrate on something else as Johanna underwent a detailed examination.

"Seven centimeters dilated," the midwife said, looking at Mellberg as if she assumed he needed to know this. He nodded, wondering what it meant. Was that good? Bad? How many centimeters were required? With mounting horror he realized that he was probably going to find that out, along with a whole bunch of other stuff, before this experience was over.

He took out his cell and tried Paula's number, but it went straight to voice mail. The same with Rita. What was the matter with these people? How could they not have their phones on when they knew that Johanna was due at any time? He slipped his cell back in his pocket, wondering once again if he could possibly slip away when no one was looking.

Two hours later, he was still there. They had moved into a delivery suite, and he was now rooted to the spot by Johanna, who was holding his hand in an iron grip. He couldn't help feeling sorry for her. He had been informed that the seven centimeters would need to increase to ten, but the last three seemed to be taking their time. Johanna was clutching the nitrous oxide mask, and Mellberg wouldn't have minded having a go himself.

"I can't do this anymore . . . ," Johanna said, her eyes glazed from the effects of the gas. Her hair was plastered to her forehead with sweat, and Mellberg reached for a towel to mop her brow.

"Thanks . . . ," she said, looking at him with an expression that immediately dispelled all thoughts of flight. He couldn't help feeling a certain fascination at the events being played out before him. Obviously he had known that giving birth was a painful business, but he had never realized what a Herculean effort was involved, and for the first time in his life he felt a deep respect for the female of the species. He would never have been able to do this—that was for sure.

"Try . . . calling . . . again," Johanna said, breathing in the gas as the machine hooked up to her abdomen indicated that another contraction was on the way.

Mellberg extricated his hand and tried the two numbers yet again; he had called countless times over the past two hours, and there was still no reply. He shook his head sadly at Johanna.

"Where the hell—" she began, but the next contraction followed immediately, and her words disintegrated into a yell.

"Are you sure you don't want that . . . edipural or whatever it was the nurse asked about?" Mellberg said anxiously, wiping Johanna's brow once more.

"No . . . I'm so close now . . . I can do this. . . . And it's called an epidural. . . ." She cried out again, arching her back. The midwife returned and checked to see how dilated Johanna was, as she had done at regular intervals.

"She's fully dilated now," she said, sounding pleased. "You hear that, Johanna? Well done. Ten centimeters. You'll be able to start pushing before long. You've done brilliantly. Your baby will be here very soon."

Mellberg took Johanna's hand and squeezed it hard. He had the strangest feeling in his chest; the closest word he could find to describe it was "pride." Pride in the fact that Johanna was being praised, that they had worked together, and that Johanna and Paula's baby would soon be here.

"How long does the next bit take?" he asked the midwife, and she was happy to answer his question. Nobody had asked about his relationship to Johanna, so he assumed they thought he was the child's father, albeit a little on the old side. He didn't bother to disabuse them.

"It varies, but I would guess that this baby will be with us in no more than half an hour," she said, smiling encouragingly at Johanna, who was resting for a few seconds between contractions. Then her face contorted and her body tensed again.

"It feels different now," she said through clenched teeth, reaching for the mask.

"Time to push," the midwife said. "Wait until you feel a really strong urge to bear down; I'll help you, and when I tell you, I want you to draw up your knees, put your chin on your chest, then push as hard as you can."

Johanna nodded wearily, squeezing Mellberg's hand. He squeezed back, then they both watched the midwife as they waited for further instructions.

After a few seconds Johanna started panting, and she looked to the midwife for guidance.

"Wait, wait, wait . . . not yet . . . wait until it's really strong. . . . NOW push!"

Johanna did as she was told, pressing her chin against her chest, drawing up her knees and pushing until she was red in the face and the pain subsided.

"Good! Well done! Wait for the next one—this will be over in no time!"

The midwife was right. Two contractions later, the baby slid out and was immediately placed on Johanna's stomach. Mellberg stared in fascination. He knew how it worked in theory, but to actually see it for real. . . . To see a baby come out, waving his arms and legs and yelling in protest before he started wriggling around on Johanna's chest.

"Let's help your little boy to the breast—that's what he's searching for," the midwife said kindly, guiding Johanna until the new little life found her breast and began to suckle.

"Congratulations," the midwife said to both of them, and Mellberg felt himself beaming like the sun. He had never experienced anything like it. Never!

A little while later, the baby had finished feeding and had been washed and wrapped in a blanket. Johanna was sitting up in bed with a pillow behind her for support, gazing adoringly at her son. Then she looked at Mellberg and said, quietly, "Thank you. I couldn't have done it on my own."

Mellberg could only nod. There was some kind of lump in his throat that was preventing him from speaking, and he swallowed and swallowed to get rid of it.

"Would you like to hold him?" Johanna asked.

Once again Mellberg could only nod. Nervously he held out his arms as Johanna gently passed him her son, making sure the head was properly supported. It was a strange feeling, to have this warm, new little body in his arms. He looked down at the tiny face, and the strange lump in his throat grew bigger. And when he gazed into the boy's eyes, he knew one thing for certain. That from this moment on, he was helplessly, hopelessly in love.

48
Fjällbacka 1945

Hans smiled to himself. Maybe he shouldn't be smiling, but he couldn't help it. No doubt things would be hard for them at first. Lots of people would express their opinions, condemning them and talking of sin in the eyes of God, along with plenty of other comments in that vein. But when the worst had passed they would be able to start building a life together, he and Elsy and the child. How could he feel anything but joy at the prospect?

But the smile on his lips died away when he thought about the task that lay before him. It wasn't going to be easy. Part of him wanted to ignore what had gone before, to stay here and pretend he had never lived another life. That part of him wanted to believe that he had been born into a new life, a clean, blank page the day he crept aboard Elsy's father's boat.

But the war was over now, and that changed everything. He couldn't move on without first going back. It was mostly for his mother's sake. He had to make sure that she was all right, to let her know that he was alive and had found a home.

He reached for a suitcase and began to pack enough clothes for a few days. A week. He had no intention of being away any longer; he didn't want to be parted from Elsy. She had become so important to him that he couldn't even entertain the idea of being separated from her, but once he got this trip out of the way, they would be together forever. They would go to bed together every night and wake up in each other's arms, without shame or the need for secrecy. He had meant what he said about seeking permission to marry; if it was granted, they could wed before the child was born. He wondered whether it would be a boy or a girl. The smile broke through again as he stood there folding his clothes. A little girl, with Elsy's sweet smile. Or a boy, with his curly blond hair. He didn't care which it was; he was so happy, and would gratefully accept whatever God chose to give them.

Something hard wrapped in a piece of fabric fell on the floor with a metallic clang as Hans took a sweater out of the drawer, and he quickly bent down and picked it up. He slumped down on the bed, gazing at the object in his hand. It was the Iron Cross that had been awarded to his father in recognition of his efforts during the first year of the war. Hans stared at it. He had stolen it from his father, brought it with him as a reminder of what he was running away from when he left Norway, and as a kind of insurance in case the Germans caught him before he managed to reach Sweden. He should have gotten rid of the medal, he knew that. If anyone was poking around among his belongings and found it, his secret might be revealed. But he needed it. He needed it so that he would remember.

He had felt no sorrow at leaving his father behind. If he could make a wish, it would be never to have anything to do with that man again. He represented everything that was wrong with the human race, and Hans was ashamed that he had once been too weak to stand up to him. Images came into his mind—cruel, ruthless images of acts that had been carried out by a person he no longer had anything in common with. A weak person who had bowed to his father's will, but who had eventually managed to free himself. Hans was squeezing the medal so hard that its edges were cutting into his skin. He wasn't going back to see his father. Fate had probably caught up with him in the end, and with any luck he had received the punishment that was coming to him. But he had to see his mother. She didn't deserve the anxiety she must be feeling; after all, she didn't even know whether Hans was dead or alive. He had to talk to her, show her that he was fine, and tell her about Elsy and the baby. In time he hoped to be able to persuade her to come and live with them; he didn't think Elsy would mind. One of the things he loved the most about her was her warm heart. He thought she and his mother would get on well.

Hans got up from the bed, and after a moment's hesitation he put the medal back in the drawer. It could stay there until he came back, as a reminder of the person he would never be again. A reminder that he would never be a weak, cowardly boy. For the sake of Elsy and the child, he had to be a man now.

He closed the suitcase and looked around the room where he had experienced so much happiness over the past year. His train was leaving in a couple of hours. There was only one thing he had to do before he left. One person he had to speak to. As he left the room and closed the door behind him, he suddenly had a premonition of doom. A sense that something was not going to go well. Then he shook off the feeling and went on his way. He'd be back in a week, after all.

49

Erica had insisted on driving to Gothenburg alone, even though Patrik had offered to go with her. This was something she had to do by herself.

She stood outside the door for a while, unable to lift her hand and press the doorbell, but eventually she couldn't put it off any longer.

Märta opened the door and looked at her in surprise, but immediately stepped aside to let her in.

"Sorry to disturb you," Erica said, her mouth suddenly dry. "I should have called you first, but. . . ."

"It's fine." Märta smiled warmly at her. "At my age I'm grateful for the company, so I'm delighted to see you. Come in, come in."

Erica followed her into the living room, and they sat down. She was feverishly wondering how to begin when Märta spoke first.

"Did you get anywhere with those murders?" she asked. "I'm sorry we couldn't be of more help the last time you were here, but, as I said, I didn't have anything to do with our finances."

"I know what the payments were for. Or, rather, who they were for," Erica said, her heart pounding wildly.

Märta looked at her curiously, but didn't seem to understand what she meant.

Slowly, her eyes fixed on the old lady, Erica said, softly, "In November 1945, my mother had a son who was given up for adoption right away. She gave birth to him at my grandmother's sister's house in Borlänge. I believe that the man who was murdered, Erik Frankel, was making regular payments to your husband for that child."

There was complete silence in the living room. Then Märta looked away; Erica could see that her hands were shaking.

"The thought did cross my mind. But Wilhelm never said anything about it to me, and . . . well, I suppose a part of me didn't want to know. He's always been our son, and, even if this sounds horribly cold, I've never really considered the fact that someone else gave birth to him. He was ours, mine and Wilhelm's, and we've never loved him any less than if I'd given birth to him myself. We wanted a baby for so long, we tried for so long, and . . . well, Göran was like a gift from God."

"Does he know . . . ?"

"That he's adopted? Yes, we've never kept it from him. But I don't think he's ever really been bothered about it, to be honest. We were his parents, his family. We talked about it occasionally, Wilhelm and I, wondered how we would feel if he wanted to find out more about his . . . biological parents. But we always said we'd cross that bridge when we came to it, and Göran never seemed to show any interest, so we let it lie."

"I like him," Erica said spontaneously, trying to get used to the idea that the man she had met on her previous visit was her brother. And Anna's brother, she corrected herself.

"He liked you, too," Märta said, her face lighting up. "And I think a part of me subconsciously reacted to the fact that you were alike. There's something about the eyes that . . . oh, I don't know, but there's definitely a resemblance."

"How do you think he'd react if. . . ." Erica didn't dare to complete the sentence.

"He used to go on and on about having brothers and sisters when he was a child, so I'm sure he'd welcome a little sister with open arms." Märta smiled; she looked as if she was beginning to relax after the initial shock.

"Two sisters," Erica said. "I have a younger sister named Anna."

"Two sisters," Märta echoed, shaking her head. "Well, I'll say this: life never stops coming up with surprises, not even at my age." Then she grew serious. "Would you mind telling me about your mother . . . his mother . . . ?" She looked searchingly at Erica.

"Not at all," Erica said, and started talking about Elsy and how she came to give up her son. She spoke for over an hour, trying to do justice to her mother and the situation in which she had found herself as she told the story to the woman who had raised and loved the son Elsy had been forced to give up.

When the front door opened and a cheerful voice called out from the hallway, they both gave a start.

"Hi, Mom, have you got visitors?" Footsteps approached the living room.

Erica glanced at Märta, who gave a faint nod to indicate her consent. The time for secrets was over.

Four hours later, they were beginning to despair. They felt like moles, sitting there locked in the pitch-dark cellar, in spite of the fact that after a while their eyes had grown sufficiently accustomed to the darkness to allow them to make out the contours of the room.

"This isn't exactly how I expected things to turn out," Paula said with a sigh. "Do you think they'll send a search party anytime soon?" she joked, but couldn't help sighing again.

Martin, who hadn't been able to stop himself from going a couple more rounds with the door, was sitting there rubbing his shoulder, which was very sore by now. No doubt he would have an impressive bruise to show for his efforts.

"He must be long gone by now," Paula said, feeling a surge of frustration.

"I guess so," Martin agreed, which didn't help at all.

"He's got a hell of a lot of stuff down here." Paula squinted so that she could make out the shapes of all the things cluttering the shelves.

"I should imagine most of it belonged to Erik," Martin said. "I think he was the collector."

"But all these Nazi artifacts—they must be worth a fortune!"

"Probably. But if you spend most of your life collecting, you end up with a whole heap of stuff."

"Why do you think he did it?" Paula stared into the darkness, trying to gather her thoughts about what they now considered to be fact. To be honest, she had been completely convinced as soon as she started to think about his alibi. She had decided to see whether Axel Frankel's name appeared on the passenger lists of any other flights during the month of June; when they checked his alibi, they had simply verified that he had left the country on the date he had given them, without considering the possibility that he might have made other journeys. And there it was, in black and white. Axel Frankel had flown from Paris to Gothenburg on June 16, and had taken the return flight the same day.

"I don't know," Martin replied. "That's what I still don't understand. The brothers seemed to have had a good relationship, so why would Axel kill Erik? What was it that triggered such a violent reaction?"

"It must have had something to do with the renewed contact between Erik, Axel, Britta, and Frans. It can't just be a coincidence. And somehow there must be a link to the murder of the Norwegian."

"That's what I thought too. But how? And why? Why now, after sixty years? That's what I don't understand."

"We'll just have to ask him. If we ever get out of here. And if we ever catch up with him. He'll be on his way abroad by now," Paula said miserably.

"Perhaps they'll find our skeletons down here in twelve months' time," Martin joked, but his colleague didn't seem to appreciate his humor.

"Or if we're lucky, maybe one of the local kids will break in again," she said drily, which provoked a forceful poke in the ribs from Martin.

"That's it!" he said excitedly as Paula rubbed her side where his elbow had jabbed her.

"Whatever it is, I sincerely hope it's worth a broken rib," she said sourly.

"Don't you remember what Per said when we interviewed him?"

"I wasn't there—it was you and Gösta who questioned him," she reminded him, sounding interested in spite of herself.

"He said he got in through a cellar window."

"There aren't any windows, otherwise it would be a lot brighter in here," Paula said skeptically, trying to look around the walls.

Martin got up and felt his way to the outside wall. "That's what he said, though. There must be windows, but there might be something covering them. As you said, this stuff must be worth a fortune, so maybe Erik didn't want anyone to be able to see his collection of treasures."

Paula got to her feet and followed Martin. She heard an "Ouch!" as he bumped into the wall, but when it was followed by an "Aha!" she felt her hopes begin to rise. Hope turned to triumph when Martin tore down the heavy curtain covering one window and daylight suddenly poured into the cellar.

"Couldn't you have thought of this a couple of hours ago?" Paula said crossly.

"Just be grateful that I've solved the problem," Martin said cheerfully as he opened the catch and pushed the window outward. He grabbed a chair and placed it directly below the window.

"Ladies first!"

"Thanks," Paula muttered. She stepped onto the chair and wriggled out through the window.

Martin followed her, and they stood outside for a moment so that their eyes could get used to the harsh daylight. Then they ran around to the front door; it was now locked, and this time there was no key hidden above the porch. This meant that their jackets were locked inside, along with their cell phones and car keys. Martin was just about to run across to the nearest neighbor when he heard a loud crash. When he turned to see where the noise had come from, he realized that Paula was looking very pleased with herself, having thrown a stone through one of the ground-floor windows.

"We got out through a window, so I thought we could get in the same way." She picked up a stick and cleared away the fragments of glass around the frame, then gave Martin a challenging look.

"So? Are you going to give Axel even more of a head start, or are you going to help me get inside?"

Martin hesitated for no more than a second before boosting his colleague in through the window and clambering in after her. They had to try to catch up with Erik Frankel's killer. Axel had been gone for hours, and they still had far too many unanswered questions.

He had gotten no farther than Landvetter airport. Then he just sat there. Adrenaline had coursed through his veins as he locked the police officers in the cellar, threw his bags in the car, and drove off; but now it had gone, leaving only a great emptiness in its place.

Axel sat perfectly still, staring out of the windows as one plane after another took off. He could have boarded any one of them. He had the money, and he had the contacts. He could disappear to anywhere he wanted, however he wanted. He had been a hunter for so long that he had learned every trick in the book if you were the quarry and wanted to lie low. But he didn't want to. That was the conclusion he had eventually reached. He could run. But he didn't want to. That was why he was sitting here in no-man's-land, watching the planes landing and taking off. Waiting for fate to catch up with him at long last. And to his surprise, it didn't feel as terrible as he had expected. Perhaps this was the way the people he had hunted down had felt when someone finally knocked on the door and called them by their real name: a strange mixture of fear and relief.

But in his case the price had been too high. It had cost him Erik.

If only Elsy's daughter hadn't turned up with that medal. It symbolized everything they had tried to forget, tried to live with. At a stroke she had brought everything back to life, and Erik had taken it as a sign that the time had come. He had talked about it before, saying that they ought to do what they could to put things right, or at least take responsibility. Not before the law; it was already too late for that. No one would be able to secure a criminal conviction at this stage. But Erik had insisted that they should own up to their peers, their fellow human beings—admit what they had done. On a human, moral level. They deserved the shame, the condemnation. They had managed to evade judgment for far too long, he had insisted with increasing stubbornness.

But Axel had always managed to calm him down, convince him that there would be no point. It would only cause damage. Nothing that had happened could be changed, after all. It was as it was, and if they left it behind them, Axel could devote his time to making amends, to putting things right. He couldn't fix what they had done, but through his work he fought evil and served good. He couldn't do that if Erik continued to maintain that they should answer for past sins. What was done was done, and it would be pointless to sacrifice all the good he had done and could do, simply to facilitate a penance that would change nothing. Even the law was indifferent and toothless when it came to their crime.

And Erik had listened, tried to understand. But deep down Axel had known that the guilt was eating away at Erik, consuming him from the inside until eventually only the shame remained. Axel had tried to convince his brother that the world existed in shades of gray, even though he should have known that it was never going to work in the long term. Because when it came down to it, Erik's world was black and white. Erik dealt in facts. Not ambiguities. The world consisted of names and dates, times and places, written in black on a white background. Axel had fought against it, and for a long time he had succeeded—for sixty years, in fact. Then Erica Falck had turned up on their doorstep with a symbol from the past, while at the same time Britta's defenses had begun to crumble, eroded by an illness that was slowly destroying her brain.

Erik had begun to waver more and more, and Axel had felt the panic rising with every passing day. He had tried desperately to plead with Erik, to reason with him. He couldn't be expected to answer for something that was no longer a part of him. That wasn't how others thought of him. Everything he was, everything people saw in him, would melt away like early morning mist, and only the terrible thing he had done would remain. His entire life's work would collapse in ruins.

That day in the study . . . Erik had called him in Paris to say that the time had come. Just like that. He had sounded drunk, which was extremely alarming, because Erik drank only in moderation. He had wept on the phone, saying that he couldn't put it off any longer, and that he had been to see Viola to say good-bye so that she wouldn't have to be tainted by the shame when the truth came out. Then Erik had mumbled something about the fact that he had already set the ball rolling, that he couldn't wait any longer for someone else to reveal their dirty secret, the thing he had never dared to confess. But now there was to be no more cowardice, no more waiting, he had slurred as Axel gripped the receiver with sweaty hands.

Axel had caught the first plane home, determined to make an attempt to reason with Erik, to make him understand. He had found his brother in the study. Axel closed his eyes and his heart ached as he pictured the scene. Axel had rushed in to find Erik sitting at his desk, idly scribbling on a notepad as he spoke in a dry, toneless voice, saying the words that Axel had dreaded for six decades. Erik had made up his mind. The guilt was eating away at him, and he couldn't cope with it any longer. He had made it very clear to Axel that he had begun to take steps to ensure that they would both finally accept responsibility for what they had done.

Axel had hoped that what Erik had said on the telephone was no more than empty words, and that his brother would have come to his senses when he sobered up. Now he realized that he had been wrong. Erik was sticking to his decision with terrifying resolve.

Axel had begged, he had pleaded with Erik to leave things as they were, to let the past remain buried, but for the first time he had seen an implacable side to his brother. This time Axel wasn't going to be able to reason with him to put things off. This time Erik had decided that the truth must come out. He had spoken about the child too. For the first time, he had told Axel that he had done some research long ago, and had managed to find out where the child had gone. A boy. He had been transferring money for him every month, ever since he started earning, as a kind of penance for what they had taken away from him. The boy's adoptive father had probably thought Erik was the biological father, and had accepted the money for his son without asking any questions. But it hadn't been enough. The penance had not eased the pain that was tearing him apart, it had simply made the consequences of what they had done even more real. Now it was time for the true penance, Erik had said, looking his brother straight in the eye.

Axel had watched his life pass before him. He had seen himself from the outside, the way people looked at him. A life of admiration, of respect. All gone. With one click of the fingers it would all be gone. Then he had remembered the camp. The prisoner beside him who was pushed into the grave they were digging. The hunger, the stench, the degradation. The dead man leaning against him on the bus as they traveled across Europe to Sweden. He was back there. He heard the sounds, experienced the smells, felt the rage that had constantly simmered away inside him, even when he had no strength left and could only focus on surviving, one day at a time. He no longer saw his brother sitting there in front of him. He didn't see Erik, he saw every single person who had humiliated him, hurt him.

And now they were all grinning scornfully at him, reveling in his situation, delighted that this time it was his head that was on the block. But he couldn't give them that satisfaction. All the dead and the living were standing there grinning at him. He wouldn't survive it. And he had to survive—that was the only thing that counted.

The buzzing in his ear was worse than usual, and he couldn't hear a word Erik was saying; all he could see was his lips moving. But it wasn't Erik any longer. It was the blond boy at Grini who had been so friendly, making Axel believe he was a fellow human being, the only trace of humanity in an inhuman place. The same boy who had raised his rifle and then, looking Axel right in the eye, had brought the butt down on his ear, breaking his heart at the same time.

Filled with pain and rage, Axel had grabbed the nearest thing at hand. He had picked up the heavy stone bust and raised it high above Erik's head as his brother continued talking and scribbling on the pad on his desk.

Then he had dropped the bust. He hadn't smashed it down, he had simply let it fall on his brother's head, carried by its own weight. No, not on his brother's head. On the guard's head. Or was it Erik after all? Everything had felt so confused. He had been at home in the library, but the smells and the sounds were so vivid. The stench of dead bodies, boots marching in time, German commands that could mean one more day of life, or death.

Axel could still hear the sound of the heavy stone striking skin and bone, and then it was all over. Erik had let out a single groan, then collapsed, his eyes wide open. But, strangely enough, after the initial shock, the realization of what he had done, Axel had felt completely calm. There was nothing he could do about it now. He had carefully placed the stone bust under the desk, pulled off his bloodstained gloves, and put them in his pocket. Then he had closed all the blinds, locked the front door, gotten in the car, driven back to the airport, and caught the first plane back to Paris. He had tried to suppress everything, throwing himself into his work until the police had called him.

Coming home had been difficult. At first he didn't know how he was going to cope with setting foot in the house again, but after the two kindly police officers had driven him back from the airport, he had pulled himself together and simply done what he had to do. As the days went by, he had made a kind of peace with Erik's spirit; he still felt its presence in the house. He knew that Erik had forgiven him. On the other hand, Erik would never be able to forgive him for what he had done to Britta. He might not have laid a hand on her himself, but he had known what the consequences would be when he made that call to Frans. He knew exactly what he was doing when he told Frans that Britta was going to reveal everything. He had chosen his words very carefully, worked out how to put things. He had said what needed to be said in order to send Frans on his way like a speeding bullet, fired with deadly precision. He knew that Frans's political aspirations, his desire for status and power, would make him react. Even during their conversation he had heard the fury that had always been the driving force behind Frans, and so he was just as guilty as Frans when it came to Britta's death. And he was finding that very difficult to deal with. He still remembered the way Herman had looked at her, with a love that Axel had never even come close to. And he had robbed them of that love, that companionship.

Axel watched as yet another plane took off for an unknown destination. He had come to the end of the road. There was nowhere to go now.

It came as a relief when, after many hours of waiting, he finally felt a hand on his shoulder and heard his name.

Paula kissed Johanna on the cheek and her son on the top of his head. She still couldn't believe she had missed the whole thing—and that Mellberg had been there.

"I'm so, so sorry," she said for the umpteenth time.

Johanna smiled wearily. "I don't mind admitting that your name was mud when I couldn't get hold of you, but I realize it wasn't your fault that you got locked in. I'm just glad you're okay."

"Me too. I mean, I'm glad you're okay," Paula said, kissing her again. "And he's just . . . amazing." She looked at their son in Johanna's arms; she couldn't believe he was here, that he was actually here at last.

"Here, you take him," Johanna said, passing him over to Paula, who sat down by the bed, rocking him gently. "And what were the odds of Rita's cell choosing today to stop working?"

"Yes, Mom is devastated," Paula said, bouncing her newborn son up and down. "She's convinced you'll never speak to her again."

"It wasn't her fault. And I did get some help eventually," she said with a laugh.

"Oh, my God, who'd have thought it?" Paula was still in shock at the realization that her boss had been Johanna's birthing partner. "You should hear him out there in the waiting room with Mom. He's boasting to anyone who'll listen about what a 'terrific boy' we have, and how brilliant you were. If Mom wasn't in love with him already, she certainly looks as if she is, now that he's helped her grandchild into the world. What a day," Paula said, shaking her head.

"For a while there I actually thought he was going to make a run for it, but I have to admit he's made of stronger stuff than I expected."

As if he had heard them talking about him, there was a knock on the door and Bertil appeared, with Rita behind him.

"Come on in," Johanna said.

"We just wanted to see how you were all getting on," Rita said, coming over to join Paula and her grandson.

"Obviously—it's been at least thirty minutes since you were in here," Johanna teased.

"We need to check if he's grown, and if he's got a beard yet," Mellberg said, beaming as he slowly edged closer to the boy, his eyes filled with longing. Rita gazed at him with an expression that could only be interpreted as love.

"Can I hold him again for a minute or two?" Mellberg couldn't help asking.

Paula nodded. "I guess you've earned it," she said, passing over her son.

Then she leaned back and watched the way Mellberg was looking at the baby, and the way Rita was looking at the two of them. And she realized that even if she had thought it might be good for her son to have a male role model in his life, she had never imagined it would be Bertil Mellberg. But now that she was facing the prospect, she thought it might not be such a bad idea after all.

50
Fjällbacka 1945

He had taken a chance that Erik would be at home; he felt it was important to speak to him before he left. He trusted Erik. There was something genuine, something honest behind that slightly dry façade. And he knew that Erik was loyal; he was counting on that more than anything. Because Hans couldn't rule out the possibility that something might happen to him. He was going back to Norway, and even though the war was over, he had no way of knowing what was waiting for him. He had done things, unforgivable things, and his father had been one of the most prominent symbols of the evil power of the Germans in Norway. So he had to be realistic; he had to be a man and think of every eventuality now that he was going to be a father. He couldn't leave Elsy without a safety net, without a protector, and Erik was the only person he could think of who could fulfill that role. He knocked on the door.

Erik wasn't alone. Hans sighed to himself when he found Britta and Frans in the library, listening to records on Erik's father's gramophone.

"Mom and Dad are away until tomorrow," Erik explained, sitting down in his usual place behind the desk. Hans remained standing in the doorway, unsure what to do.

"It was actually you I wanted to speak to," he said, nodding to Erik.

"What secrets are you two cooking up?" Frans teased, swinging one leg over the arm of the chair he was sitting in.

"I just need to speak to you," Hans said stubbornly to Erik.

Erik shrugged and got up. "We can go outside for a while," he said, leading the way onto the porch. Hans followed and made a point of closing the door behind him. They sat down on the bottom step.

"I have to go away for a few days," Hans said, drawing circles in the gravel with his shoe.

"Where are you going?" Erik said, pushing up his glasses, which kept slipping down his nose.

"To Norway. I need to go home and . . sort out a few things."

"Right," said Erik, who wasn't really interested.

"And I'd like to ask you a favor."

"Okay." Erik shrugged once more. They could hear the music from inside; Frans must have turned up the volume.

Hans hesitated, then said: "Elsy's pregnant."

Erik didn't say anything; he just pushed his glasses back up his nose yet again.

"She's pregnant, and I want to apply for permission so that we can get married. But I have to go home and take care of a few things back there first, and if . . . if anything should happen to me—would you promise to look after her?"

Erik still didn't say anything, and Hans waited nervously for his answer. He didn't want to leave without a promise that someone he trusted would be there for Elsy.

Eventually Erik spoke. "Of course I'll take care of Elsy, even if I think it's unfortunate that you've put her in this position. Anyway, what could happen to you?" He frowned. "I should think you'll be welcomed as a hero when you get home. Surely nobody will blame you for escaping when things got too dangerous, will they?" He turned to look at Hans, who ignored Erik's question. He got up and brushed off his pants.

"Of course nothing's going to happen to me, but I wanted to talk to you just in case. And now you've promised."

"Okay, okay," Erik said, also getting to his feet. "Are you coming in to say good-bye to the others before you leave? My brother's home too—he arrived yesterday," Erik said, his face lighting up.

"I'm so pleased to hear that," Hans said, squeezing Erik's shoulder. "How is he? I heard he was on his way home, and that he'd had a bad time."

"You're right." Erik's face darkened. "He has had a bad time, and he's very weak. But he's home!" he said, brightening up again. "So come in and say hello—you two have never met."

Hans smiled and nodded as he followed Erik back indoors.

51

For the first few minutes the atmosphere around the kitchen table had been slightly strained. Then the nervousness had gone and they had been able to talk to their brother in a cheerful and relaxed way. Anna still looked a little shocked at the news, but she was gazing across the table at Göran in fascination.

"Did you never wonder about your biological parents?" Erica asked curiously, reaching for a chocolate caramel from the bowl of assorted candies she had placed on the table.

"Of course I did, now and again," Göran replied. "But at the same time, Mom and Dad, Wilhelm and Märta, I mean, were somehow enough. But yes, sometimes I thought about it, I wondered why she'd given me up and so on." He hesitated. "I believe she had a hard time."

"Yes," Erica said, glancing at Anna. She had found it difficult to decide how much to tell her younger sister; she had always had a tendency to be overprotective. But eventually she had realized that Anna had survived far more harrowing experiences than she had, and at that point she had given her sister all the information she had, including the diaries. Anna had taken everything in stride, and now they were gathered together in Erica's kitchen. Three siblings. Two sisters and a brother. It was a strange feeling, yet in some peculiar way it felt perfectly natural. Perhaps it was true that blood was thicker than water.

"I presume it's too late to start wanting to inspect your boy-friends," Göran laughed, pointing to Patrik and Dan. "I guess I've missed that stage, unfortunately."

"I guess so," Erica smiled, taking another caramel.

"I heard they caught the killer, the brother," Göran said, suddenly growing serious.

Patrik nodded. "Yes, he was sitting waiting for them at the airport. Odd, really, because he could easily have gotten away if he'd wanted to, and I don't think we would ever have caught up with him. But according to my colleagues, he's been extremely cooperative."

"But why did he kill his brother?" Dan said, putting his arm around Anna's shoulders.

"They're still questioning him, so I don't really know," Patrik said, passing a piece of chocolate to Maja, who was sitting on the floor beside him playing with the doll that Göran's mother had given her.

"I can't help wondering why the brother who died was paying money to my dad for all those years. As far as I understand it, he wasn't my father; it was a Norwegian. Or have I got it all wrong?" Göran said, looking at Erica.

"No, you're absolutely right. According to my mother's diaries, your father's name is Hans Olavsen—or Hans Wolf, to be more accurate. I don't think Erik and my mother ever had any kind of romantic relationship, so I don't know. . . ." Erica chewed her lower lip, looking pensive. "I'm sure it'll all become clear when we find out what Axel Frankel has to say."

"Absolutely," Patrik nodded in agreement.

Dan cleared his throat and everyone turned to look at him. He and Anna exchanged glances, and eventually Anna said, "Actually . . . we've got some news."

"What?" Erica demanded, shoving yet another caramel in her mouth.

"Well . . ." Anna took her time, but then the words came tumbling out: "We're having a baby! In the spring."

"Noooo! That's fantastic!" Erica shrieked, racing around the table to hug first her sister and then Dan, before sitting back down again, her eyes shining.

"How are you doing? How do you feel? Are you okay?" Erica fired off the questions at high speed, and Anna laughed.

"I'm as sick as a dog, but I was exactly the same with Adrian. And I'm craving peppermint candies all the time."

"Peppermint candies, of all things," Erica laughed. "Mind you, I shouldn't talk; I was always stuffing myself with chocolate caramels when I was pregnant with. . . ." She broke off in midsentence and stared at the pile of wrappers on the table. She looked up at Patrik, and could see from his open mouth that he had noticed the same thing. Feverishly she started to think. When was her period due? She had been so caught up in this business with her mother that it hadn't even occurred to her. . . . Two weeks ago! She had been due two weeks ago. She looked back at the pile of wrappers once again, completely dumbfounded. Then she heard Anna burst out laughing.

52
Fjällbacka 1945

Axel could hear voices from downstairs. With a huge effort he hauled himself out of bed. It would take time before he was fully recovered, according to the doctor who had examined him on his arrival in Sweden. His father had said the same thing, looking deeply concerned, when Axel finally got home the day before. Coming home had been blissful. For a moment it was as if all the fear, all the horrors he had experienced had never existed, but his mother had burst into tears when she saw him. She had wept as she put her arms around his frail, wasted body. That had hurt, because they were not only tears of joy; she was weeping because he was no longer the same person. He could never be the boy he had been. The fearless, daring, cheerful Axel no longer existed. The years had beaten that out of him, and he could see in his mother's eyes that she grieved for the son she would never get back, while at the same time rejoicing in the little bit of him that had come home at last.

She hadn't wanted to go away overnight with his father, even though it was a long-standing arrangement, but his father had understood that Axel needed a little peace and quiet, and had insisted that they should go anyway.

"The boy is home now," his father had said. "We'll have plenty of time to spend with him. Right now we're going to leave him in peace so that he can get some rest; after all, Erik is here to keep him company."

Eventually she had given in, and Axel had welcomed the opportunity to spend some time on his own; getting used to being back home was difficult enough. Getting used to being Axel.

He turned his right ear toward the door and listened. He would probably have to accept that the hearing in his left ear was gone for good, the doctor had said. This hadn't come as a surprise. As soon as the guard hit him with the butt of his rifle, he had felt something burst. The damaged ear would be a permanent, daily reminder of what he had gone through.

He shuffled onto the landing. His legs were still very weak, so his father had given him a walking cane to provide extra support for the time being. It had belonged to his grandfather before he died: a sturdy, solid, silver-tipped cane.

He had to hold on tightly to the banister as he laboriously made his way down the stairs, but he had been resting in bed for a long time and was curious to see who the voices he had heard might belong to. And in spite of the fact that he had longed to be alone, now he wanted some company.

Frans and Britta were sitting in armchairs, and it felt strange to see them there, as if nothing had happened. For them, life had continued as normal. They hadn't seen piles of dead bodies, or watched the friend working beside them jerk backward and collapse thanks to a bullet in his forehead. For a moment, he felt a spurt of rage at the injustice of it, but then he reminded himself that he had chosen to expose himself to danger, and therefore he had to accept the risks. But some of the anger remained, bubbling away beneath the surface.

"Axel, you're up! Good to see you," Erik said, sitting up straight behind the desk. His face lit up when he saw his brother. That was what had warmed Axel's heart the most when he got home: seeing his brother's face again.

"Yes, the old man has made it with the help of his stick," Axel laughed, pretending to wave the cane threateningly at Frans and Britta.

"There's someone I want you to meet," Erik said eagerly. "Hans is from Norway; he was a resistance fighter, but he stowed away on Elof's boat when the Germans were after him. Hans, this is my brother Axel." Erik's voice was bursting with pride.

Only now did Axel notice someone standing by the wall. He had his back to the door, so all Axel saw was a slender figure with curly blond hair. Axel took a step forward to shake hands, and the boy turned around.

At that moment the world stopped. Axel saw the rifle butt, saw it being raised in the air, then coming down toward his ear. He relived the betrayal, how it felt to have trusted someone he thought was one of the good guys and then to be let down. He saw the boy and recognized him immediately. He heard a rushing sound in his ear and the blood raced in his chest. Before Axel knew what he was doing, he had raised the cane and swung it straight across the boy's face.

"What are you doing?" Erik yelled, rushing over to Hans, who had fallen to the floor, clutching his head as the blood seeped through his fingers. Frans and Britta had jumped to their feet and were staring wildly at Axel.

He pointed at the boy with his cane, his voice trembling with hatred. "He's been lying to you. He's not a Norwegian resistance fighter. He was a prison guard at Grini when I was in there. He's the one who robbed me of my hearing; he smashed his rifle butt into my ear."

You could have heard a pin drop in the room.

"Is this true?" Erik said quietly, sitting down next to Hans, who was lying on the floor whimpering. "Have you been lying to us? Were you with the Germans?"

"At Grini they said he was the son of an SS officer," Axel said, his whole body shaking.

"And someone like you has gotten Elsy pregnant," Erik said, looking at Hans with loathing.

"What?" said Frans, the color draining from his face. "He got Elsy pregnant?"

"That was what he wanted to tell me just now, and he had the nerve to ask me to take care of her if anything happened to him. Because he has things to sort out in Norway." Erik was so angry that he too was trembling. He kept clenching and unclenching his fists as he stared at Hans, who was now trying in vain to get to his feet.

"I can well imagine that he has things to sort out. He's probably running home to Daddy," said Axel, raising the cane once more. He struck Hans with all his strength, and the boy collapsed with a groan.

"No, I was going . . . to see my mother," Hans said with difficulty, looking up at them with pleading eyes.

"You fucking bastard," Frans said through gritted teeth, giving Hans a vicious kick in the abdomen.

"How could you do it? Lie to our faces? When you knew that my brother—" Erik had tears in his eyes, and his voice broke. He stood up and moved back a few steps. He wrapped his arms around his body, shaking even more.

"I didn't know . . . your brother . . . ," Hans said indistinctly, making another attempt to get up.

"You were planning on making a run for it, weren't you?" Frans yelled. "You got Elsy pregnant, and you were going to take off. You bastard! If it was any other girl . . . but not Elsy! And now she's going to have a German brat!" His voice rose to a falsetto.

Britta was staring at Frans in despair. It was as if she had only just realized the depths of his feeling for Elsy. The pain in her heart was unbearable; she sank to the floor, sobbing uncontrollably.

Frans turned to look at her; he gazed at her for a few seconds, then, before any of the others had time to react, he walked over to the desk, picked up the letter opener that was lying there, and thrust it deep into Hans's chest.

The rest of them were frozen in horror. Erik and Britta seemed to be paralyzed by the shock, but it was as if the sight of the blood welling up around the blade triggered some kind of animal instinct in Axel. He directed his rage at the bundle lying motionless on the floor. Blows and kicks rained down on Hans as Frans and Axel uttered primitive grunts; by the time they stopped, breathless and exhausted, the boy was no longer recognizable. They looked at each other—afraid, yet somehow excited. The feeling of releasing all the hatred, everything that was inside them and needed to come out, had been liberating and powerful, and they could see it mirrored in each other's eyes.

They stood there for a while, sharing the experience, drinking it in, their hands, clothes, and faces covered in Hans's blood. It had spattered in a wide circle all around them, and a dark pool was slowly spreading beneath his body. Some of the blood had splashed onto Erik, who was now shaking violently, his arms still wrapped around his body. At first he couldn't take his eyes off the bloody heap on the floor, and his mouth was wide open when he eventually turned to his brother. Britta sat there gazing at her hands, which were also spattered with blood, and her eyes were as blank as Erik's. Nobody said anything. It was like the awful silence after a storm; everything is quiet, but the stillness still carries with it the memories of the howling gale.

It was Frans who eventually spoke.

"We need to get this cleared up," he said coldly, giving Hans a shove with his foot. "Britta, you stay here and clean the room. Erik, Axel, and I will get rid of him."

"But where?" Axel said, trying to wipe the blood off his face with the sleeve of his sweater.

Frans thought it over, then said "Okay, here's what we're going to do. We wait until dark before we carry him out. We'll have to put him on something so that he doesn't make any more mess. Then we'll all stay here and clean up, and we'll need to wash ourselves too."

"But . . . ," Erik began, before realizing that he was incapable of formulating the question. He sank down on the floor instead, his eyes fixed on a point beyond Frans.

"I know the perfect place. He can join his fellow countrymen," Frans said, with an undertone of amusement.

"His fellow countrymen?" Axel echoed in a hollow voice. He was staring at the cane, which was covered in blood and hair.

"We'll bury him in the Germans' grave. In the churchyard," Frans said, his smile growing broader. "There's a certain poetic justice in that, don't you think?"

"*Ignoto militi*," Erik mumbled, his eyes still blank. Frans looked inquiringly at him. "To the Unknown Soldier," Erik explained quietly. "That's what it says on the grave of the Unknown Soldier."

Frans laughed. "There you go—perfect!"

None of the others laughed, but they also didn't object to Frans's suggestion. Moving stiffly, they began to do what had to be done. Erik got a large paper sack from the cellar, and they placed the body on top of it. Axel provided the necessary cleaning materials, and Frans and Britta began the laborious task of scrubbing the library clean. It proved to be more difficult than they had expected. The blood was beginning to congeal, and at first they just seemed to be smearing it around. Britta wept hysterically as she worked, stopping from time to time and sobbing helplessly as she knelt on the floor, the scrubbing brush in her hand, while Frans barked at her to keep going. He himself was working so hard that the sweat was pouring off him; but unlike the others, there was no sign of veiled shock in his eyes. Erik scrubbed away with mechanical movements, and stopped insisting that they must report what had happened. Eventually he had realized that Frans was right; Axel had just come home, having survived the hell of the concentration camps, and Erik couldn't risk his being arrested by the police and thrown into jail.

After over an hour's hard work, they wiped the sweat from their brows, and Frans noted with satisfaction that no trace remained of what had taken place in that room.

"You'd better borrow some of Mom and Dad's clothes," Erik said in a subdued voice, and went upstairs to get them. When he came back, he stopped and looked at his brother, who was slumped in a corner of the library, his eyes fixed on the hairy, bloody clumps stuck to the end of his cane. He hadn't said a word since the rage left him, but now he looked up and asked "How are we going to get him to the churchyard? Wouldn't it be better to bury him in the forest?"

"You've got a motorbike with a platform; we'll use that," Frans said, unwilling to give up his idea. "Come on. If we bury him in the forest, some animal will come along and dig him up, but no one would ever imagine that there might be another body in the Germans' grave. I mean, there are already a few corpses in there, and if we put him on the motorbike platform and cover him up with something, nobody will see a thing."

"I've dug enough graves . . . ," Axel said absently, fixing his attention on the cane once more.

"Frans and I will do it," Erik said quickly. "You stay here, Axel. Britta, you'd better go home; your parents will be worried if you're not back in time for dinner." He spoke quickly, the words rattling out like bullets from a machine gun, and he never took his eyes off his brother.

"Nobody cares whether I'm home or not," Frans said dully. "So I can probably stay. We'll wait until about ten o'clock; there aren't usually many people around by then, and it will be dark."

"What about Elsy?" Erik said, speaking more slowly and quietly this time. He looked down at his shoes. "I mean, she'll be waiting for him to come back. And now she's pregnant. . . ."

"Yes, with a German brat! She'll just have to take the consequences!" Frans snapped. "Elsy can't know anything! Get it? She'll just have to believe that he's gone away and abandoned her, which is no doubt what he would have done anyway! I have no intention of wasting my sympathies on her. She'll just have to manage on her own. Anyone have any objections?" Frans stared at each of the others in turn. No one said a word.

"Right, then! That's agreed. This is and will remain our secret. Go home now, Britta, so they don't come looking for you."

Britta got up and with trembling hands smoothed down her bloodstained dress. Silently she took the dress Erik passed her, then went to wash herself and get changed. The last thing she saw before she left the three boys in the library was the expression on Erik's face. All the anger she had seen in his eyes when Hans's secret was revealed was gone now. Only shame remained.

A few hours later, Hans was laid in the grave where his body would lie undisturbed for sixty years.

53
Fjällbacka 1975

Carefully, Elsy placed Erica's drawing in the chest. Tore had taken the girls out in the boat, and she had the house to herself for a few hours. She would often come up here when she had the chance. Sit for a while and think about the way things had been.

Life had turned out so differently from what she had imagined. She picked up the blue diaries and distractedly ran her fingertips over the cover of the top one. She had been so young. So naïve. She could have saved herself so much pain if she had known then what she knew now. You couldn't afford to love too much; the price was always too high. That was why she was still paying for that one time, so long ago, when she had loved too much, but she had kept the promise she had made to herself: she would never love like that again.

Admittedly, she sometimes felt tempted to give in, to let someone into her heart once more. When she looked at her two blond girls, at their faces filled with longing as they gazed up at her, she could see a kind of hunger in them, a hunger for something that she was expected to give them, but was unable to provide. Particularly Erica. She needed it more than Anna. Sometimes Elsy would catch Erica watching her with an expression that betrayed all the unrequited love contained in a little girl's body. And a part of Elsy just wanted to abandon the promise she had made, to go and put her arms around her daughters and feel their hearts beating in time. But something always stopped her. At the last minute, before she got up, before she went to hug her daughters, she always felt the sensation of his tiny warm body in her arms. She saw his brand-new eyes gazing up at her, so like Hans, so like her. A child born out of love, a child she had thought they would raise together. Instead she had given birth to him alone in a room with strangers, felt him slide out of her body and then out of her arms as he was taken away to a different mother she knew nothing about.

Elsy reached into the chest and took out the child's dress. The stains left by her blood had faded over the years and now looked more like rust. She brought the dress to her nose, sniffing to see if she could still detect any trace of his smell—the sweet, warm smell of him when she held him in her arms. But there was nothing left, only a stuffy, musty odor. All those years in the chest had eradicated the smell of the child; it was gone.

Sometimes she had thought about trying to trace him, just to make sure that he was all right. But it had never gotten beyond an idea, just like the idea that she might be able to stand up, walk across the room, and put her arms around her daughters, releasing herself from the promise that she would keep her heart closed.

She picked up the medal at the bottom of the chest and weighed it in her hand. She had found it when she was going through Hans's room, before she was sent away to give birth to his child. When she still thought there was hope, that if she went through the things he had left behind she might find some explanation for why he had never come back to her and their child. But the only thing she had found, apart from a few items of clothing, was this medal. She had no idea what it meant, didn't know where he had found it or what role it had played in his life. But she felt that it was important, and she had kept it. Carefully she wrapped the medal in the child's dress and put the little package back in the chest. She put back the diaries and the drawing Erica had done for her that morning. Because this was the only thing she could give her girls: a few moments of love when she was alone with her memories. In those moments she could allow herself to think of them not only with her head, but with her heart. But as soon as they looked at her with their hungry eyes, her heart closed up with fear once more.

Because if you didn't allow yourself to love, you didn't risk losing everything.

Acknowledgments

Once again, Micke has provided a great deal of support, and therefore comes first in the list of those I would like to thank. As always, my publisher, Karin Linge Nordh, has made my manuscript a better book and me a better writer, with her warmth and meticulous attention. And everyone else at Forum has continued to provide me with both reassurance and encouragement. It is a great pleasure to work with all of you.

The best Bengt in the world and the best Maria in the world are, of course, Bengt Nordin and Maria Enberg at Nordin Agency, who always manage to sound utterly delighted and happy on my behalf when they have some good news for me. Without you, this would be a much lonelier job.

I have also had invaluable help with the checking of factual information, and with opinions on content. As always, the police officers at Tanumshede police station have been more than helpful, and I would particularly like to thank Petra Widén and Folke Åsberg. Martin Melin has also read the text and offered valuable insight on the details relating to police procedure, and, as a bonus, his father, Jan Melin, helped with the historical details relating to the 1940s and Sweden during the war. Once again, Jonas Lindgren at the Forensics Medicine Lab in Gothenburg has been kind enough to allow me to consult him.

Thanks also to Anders Torevi, who once again read my manuscript and corrected a number of details relating to Fjällbacka, as it has been a number of years since I lived there. My mother, Gunnel Läckberg, also provided information about Fjällbacka; she was also invaluable when it came to child care! The same applies to Hans and Mona Eriksson; in addition, Mona read the manuscript as usual and offered her comments.

I would also like to thank Lasse Anrell for allowing me to use him for a brief guest appearance in the book. He has also promised to give me some tips on growing pelargoniums the next time we meet. . . .

As always, I have been able to work in peace and quiet at Gimo Herrgård. They always take such wonderful care of me when I turn up with my computer and check in.

And then there are the girls. . . . You know who you are. . . . What would this writer's life be like without you? Desolate and lonely and boring. . . . And my readers and blog readers—a huge, huge thank-you to all those who continue to get involved in book after book.

Finally, I want to thank Caroline, Johan, Maj-Britt, and Ulf, who led us to the paradise where I now find myself and helped us to settle in. . . .

—Camilla Läckberg